Diseases of the Teeth

Diseases of the Teeth

Simon Kurt Unsworth

BLACK
SHUCK
BOOKS

First published in Great Britain in 2016 by

Black Shuck Books
Kent, UK

'Into the Water' first published in *Weirder Shadows over Innsmouth* (Fedogan & Bremer, 2013)
'Left Behind' first published in an earlier version as a private chapbook.
'Little Traveller' first published in *The 2nd Spectral Book of Horror Stories* (Spectral Press, 2015)
'N is for Noodle' first published in *M is for Monster* (Dark Continents, 2010)
'Child' first published in *Black Static 22* (TTA Press, 2011)'
'H is for Hrace' first published in *The Demonologia Biblica 1: Tres Librorum Prohibitorum* (Western Legends, 2013)
'The Cotswold Olimpicks first published in *Terror Tales of the Cotswolds* (Gray Friar Press, 2012)
'Christmas Eve, 5.24' first published online by *This is Horror* (2011)
'Hurting Words' first published in *Haunts* (Ulysses Press, 2011)
'The Pyramid Spider' first published in an earlier version as a private chapbook
'Vernon, Driving' first published in *Lovecraft Unbound* (Dark Horse Publishing, 2009)
'Private Ambulance first published in *Noir* (New Con Press, 2014)
'Photographs of Boden' first published in an earlier version as a private chapbook
'Rough Music' first published as a limited edition chapbook (Spectral Press, 2012)
'The Poor Weather Crossings Company' first published in *Terror Tales of the Seaside* (Gray Friar Press, 2013)
'Chapter Bank' first published in *Siblings* (Hersham Horror, 2012)
'The Fourth Horse' first published in *Postscripts 28/29: Exotic Gothic* (PS Publishing, 2012)
'Qiqirn' first published in *Phobophobia* (Dark Continents Publishing, 2011)
'Day 34' first published in *Reality Bites* (KnightWatch Press, 2015)
'A Place for Feeding' first published in *Never Again* (Gray Friar Press, 2010)

Cover design and interior layout © WHITEspace, 2019

978-1-913038-16-8

This book is dedicated to my beautiful soulmate and wife Rosie, my wonderful son Ben and my equally wonderful stepdaughters Mily and Lottie, the four most important people in my life. Each minute spent with you matters more than you'll ever know, and each minute spent away from you feels like a waste. I love you all.

Nothing is created in a vacuum and this collection is no exception. Although all of its imperfections can be laid at my feet, without the following people *Diseases of the Teeth* wouldn't be the book it is now and they deserve a tip of the hat and a cheery wink as thanks. Although, to be honest, they shouldn't get too big-headed about it because I put most of the hard work in.

My wife Rosie, who loves me the way I love her and who I let pick me up when I'm feeling low.

My children (they're all my kids, whether I was involved their actual creation or not) Mily, Ben and Lottie, who are clearly lucky to have me as a role model, father-figure and guide.

My parents, Diane and Kurt, and sister and brother-in-law Rebecca and Adam, who are blessed to have me in their lives.

Steve Shaw, publisher *par excellence*, who benefitted from drinking wine and eating home-made pasta with me while I pitched to him, and then took a chance and said 'Yes'.

Andrew Worgan, the whiskey fairy, who ate keema mutter in my lounge and then watched movies with me while we drank whiskey and I told him stories.

Steve Marsh, who I graciously remember to text every now and again because he's my oldest friend.

All the editors who realised they wanted my stories in their anthologies, because why wouldn't they?

I've probably missed people; apologies, but never mind because there's always next time.

Into the Water

Kapenda watched the water, and the water ate the earth.

"Isaac, the high street's finally going under, we need to go and catch it," said Needham from somewhere behind him. Kapenda raised his free hand in acknowledgement but didn't move. Instead, he let his eye rise, up from the new channel of brown and churning floodwater to the bank above. The house's foundations were exposed by the water so that it now teetered precariously on the edge of a gorge. *Fall*, thought Kapenda, *fall, please*. The house didn't fall but it would, soon, and he hoped to be here when it did.

"Isaac!" Needham again. The talent was already at the high street, waiting. The talent was like a child, got fractious and bored if it wasn't the centre of attention. *Don't keep the talent waiting* was the motto. *Don't annoy the talent* was the rule. Sighing, Kapenda finally lowered the camera and turned to go.

It had rained for months, on and off. Summer had been a washout, the skies permanently thick with cloud, the sun an infrequent visitor. On the rare occasions the clouds broke and the sun struggled through, grounds steamed but didn't dry out. The water table saturated upwards, the ground remaining sodden until the first of the winter storms came and the rivers rose and the banks broke and the water was suddenly everywhere.

They were less than a mile from the town but the journey still took several minutes. The roads were swollen with run-off, thick limbs of water flowing down the gutters and pushing up from the drains, washing across the camber and constantly tugging at the vehicle. Kapenda wasn't driving but he felt it, the way they pulled across the centre line and then back as Needham compensated. It had been like this for days now all across the south of England. Kapenda leaned against the window, peering at the rain and submerged land beyond the glass.

There were figures in the field.

Even at their reduced speed, they passed the little tableau too quickly for Kapenda to see what the figures were doing, and he had to crane back around to try and keep them in view. There were four of them, and they appeared to be crouching so that only their shoulders and heads emerged from the flooded pasture. One was holding its arms to the sky. There was something off about the shape of the figures; the arms held to the clouds were too long, the heads too bulbous. Were they moving? Still? Perhaps they were one of those odd art installations you sometimes came across, like Gormley's standing figures on Crosby beach. Kapenda had filmed a segment on them not long after they had been put in place, and watching as the tide receded to reveal a series of bronze, motionless watching figures had been quite wonderful and slightly unnerving. Had they done something similar here?

The rain thickened, and the figures were lost to its grey embrace.

The talent, a weasel of a man called Plumb whose only discernible value was a smoothly good-looking face and a reassuring yet stentorian voice, was angry with Needham and Kapenda. As Kapenda framed him in shot so that the new river flowing down Grovehill's main street and the sandbagged shops behind it could be seen over Plumb's shoulder, Plumb was moaning.

"We've missed all the dramatic stuff," he said.

"We've not," said Needham. "Just trust in Isaac, he'll make you look good."

"It's not about me looking good," said Plumb, bristling, brushing the cowlick of hair that was drooping over his forehead. "It's about the story."

"If course it is," said Needham. "Now, have you got your script?"

They didn't get the lead item on the news, but they did get the second-string item, a cut to Plumb after the main story so that he could intone his description of Grovehill's failed flood defences. Kapenda had used the natural light to make Plumb seem larger and the water behind darker, more ominous. He was happy with the effect, especially the last tracking shot away from the talent to look up the street, lost under a caul of fast-moving flood whose surface rippled and glittered. The water looked alive, depthless and hungry, something inexorable and unknowable.

Now that, thought Kapenda, *is how to tell a story*, and only spotted the shape moving through the water when he was reviewing the footage a couple of hours after it had gone out. It was a dark blur just below the waves, moving against the current and it vanished after perhaps half a minute. Something tumbling through the flow, Kapenda thought, and wished it had broken the surface; it would have made a nice image to finish the film on.

Plumb had found an audience.

They were in the bar of the pub where they were staying, the tiny, cramped rooms the only place available. The flood had done the hospitality industry a world of good, Kapenda thought; every room in the area was taken with television and print reporters.

"Of course, it's all global warming's fault," Plumb said.

"Is it?" said the man he was talking to. The man's voice was deep and rich, accented in a way Kapenda always thought of as old-fashioned. It was the voice of the BBC in the 1950s, of the Pathé newsreels. He punctuated everything he said with little coughs, as though he had something caught in his throat.

"Of course," said Plumb, drawing on all the knowledge he had gained from reading one and two minute soundbite pieces for local and, more latterly, national news. "The world's heating up, so it rains more. It's obvious."

"It's as simple as that," that said the man, and caught Kapenda's eye over Plumb's shoulder. One of his eyes was milky and blind, Kapenda saw, and then the man, disconcertingly, winked his dead eye and smiled.

"He really is an insufferable fool, isn't he?" the man said later to Kapenda, nodding at Plumb, who was now holding court in the middle of a group of other talents. *What's the collective noun for the talent*, thought Kapenda? *A show-off? A blandness? A stupidity?* He moved a forefinger through a puddle of spilled beer on the table, swirling it out to make a circle. The man, whose name was David, dipped his own fingers in the puddle and made an intricate pattern on the wood with the liquid before wiping it away.

"He thinks he understands it," said David, and gave one of his little coughs. "But he doesn't."

"What is there to understand?" asked Needham. "It's rain. It comes down, it floods, we film it and he talks about it and tries to look dramatic and knowledgeable whilst wearing an anorak that the viewers can see and wellingtons that they can't."

"This," said David, waving a hand at the windows and the rain beyond. He was drunk; Needham was drunker. "It's not so simple as he wants to believe. There are forces at work more complex than mere global warming." He coughed again, a polite rumble.

"Pollution?" said Needham. Kapenda thought of his camera, of the eye he held to his shoulder to see the world, about how he'd frame this discussion. One at each edge of the screen, he decided, in tight close up, David's opaque eye peering into the lens as Needham's head bobbed back and forth, up and down, like a bird. Needham was a good producer and director because he stressed over the little details but a bad drinking companion because he got like a terrier over tiny fragments of information.

"Pollution? Possibly, but no answer about the earth is that simple. Why is the water rising so fast? So far? Mere geography, or something more? My point is that we look to the wrong places for answers, because the real answers have faces too terrible to contemplate," said David and then stood. He was tall and solid, not fat exactly but well-built, his waistcoat straining under the pressure from his ample belly.

"You're looking in the wrong place, all of you." And with that, nodding his thanks for the company, David turned and walked away. Kapenda grinned at the look of confusion on Needham's face, saw that Plumb was heading back their way and quickly rose himself.

"I need a walk," he said.

"A swim, surely?" said Needham, and he and Plumb laughed. Kapenda did not reply.

The pub was on a hill, which was why it remained mostly unaffected by the storms and the rising floodwater. The rain was coming in near-horizontal sweeps now, gusting along in cold breaths that made Kapenda shiver. Lightning crackled somewhere over the fields, followed by thunder that reminded him of David's voice and cough. The forecasters were saying that this storm would burn itself out in the next day or so, but they'd said that before and been wrong; the previous week, the rains had continued through the period they'd confidently predicted would be dry, and the groundwater rose and rose. What had he come outside for? Not air, not even to be away from Needham and Plumb, not really.

Kapenda went down towards the lights that were strung out along Grovehill's main street. Generators, housed in the nearby community hall, powered the lamps and rope barriers prevented him from getting to the water. Even at this time of night, news crews were clustered along the ropes, each filming or preparing to film. He tried to look at the scene as though he was holding his camera; was there something here not about the floods but about the press response to it? No, that had been done.

There had to be something new, some fresh angle. As the rain pattered down around him, Kapenda thought. What was the weirdest thing he'd seen since this all started? He'd been in the tiny town of Chew Stoke a few weeks earlier, filming the remains of a vehicle that had been washed into a culvert and whose driver had died; in Grovehill, no one had died yet but there were abandoned cars strewn along the streets and tracks around it, hulking shapes that the water broke around and flowed over in fractured, churning flurries.

That was old. Every television station had those shots. He'd been there the year before when the police had excavated a mud-filled railway tunnel and uncovered the remains of two people who had been crushed in a landslide; what they needed was something like that here, something that showed how weak man's civilised veneer was when set against nature's uncaring ferocity. He needed something that contrasted human frailty and natural strength, something that Dali might have painted; a boat on a roof or a shark swimming up the main street. He needed that bloody house to collapse.

What about figures in the field?

Actually, the fields were a good starting point. They had flooded heavily and most were under at least four or five feet of water, but due to some quirk of meteorology or geography the water on them was sitting calm. Somewhere, he thought, somewhere there's an image in that smooth expanse that I can use.

Kapenda waited until morning, and such light as came with sunrise, before investigating. He left a note for Needham, who likely wouldn't be up until mid-morning anyway, and drove back along the roads towards the fields. Through the windscreen, the road ahead of him moved like a snake, constantly surging and writhing.

The dark shape was in the first field he came to, drifting slowly along, spinning. Kapenda saw it through the tangle of hedgerow and stopped, climbing out into knee-high water and lifting his camera to his shoulder. He couldn't see well, was too low, so climbed onto the vehicle's door sill and then higher, onto its roof. Was this the field where he had seen the figures? He thought it was, although there was no sign of them now. From his raised vantage point, he saw what the shape was, and started filming.

It was a dead cow. It was already bloating, its belly swelling from the gases trapped within, and its eye peered at him with baleful solemnity.

Its tongue trailed from its open mouth, bleached to a pale grey by the water. Its tail drifted after it like an eel. There was another beyond it, he saw, and more beyond that. A herd, or flock, or whatever a group of cows was called, trapped by the water and drowned.

Drowned? Well, probably, but one of the further animals looked odd. Kapenda zoomed in, focusing as he did so; the dead creature's side was a ragged mess, with strips of peeled flesh and hide along its flank exposing the muscles below. Here and there, flashes of white bone were visible. Its neck was similarly torn, the vertebrae visible through the damaged flesh. As he filmed, the creature spun more violently as a current caught it, slamming it into a tree trunk; the collision left scraps of meat clinging to the bark. Kapenda carried on filming as the cow whirled away, watching as it caught on something under the water, jerked and then suddenly submerged, bobbing back up before vanishing again. A great bubble of air, so noxious Kapenda could smell it from his distant perch, emerged from where the cow had gone down.

It was as Kapenda climbed down from the roof that he saw the thing in the hedgerow.

It was jammed, glinting, into the tangle of branches and leaves about four feet from the ground. From the surface of the water, he amended. Leaving his camera in the jeep, he moved cautiously towards the glint, feeling ahead with his feet. The ground dropped away as he stepped off the solid surface of the road, the water rising against him. It came to his thighs and then his waist; he took his wallet and phone from his jeans and zipped them into his jacket's inner pocket; they were already in plastic bank bags, sealed against the damp. Carefully, not wanting to slip, lose his footing and be washed away like the cows, he leaned into the hedgerow and pushed his arm into it. The thing was tantalisingly out of reach. He pushed in harder, felt his feet shift along the submerged earth and then he was over, falling into the water and going under.

It was cold, clenching his head in its taut embrace and squeezing. Kapenda kicked but his feet tangled into something, branches or roots, and were held fast. Something large and dark, darker than the water around him, banged into him, began to roll over him and force him further under the water. He wanted to breathe, but knowing if he opened his mouth he'd take in water and drown, he clenched his jaw. The thing on him was heavy, clamped onto his shoulder and was it biting him, Jesus yes, it was biting him and pushing him down and he was trapped, was under it and couldn't shift it and then something grasped his other shoulder, hard, and he was pulled up from the water.

"No! No! Let him be!" It was David, hauling Kapenda from the water, pulling him back to the jeep. "What were you doing in the water? You could have bloody drowned!"

Kapenda collapsed to his knees, back into the water but held up by the jeep, and vomited. His breakfast came out in a soup of dirty liquid, the sight of it making him retch even more.

"Are you okay? Do you need to go to the doctor? The hospital?" David was calmer now, more concerned than angry.

"No," said Kapenda after a moment. "I think I'm okay. What was it?"

"A dead cow," said David after a moment. "What were you doing, going into the water?"

"I saw something in the hedge," said Kapenda, and it sounded ridiculous even as he said it. He managed to rise to his feet, using the side of the jeep as a support. Water dripped from him.

"Let me see then," said David. The man looked paler in the daylight, as though he was somehow less there, his dead eye bulging from a face that was round and wan. Its milky iris peered at Kapenda. His other eye was dark, the sclera slightly yellowing. Was he a heavier drinker than he'd appeared the night before? He had patches of rough skin, Kapenda saw, dried and peeling. There was a bike leaning against the back of the jeep and Kapenda was suddenly struck with the image of David cycling down the centre of the road, his front wheel cutting a V though the water, his feet submerging and re-emerging with each revolution of the pedals, and it made him smile.

"Now, let's see this thing you were prepared to drown to get," said David, also smiling.

"Oh, I–" started Kapenda, about to say that it was still in the hedge and then realised it wasn't; he was holding it.

It was a small figure, made from some dull metal. It had a suggestion of legs and arms and a face that was nested in tentacles, its eyes deep-set and its mouth a curved-down arc. Was it an octopus? A squid? A long chain dangled from it, fine-linked and dully golden. More figures were hooked to some of the chain's links, tiny things like toads with swollen genitalia and fish with arms and legs. David held the figure up by the chain, peering at it.

"What is it?" Kapenda asked.

David didn't answer. Instead, he spun it, watching as it caught the pallid light. Its surface was smooth, but Kapenda had the impression it was the smoothness of age and wear, that the ghosts of old marks still lay under its skin. Finally, David spoke, muttering under his breath, words that Kapenda didn't catch.

"Do you know what it is?" asked Kapenda. He was starting to shiver, the shock and the cold catching him. He wanted to go back to the hotel and dry off, warm up.

"Yes," said David. "I saw one once, as a child, and I hoped not to see one again so soon. Still, I suppose it explains a lot." He rubbed one of the patches of dry skin on his neck slowly.

"The water's coming, my friend," he said, "and there's nothing we can do to stop it. Its time is here again. Well, if you're sure you're okay to drive, I'll leave you be. Take my advice, stay out of the water."

"I will," said Kapenda, "and thank you."

"Think nothing of it," said David and coughed again, his own private punctuation. He winked his sightless eye once more and then went and mounted his bike, wheeling it around to point back to Grovehill. Moments later all Kapenda could see of him was his back, hunched over the handlebars as he went down the road. Behind him, tiny waves spread out across the water and then broke apart.

It was only when Kapenda got back into the jeep he remembered the bite; sure enough, his jacket was torn in two semi-circles, to the front and rear of his shoulder, and the skin below bruised but not broken. He got back out of the jeep to try and see the cow but it must have floated off and the only thing to see was the flood, ever restless and ever hungry.

The house collapsed just after lunch.

They were filming at the rope barrier again, this time framing the talent against a shot down the street to show how the water wasn't retreating. "Forecasters say that, with the recent rainfall, the water levels aren't expected to recede until at least tomorrow, and if more rain comes it could conceivably be several days or more," Plumb intoned. "Great sections of the south west are now under water, economies ruined and livelihoods and lives destroyed. Even today, we've heard of two more deaths, a woman and child who drowned in their lounge in the village of Arnold, several miles from here. Questions are being asked of the defences that the government installed and why the Environment Agency wasn't better prepared. Here, the people merely wait, and hope."

Kapenda waited until Plumb had done his turn, letting him peer meaningfully down the flooded street, before lowering the camera. One of the other crews had found a flooded farm earlier that day and had proudly showed their footage to everyone, of the oil slick forming across the surface of the water in the barn and around it as the water worked its way into the abandoned vehicles and metal storage canisters, teasing out the oil and red diesel they contained. The rainbow patterns had been pocking and dancing in the rain, and the image had been oddly beautiful; Kapenda had been professionally impressed, and privately jealous.

"Was that good?" asked Plumb, and then stopped and listened as the air filled with a dense rumbling, grinding sound like something heavy being pushed over a stone floor.

"The building's gone," someone shouted, a runner with a phone clamped to his ear, "it's completely collapsed. The flood's surging!"

As the man spoke, a fresh wall of water appeared between the furthest buildings, higher than those that had come before it, driven by the tons of brick and wood and belongings that had suddenly crashed into the flow. The wave was a dirty red colour, curled over like a surfer's dream. Somewhere, it had picked up trees and a car, a table, a bed and other unidentifiable shapes; all of these Kapenda saw even as he was raising the camera. In the viewfinder, he caught the things in the water as they hit the buildings, saw the car crash through the window of a chemist, saw the bed hurtle into and buckle a lamppost, saw bricks bounce and dip like salmon on their way to spawning, and then the wave was upon them.

He moved back, never stopping filming, cursing under his breath that he'd missed the actual collapse. Things churned through the water, dark shadows darting back and forward under the surface, their edges occasionally breaking through to the air only to roll back, splash their way under again.

The water level rose rapidly, submerging the makeshift barriers and eating away at the bottom of the hill. As Kapenda and Needham and the talent moved rapidly back, jostling in amongst the other film crews, cars were lifted out of the side streets and began to jolt through the water. One of the lights exploded as the water reached the electric cables, and the others shorted in a series of rapid pops that left behind ghost spots in Kapenda's eyes and an acrid smell of smoke in the air. Moments later, one of the generators made a series of groaning sounds from inside the community hall and black smoke breathed out from the windows as it, too, shorted out. The police pushed the crowd back, followed all the while by the water.

By nightfall, Grovehill was lost. The rains, which had continued to fall all day, had finally abated as the light faded, but the floodwater had continued to rise, submerging most of the houses and shops up to their roofs. In the pub, the conversation was subdued, slightly awed. Most of the crews had worked on weather stories before; Kapenda himself had been at Boscastle in 2004, filming the aftermath of the flash flood, but this was worse; it showed no signs of receding.

Two cameramen had died when the building collapsed. One had been caught in the initial surge of water, swept away like so much flotsam. The other, further down the torrent, had been on the edge of the bank when something turning in the water, the branches of an uprooted tree it was supposed, had reached out and snagged him, lifting him from his feet and carrying him off. His talent, a pretty blond stringer for a local news programme, had been taken off in shock talking about how the water had eaten the man.

"I saw one of those in Russia," said a voice from behind him.

It was one of the other cameramen – Rice, Kapenda thought he might be called. Rice nodded at the thing Kapenda had pulled from the hedge, sat on the table by his glass of beer.

"Russia?" asked Kapenda

"I was in Krymsk in 2010 and in Krasnodar," said Rice, "back in 2012, when the flash flood killed all those people. We found a few of those around the port in Krymsk and in the fields about Krasnodar. We did a segment about them but it was never shown." He picked up the figure and dangled it, much like David had done, eying it.

"It's almost identical," he said. "Strange."

"What is it?"

"We never found out, not really. I always assumed it was some kind of peasant magic, some idol to keep the floods away. If that's what it was, it didn't work though, the damn things were always where the water was at its highest. I found one hanging from a light fitting in the upper room of a school that was almost completely submerged." He put the thing back on Kapenda's table.

"What happened to your segment?"

"Got archived, I suppose," said Rice. "Pretty much what we expected. I didn't mind, not really; Russia was a nightmare, and I had bigger things to worry about than whether the piece I filmed got shown."

"Really?"

"Really. It was chaos, thousands of people made homeless, streets full of mud and water and corpses. In Krymsk, everything got washed into the Black Sea, and the harbour was blocked with debris for weeks after. The local sea life was well fed, though."

"Jesus," said Kapenda.

"Yeah," said Rice. "You'd see them, dark shapes in the water, and then some floating body would suddenly vanish. The official estimate for Krymsk was one hundred and seventy dead, or thereabouts, but I'll be damned if it wasn't far higher though. I had a friend covered the Pakistan floods, was in Sindh and Balochistan, and he told me there were things like that there as well, hanging from the trees just above the floodline."

"The same things?"

"Yeah," said Rice again. "And I'll tell you one other thing that's odd."

"What?"

"That old woman that died in the flood at St Asaph the other week? That drowned in her home? There was one hanging outside her house, and one outside the house of the mother and child that drowned yesterday."

"What? How do you know?"

Rice merely smiled at Kapenda. *I have my sources*, the smile said, *and I'm keeping them secret*. "Keep it safe," he said as he turned and went back to the bar, "you never know when you might need protection against the water."

Needham was in a bad mood.

It was the next morning, and he had been trying to find someone local to interview. He wanted the talent to do some empathy work, get Plumb to listen sympathetically and nod as some teary bumpkin showed them their drenched possessions and talked about how their pictures of granny were lost forever, but there wasn't anyone.

"They won't talk to you?" asked Kapenda.

"They've all fucking vanished!" said Needham. "There's no one in the emergency shelters, no one worth mentioning anyway, and they certainly aren't staying at any of the farms, I've checked. Most of them have been abandoned too. The police aren't sure where anyone's gone, or they're not saying if they know."

"They must be somewhere," said Kapenda.

"Must they? Well I don't know where to fucking find them," said Needham.

"Perhaps they all swam away?" said Plumb and laughed. Neither Kapenda nor Needham joined in.

"It'll be dead cows and flooded fucking bushes again, you'll see," said Needham, disconsolate. "Isaac, can't you find me something new?"

"I'll try," said Kapenda.

David was standing in the water in one of the fields a little further out from Grovehill. Kapenda saw his bike first, leaning against the hedge and half under water, and pulled the jeep over to see what the man was doing. There was a stile in the hedge and David was beyond it, out into the field proper. Kapenda waded to the wooden ladder and climbed it, perching on the top and calling, "Hello!"

"'For Behold'," said David loudly, his voice rolling across the water, "'I will bring a flood of water upon the earth to destroy all flesh in which is the breath of life under heaven'. Hello, Isaac. They knew, you see; they understood."

"Who knew? Understood what?"

"We have always waited for the water's call, those of us with the blood, waited for the changes to come, but now? Some of us have called to it, and it has come."

"I don't understand," said Kapenda. He wished he had brought his camera; David looked both lonely and somehow potent, standing up to his chest in the water, his back to Kapenda. It was raining again, the day around them grey and murky.

"What are you doing?"

"It has been brought this far but I worry," said David, his voice lower, harder for Kapenda to hear. "How much further? How much more do we want? And what of what comes after us? The sleeping one whose symbol you found, Isaac? It wants the world, drowned and washed clean, but clean of what? Just of you? Or of everything, of us as well? We should have stayed in the deeps, but no, we have moved into the shallows and we prepare the way as though we were cleaning the feet of the sleeping one, supplicants to it. We might be terrible, Isaac, but after us? Do you have a god? Pray for its mercy, for the thing comes after us, the thing we open the way for, will be awful and savage beyond imagining."

"David, what are you talking about?"

"The water, Isaac. It's always about the water." David turned; in the fractured, mazy light, his face was a white shift of moonlike intensity. His eyes were swollen, turning so that they appeared to be looking to opposite sides of his head. His skin looked like old linen, rough and covered in dry and flaking patches. He seemed to have lost his hair and his neck had folded down over itself in thick, quivering ridges. "It would be best for you to leave, Isaac. You have been saved from the water once, but I suspect that once is all."

"David, please, I still don't know what you mean. Tell me what you're talking about."

"I thought we had time, that the calling that cannot be ignored would never come, but it is too late. Others have hastened it, and the water calls to us even as they call to it. I can't stand against it, Isaac. The change is come."

"David–" Kapenda began but the older man turned and began to move off across the field, bobbing down shoulder deep into the water with each long stride, sweeping his arms around as though swimming.

"David!" Kapenda shouted, but the man didn't turn. Just before he was lost to view, the water around him seemed suddenly full of movement, with things rising to the surface and looking back at him. Kapenda, scared, turned away and returned to the jeep.

"I've found us a boat!" said Needham when Kapenda got back. He didn't seem bothered that Kapenda hadn't found anything new to film.

"Your idea about the fields yesterday, about how smooth they are, it got me thinking," Needham continued. "Now the flow's slowing down, it's safe to go out in a boat, not in the fields but around the houses. They got film of the barns yesterday, didn't they? Well, we'll go one better, we'll get film of the houses, of Grovehill!"

Plumb was already in the boat, bobbing gently at the edge of the flood. It was a small dinghy with barely enough room for the three of them; Kapenda had to keep the camera on his shoulder as Needham steered the boat using the outboard on its back. Why had he come? Kapenda wondered.

Because, he knew, this was where he belonged, recording. Whatever David had meant, whatever this flood and the ones that had come before it were, someone had to catch them, pin them to history. Here, in this drowned and drowning world, he had to be the eyes of everyone who came after him.

Needham piloted the boat away from the centre of Grovehill, down winding lanes among houses that were under water to their eaves. They went slowly; here and there, cars floated past them, and the tops of signs and traffic lights emerged from the flood like the stems of water plants. Kapenda filmed a few short sequences as they drifted, Plumb making up meaningless but portentous-sounding phrases; mostly, the imagery did the talking. At one point, they docked against a road emerging from the water that rose up to a hill upon which a cluster of houses sat, relatively safe. Kapenda focussed in, hoping for footage of their occupants, but no one moved. Had they been evacuated already?

Several minutes later, they found themselves drifting over a playing field, the ghostly lines of football pitches just visible through the still, surprisingly clear water. While Plumb and Needham argued a script point, Kapenda had an idea; he fixed the water cover to the lens of the camera and then held it over the side of the boat and into the water. The surprising clarity would hopefully allow him to obtain good images of the submerged world, eerie and silent. Leaning back and getting as comfortable as he could, Kapenda held the camera so that it filmed what was below while he listened as the talent and the director argued.

"Hey!" a voice called, perhaps twenty minutes later. It was distorted, the voice, coming from a loudhailer. Kapenda looked up; bouncing across the surface towards them was one of the rescue boats, a policeman in its bow waving at them.

"Oh fuck," said Needham.

"What?" asked Plumb.

"I didn't actually ask permission to come out here," said Needham.

"Shit!" said Plumb. "We'll be fucking arrested!"

"We won't. Isaac, have you got enough footage?"

"Yes."

"Then we play innocent. Plumb, charm them if you can."

"You have to go back!" the policeman called. Needham raised an arm at him and as the launch pulled alongside them, the talent began to do his stuff.

By the time they sorted out the police, with many *mea culpa*s from Needham and much oleaginous smiling from Plumb, it was late. The water had continued to rise, its surface now only a few feet down the hill from the pub's door. Plumb made a joke about being able to use the boat to get back to it, but it was almost true and none of them laughed.

Inside, most of the crews were quiet and there was little of the talking and boasting and arguing that Kapenda would have expected. There were less of them as well; some had already left, retreating north to the dry or hunting for other stories. In Middlesbrough and Cumbria, rivers were bursting their banks and Kapenda watched footage on the news of flooded farmland and towns losing their footing to water. In one tracking shot, he was sure he saw something behind the local talent, a tiny figure hanging in a tree, spinning lazily on a chain as the water rose to meet it.

Back in his room, Kapenda started to view the film he had taken that day. The first shots were good, nice framings of Plumb in the prow of their dinghy with Grovehill, drowned, over his shoulder. He edited the shots together and then sent them to Needham, who would work on voiceovers with Plumb.

Then he came to the underwater footage.

They were good shots, the focus correct and imagery startling. The water was clear but full of debris; paper and clothing and unidentifiable things floated past the lens as it passed over cars still parked in driveways, gardens in which plants waved, houses around which fishes swam. At one point the corpse of a cow bounced languidly along the centre of a street, lifting and falling as the gentle current carried it on. The dead animal's eyes were gone, leaving torn holes where they used to be, and one of its legs ended in a ragged stump. It remained in the centre of the shot for several minutes, keeping pace with the boat above, and then it was gone as they shifted direction. Kapenda's last view of it was its hind legs, trailing behind as it jolted slowly out of sight.

They were in a garden.

At first, he thought it was a joke. Someone had set four figures around a picnic table, seated in plastic chairs, some kind of weird garden ornamentation, and then one of the figures moved and Kapenda realised that, whatever they were, they were real. Three were dark, the fourth paler, all squat and fat and bald. One of them held a hunk of grey meat in its hand, was taking bites from it with a mouth that was wide and lipless. Their eyes, as far as Kapenda could tell, were entirely black, bulging from the sides of their heads. All four were scaly, their backs ridged. As Kapenda watched, one of the figures reached out and caught something floating past and its hand was webbed, the fingers thick and ending in savage, curved claws.

As the figures moved off the side of the screen, the palest looked up. Thick folds of skin in its neck rippled, gill-slits opening and closing. Its mouth was wide, open to reveal gums that were bleeding, raw from tiny, newly-emerging triangular teeth. It nodded, as though in greeting, and raised a webbed hand to the camera.

One of its eyes was a dead, milky white.

Kapenda turned off the camera and went to stand by the window. He took the little figure from his pocket, turning it, feeling its depth-worn smoothness as the chain moved through his fingers. He watched as figures swam through the ever-advancing water below him, never quite breaking the surface, forming intricate patterns of ripple and wave. Rice had called the thing from the hedge an idol. Was it simple peasant magic? No, this was nothing simple, nothing innocent. The idol looked nothing like the figures in the flood, was something harsh and alien. What had David said? That it was the thing that came after?

What was coming?

The rain fell, and the water rose to eat the earth.

Anodontia :
The lack of development of teeth.

Left Behind

Everyone liked working the shop floor because you got to talk to the people that came in to browse and buy things. Most of the volunteers said it was their preferred job, and asked to do that one before any of the others, all except Alice. Alice's favourite job was sorting the stock out on the first floor, where it was warm and airy and where all the things that were donated or left behind got taken.

The stock rooms, which filled the upper floors of the building, were usually in a state of controlled chaos. There were shelves piled high with CDs and DVDs and books that there was no room for downstairs, or which were duplicate copies, and rack after rack of clothing dangling from cheap metal hangers. Bags were piled up high against most walls and across most of the floor space, some open and others still closed, and in the main room two tailor's dummies had been stood by the windows looking out over the street and, on Hazel's desk, an ancient computer hummed away among the invoices and scribbled telephone messages and printed messages from head office. Alice liked the upper floors for all of those things, and for their heat and the humidity from the steam irons and for the friendship that she found there from the other volunteers, but mostly she liked it for the things that came out of the bags.

Opening the bags was always exciting; the things people gave away were just amazing. Alice had found entire dinner services, dresses from the seventies and sixties, jackets with designer labels that she had never heard of, films and music from groups she knew and more that she didn't, strange pieces of technology that had aged and become forlorn in their aging, and she had only worked at the charity shop for 4 months. People gave away things that were new, old, decaying, ugly, beautiful, and it was never boring, even when it was hard work. Of course, she would tell people, it wasn't all pleasant. On her third day, she had pulled a used disposable nappy, neatly tied into a thin plastic bag, out of one of the donation sacks. The nappy had burst inside its bag, leaving dark smears across the inner surface of the bag's skin, and Alice had screamed. One of the other volunteers had put the nappy in the bin while Hazel had calmed Alice, telling her, "It happens."

"People," said Hazel, "are either lovely or they're horrible, and the horrible ones use the shop as a way of getting rid of the stuff they can't be bothered getting rid of themselves, or they think it's funny, imagining you finding one of their baby's old nappies." She was right; during the last months, in amongst the things that had been cared for, loved, that could be sold, Alice had also found clothes filthy with mud or sweat or worse, books bloated with damp that fell apart into clinging, wet flakes across her fingers when she picked them up, and other unidentifiable, useless things. For every stuffed toy whose fur was clean, they would find another whose filling spilled out in grey clouds, and they often received kitchen equipment in a dreadful state, pans with food still burned on to them or kettles whose elements were furred to a bilious yellow.

"Always look in the bags before you put your hand in," said Hazel, "and try not to dwell on the horrible stuff, and you'll soon learn to deal with it." As ever, Hazel was right, and Alice had a good time volunteering at the shop, and looked forward to her time there, until the day the hangers moved by themselves.

It was early, before the shop opened, and Alice was getting ready for the shift ahead. She was just checking to see if the previous day's volunteers had left any messages when she heard a noise from behind her. At first she assumed it was another volunteer but when she looked around there was no one there. On the other side of the room, however, the metal hangers dangling on an empty rack were spinning and twisting slowly, as though someone had just brushed past them. They clinked quietly as they touched against each other, like birds chirping.

Alice went to the head of the stairs, wondering if there was someone down in the shop. "Hello?" she called, her voice bouncing slightly off the painted walls. There was no reply. Behind her, the hangers continued their quiet whispering. There was no breeze, so why were they moving? She turned back, and the hangers were still spinning, if anything slightly more now, as though someone had gone back along them, brushing against them, setting them into a lethargic waltz.

The shop and the floors above it were actually an old house, with the various bedrooms and boxrooms and strange mezzanine floors used now for storage, and Alice searched each one carefully. There was no one else in the building, of this she soon became certain. She even ventured into the loft, where the stock that no one thought would ever sell, the torn suitcases and the bags, the old paperwork, was all haphazardly stored, waiting for the yearly clearout. By torchlight, the shadows seemed to move and sway, but became static when Alice steadied the light, and no one lurked within the room. Eventually, she went back to the first floor and carried on working, convinced that she'd imagined it or heard someone outside.

It was a couple of days later, when she was having a coffee with Hazel, that Alice mentioned what had happened, laughing. Hazel smiled at her and said, "I wondered if she might say hello."

"Who?" asked Alice.

"Maudie," said Hazel. "She's our ghost."

"Maudie's been here about three years," said Hazel later. "She died at home, alone, and she wasn't found for a couple of weeks. She's got two sons, but they didn't visit her often. It was one of them that found her. She'd had flu, but didn't want to bother anyone, so she didn't call her sons or an ambulance. She wrapped herself in her favourite coat and sat in her comfiest chair and very quietly, very slowly, died."

Alice thought Hazel was joking at first, but quickly realised she wasn't; she was entirely serious. "It's this place," said Hazel. "We get all the things people don't want, all the old and the tired things, but we get other things as well. Maudie's sons didn't know how much she liked her coat, how much it meant to her, how it was the last thing her husband had bought her before he died and how she thought about him every time she put it on. To them, it was just a coat, old and ugly, and they just put it in a bag with all the other things of hers they didn't want and sent it here, and Maudie came with it. She'd nowhere else to go, you see."

"What about–" but Alice couldn't finish the sentence, unsure of what she meant.

"Heaven?" said Hazel. "Hell? Well, I don't know. I think some people go on to somewhere else, and some of them just fade away. Maudie'll be one of the ones who goes on, I think, and it'll be soon. She misses her husband, more every day."

"How do you know?"

Hazel didn't reply for a moment, looking into her coffee cup with an expression on her face that Alice couldn't read. Steam curled up around her head, wreathing her in vapour. "I just do," she said eventually. "I've known things like this all my life. Most of the time it's just flashes, like flicking through a magazine and seeing the pictures but not reading it. Sometimes, though, with people like Maudie, they're stronger. I don't know why it's like that but when it is, they can tell me things. It's not talking, exactly, it's more like I can sense their moods, know things about them. Maudie's strong enough to make herself known to others as well, when she likes them. She likes you, that's why she rattled the hangars at you. When they're like Maudie, I try to find the thing they're attached to and I look after it until they let go of it."

The cupboard, stuck in a weird little alcove off the stairs between the second floor and loft, was full and locked, the key hanging on a nail piercing the wall next to it. As well as Maudie's coat (long and green and lined with fur and smelling faintly of talcum and perfume), there were other clothes, books, children's toys, even an old typewriter, its keys bent and tangled. "They all belong to someone who's stayed," said Hazel. "I don't want to pass them on, they've had enough upheaval and upset. When they're gone, really gone, I could sell the things they were attached to, I suppose, but I don't like to. It seems, I don't know, disrespectful somehow."

"How many of them are there?" asked Alice.

"At the moment? Just a few. They're nothing to be scared of, Alice. They're just like us, they just want somewhere to belong and someone to be with. We keep them safe as long as they want to be here, that's all."

"Yes," said Alice, and over the next couple of months, she met them all. There was the Colonel ("I don't know his name, or whether he was in the army or not, but he seems military," said Hazel), who didn't do much and was noticeable only as a smell of stale pipe smoke; Peg, whose typewriter was in the cupboard, was the only one that spoke, a polite 'Hello' from behind Alice whenever she was alone in the tiny kitchen of the shop. The first time Alice heard her, she nearly dropped her tea but after that it became easy to reply a cheery 'Hello!' back and get on with whatever she was doing. There was Ken ("Older," said Hazel, "and confused. I think he had some kind of dementia and he's brought it with him."), who liked to turn the lights on and off, but only when there was no one in the room with him. He tended to do it as Alice or one of the others was walking up the stairs so that the darkness leapt up around them and then fell back; if you waited a few minutes, he stopped and you could carry on up the stairs without further incident, Alice found. Suzy liked to sing, distant and mumbled, as though she didn't know all the words, and The Gentleman ("He's so polite he's almost embarrassed to be haunting us," said Hazel, "and he's not ready to go on because I think he's embarrassed about that as well!") tended to follow Alice around the shop floor early in the mornings or in the evenings after the public had been locked out; Alice never had any sense of him other than someone being interested in what she was doing. The Lady in Waiting only ever appeared at the corner of Alice's eye, a figure caught in the shadows by doorways, never moving.

Maudie was Alice's favourite, though; it got so Alice could tell what she was saying by listening to the different tones the hangers made as they rattled together. They were softer for hello and goodbye, more strident when Maudie was lonely and wanted someone to talk to her or when something had disturbed her, a difficult customer or a donation that had something unpleasant in it. Maudie and the others, they were oddly reassuring, Alice thought; like having friends without seeing them, there but keeping their distance, not interfering. When Alice said as much to Hazel, Hazel said, "Yes. Not all the volunteers think so, of course, but most times they don't really notice them. You're like me, though, tuned in to them somehow. It's funny, but I'd miss them if they weren't here as well; they make me feel like I'm never really alone here. They're nice to have about." And so it went, until the bags from the Morecambe house clearance arrived, and the scarecrow came with them.

Alice first saw the scarecrow one autumn evening, a night where the chill tautened the air rather than simply teased at it, the first shadows of what was going to be a cold season. She was in the office, alone, when the hangers rattled. "Hello Maudie," she said, not looking around. She was totting up the day's figures, a job she hated, and she needed to concentrate. The hangers rattled again, metallic and insistent, loud, and this time she said, "Not now, Maudie, give me a minute, please."

Another rattle of the hangers. Another. Another, louder still, and this time there was something so odd about the sound that Alice sighed and turned.

The hangers were shifting wildly on the rail, agitatedly dancing back and forth. They caught the light and sent it darting around the room in splintered fragments, making it snake up the walls and across the ceiling.

"Maudie, what's wrong?" asked Alice, because something *was* wrong, she knew it without quite knowing how she knew it. It wasn't simply the hangers, it was something else, some unidentifiable feeling of things suddenly tilting off-kilter, of wrongness.

"Maudie?" and her reply was the hangers chittering again, bouncing violently, sending one or two jangling loose from the rack, and then the ones at the end of the rail began to stretch out, their hooks unbending as though pulled from below, clattering to the floor in a tangle. More began to stretch, quicker and quicker so that the sound of them coming of the metal rail was like the twang of distant catapults. They bounced on the floor, spinning towards her and off behind the rack where they punctured the black plastic bags that were still waiting to be sorted. Alice heard rustling, thought briefly of snakes slipping through dry grass, and then the bags behind the rack were slipping forward, spilling out their contents and the scarecrow was capering across the room towards her.

It was a pair of trousers and a shirt, moving with exaggerated gestures, the knees kicking high, the arms waving wildly above it. The clothes hung loose and Alice had a sense of something skinny and dry within them, like sticks, and it made her think of scarecrows, of figures that danced, spindly, in the wind. The scarecrow had no head but there was something above the shirt collar, a patch of shade that might have been a face, a smear of eyes and pale lips and teeth that gleamed, and then Alice screamed and she was running.

The scarecrow followed her, still running with its legs kicking high and its arms describing uneven circles about it, dervish-like. She saw the label at the back of the shirt, saw the tails flapping up to reveal the waistband of the trousers, and she ran down the stairs towards the shop floor. As she ran, she heard the flapping of cloth from behind her even over her scream, and then she was through the door and across to the counter.

The room was dark, the racks of clothes and shelves of books about her, hemming her in, the gloom pressing up against the windows at the front of the shop, and the scarecrow was coming through the door, still capering, still dancing to a beat she could not hear. Alice screamed again and smelled dirt and urine and old cigarette smoke and then the scarecrow was up against her, its arms falling over her shoulders and she felt the thing inside it, the scarecrow's bones, pressing down on her. She punched out, her hands wrapping into the material of the shirt, clutching at it, feeling a writhing hardness under her fingers and she yanked, tore at it, kicking at the trousers, feeling them tangle around her and she screamed again and then she was tearing at it frenziedly and the scarecrow collapsed to the floor.

It was just a shirt and a pair of trousers; they were flat, empty, lying at her feet like shed skin. Alice reached out a cautious foot and pushed at them. The movement released another breath of the smell, now faded and pale. The hair on Alice's arm, across her whole body, began to settle back against her skin; she hadn't realised that it had been stood up. She was shivering, she discovered, and starting to feel sick. Trembling, she stepped over the clothes and went to the door, intending to leave, but stopped.

Her keys were upstairs. Her keys, her bag, her coat. Everything. The shop door was locked, and her keys were upstairs.

Maudie was upstairs.

Alice stepped away from the door and its tantalising glimpses of the safe outside, moving towards the stairwell, and then came to a halt. The trousers and shirt had risen from the floor and were standing behind the counter. The cuffs of the shirt tilted above the counter's surface as though their occupant was leaning against it and surveying the shop like it was theirs, the shoulders dangling down around something that came nowhere near filling the space within the material, the trousers hanging loose around hips that weren't there. Alice tried to scream again but made only a kind of wretched choking sound and the scarecrow set to dancing, throwing its arms up as though she had startled him. In the darkness around its shoulders, a head made of shades and glints bobbed merrily. Its dance took it to the end of the counter and out into the body of the shop, where it jigged and cavorted but came no closer. She heard the flap of the material around it, heard the crack of the heavy trousers, and she knew, she knew, that it was enjoying her fear, enjoying the way the terror was stealing through her, faster and faster until it felt as though it might drown her.

It was the thought of Maudie that made her move in the end, the thought of the hangers jangling furiously and then bending out and snapping off the rail, of her fear and Maudie's fear. She dashed back up the stairs, not liking the way the walls hemmed her in, trapping her between two narrow exits, and then was into the stock room. She shut the door into the stairwell, not knowing if it would help but reassured by the solidity of the thud as the door closed into place. The scarecrow hadn't followed her, was presumably still dancing in the now-empty shop, down amongst the books and clothes and old VHS tapes that few people bought these days.

"Maudie?" Alice said when her breathing had calmed. "Maudie?'

At first, there was no response, and then the remaining hangers span slightly on the rail, turning and clinking against each other quietly. Alice sniffed, smelling a faint whiff of The Colonel's pipe smoke, and glimpsed the Lady in Waiting in the corner of her eye. The lights flickered briefly. She had the impression that the shop's ghosts were emerging from hiding, peering out from around corners only they knew where to find. "Maudie, are you okay?" she asked, and the hangers swung a little more firmly for a moment: yes.

"Maudie, what is that?" Alice said. "Who is that?" In response, the hangers jerked violently and then stopped. There were no words but Maudie's meaning was clear: she was scared.

"We need to find what he's attached to," said Hazel.

It was the next day. Alice had stayed in the shop for another hour last night before finally turning all the lights on from the panel upstairs, wrapping herself in her coat and going as silently down the stairs as she could. The trousers and shirt were piled in the centre of the shop's floor but she ignored them, hurrying to the door and leaving as fast as she could. There was no sign of the scarecrow, and the clothes it had inhabited earlier remained motionless as she left. The next morning, she told Hazel what had happened, whispering to her so that the other volunteers wouldn't overhear her and think her mad. Truthfully, in the autumnal morning light, the fear she had felt for a pair of dancing trousers and shirt seemed silly somehow, distant and unreal.

Hazel didn't seem particularly worried, although she did keep asking Alice is she was okay or if she wanted to go home. Alice didn't, though; she had spent the evening thinking about the scarecrow, about the shop, about the friends she had made there and the work they did, and she had decided no. She was not going to be scared off by this new thing, and she was not going to let it scare Maudie or the Colonel or the Lady in Waiting, or any of the others.

"How can we tell?" asked Alice, looking at the black bin bags lining the walls of the stockrooms.

"We do what we always do," said Hazel. "We sort this stuff out, as quickly as we can. Whatever he's attached to, I'll know when we find it. He can't harm you, Alice, he's just angry and confused and frightened. He's not dangerous."

"No," said Alice, but she was thinking of the others, hiding from him, and the way he had jigged and then stood behind the counter like the lord of a manor and of her fear, and she wasn't sure Hazel was right.

By the end of the first day's sorting, they'd unpacked maybe a third of the bags. Most of the contents were clothes, older but in good condition; Alice found it fascinating, uncovering a strata of fashion that she had little knowledge of, where wider lapels and thick shirt collars that came down to long points like dog's teeth were the norm and the suits were heavy and woollen and smelled of must and sweat. There were books as well, and old kitchen equipment, and boxes of records by people that Alice had never heard of, Art Blakey and Bix Beiderbecke and others. Most of the clothes were put for cleaning and then selling, although the threadbare underwear they found in one bag was put into the rags pile, and the records were put on one side to see if they were rare enough to interest a collector. They didn't find anything that might explain the scarecrow, though, and at the end of the day Hazel said to Alice as they were leaving, "I'll come in early tomorrow and carry on."

"Will you be okay?"

"Of course," said Hazel. She hugged Alice briefly, and then turned and went towards her car. The lights from the streetlamps rolled orange over her shoulders and dark hair and she looked confident and strong, just like Alice wanted to be, and then she gone around the corner. It was the last time Alice saw her.

Hazel was found the next morning at the bottom of the stairs, sprawled out onto the shop floor with her neck broken and her head twisted around so that she was almost looking back up the steps towards the stockrooms. She was cold when she was found and had been dead at least a couple of hours.

~

The shop was closed for a week afterwards; the first day was a chaos of flashing lights and police and ambulances, and then there were people from head office and a few local reporters and Alice was pinballing from one to another, telling them what she'd seen, which was nothing really, and yes, the stairs were steep and yes, it must have been a terrible accident. She didn't mention the scarecrow, or Maudie and the others, and no one asked.

When head office found a temporary manager and called everyone to ask if they'd come back, Alice agreed because she wasn't exactly sure how to say no. Besides, she liked her time there; it got her out of home and away from her mum and dad, who were going through another of their argumentative spells. Their tensions with each other kept spilling out into nagging Alice about when she was going to do something with her life, when was she going to get a job, make something of herself? They never offered her any help, only pointed questions with their riptide currents of pressure and implication and disappointment, and what could she say? There were no jobs and besides, she liked volunteering at the shop; it made her feel wanted, important, part of something bigger than her own tiny life. She had liked it, anyway, before Hazel died.

Before the scarecrow.

The temporary manager was a large, red-faced man who insisted everyone called him Mr Pitt, and who held Alice's hand for a moment too long the first time he met her. He told them he was going to see to 'front of house', and asked her to see to the stock, which suited her perfectly well. At least the stockroom was quiet, and it was warm.

Only that day, it wasn't, it was cold and dull. No, more than that, cold and empty; it wasn't that there were no people, that she was the only one upstairs, it was more than that. It wasn't just that this was the first time she had been there since Hazel's death, either; it was something even more cavernous, something that made her think of places abandoned and left to decay in the dark, and then, with a sad little jolt, she understood what the problem was.

It wasn't just Hazel; the ghosts were missing.

"Maudie," called Alice and then waited for the reassuring rattle of hangers, but nothing came. She called again; still no response. She narrowed her eyes slightly, letting her focus loosen in the hope of catching the Lady in Waiting at the corner of her vision, but she wasn't there. None of them were, she realised as she searched the building, growing frantic as she went; they were all gone. She hadn't understood how much she enjoyed their presence until then, until they weren't there. They had filled the building, adding comfort to its corners, like the smell of baking bread or the warmth from a radiator, and their absence bled the rooms cold.

She started to cry; it was so stupid, she thought, crying about something, the absence of something that most people wouldn't even have accepted had been there in the first place, but it was horrible. First Hazel and now Maudie and the others, and she knew, just knew, that it was the scarecrow that had driven them out, had somehow scared them from the shop and into... what? Somewhere beyond, that they did not want to go? Outside, where they would wander the streets like wraiths from some fairy story? It was so awful, so unfair! And Hazel? She couldn't even ask herself the question, so enormous were its implications. But yes, she thought. Yes.

Alice went to the chair, to Hazel's chair, and sat, suddenly exhausted, helpless tears rolling down her cheeks. And then, with a rustle of old cloth, the scarecrow rose up from the bags on the other side of the room.

There was something different about it; it was taller somehow, less scrawny. Less like a scarecrow. The shirt it was using to create itself seemed fuller, less held up by sticks, padded out from within, as did the trousers, and the dark smudge of air above the shirt collar was thicker, fuller. More feral. For a moment, Alice was too frightened to move, too frightened to scream, too frightened to even breathe. It capered out of the bags, trouser legs kicking them away. Clothes fell from them, scattering across the floor in drifts of old-fashioned stripes and patterns and fraying cuffs and turn-ups and then it was free and was whirling across the room at her.

Alice's legs pistoned, pushing the chair back, but it only moved an inch before hitting the desk, making the ancient computer on it shake and jolting her. At the same moment, something jangled the hangers on the rail violently, snapping them so that they jerked and leapt. The scarecrow turned, racing away from her and towards them in that ridiculous, dancing run, covering the short space incredibly quickly. Something that Alice couldn't see but could feel broke from behind the clothes rail, darting across the room ahead of the scarecrow. It veered, a shadow made not of darkness but of a distortion of the air, and then something else, a paler smear at the corner of Alice's eye, was moving fast as well. *Maudie!* she thought, *and the Lady! They're here!*

Maudie made it to the front stairs and started down whilst the Lady went the other way, towards the rear stairs up. The scarecrow veered again, starting after the Lady, dashing past Alice in a blur of flapping cloth and a thick smell of body odour and something oily that she couldn't recognise but instinctively thought of as old fashioned. She managed to loose the scream that had been building inside her for the last few minutes and then the scarecrow was lurching up the stairs after the Lady. Alice heard someone shout from downstairs and then there was shriek, not from downstairs but from above her, from upstairs.

From the Lady in Waiting.

It was terrible, a drawn out thing like someone scratching a nail over glass, hopeless and lost and desolate and agonising, but it trailed away to nothing so quickly Alice wondered if she'd heard it all. She started to rise and then Mr Pitt burst into the stockroom shouting, "What the devil is going on?" and didn't see the small pile at the bottom of the stairs made from a pair of trousers and a shirt, now still and flat, that had tumbled to a halt moments before from out of the shadows of the upper floor.

The Lady was gone.

The next day, Alice tried everything, but she was never there in the corner of her eye. Making sure she was never alone, Alice went into every room in the building, from the shop floor right up to the loft with its spilling guts of old folders and broken suitcases, and nowhere could she find the smudge of movement in her peripheral vision that meant the Lady was there. The other ghosts remained hidden, tense, behind things, and only Maudie made her presence felt, shifting the hangers so slightly as Alice passed that she might have been a breeze coming in through the rotting wooden window frames or the breath of a distant god.

Eventually, Mr Pitt got tired of Alice walking about the shop and demanded that she carry on sorting out the stock from the house in Morecambe. She didn't want to, remembering the scarecrow rising up from the clothes like some malignant jack-in-a-box, but there was no way to tell Mr Pitt that; her protestations evaporated like steam in the face of his fat and his bluster and his arm-touching. Another volunteer, Jennie, was pricing records at the desk behind her, though, so maybe it would be okay.

The first bag contained old vests and a torn waistcoat. The vests were stained yellow under the arms and around the neck and she put them into the rags pile; the waistcoat followed, as did the contents of the next bag, mismatched tablecloths with stains puddled across them that looked dried-in and old. Alice managed to lose herself in the rhythm of sorting, pulling things out and scanning them, separating them into piles for rags and cleaning. There were books with yellowed pages that breathed the smell of cigarettes at her as she pulled them out of the bags, a mess of cufflinks and ties, shirts with curled collars, a whole life thrust into black plastic waiting for her to unearth.

Something rustled, deep in the bags, and began to move.

It's okay, Alice told herself, it's okay, Jennie's here, just behind me. She turned, the rustling sound increasing, the bags beginning to shift and slide, to find that the chair behind her was empty. Jennie was gone.

She couldn't even cry out as it rose up in front of her. It was in a new outfit now, a ragged jumper and heavy twill trousers, and he looked even fuller, the V neck not dangling but lying taut against a chest that she couldn't see, the trousers kicking out, and then it was coming. Bags flew up around it as it surged forward, clothes leaping into the air, plastic tearing, and still she couldn't scream. One of the ties landed on its shoulder and flapped obscenely like a tongue and she was suddenly sure that it was deliberate, that the scarecrow wanted it to fall that way, wanted it to waggle at her, and then she started to scream and it was on her.

It was almost weightless, volume without mass, but she fell back nonetheless, the black shadow of its head pressing against her face and smelling of shaving soap and nicotine and an old man's exhalations. Its breath pressed against her, clammy on her teeth and filling her mouth and lungs, and Alice suddenly knew that this was the last thing Hazel had smelled as she died, this broth of aged scents, and it was bearing down on her hard, so hard, and then the scarecrow was jerked away.

Alice caught a whiff of pipe smoke and thought, *The Colonel!* She rolled over on to her front, the scarecrow on the floor next to her. It was struggling, fighting with something beneath it that she could not see and she thought again, *The Colonel* and then there was another of those screams, like wire dragging across wire, escalating, rising. The unseen shape beneath the scarecrow collapsed, disappeared, the scarecrow sinking to the floor in a mess of musty cloth and shifting, dwindling blackness. He...it...seemed thicker somehow, fatter, filling its clothes more, and then it flipped over onto its back, sat up, rose to feet it didn't possess and was coming towards her again.

Two more things darted from the edges of the room, ripples in the air and there was singing, something old and mumbled and Alice had time to think *Suzy! Peg!* and then they were on the scarecrow. One of them, Suzy she thought, wrapped itself around the scarecrow's legs and pulled at the pants and they twisted, tangling and kicking. Peg clung to the scarecrow's chest, dragging one of its woollen arms around. It thrashed, rippling, its shade head bobbing, its afterimage teeth gnashing and champing. With its free arm it reached down and grasped at the air around its legs, yanking on Suzy so that she came up with a howl like an electric filament burning out, and then she was gone. Peg, shifting around it in a frenzy, trying to avoid its grip, was gone a moment later. Her last sound was a torn, drawn-out yelp that might have been a word and might have been a simple scream of agony and terror, and then the scarecrow turned back to Alice and began its dance.

Alice ran. The scarecrow was between her and the stairs down, so she dashed to the other set and started upwards. Not all the way, though, not to the loft with its low roof and mounds of abandoned detritus and its closed, trapping walls, but to the next floor up. She came off the stairs, running into the first room; paintings and prints and ornaments surrounded her, chipped and glazed eyes staring on as she ran. An ornate mirror on the other side of the room showed the room around her, the scarecrow behind her, no longer spindly but grown to a thick, terrible vitality, capering after her. It still ran exaggeratedly, like a clown, as though this was a game, as though this was something joyous, to be revelled in. She hardly recognising the dusty, crying girl she saw in the mirror in front of the scarecrow as herself.

Alice ran though the doorway at the back of the room, her last glimpse of the thing chasing her a blurred darkness in the silvered glass, and then she was in the next room. Racks of clothes greeted her, summer dresses and tops, shorts, Hawaiian shirts, waiting for the warmer weather to come around again. She buried herself between the racks, hoping that it might not see her in amongst the gaudiness. She wrapped herself in the colours of sunlight, and tried to become motionless, silent.

The scarecrow did not follow her into the room.

Alice wasn't sure how long she waited; a minute maybe, possibly longer. She began to wonder if it had stopped, if she would find its latest skin abandoned in the other room much as she had before, and very slowly stepped out from her hiding place. The garments swung around her, but their movement was slow and easy, natural. Normal. The doorway was dark, weak light glimmering through it. Nothing moved, nothing capered or danced or ran. Was it gone? Really? Alice took a step towards it, wanting it to be true, unsure.

There was another of those thin, terrible screams and for a moment lights flickered violently in the far room, on and off, off and on. *Ken*, thought Alice, and then the scarecrow gambolled through the doorway and she was running again.

The next room along wasn't really a room, was just a blister between spaces, an afterthought, and it was full of games and jigsaws, stacked high and unevenly. They teetered as she passed them, finally crashing down behind her in a spray of cardboard pieces and die and counters. She was at the back of the building now, into the next room where the larger items and the kitchenware were stored, the view out of the windows drab and grey and God how she wished she was out there now, out in the greyness and the rain and the litter, with water running down her coat and off her hair and the Morecambe air dirty against her skin. The scene on the far side of the glass was as distant as a painting, though, distant and untouchable and unreachable.

The scarecrow was in the room, kicking through the jigsaw pieces, segments of coloured card leaping up around it, and Alice carried on running because there was nothing else she could do.

She had almost completed a loop now, was back at the entrance to the stairs and her head was saying *Down! Down!* but her feet took her to the stairs up and it came after her, its feet made of murk and shade and as silent as she imaged a predatory cat's to be. She stumbled as she ran, her feet dragging across the cheap nylon nap of the carpet, and then fell. Her knees and hands hit the steps and raised clouds of dust that smelled of plaster and moths and mildew. It was almost on her, its shadow falling across her, the only sound apart from her breathing the grim sibilance of its jumper and trousers and tie flapping. She scuttled forwards and upwards, just out of its grasp, and finally reached the alcove between the floors, another of the building's weird little unexpected spaces, and yanked open the cupboard doors.

She didn't know why she hadn't thought to check before; the cupboard, where Hazel put the ghosts' anchors, where Peg's typewriter and Maudie's coat and all the other things were kept. In its depths were the little lost treasures and loved things, the things the dead couldn't bear to leave behind, and she hoped, desperate, that there was something new here. She fumbled the key off the wall and unlocked it quickly, pulling open the door and staring at the things within.

It was at the side, hanging by itself, the rest of the clothes pushed away as though they didn't want to be near it; a man's overcoat, heavy and woollen with a collar of some other, darker material. *Astrakhan*, she thought abstractly, dragging the coat from the hanger, holding it in front of her like a matador's cape and spinning around to face the approaching scarecrow. She hoped; it was all she had left.

She hoped

It was his; as the coat flapped in Alice's hands, she caught a taste of the scent that had been with the scarecrow as it had been on top of her in the stockroom. The coat's lining hung down like half-shed snakeskin, frayed loops of material swaying below the hem. The scarecrow stopped scant feet from her and watched, its blurred head tilting to one side in a way that seemed quizzical and amused and somehow dismissive. *Little girl*, it seemed to say, *what do you hope to do with that coat? What can you do to me?* And, she realised, she didn't know, had no answer for him. It took a deliberate step towards her, subtle and stealthy now, all exaggeration gone. Another.

Another.

Alice backed away, bumped into the cupboard and had a momentary vision of stepping inside it, locking it somehow, falling through its back and into the dreary Morecambe night, stepping back out from this terrible Narnia into reality. The coat flapped in her hands and the scarecrow took another step, reached out its sleeves with their worn cuffs and Alice knew that its hands beyond the cuffs were curled into claws, and then the coat flapped again. It was moving in her hands, the heavy wool jerking through her fingers. The garment was filling out, the sleeves rising, the shoulders swelling, and Alice thought it was the scarecrow itself and then realised it wasn't, it was something else, someone else.

It was Maudie.

For a moment the two ghosts faced each other, and then the coat,

Maudie, suddenly leapt, crashing into the scarecrow. Instead of falling back, the two tangled and rolled up the upwards steps, flapping, coming apart and then together again in a writhing mess. The clothes struggled against each other, flailing up the stairs and finally collapsing through the doorway into the loft. Alice stepped forward so that she see better but there was nothing there, just the dark regularity of the doorway. Something brushed past her, the Gentleman, the quietest of the shop's ghosts, normally so diffident but now moving determinedly upwards. Something crashed in the loft and then the shadows of the doorway wavered slightly as something passed through it. *That's him,* Alice thought, *the Gentleman. That's the first time I've ever seen him.* It was a strange thing to think, she knew, but what about her life wasn't strange now?

There was another crash, louder, more metallic. One of the old ornaments, perhaps? A piece of household equipment? She couldn't tell.

"Alice?" called a voice from downstairs. Mr Pitt; she'd almost forgotten she wasn't here alone. "What's going on up there? What are you doing?"

"Nothing," she called, and hoped he wouldn't come up. There was another crash, and then a scream, thin and drawn out. The Gentleman. He and Maudie were fighting the scarecrow, fighting it for Alice's safety and for their home, and the Gentleman had been... what? Injured? No, worse; killed.

Murdered.

"Alice!" called Mr Pitt. "What on earth are you doing?" He was closer, off the shop floor. Coming up.

Another crash, the sound of things falling, of two people, two dead people, fighting from one end of the room to the other. She felt suddenly exhausted; she heard Mr Pitt walking across the stockroom below her, the floor creaking under his bulk, and then start up the next set of stairs. "Alice!" he shouted again, angry now.

Something else crashed in the loft and a window broke, the shattering of glass a descant to the sounds of the fight. There was a thud as something heavy hit the floor, and more crashes, and then a second scream, longer than the first, drawn out, stretching and metallic, breaking apart after a second into noises like flies dying, fading to nothing. She wanted to believe that it was the scarecrow, that it was his death rattle, that he was gone.

Something shifted in the doorway, bobbed through, hidden in the shadows for a moment before emerging into the light at the top of the stairs. It was the overcoat, its shoulders slumped, its collar dark. She caught a faint scent, of perfume and talcum. "Maudie?" Alice whispered, her heart leaping in her chest. The figure stepped forwards, emerging from darkness into light.

"Alice," said Mr Pitt from behind her as the coat fell to the floor. Alice couldn't reply as the scarecrow, kicking its legs high and waving its arms above its head in a triumphant jig, danced down the stairs the stairs towards them.

2.23 a.m.

My wife woke me from a dream sometime in the early hours of Christmas morning when she rolled over and came to rest against me. Her arm slipped across my chest and she pressed, warm, against me. Her smell filled my nostrils, perfume and soap and skin, and I put my arms around her and marvelled again at the way she fitted into me as though she was a missing piece sent to make me whole. In the safety of our bed, she was all curves and smooth hollows whereas I was all lines and edges, she soft and I brittle, and I loved her. She murmured something that might have been "Happy Christmas," and then was silent.

Later, on the edge of sleep, I remembered that I was not married and never had been, and the cold space in my arms smelled of nothing but misery and loneliness and of dreams I did not want.

Little Traveller

Ghedi jittered.

The scow lifted and dropped, buffeted by the arrhythmic chopping of the swell surging at them from the ocean at their backs and the container ship's hull at their fronts. Everything trembled, everything shook, the water trying to unsettle Ghedi but failing because of the steel that ran through his bones and the density of his muscle. All around the world had tautened, become bright, diamond-edged and clear, sharp; this was the most dangerous part, these next few minutes, when Ghedi and the others would be at their most vulnerable.

There was a boom from the scow in front as Korfa fired the gas-powered grappling hook; he had stolen that two or three ships back and it was one of his proudest possessions. Ghedi only had a welded mess of fishing gaffs at the end of a rope and he threw it now, watching as it arced into the sky above him, leaving black trails behind itself like shed snakeskin before it disappeared over the ship's rail. He tugged, felt the hooks drag and then find purchase, and then he was swarming up the rope, antlike and quick, fingers sure on the rope as it writhed in his grip. His gun chittered to itself on his back, little satisfied metallic clinks as it readied itself for what was coming and looked forward, excited. Hand over hand he went, feet walking the skin of the ship, silent and intense, letting his lack of fear, his ferocity and preparedness to kill go ahead of him like the scent of a lion's musk as it charged its prey.

He reached the rail without incident; no water cannon, no gunshots from the fat white men that the companies sometimes hired to protect the ships, men with shaven heads and tattoos who thought they understood violence and fear but who did not. Ghedi understood violence and fear; Ghedi was violence and fear.

Despite his gas grapple, Korfa was over the rail later than Ghedi, slow and old and weighted by a belly that was growing fat and soft; Ghedi would smile about that later, but not now. Now he crouched and peered about, as Korfa was doing a hundred feet along the deck from him. The container ship was deserted, the deck silent apart from the rapid echoes of Ghedi's own breathing, coming back at him from the sides of the containers stacked high and running down the centre of the ship like a vast, segmented spine, doubling his inhalations and exhalations so that he sounded like two men, two warriors, weapons made flesh. He scuttled forward, drawing close to the containers, wary of the occasional gaps between them but grateful of the cover they offered. Korfa, more brazen, stayed by the rail, leaning back and peering up. He had a quizzical look upon his face and as Ghedi came alongside him he said, "Up there, little traveller."

Little traveller; how Ghedi hated that nickname, bestowed upon him simply because he was younger than Korfa and the others and because of his name's meaning. Ghedi sometimes imagined his parents hoping that his name would encourage him to see the world; little people with big ideas, lost now in the somewhen of his past. He couldn't remember their faces, nor their voices or the touch of their hands. Little traveller. Would they ever have guessed where he would travel to, he wondered? Probably not.

"What?" Glancing up. Nothing.

"Shadows, most likely," said Korfa, not looking down yet, "but maybe one of the *hooyadiis wase*." His voice sounded distant, thoughtful, as though he were contemplating which of the camp's whores to fuck.

Ghedi scanned along the tops of the containers. They were stacked high, four up, the edges deep in shadows, the sky beyond them the blue of forever. It wasn't unheard of for the fat white *dufarr* to position themselves on top of the containers when they saw the attack coming, for them to fire down or drop things. One of Ghedi's friends had been hit by a dropped stanchion on an earlier raid, bursting his head open so that his brains had spattered out and ended up looking like worms on the deck, pink and crawling. Today, though, Ghedi saw nothing.

"We should move," said Korfa, snapping back into reality and glaring at Ghedi, as though the delay hadn't been his fault. Ghedi nodded and swung his rifle around from his back, took it by the neck and stock and held it calm, and they went forward. Ghedi, still dancing along close enough to the containers to feel their breath on his back, watched as Korfa moved along the rail, continually glancing up. What had he seen, or thought he had seen, Ghedi wondered, because Ghedi could hear and see nothing.

Nothing.

That wasn't usual, was it? In all of their incursions (a word he had heard in a crackling radio broadcast by a faraway white man about what he and Korfa and the others did, and liked for its rolling, jagged sounds and the way it caressed his tongue), their time on the boats had been built of noise and fragments, of the stenches of fear and sweat and gunfire and sometimes of blood. Now, however, all was silent except for the scuff of their feet and the muttering of his gun, and the only smell was that of burning.

Ghedi stopped. It had only been a whiff, as though his nose had touched against a tendril drifting in from some vast distance, but it had been there nonetheless, there and now gone. He sniffed again, smelled nothing.

"What?" asked Korfa, turning. The man's skin was slick with sweat, and suddenly all Ghedi could smell was him, the smell of his body and the things he smoked, that they all smoked, thick, seeping out from his pores as though Korfa was more drug than man. Perhaps he was.

"Nothing," said Ghedi after another sniff.

"Then come on," said Korfa, looked up again at the top of the containers and screamed.

It made Ghedi jump, the scream, and he pulled the trigger on his rifle unthinking. The weapon, exultant, screamed the song of its soul and spat fire and Korfa's chest and belly bloomed open into flowers that had rich red petals. The man screamed again, staggering back against the rail, pushed by the weight of the rifle's touch on him, then teetered and fell forward. He rolled, flopping like a gaffed fish, ended up on his back, staring still at the top of the containers and screaming. Ghedi dropped to his knees, sorry but needing Korfa to shut up, to shut the fuck up before someone came, holding a hand over his mouth to stifle the noise of him. Gradually, Korfa quietened, and his silence was somehow worse than his noise.

"Little traveller," said Korfa after a second. He was still staring up, looking not at Ghedi who had shot him but beyond, focussing on something and scared of the something, a something that Ghedi could not see even when he turned and looked to the same place. "Little traveller," said Korfa again, his voice stinking of meat because of the blood in his mouth and the terror in his eyes, "run." He coughed once, spraying Ghedi with warmth, and then died.

Gone. Korfa was gone and in the past and no longer part of the present, and a smell of burning again, just for a second and then drifting away.

There was no decision to be made; forward, the only way for Ghedi now. They had a job to do, an incursion to complete, he and his fellow sailors. He might mourn Korfa later, but now there were fat white pickings to take, a ship and its cargo and crew to place his hands around so that money could be strangled out of the even fatter, whiter insurance companies. Forward.

Ghedi dashed down the deck, all thoughts of caution gone now, running and wearing Korfa's death across his face like warpaint, I am fear, I am terror, running past the shadowed gaps between the containers and beginning to scream himself, a howl of fury, a roar to show his teeth. From somewhere on the other side of the containers he heard the sound of another grapple hitting the deck and dragging, the metal yammer of it piercing, and then another, the other two boats looped around and finally catching up with him and Korfa, then the duller thumps of feet and hands.

Past the end of the piled spine of containers now, approaching the ladder that led to the observation decks and helm, still no sign of movement other than his own beading sweat and leaping shadow, his other self, the darkness from his own heart allowed out, urged on before him. From the other side of the containers Erasto and Labaan appeared, also screaming lionlike, seeing Ghedi and making for the other stairway. Ghedi kept moving, rushing through sun that was like water on his skin, making the foot of the metal stairs and starting up. He lost sight of Erasto for a moment, caught a whiff of burning wood, burning flesh, saw a memory flash of a house with flames in the window, heard gunfire.

Labaan, not quite at the foot of the other stairs, stepped behind Erasto, looked up and howled, not a lion now but a hyena faced with a lion. Erasto's rifle, an American M16 stolen from the last ship's cowering security officer, clattered down and bounced at Labaan's feet; Ghedi, despite the need to move, slowed and watched as Labaan backed away, feet tangling, and fell. He shrieked again, brought his own gun up and fired, the bullets striking sparks off the rail and risers that were bright even in the shadeless sun, crabbing backwards like a child, tears on his face. Another wave of the burning stench and then Labaan flipped himself over, a rib of meat on a grill, and scuttled back behind the edge of the containers. There was another burst of firing, the sound of frayed ricochets, and then from the stairway a crunch and a scream that rose, rose again, cut off.

Ghedi glanced over; the scows were still circling out on the chopping blue surface of the ocean, sharks waiting for their prey to weaken. How many others had come on board? Were any of them left? Should he signal, bring them in and leave?

No.

This ship was theirs, was his, by the rights of terror and strength and by the rules that they themselves had decided; it was theirs because they wanted it, because they had nothing besides that which they took themselves, not families nor homes, not anything except each other. Besides, to bring it in alone, without Korfa or the others? To make it his? He would never be Little Traveller again, never be left the scraps of the drugs or women, never be left on the edges, never be beaten or teased with match or flame, there would be no more jeering about the little lost one, the cast-off, the child he had been once and never outgrown.

Ghedi jittered and ran, upwards and onwards, his gun leading him, his brother during day and night. It spoke to him, urging him on, up and up because they were travellers together, no longer little, no longer weak, the roar and terror of him huge, and still there were no signs of life on this flabby western ship.

As Ghedi reached the top of the staircase he caught another scent of burning, gone as quickly as it had arrived, a memory in his nostrils that reached back through the years to a place he had vowed never to visit again. It was the past, dark to him now except in flashes of brightness at the centre of the cooking fires or the waved torches that Korfa and the others had sometimes brandished, laughing at him as he cried out or jumped back from them, weeping.

Across the flat expanse of the upper deck towards the wheelhouse, a metal cabin fronted by a huge window. The sun glared across the surface of the glass, hiding what was behind it, blinding him. Ghedi roared so that they would know he was coming, was surging towards them unstoppable and terrible, would know that no glass or metal walls would stop him. Ghedi was arrived, Ghedi the traveller was come, and he was death and fear and violence.

Closer to, and the sun's fiery reflected eye shifted, sliding along the glass to reveal the room behind. It held banks of equipment and flashing dials and lights, computer displays, a large wooden wheel that was almost certainly for display rather than for any actual purpose. At its rear, a door to the lost depths of the ship was shut, bolts clearly locking it from the inside; another door, also bolted, in the side wall led out onto the deck. A shelf on the rear wall held plastic folders in rainbow colours, and logs and books, and a table under it was covered in cups and a map held down at its corners by pencils.

And there were crew.

Four of them, all standing still, looking at him, faces blank. *They fear me, know what I am*, Ghedi thought, and raised his rifle, letting its mouth open, letting it show its teeth. He tapped it against the glass and gestured at the side door, moving along the front of the glass towards it, a lethal, venomous spider clinging to the window's surface and dancing towards its prey.

The crew did not move other than to follow him with their eyes.

"I will kill you!" Ghedi shouted. He shouted it first in English, then repeated it in French and German. He didn't like the way the words felt in his mouth, the English slimy, the French too smooth and the German angular, digging into his throat like hooks as he spat the phrase out. He could speak none of those languages, of course, Korfa had simply taught him the expression; Korfa, now gone. The realisation made Ghedi pause for a moment, looking at the crew. His own face would be dark to them, its covering of Korfa's blood like a mask, just as theirs were pale to him, little more than hovering white discs in the gloom of the room, their eyes depthless hollows in which glints flickered in time with the ever-changing displays on the computer screens. Ghedi gestured again at the door, and again the crew merely looked at him.

There was little point in firing at the glass; it would be bulletproof. Ghedi had learned that on an earlier incursion when one of the others, Labaan he thought, had shot at the window and the bullet had leapt back between them singing a song like an enraged hornet. It had torn through the skin of Korfa's shoulder, Ghedi suddenly remembered, making the man shriek like a child. Fat westerners, trying to keep themselves safe behind thick glass and bolted metal and still they fell at Ghedi and his companions' feet. Instead, he tapped the rifle against the glass in a regular threat, still moving around towards the wheelhouse door.

"I will kill you!" he called again, gagging on the words now, and still the crew did not move. Did they really think they were safe, he wondered, that he could not get through the door?

His own face shone on the surface of the glass, ghosting across it, covering the closest crewmember's face for a moment so that the man appeared to be wearing a mask, his face becoming a satire of Ghedi's own, distorted and ugly, and then something behind Ghedi moved in the reflections, something orange and black.

He whipped about, fast, rifle an extension of his arm, ready to deal with any fat *eey* creeping up behind him – but the deck was empty. He looked about, squinting into the sun. It had been there, hadn't it? Hadn't it? Something behind him, shifting and changing but still somehow peering at him, sweating sadness.

Sadness? Why had he thought that? But yes, sad, it had been sad as it looked at him, something at its centre that was without eyes but that looked at him nonetheless. And it smelled, that burning stench, of wood and material crackling and hair shrivelling, of fat roasting. What trickery was this? The crew, he thought, operating a film projector or some other device to fool or frighten him. Well, they would soon know that Ghedi was fearless, would not be stopped.

He spun back about, jabbed his rifle against the glass once more and shouted "Open up!" They wouldn't understand, he wasn't speaking English or French or German but his own tongue, the language of his father, but his meaning was clear. Angling the rifle so that it pointed away, he fired, the shot careening across the glass with a sound like a dry bone breaking and leaving a silvered streak that trailed from fat to thin like a snake. A wisp of smoke rose from it like a kiss and then was gone.

The crew didn't react.

The man nearest the glass, his face still little more than a pale distortion in the gloom, carried on staring at Ghedi. Ghedi raised the rifle and pointed it directly at the man and fired. The shot impacted against the glass, cracking through its upper layer before being stopped, spreading and leaving an uneven grey mass trapped in the pane, as though the window had grown some distorted eye that stared at Ghedi. Still the man did not react, did not move or jump, did not blink.

Ghedi peered at the man, who simply stared back. After a moment the man opened his mouth and spoke, the words clear despite the layer of glass between them. "Little Traveller," he said, "run."

Something was burning.

It wasn't a whiff or a hint as before, but the thick, sour stench of encroaching flame. At first, he thought it was the spore of his rifle and then it rose up from behind Ghedi in reflection, an entire house aflame, windows ringed in fire, door buckling in the heat. He could see it, despite the impossibility of it, feel it, feel the hair on the back of his neck singe and the prickle of heat across his skin, smelled it and then he was running and the crew merely stared as Ghedi fled from the house that couldn't be there.

Down the steps and away from the wheelhouse he went, the steps that Labaan and Erasto had been at the bottom of when whatever happened to them had occurred. He ran, thoughtless, rifle screaming at him in fury, sweat covering him like oil, away from the house and the flame and the smell and the thing behind the house's window. Ten steps down, twelve, twenty, how many? Something grated behind him, wood grinding across metal, and then his shadow was ringed ahead of him by an orange halo that flickered and jumped and he ran faster, the little traveller running, thirty steps, forty, taking four and five at a time and then there was Erasto.

He was sitting with his back against the stairwell wall, legs stuck out in front of him like the limbs of the stickmen that Ghedi's father used to make him when he was a small boy. Erasto, normally the darkest of them, had paled to something the consistency of goat's milk, and his skin was covered in ragged tears and punctures that were scored across his chest and abdomen. He jerked, twisting, not alive but moving nonetheless, moving in a way that reminded Ghedi of the victim of the crocodile attack that Erasto had described witnessing as a child and which had scared him so much that he would never enter the waters of river or sea. Blood sprayed from the holes in the man's skin, staining Erasto's T-shirt, darker than the ancient sweat rings that clustered around his armpits. Ghedi leapt over him, landing steps down, catching a glimpse as he passed over of something covering Erasto like a second skin, something green and grey and thrashing, ridged back hunched and eyes like glass peering up at him.

More steps and just as Ghedi was beginning to despair of ever reaching the bottom, thinking that he would simply dash further and further until he reached Hell itself, there was the deck. Out and moving faster now, rifle swinging behind him, something crashing down in his wake, heat on his back, the smell of flame and fat bubbling, flesh roasting and burning, and Ghedi screamed now, no longer the maker of fear and terror but made of it, the little traveller again, helpless and lost and afraid. *Back to the rope and down*, he thought, *and hope the others see me, come in close to catch me before it does, or before I fall.*

The others. His friends, who teased him and mocked him but who had been the only people he had been able to rely on since it had happened, since the day Ghedi had been untethered from the life of his birth, the others who had taken him in and given him bed and food and safety, of a sort.

Ghedi stumbled, spinning and falling in one ungainly stutter of movement and came to a rest with his back against the cargo container facing back up the stairs. His rifle yelped and spat, his finger jerking on the trigger without instruction, sending tiny bolts of fire spraying across the stairs and careening across the deck.

There was nothing there.

The air in Ghedi's lungs felt curdled, thick and clotted, making breathing difficult. He tried to take in a breath, failed, sucked again and hitched, drew hard and finally something in his chest popped as though a bubble of mucus had risen to the surface and finally worked itself loose. There was nothing there: no fires, no shadows, nothing chasing him down the steps. *It must be the drugs*, he thought, a bad batch cooked up with poison and bile at its heart.

He risked a glance behind him, back along the deck. Erasto and Labaan's grappling hooks were still clinging to the rails, the ropes dangling from them threads connecting him to the ocean and the boats and his life beyond.

Past them, in the centre of the deck, Labaan was standing, head bowed and with his back to Ghedi.

He was shaking, a violent shudder that seemed to consume his whole body so that he was bouncing, shoulders spasming and hands hanging at his sides, flapping like boneless crabs. Ghedi dragged himself to his feet, using the container to steady himself as he rose. He felt full of sickness, the toxins of his unspent fear gathering at his joints and in his stomach. He started along the deck towards Labaan, watching as the man's movements grew more and more pronounced, his arms and legs now dancing spastically, a vicious palsy that eventually dropped him to his knees.

Still he shuddered, faster and faster.

As he came around Labaan, Ghedi caught a glimpse of the man's face; his eyes were wide and weeping tears of blood, rolled back to complete whiteness, blind and staring. His mouth was open, tongue protruding, a fat saliva-dressed worm questing forth into the daylight, its end squirming back and forth. He was shaking so fast now that he blurred, his edges collapsing into the brightness, his core dark and indistinct, and then he pitched forward and was suddenly still.

Ghedi prodded him with the barrel of his gun; Labaan didn't move. He prodded again and then, when there was still no response, he crouched and leaned in to see if he could detect inhalations or exhalations. Nothing. Was he dead? Ghedi prodded again, trying to roll Labaan over.

Veins bulged under the skin of Labaan's scalp, crawling down his face and neck and disappearing into his shirt. His arms and legs were tensing now, clenching, becoming rigid. Smoke drifted out from his short hair and from the skin of his neck, the smell of it bitter, reminding Ghedi of something Labaan had once said, something about electricity, about electrocution, about his fear. The man's arms and legs were stiff now, skin a mass of swelling veins, no longer shaking but somehow vibrating, banging against the deck in a rapid, violent tattoo and then someone called Ghedi's name.

It was a voice filled with love and pain, reaching out to him through smoke and the sound of wood expanding in flame and then something emerged from between two containers, ahead of him now, something that could not possibly have been hiding in the gap it came from, something too wide and too long, something that shouldn't be able to move but was, gliding like a snake to fill Ghedi's vision and his nose and ears, filling his whole head with its impossibility and its reality.

It was almost burnt flat now, its walls crumbling, the roof gone, and they were dead, had to be dead, but still Ghedi heard them screaming from within its raging heart, could see their shapes at the window burnt scrawny and he hadn't meant to, had only been playing with the stove and the paper, hadn't meant to make the flames come. *Please*, he thought and then said the word aloud and then there was no more travelling and no more words and the house came to him and the heat placed its arms around him and his father's voice spoke his name.

Dental Caries:

Decay causes certain strains of bacteria that, especially when exposed to excess sugars, attack teeth and gums.

N is for Noodle

"I wouldn't eat that."

Jimmy leaned back in his seat and sipped at his Sapporo, looking seriously at Glyn. Glyn sipped at his own beer and looked down at the bowl in front of him; noodles, the liquid breathing steam and swimming with tiny golden globules of fat, the pale strands twisting around the lumps of vegetables and meat that swam below the fat. Experimentally, he swirled the contents of the bowl with his chopsticks, watching as they span about and smelling its rich scent. He caught a frond of noodle and lifted it, sniffing it and then popping it into his mouth. Smelled good, tasted fantastic. Noodles.

"I really wouldn't," said Jimmy again. He swallowed the last of his beer and raised his finger to the waiter behind the counter. Across the quiet restaurant, the man nodded almost imperceptibly. Glyn nodded as well, and the man busied himself with drawing two more Sapporo.

"Why? It tastes good. Great actually. There's nothing wrong with noodles," said Glyn.

"I never said there was," said Jimmy, "I just wouldn't eat the noodles from here."

"Why?" asked Glyn again, ladling more into his mouth. It was good.

Jimmy waited while the man from behind the counter, who seemed to serve as both waiter and chef at the small noodle house, placed their beers on the table and then walked away. When he had gone, returning to his position behind the counter that ran along the rear wall and which separated the seating area from the kitchens, Jimmy leaned forward conspiratorially and said, "I had this cousin. He worked in the public health department not far from here, and his job was to investigate outbreaks of suspected food poisoning."

Glyn settled back; Jimmy's stories could take a while to tell, but they were always entertaining. He ate another mouthful of noodles, chewing on lumps of what tasted like mushroom and chicken as he listened. Their flavour was rich, flooding his mouth and settling into his stomach like an old friend.

"Like I said," said Jimmy, "his job was to investigate suspected outbreaks of food poisoning to see if there was a link between outbreaks and if they could be traced to a particular food venue, whether the link could be proved, that kind of thing. Anyway, a while ago, he investigated an outbreak of what looked like severe gastroenteritis; people were shitting and puking fit to burst. The initial cluster was about forty people, and new cases were coming in every day. People were being hospitalised, one man was found so badly dehydrated that he needed intensive care for a week, another woman didn't come out from her toilet for over twenty four hours and was found by her family sitting on a toilet full of blood. It was serious stuff, even pretty healthy people were getting hit by it, really knocked out. The number of cases kept going up, more every day. Eventually, one old guy had it so bad that he died, just shit his insides out, crapped and puked himself to death, and then things got really serious. My cousin was really under pressure to identify the source of the outbreak and to get it stopped. He spoke to as many of the people who had been ill as he could, and he soon found that the link was likely to be a new noodle bar just like this one. They'd all eaten in it or bought food to take away from it."

"What's your cousin's name?" asked Glyn. Another mouthful of noodles, and chew and swallow. They were hot enough to pretty much disintegrate in his mouth, just the way he liked them. He took another sip of beer; so did Jimmy.

"Gerard, but he hated that and called himself Gerry. I used to go for a drink with him about every month, that's when he told me this, at the end of that first week of investigating; we got on fairly well, which was odd considering he was from my dad's side of the family." Jimmy and his dad didn't get on, and hadn't for as long as Glyn had known him. Given an opportunity, Jimmy could rage about his dad and his paternal relatives for long, uninterrupted periods. Jimmy's dad was a redneck turd, and he apparently hated his son for his intelligence, for his easy way with people and for what he saw as his lifestyle choices. To get Jimmy back on track, Glyn said, "I bet that's an interesting job."

"Christ, the stories he could tell!" said Jimmy. "Restaurants that tried to pass ratshit off as capers, that had fruit trays in the kitchens that were so mouldy that you couldn't tell what sort of fruit it was under the green fur, that had mice nests in the cupboards and maggots in the meat. He once found a dead dog in the freezer of a bar he was investigating. A dead dog! Apparently, it was the chef's, it had been knocked down and he wanted to get it stuffed rather than bury it but he didn't have a shift off for another week so he'd put it in the freezer until he could get to the taxidermist. The owner offered to give Gerry a blowjob if he stayed quiet and didn't report her; I mean, he didn't take her up on it, he was good at his job and mostly honest. Like I said, he was an okay guy. Plus, she was fatter'n a whale and uglier than the dog, he told me, and anyway, he was gay."

As was Jimmy, thought Glyn. Everyone who knew Jimmy knew it, apart from Jimmy himself, it seemed. He had a sudden image of Jimmy sitting with his gay cousin, comfortable, all defences and pretences down, laughing as they discussed the corpulent bar owner and her dead canine, and found it oddly pleasing. He grinned at Jimmy, who grinned back, although only briefly.

"Well, this night he wasn't happy. 'It's the noodle place', he told me, 'but I can't work out what that problem is. It seems clean enough although the owner's a little fucker, not exactly unhelpful, showing me enough to keep me happy, but there's nothing there'. We talked about it a bit, and he told me that the kitchens looked okay, the food storage was right, the owner and the other staff member, there was only one, seemed to understand hygiene rules. It was a mystery.

"The problem was that there was no proof of anything, but people kept getting ill and they kept telling him that they'd eaten at the noodle bar. He went back a couple of times over the next couple of weeks, he told me, but it was only on his third visit that he found something odd. He arrived there for an unannounced visit and found the staff unpacking a delivery, and he didn't recognise the boxes. They were covered in foreign writing, Japanese or Chinese or Korean or something, and all the owner would tell him was that they were the herbs and spices he used in the various noodle recipes he used, all imported from his homeland. Well, that made Gerard suspicious; he knew every import company that delivered to the restaurants in the city, and this wasn't one of them. Plus, they didn't have any customs documentation."

Jimmy finished his drink and ordered another. Glyn, who had been balancing drinking and eating, turned down Jimmy when he offered to buy him another. His glass was still almost full, although his noodle bowl was over half empty now.

"Most of the boxes held dried leaves, ground herbs, that kind of thing," continued Jimmy, "normal restaurant stuff. The last two, however, were full of pieces of dried meat. Gerry told me they weren't packed well, that although they were vacuumed into sheets of plastic they looked like really cheap cuts of meat and air had got into them. Some of it looked fucking green, he said. The owner couldn't or wouldn't tell him what meat it was or where it was from, and that plus the lack of import documents meant he decided to shut the restaurant with immediate effect.

"The owner was really pissed, which Gerry was used to, and anyway, he had the law on his side. He had enough suspicions and circumstantial evidence to close the place down as a public health hazard. I think he quite enjoyed the power on the quiet."

Glyn looked around. There weren't many other diners in the restaurant, which was small and had only opened the week before. The waiter had been joined by another member of staff and they looked to be chopping vegetables and placing them in plastic storage trays. Both of the men were Asiatic, and they kept looking over at Glyn and Jimmy. Jimmy was getting louder as he drank more.

"So Gerry now has the time to really strip the kitchen, pull it apart and look for something that might be causing the illness, and that's what he does. All the time he's working, the owner's watching him, sometimes speaking to him or shouting at him in a language Gerry doesn't recognise.

"Is there a point to this story?" asked Glyn. "I've almost finished my noodles, so if you were hoping to put me off them, you've fucked up, haven't you?"

"Bugs," said Jimmy, grinning broadly and without humour. "My cousin found evidence of bugs in the meat. Not the bugs themselves, but of their eating and their leavings."

"Leavings?"

"Their shit, but also things like bits of egg casings, that sort of stuff. Whatever the meat was, wherever it was coming from, it was infested with something. I didn't hear from him for a few days, and when he did get in touch, he was exhausted. He'd been working non-stop for the past few days, trying to work out what had happened. The noodle place had stayed closed, of course, and they'd not had many more new cases of illness since they'd shut it, but they still had to try to work out exactly what had happened, who was at fault, that kind of thing. 'I've been at the restaurant, the noodle place,' he told me. 'We started with the boxes, trying to track the company that sent the meat over, but there's no record of them anywhere. The name on the boxes is The Big Sky Noodle Company, but we've not found any trace of them, no import licences granted, no tax records, nothing. The meat itself is a mix of beef and chicken and pork, and it's okay as far as it goes, but there's definitely been something in the box with it. We've got egg casings, pieces of wing and exoskeleton, one or two pieces of leg and pincer, lots of shit. It's a bug, but God only knows what sort. It's no wonder the fucking diners were ill, if this is what the owner was using.'"

Glyn looked down at his bowl. Most of his noodles were gone and what was left was a broth of vegetable and meat pieces and a slick of golden juice. Small pieces of noodle floated in it. Jimmy finished his Sapporo and ordered another without looking around. Glyn joined him this time, using his chopsticks to collect some of the fragments from his bowl and insert them in his mouth. Even now, as it cooled, the taste was dense and heavy. Joyous.

"The owner and the other staff member refused to tell them anything about where they got their ingredients from, and they didn't turn up any paperwork that might show them where to look. The more they looked, he said, the more evidence they found that the bugs had got everywhere in the kitchen. Nothing obvious, just little things, the odd fragment of shell in the dried herbs or something that might have been a part of a body in a sauce. Enough to confirm suspicions, he said, but not to track anything or identify the bug involved.

"Do you know what's in that?" asked Jimmy suddenly. "Really?"

"What? Yes, of course," said Glyn. "There's mushrooms, I think pork, some chicken, carrots, spring onions. There was a dumpling but I ate it."

"You're sure? Nothing else? And how do you know it's pork?"

"Well," started Glyn, but was interrupted by the arrival of their drinks. Jimmy ignored the waiter, leaning forward and taking the chopsticks from Glyn's unresisting fingers. He whisked Glyn's remaining food around and then dug into it, removing a long black tendril and draping it over the rim of the bowl.

"What's that?" he asked quietly.

"It's part of a vegetable," said Glyn. "It looks like a piece of skin from something like a courgette, or maybe mushroom."

"Or a bug's leg," said Jimmy. "Or maybe an antennae, do you think?"

"No," said Glyn.

"Really? You're sure? You don't sound convinced," said Jimmy, and that humourless grin flashed across his face again.

"Of course I am," Glyn replied, although now Jimmy mentioned it, the black tendril, about two inches long, did look faintly insectile.

"That's just it, isn't it? We order our food and we hope that we get what we asked for, but we're never sure, are we? Even something like steak and potatoes, how do we know that the meat has been stored properly? That the chef hasn't spat on it? Or masturbated into the creamed potatoes?"

Glyn knew Jimmy of old; if you rose to these provocations, he would make wilder and wilder claims in an effort to generate disgust or humour, or both. He reached over and took his chopsticks back from his companion and said, "Well, insect or not, it tastes good." He lifted the draped thing to his mouth and ate it; it was slimy rather than crunchy, not insect, he was sure, but vegetable despite its rich flavour.

"Your choice," said Jimmy. "Anyway, Gerry had done what he could; he'd closed the place, reported it to the police, and there were other things he needed to investigate. He presented his findings to the city's sanitation board and they decided to revoke the owner's licence. He didn't turn up to defend himself at the hearing, and when Gerry went to tell him the board's decision, the last thing he needed to do, he found the noodle place deserted, cleaned out.

"It happened a few times over the next year or so, outbreaks of the shits and vomiting that got traced to small noodle bars, and they'd find boxes from the Big Sky Noodle Company somewhere in the kitchen, and the boxes would be full of signs of bugs. Never the bugs themselves, though. He used to get angry about it when we met for drinks, pissed off that he couldn't find out anything about the company even though they were clearly importing meat that was like ground zero for some sort of infestation, and that it was making people ill. There were never any outbreaks as serious as the first one, no one else died, but still, it bothered Gerry. His job mattered to him, and I think he really thought he was failing by not finding Big Sky and closing it down. All he could do was keep sending bulletins out about it, hoping that someone would get in contact, that they'd catch a break."

Jimmy swallowed the remains of his beer and looked at the empty glass for a moment. Glyn managed to snag the last piece of food from his bowl, a tiny piece of torn chicken, and then put his chopsticks aside.

"One more," said Jimmy quietly, raising the glass and tilting it at the waiter. "There isn't much more to tell, but I need beer to get through this bit." He waited until the two new glasses of Sapporo were set upon the table and the empties and Glyn's bowl removed, and then said, "Gerry called me one night.

"I was supposed to be visiting him the next day, but he said we had to cancel. One of his bulletins had paid off, someone had been in contact and he'd had an anonymous call, a lead on where Big Sky were based, and he was going to investigate. I offered to go with him, seeing as at that point he was going unofficially just to see what he could find, but he turned me down. I wish I'd pressed him, but he'd been being a bit funny that last few times I'd seen him and I didn't want to spend another evening talking to him about bugs. He'd got funny, you see, anxious and nervous about something. He told me that he had started to hear things in his apartment whenever he turned the lights off, the sound of something, lots of somethings, moving around. A few times, he'd caught sight of things moving in the corner of his eye but they'd be gone by the time he turned around.

"He was getting obsessed, I thought. He was convinced that the bugs from Big Sky had somehow found him and were keeping watch on him. He told me he thought Big Sky were bringing the bugs in deliberately, that the owners of the noodle bars were part of some plot, although he was never sure what, or whether people getting ill was part of the plot or simply an accident. He told me he thought the bugs were smart, much smarter than normal bugs. They'd never managed to catch one, and since the first outbreak none of the rest had been so serious. 'They know to be careful,' he said to me once, 'to not draw attention to themselves. Christ only knows what they're planning. I wouldn't be surprised if they ate that first owner to keep him quiet and to punish him for letting us get so close to discovering them'. I thought he was going paranoid. I didn't surprise me, really, given that he was from my dad's side of the family and they're mostly fucking nuts anyway."

"And that's it? I'm supposed to avoid to eating noodles because your cousin once had to close a noodle bar and then got weird about the bugs that made people ill?"

"No," said Jimmy, his face serious, catching shadows under his eyes and in the frownlines of his forehead, "that's not quite it. I don't know what Gerry did that night after I spoke to him; no one does. His body was found about 4 months later in an abandoned parking lot near an industrial estate. The body, *his* body, was in a terrible state. Something had been at it, had eaten him down to fucking nothing. Not a big scavenger either, but something small. The skeleton was picked damn near clean. The coroner said it was the normal, although severe, predation of a body left in the open, but I had my doubts. I still do. I checked around and found that a company that might have been the Big Sky Noodle Company had had a unit in the nearby industrial estate until about the time that Gerry disappeared, and I started to think. What if he was right? What if the bugs were smart, and they found him? And what if they started to see him as a threat? What if there was an anonymous call, luring him to where they could deal with him without being disturbed?"

"Jimmy, man," said Glyn. This was getting silly. "I'm sorry about your cousin, assuming you aren't joking, but I'm supposed to believe that the bugs found him? Killed him? That, what? There's a bug running around that's intelligent, that it's planning something and that it's working with human servants or partners to achieve what? World domination? From a fucking noodle house base? And no one's fucking noticed? Please. Bugs aren't smart, Jimmy, they don't plot and they can't plan."

"They never found a dead one, not ever," said Jimmy. "Not one dead bug. All the traps they set, all the places they searched, and not one dead bug they could identity or analyse, that would let them explain the illness. How do you figure that?"

"Because they were unlucky," said Glyn. "I'm sorry about your cousin, seriously, but it's a hell of a leap to go from believing that there are unclean kitchens using cheap imported meat to believing that there's a company sending bugs into kitchens, that the bugs are smart enough to hide when people come looking, and to kill someone that they see as a threat. I mean, come on."

"Believe what you want," replied Jimmy, and he sounded weary. "You asked why I said not to eat here, and I've told you."

"What, because all noodle bars have bug-infested kitchens? Come on Jimmy, that's not funny, it's racist."

"I didn't say all noodle bars," said Jimmy, defensive. "I never said not to eat at noodle places, just some. The ones where the bugs might be."

"Bullshit," said Glyn, grinning and expecting Jimmy to return it. He didn't. Instead, he rose, saying, "I have to piss. I'm not joking about this, Glyn. Have a look at the containers on the shelf behind the counter while I'm gone. I saw them after the food arrived. If I'd seen them before, I'd've left."

Glyn looked over as Jimmy walked away. A shelf above the waiter's head held a number of white boxes, and on the largest he saw printed The Big Sky Noodle Company. He burped, tasting lager and noodles.

The other diners had gone, paying and leaving without Glyn noticing. He looked at his watch; it was late, later than he thought. Jimmy's story had taken a while to tell and the waiter-cum-chef was already turning out the lights in the kitchen. Some of the overhead lights in the dining areas had been dimmed so that the room had filled with shadows the colour of dirty water. He signalled to see if he could get him and Jimmy one last beer but the waiter didn't see him or ignored him, instead going through a door into an area behind the kitchen that Glyn assumed was for storage and cleaning. The waiter left the door open so that Glyn saw the lights going off in there as well. There was a low rustling and the sound of pots rattling and lids being opened and closed.

What was keeping Jimmy?

There was a bump and then a thud from the toilet and the door swung open a few inches before drifting back in. "Jimmy?" called Glyn. There was no reply. He looked back to the counter, hoping to see the waiter again, but there was no sign of him. Instead, the rustling was louder and the darkness thicker. Had he turned off all the lights behind the counter as well as in the kitchen? It looked like it; the shadows were everywhere, creeping down the counter and across the floor, sidling between the remaining pools of light.

How loud had Jimmy been talking? He had started out like he was spinning a yarn, but by the end he had seemed deadly serious, that the dead cousin, Gerry, and the bugs weren't part of some frantic friend-of-a-friend story he was making up at all. Had the waiter heard Jimmy's bizarre story? Was that why he had vanished, because he was offended by what he had overheard?

Had something else heard?

The shadows were moving faster and faster, in great drifts like oil spilled on smooth floors. There was another thumping from the toilet, and a noise like a groan. The rustling grew louder. The darkness flowed from the kitchen towards him, chittering and clicking as it moved. Glyn saw that it was fragmented, made of a myriad separate pieces all scurrying together, revealing scuttling legs and antennae that waved and eyes that glittered with intelligence.

He had time for one scream before they were on him.

Gingivitis:

An inflammation of the gum causing pain and discolouration, caused by the body's response to bacterial biofilms.

Child

I step to the doorway as the sound echoes in the chill air, orchestral and layered around me. My naked flesh ripples with goose bumps, what I can hear and the midnight cold making the hairs across my arms and chest rise in an attempt to trap the frigid atmosphere and warm it. I take another step away from my bedroom and the sound clarifies, tautens. It keens, this sound, is a swooping thing of sharpness and inexorability. I look around, hoping for an open window, hoping that it is a cat tearing the night open with its cries, but all are closed.

Behind me, my wife lies sleeping in our bed. Her face is slack in repose, calm and smooth like a Japanese mask. She seems like a stranger to me at that moment, someone distant and lost and nameless. Usually the lightest of sleepers, disturbed by the slightest thing, this sound leaves her untouched, a small mercy. The smallest mercy, maybe, and one that has not been extended to me, for it has woken me every night over the last weeks, filling the hallway like tainted water and louder each night. It is a private noise, private and personal and, much as I might not want it, mine. Despite my hopes, it has not left me alone, does not let me remain asleep; it calls, its voice as impossible to resist as the barbed wires that draw deep-sea fish from their lairs.

This is the first night that I have risen from my bed and followed the thread of sound, the first time I have stepped into the darkness and away from the security of my bed. Its pull, fiercer each night, has become fevered, insistent, and I can resist it no more. I find that walking is not the automatic thing it once was but has become a thing of consciousness; I must raise my feet, let myself fall, catch the floor with my foot, move forward, move on and all the while I am fighting the urge to hurry back to where my wife sleeps, wishing I could go to her. I want to drag myself under the covers, to try to warm my cold flesh against hers and block the sound with the sheets above me and the rush of blood in my ears, but I know I cannot; if I do not answer, the sound will simply come again tomorrow and the night after that and the night after that and perhaps every night without cease. It may never leave me alone.

Away from the cocooned warmth of the bedroom, the sound reveals its irregular pitch, rising and falling, falling and rising. It is a pale shriek, pulls and pushes at me like uncontrollable tides, at once both tiny and vast, the centre of the world and something apart from it. Like fishhooks, its upper cadences snare my skin; like lassoes, its lows drag me on. My feet rise and fall, ensnared, commanded. I have not dressed to make this journey but travel unprotected, helpless and naked as a child. I am cold; my scrotum puckers and withdraws, my penis becoming small and shrivelled and dark. My nipples are tight, tiny protuberances like flecks of ice upon my chest, the aureoles ringed in hair. A sign of my age, my beard is flecked with grey. I am balding, running to fat in my belly and thighs, and to intolerance in my attitude. I have no time for noises that come in the night-time, do not believe in them, and yet here they are and here I am and here I walk.

My journey is short but lasts an age, brings me to a halt outside the room I know I have been called to enter, to where the sound has been pulling me these last cold nights. I have been inside it recently, often, but only in daylight; my wife has not been in here in daylight or in darkness for many weeks. I will not pressure her to enter, trusting that she will feel when the time is right. I wonder briefly what sounds will call her to it, whether they will ever have volume enough to smother her yearning and sorrow, and know that I cannot know. These thoughts are only a way of avoiding raising my eyes, of course; of avoiding what is in front of me. The breathless, urgent crying that has pulled me from sleep over these last nights comes from within the room.

I face a perfectly normal door. There is nothing sinister about it, no gothic arches or rusting locks or drifting cobwebs, merely panelled wood, new paint, a simple frame. I know that the room beyond is empty of people, yet from it something that cannot be continues to wail in a voice as bleak and empty as the silence of tombs. No, not of tombs, but of those times before the tomb, of mourning and loss and crow-black tongues, of unrest and fragility.

I cannot wait any longer, and reach out.

The door handle is cold, the bite of the metal solid and unforgiving in my curled fingers. I am shaking; I would like to claim from the cold, but I have no lies left in me now. I am scared. I am terrified, and I am moving not despite this but because of it, because I can listen no more.

I am dressed in shadows as I open the door, dressed in robes of not-light, but one step inside the room and these shadows change, deepen. They are no longer mere not-light, but are something more, containing a richness and volume that gives them solidity. Another step, and shapes loom around me, terrible things, fractured things with mouths of needle teeth and eyes that are blank and glistening and depthless.

Another step, and those things continue to shift about me, chill and mutable.

Another step, and they fall away, resolving themselves into the angular faces of the furniture I know from the sunlight hours, a chair and a high table and drawers. We bought it all, my wife and I, and we placed it here, back when my nights were unmarred by sounds like the tearing of something's heart. The distances between then and now seem vast, almost boundless, and what lies on the other side visible only in oblique patterns that I can no longer make sense of. I step to the window, open it, still hoping that the sound is coming from outside, perhaps from some nearby home or street. Cold air enters, and the sound ends. I knew this before I opened the window, but my hopes needed to be given their last breath. Sadly, gently, I close the window, latching it shut. Immediately, the wailing comes again.

A breeze ruffles my hair, although I know that I have sealed the window. Movement catches my eye, the dancing of something across the floor. It is low, scuttling, a shadow that has no shape and is all shapes, spreading to fill the whole room. It covers the walls, creeping up to join over me like the shadowed ceiling of some cathedral vault, and then something else darts across the floor. Even in the darkness, I can see it clearly; a square sheet, four inches on a side, curled and delicate. I recognise it, step towards it, my legs weakening under me, tripping and sprawling me to the floor. My hand closes on the paper, but carefully, delicately, so terribly delicately. Shuffling, I move across the floor until I can lean against the wall. I sit for minutes, simply looking.

It is not much to see. Shiny and thin, its secrets open themselves only to those who understand its peculiar language. A chiaroscuro swirl of black and white dots make a grey landscape against which a darker, irregular ovoid is visible. This patch itself contains white scatters, tiny and frail like the stars of a frozen universe.

Holding the paper, staring at the apparently senseless image upon its surface, I feel my heart stutter and wretch. This sheet should not be here. When I last looked at it, it was in an anonymous folder with a lot of other papers and records, placed there by me; before that, it was in the hands of a pleasant, sad man in a pleasant, sad room and my wife and I were crying as he told us that our child's heart had stopped beating. I remember that the paper trembled slightly in his hands, fluttering as though trying to escape the news that he brought. I remember that I put my hand over my wife's and she felt cold.

Our child lived for almost eight weeks in my wife's womb, warm and safe, and when it died, it was seven millimetres long. We had seen its heartbeat during an earlier scan, the tiny white pulse dancing vigorously to a rhythm that gave glory to a belief in a future where our happiness was assured, where the years of trying and heartbreak were at an end. We were beyond happy beyond happy; content. And then, impossible to predict or prevent, chemicals misfired or threads failed to find each other or messages warped and lost their meaning, and that rhythm stuttered, faltered.

Failed.

When our child died, it had had the beginnings of a skeleton and of a central nervous system, filaments of feeling already growing within it. The nubs that would eventually become fingers and toes had begun to sprout, and its brain had begun to develop. It was already sensitive to vibrations, had hearing of a sort, and knowing this, every night I would put my mouth close to my wife's belly and I would whisper. With the scent of her in my nostrils, I would tell our child stories.

Some of the stories were true, some not; I told of the first meeting of my wife and I, of the dragons that lived in our garden and of the fat, cheery fairies that danced across our bed when we were asleep. I told of the family that we had, that it would be born to, and I told of our hopes and fears and dreams and desires. Afterwards, my wife and I would sometimes make love; other times we would simply drape around each other and sleep with smiles on our faces. Unable to help ourselves, we began to plan the nursery. Unable to prevent it, we wept as our child's heart beat down towards its last and just a week after seeing that strong, healthy heartbeat, it was reduced to a flicker like a dying moth's wing. One week after that and it was gone, the tiny white dot motionless, and our child was dead.

I am sitting in the nursery now, a place as alien to me as the glacial drifts of ice that ride the top of the world, and I can still hear the knife-sharp mewling, a cry for attention and love and hope and safety. I can provide none of those things. The paper is warm between my fingers, as though the thing it shows has a life of its own, a vitality and heat that

I feel but am unable to protect. I wish the paper were a screen, so that I could see the heart pulse, but I cannot; it is as still as words on a page, as letters carved in wood or stone, and as I look at it, I start to cry. I hold out the picture of our child, the only picture we will ever have, to protect it from damage. Already, it has started to become worn and I am aware that one day we will not even have this; we will simply have our memories, and each other. Both mean more to me than I can say, more than I have words to encompass, but neither truly can carry forward all our knowledge and history and love. Neither is a child.

As I sit and cry, the door to the nursery swings open, a new shape moving in the entrance. The cries rise, twisting, the sound of splintered things coming together, of threads knitting, of layers merging and binding to form a shape, one I can almost see. What would he have been? What would she have been? Happy? Sad? I do not know but I wonder, have so many ideas, and all of them are collapsing together, whirling in on themselves frantically. I look at the open doorway and the shape moves, approaches, forms itself into my wife.

I stand, trying to hide the picture from her, but she sees and comes to me. She is crying as I am, her own tears silent, yet she reaches out and takes my hand, pulling it towards her. The picture rises between us, its weight impossible for such a small thing, light as snow, heavy as grave-earth. She takes it from me, looks at it and then drops it and we watch as it spirals down in slow and steady arcs. By the time it reaches the floor, it has become nothing but shadows and dust. I am unsure what to do, have nothing to say.

My wife pulls me gently forwards, leans and kisses me. She is naked. Her chest rises and falls as she breathes into my mouth. I can hear her heart beating in the suddenly quiet room, carving out space around us. My own heart joins hers, quickening. For moments, we simply kiss, and our lips are warm together. Heat flows and covers our bodies. Looking down, I see a flush creep over my skin and hers, and my flesh thaws for the first time since our child's flesh froze. I can feel my wife's body, her nearness. Her chest is against me, her hands in mine. She pulls me to the floor and still our lips do not part.

There, shadowed by the things we bought for a child whose sex we never knew, whose personality never developed, whose eyes never opened and whose name I will never know, we make love and I hear nothing but the hammer of our pulses. Afterwards, we lie together and do not talk. There are no words to say, no phrases to utter that we have not already used. Our cooling sweat and slowing breath speak to each other more eloquently than we could ever hope to, in a language that we cannot hope to fathom but whose meaning I somehow understand. How long we stay, I do not know, but it is long enough to hear a final quiet noise in darkness. It is not much, just a little thing, a sound of something sealing and mending and satisfied, a mewl of contentment. Before the heat leaves us, I walk my sleepy wife back to our bed, pulling us far down under the quilt where we wrap our arms and legs around each other and kiss a last time before sleep.

We have taken our ghost inside ourselves, given it life, and delivered it on.

Regional Odontodysplasia:
A condition affecting the enamel, dentine and pulp
leading to teeth appearing "ghostly" on radiographs.
Radiograph series of heavily affected teeth often show
a second series of dental growths emerging behind the
existing teeth. These growths can only be seen in the
radiograph images.

H is for Hrace

On the hillside ahead of him, someone was having their photograph taken.

At least, it was what Norrish thought was probably happening. About halfway up the slope, probably four hundred feet above him, a figure in a garish red coat was standing and pointing up at the crest of the hill. Somewhere below them, Norrish expected to see a second figure taking a photograph; he suspected that most visitors to the area ended up with at least one picture of themselves standing on a hill path pointing upwards at the peak beyond in a 'look what I'm about to climb' pose. There were even pictures of Norrish like that, taken when he had still holidayed with other people rather than by himself.

The path zigzagged up the steep hill, cutting first one way through the heavy scrub of bushes and grasses and then the other, and shortly after Norrish first saw the posing figure he lost sight of them, his last glance a glimmer of red against the earthen tones of the hillside. For a few minutes he enjoyed the solitude of his walk, with the rain pattering down on his head and spattering against his jacket, an old garment of beaten waterproof whose bright yellow reflective stripes had long since peeled and faded. His pack was settled well upon his back, the straps finding the grooves in his shoulders he was sure must be there by now after all the years of walking and carrying. He expected to meet the tourists at the top of the hill, pass them in a scent of mint cake and a rustle of new waterproofs and a nodded 'hello' made without eye contact. The path switched back on itself, the scrub beginning to thin, and Norrish emerged once more into the dank light of the clouded late afternoon.

The tourist in the red coat was still there.

Not just still there; still in the same pose, one arm aloft and pointing at the peak beyond them, coat flapping in the wind, head tilted back to expose a pale face to the sky. Norrish carried on, crossing back across the face of the slope with the path and feeling the incline tug at his thigh and calf muscles. This was his first walk in several weeks, and he had gotten rusty and stiff. He wondered why the person above wasn't moving, and where their photographer was; as he got closer, the pose was getting clearer. Whoever it was, they were pointing at the standing stones on the hill's peak, at this distance little more than tiny nubs of shadow like old teeth.

Lyfthelm Circle, and it was Norrish's destination as well.

Norrish smiled slightly, thinking of the hotel owner. The man had insisted on telling Norrish about the local area, about Lyfthelm ("It means 'cloud'," he had said, "and the hill is sometimes called Hrace-Tunge, but I don't know what that means and most people call it The Swallows."), thinking that Norrish was a tourist, something Norrish hadn't been for years; Norrish was a walker, and he knew this area well.

The path turned again, threading its way through another nest of gorse and bracken and tall, tangled bushes, and the posing figure was lost to view again. The rain was becoming heavy now, its sound on his hood and shoulders a skittish tattoo. Cold water rolled around the rim of his hood, seeping down the inside his collar and tickly damply at his neck. Norrish shifted his knapsack, feeling its weight moving pleasingly with him, rolling around his shoulders. Another switchback and then he was on the same stretch of path as the figure, who was still there, still posing.

Still motionless.

As Norrish came close to them, he saw that it was a man; older, perhaps fifty, wrapped in a nicely red coat and waterproof trousers. He had a small rucksack over one shoulder, the strap twisted as though he had been halfway through removing it when he had stopped. His face was tilted back, eyes open wide and staring at the crest of the hill and the circle of stones, arm still stretched out, fingers pointing loosely. He was in the centre of the path, and he did not move as Norrish approached, did not acknowledge his approach at all.

"Hello," said Norrish. The man did not respond. Norrish repeated the word, louder, wondering if the man was perhaps a little deaf; the wind was heavier up here, the exposed hillside scoured by gusts and swirls that hummed and chuckled in Norrish's ears. It carried with it the scents of damp earth and the cold of the clouds, and it surrounded them. He walked to the man, and it was only when he got close to that he realised that something was wrong.

Terribly, horribly wrong.

The man's face was the colour of day-old milk, glittering as the rain spilled across it, and his lips had coloured to a rich, chill blue. He was shivering, teeth chittering together with porcelain insistence. His outstretched arm was shaking violently, and as he came even closer, Norrish saw that the man's fingertips were also blue. The man was freezing. How long had been standing there? Norrish stepped around the man, to his front so that he was upslope of him and blocking his view of whatever it was he was looking at.

The man had a camera dangling from his outstretched arm, spinning, its strap glistening wetly.

"Hello?" he called again, loudly, clearly. "Are you okay?"

Stupid question; this man was not okay, not by a long way. Even his ears had started to show the cold, the tops of them and the lobes an angry, cyanotic blue. His hair was heavy with the rain, twisted into rattails that dancing and swung about him, framing his face.

"We need to get you moving," said Norrish. He put one arm half around the man, placing a palm into the small of his back and pushing gently. After a moment, the man took a hesitant step and then another. His arm dropped back to his side but he kept his head tilted back and he moved like a sleepwalker or a drugged thing. The camera slipped off his wrist and fell to the ground; the man ignored it. Norrish bent and retrieved it, putting into one of the man's pockets. The man did not seem to notice but simply kept walking.

"Good lad," said Norrish, despite the fact the man was at least ten years older than he was. He pulled out his mobile phone but between their isolation and the weather, the signal was non-existent. Up or down, he wondered? He looked back down the hill; no one. It wasn't a great day for walking, not really, and they were off the main tourist trails anyway. Lyfthelm wasn't as good a stone circle as Castlerigg, smaller and less dramatic and it was harder to reach; in good weather it could be busy but in this rain and with the clouds moving above them in wolfpack circles, only people who knew it tended to come here. People like Norrish, who liked his walks to be in places where there were few other people. Feeling a flash of irritation at the man for spoiling the solitary enjoyment of his day, Norrish sighed and began to guide him up the slope.

In going up, Norrish hoped that there might be others already up there, maybe even the man's party, not realising that he had got into trouble. It was unlikely that anyone would have a signal on their phone, but he could at make sure the man was warm and safe while someone went for help. Leading the man was like pulling a sheep; he was docile yet somehow skittish and hard to move, his head permanently tilting back to stare into the rain and at the hilltop ahead of them, his steps staggering. The rain was thickening, heading towards being a storm, heavier than any of the forecasters had predicted, and Norrish was getting worried. Had he been alone he would have already turned back, but the man complicated things.

Around them, the gorse danced and shook in the rain.

The first dazzle of lightning came as they reached the last switchback, a staggered crack of thunder following on its heels. For a moment, the sky above them was a fragmented mess of roiling clouds bleached to a long-abandoned ivory by the flash, and then the world darkened again, the saturated earth regaining its palate of greens and browns. Norrish blinked, pulling the man along, his feet slipping across the rutted, waterlogged surface of the path.

The man was slowing now, tugging back from him. He was making a noise, a low keening that came to Norrish as though from under layers of ice. The man was, if anything, trembling even more, his arm rising again to point up at the brow of the hill, and now he was screeching, his mouth wide open and his tongue moving in the shadows behind his lips like a worm severed and left to its death throes. Norrish pulled at him again but the man refused to move, literally digging his heels into the raw earth and leaning back against Norrish's grip.

"Come on," said Norrish, not that gently. "We need to move."

The rain thickened, closing in around them and reducing the world to a loose circle of violently writhing, sodden greenery and bruised cloud and wind and water and ahead of them, a crown of standing stones like broken, jagged teeth. The man screeched again as Norrish yanked on his arm; Norrish felt the muscles bunch and tremble even through the layers of coat and jumper underneath, and then he was moving, his feet dragging over the soil and through the sparse grass.

There was no one on the hilltop.

The gorse fringed the brow of the hill with tired snarls and ragged stems, leaving Lyfthelm Circle's stones standing alone in the centre of a exposed clearing. The grass around Norrish's feet was longer than on the path, scrawny and plastered to the ground by the rain but lifting with each gust of wind to wave wretchedly before falling back. It tangled over the tops of their boots, tearing as they moved forwards.

The man still resisted Norrish, pulling back, stumbling, but his protests were strengthless, his moans doleful and low. The fight seemed to have gone out of him, and now even his head had dropped and he stared at the stones, his chin almost on his chest and his eyes rolling.

Norrish pulled him over to the stones, standing him as best he could against the tallest of them on the lee side of the weather in the hope of keeping the man from being too exposed. He took a moment to pull the zipper of the man's jacket to the top and lift his hood over his head, pulling the toggled strings to tighten it around his face; the man simply stood like a child as Norrish did so. His eyes still rolled, darting left and right, up and round, down and about, their sockets dark. His lips were a frigid blue now, the colour of oceans under sullen skies or bodies on autopsy tables. The colour of hypothermia. Norrish dropped his bag by the man's feet and walked around the outside of the circle, looking down the hillsides as he went. The weather had closed in so much that the foot of the hill was no longer visible, only a dirty sheet of rain that was shot through with glimmers of silver where what light there was caught the falling, spinning water in its teeth. There were no people on the paths, which appeared as little more than spider-web lines running through the covering foliage. Helplessly, Norrish took his phone from his pocket again and held it up; *No Signal* sat in the top corner of its screen, stolid and absolute.

"Shit," Norrish said and stuffed the useless thing back into his jacket. This was rapidly becoming a disaster.

There was another scouring, tearing flash of lightning and almost immediately after, another growl of thunder that echoed about him. The flash left afterglow images imprinted in Norrish's eyes, swirling patterns of white and yellow that only slowly faded back to the rainswept reality in front of him. What had the hotel owner called this weather? "Hungering", he'd said it was, a "hungering sky". When Norrish had asked him what he meant, he'd laughed and said it was just a local phrase for when the clouds gathered around Lyfthelm and the top of the Swallows or one of the other hills in the area.

When Norrish looked up he couldn't see separate clouds any more, only a dirty, bruised sky that wrapped itself around him like ancient muslin. The clouds must be surrounding the hill completely now, Norrish supposed, must have lowered themselves around the land like a mouth closing around and sucking on a knob of bone. Hungry sky, he thought, hungry and vast and unstoppable.

No. He was spooking himself, giving in to panic, and that was no use. He had to think, to act sensibly, like an adult. There was little point in trying to get off the hill now, the weather was too bad to risk the walk and the nearest outskirts of civilisation too far away. He had to make what shelter he could here and hope that either someone came or that this weather blew itself out soon. He went back to where he had left the man, thinking that at least he could give the man some tea; Norrish had some in his flask. There was another flash of lightning, creating momentary shadows that leapt around Norrish from the stones, and in the flashes retreating light he saw a bag lying in the centre of the circle.

It was a rucksack; actually, it was what Norrish always thought of as a 'tourist bag', all straps and reflective panels and pockets and looking as though it was hardly used. It was lying on its side on the earth, open and with its contents spilled out across the ground. He walked over to it, and saw a lunch box, its lid still tightly sealed and the ghosts of thick cut sandwiches and an apple visible through its semi-opaque sides. Next to it, flapping desolately, was an ordnance survey map in a plastic cover and a single glove half buried in the mud, just its fingers and thumb visible, reaching to the sky. It was a woman's glove, or maybe a child's, small and delicate. A woman's, Norrish decided, given the size of the bag. He crouched and looked inside. The bag contained a sweater – also a woman's, he saw – a scarf and a flask and a camera case but no camera. Everything was wet.

Norrish looked around; there was no sign of the bag's owner. He walked swiftly around the inside of the circle looking for anything else, but there was nothing, just wind and rain and grass shifting and puddles forming as the ground became saturated. "Shit," he said again; there seemed no other word for it.

Now he had a halfway catatonic man and an apparently missing woman to deal with. There was another flash of lightning and now the thunder seemed like laughter, mocking him for the situation he had found himself in.

The man had gone.

Norrish's bag was still on the ground, tucked against the base of the stone, but there was no sign of the man. Norrish ran back between the stones, looking back down the path they had arrived along; nothing. As fast as he dared, he ran around the outside of the circle, feet slipping on the wet earth, looking down each of the other paths that led away from the hilltop for movement.

Nothing.

Nothing, and where the fuck had the man gone? How had his day gotten so bad so quickly, Norrish wondered? A long walk along trails he was confident he knew, then back to the hotel for a bath and a hot meal and to listen to more of its owner's quaint local history, a perfect day, but no; somehow he had got caught in weather as savage as he had ever seen it trying to find people he didn't know. What the fuck had happened here? Really?

Back to the other bag, still abandoned in amongst the stones. He quickly went through it, finding that the flask was empty and that beneath the jumper and scarf there were spare socks and a small first aid kit but no phone. It meant that, whoever the woman was, she knew what she was doing, was no simple weekend walker even if she was a tourist. So where was she?

Another flash of lightning, another ragged giggle of thunder. Norrish shivered; despite his waterproof clothing, rain was finding its way further down his neck and back, and it was chilling him. The wind, coming from the direction of the lakes, carried with it not just rain but deeper breaths of coldness now, bitter against his exposed flesh. There was another flash of lightning and for a moment the world disappeared in a bleach-white glare, fading back in slowly so that the puddles around Norrish appeared red for a minute, as though filled with blood.

The red colouring didn't fade.

Blood was seeping up from the ground, filling the puddles all around him with rich, rusty threads of colour. Norrish shrieked, stepping back and tripping across the bag. He landed awkwardly, knocking against the abandoned glove with one flailing hand, tearing it loose from the mud. It came free and rolled, flapping over and over like an injured animal before coming to rest pointing away from him.

The torn stump of a wrist, bones gleaming whitely, poked from the glove's cuff. The flesh around the bones was neatly sliced, the planes of meat puckering as they chilled and the rain played across them. Norrish shrieked again and struggled to his feet, staggering away from the bag and the glove and the hand. *Fuck the man, fuck the woman*, he thought, *I am going, going now.*

The earth beneath his feet heaved.

A long bulge rose up around the edge of the circle and rolled towards its centre like a wave, humping the earth with its sodden grass covering up and then dropping it in its wake with a sound like a sloppy kiss. It sent Norrish into a lope-armed sway, pitching him sideways so that he fell against one of the stones. His hand slapped its surface and it was warm, the water covering it slick and thick and somehow organic.

He pushed himself away, trying to move between the stones but the ground heaved again, reminding him of some vast tongue probing a morsel of food. He tripped, falling to his knees, and the ground pushed back against him, lifting him.

Norrish scrabbled, trying to go forwards, but the surging earth sent him back towards the centre of the circle. Around him, the stones were tilting, clashing together, their sides dripping with liquid that looked more like saliva than rain. The noise of them grinding together made Norrish's teeth ache, and he screamed again.

More lightning, and this time the flash was accompanied almost immediately by thunder that sounded like a vast anticipatory sigh. The air thickened, the clouds gathering all about Norrish as the ground bulged again. He pitched sideways, rolling over onto his back as a giant throat opened above him and Hrace-Tunge lifted him towards the hungering sky.

Pyorrhea:

Inflammation of the gum and other oral structures, leading to the destruction of the alveolar bone, the generation of pus and exudates in the soft flesh and the subsequent loss of teeth. Caused by micro-organisms invading the mouth, clinging to the surface of the teeth and growing up under the gum line, as well as the body's over-aggressive response in attempting to fight these micro-organisms.

The Man in the Corner

"Daddy, I'm afraid."

Edward didn't speak very loudly; his daddy would be grumpy if he was woken up too suddenly. Really, Edward shouldn't be in mummy and daddy's bedroom at all, because the clock didn't say 07.00 yet, but he couldn't help it. "Daddy, I'm afraid," he said again, a little more loudly.

Edward's daddy made a funny noise, somewhere between a groan and a snore, and rolled onto his side, facing Edward even though his eyes were still shut. He let out a long breath, making his lips flap slightly, and Edward might have giggled if it hadn't been a bit too dark for giggles and a bit too cold, and if he hadn't been scared and really needing his daddy to wake up. Daddy's breath smelled sweet but somehow old, like a bottle of fizzy drink that had sat in the sun for weeks without having its top on properly and had gone flat and sickly.

"Daddy," Edward began again, but this time daddy spoke, interrupting Edward before he could finish.

"Ed, what is it?"

Daddy still hadn't opened his eyes but the fact that he had spoken, not shouted, made Edward feel a bit better. Without waiting for an invitation, he climbed up onto the bed and slipped beneath the covers, cuddling up against daddy.

"I'm afraid," he said for the third time, pressing his face into daddy's chest. Daddy's chest had hair on it, and it prickled Edward's cheek but he didn't move away. After a moment, daddy wrapped his arms around Edward and hugged him tightly. He kissed Edward's forehead and then said, "Go back to your room and go to sleep, Ed."

"I can't," said Edward. "I'm frightened. It's dark."

"You can reach the light," said daddy, "and your night light works, we checked it before. Put the hall light on if you want to, but go back to bed."

"Can't you take me?"

"No, Ed, it's–" and here daddy broke off to raise himself to one elbow, looking at the pale blue light coming from the clock on his bedside table. "Three thirty in the morning, Ed. Half three. I have to be up for work in a few hours, Ed, please go back to your own room."

"Please take me," Edward said, still cuddling into daddy' chest. "I don't want to go back alone. Can't I sleep here?"

"No," said daddy, and his sleep voice was going now, being replaced by his awake voice. Edward preferred daddy's sleep voice, it was quieter and softer and it sounded stretchy, somehow, as though the words coming out were melting into each other a bit. His awake voice was louder, the words shorter, sharper, angrier. His sleeping and awake smells were like that as well; relaxed and soft and warm when asleep or just after he had woken up but somehow sharper and harder and chillier when he was fully awake and going to work or thinking about work or doing things around the house or watching the news.

"Ed," said daddy, "it's late, I'm tired, I have work tomorrow and I haven't got time for silly games. Please go back to your own room and go back to sleep. Now."

"Take me," said Edward again, "I'm scared."

"Scared of what?" asked daddy. "What is there to be scared of in your room? There's just the toys and clothes that you haven't put away, and the piles of books that you prefer to leave on the floor rather than put back on the bookshelf. They aren't scary, are they?"

"No," said Edward, "there's a man."

That made daddy sit up. His movement dislodged Edward from his chest and he ended up tumbling between daddy and mummy. He took advantage and snuggled into the warmth they had made in the bed and which smelled of perfume and soap and the mummy and daddy mixed-together smell, the one Edward liked so much. "A man?" asked daddy.

"A man, in the corner," said Edward. "He was watching me. I didn't like him, he was watching me and he wasn't nice."

"There isn't a man in your bedroom," said daddy, lying back down so that his face was inches from Edward's. "Son, it was just your imagination." He leaned forward and kissed the tip of Edward's nose, his stubble scratching lightly at Edward's skin. Edward hoped daddy might hug him again, but he didn't.

"There is a man," said Edward. "He's in the corner and he's horrible."

Edward's daddy let out a long, clenched sigh. "Ed, go to bed," he said, and he was getting angry now. "You're a big boy, you shouldn't be scared of things in the dark that aren't here. There are no monsters, no ghosts, no things in the corner. Nothing can hurt you in your room,

unless you trip over it because you've left it in the middle of the floor."
It was a joke, or a sort of one, Edward knew, but daddy didn't sound as
if he was about to laugh.

"Please let me sleep here with you and mummy," said Edward. "I
promise I'll be quiet and not wriggle and just sleep. I promise."

"No," said daddy again. "You've got a perfectly good bed of your
own, which I'd like you to go back to. Now."

"I'll take you," said mummy, stroking Edward's back. Her voice was
warm and fuzzy and Edward rolled over and hugged up against her.
"Please?" he asked.

"No, daddy's right, but I'll take you back to bed and we'll check the
room out together. Would that help?"

"I want daddy to," said Edward. It had to be daddy; mummy had to
do some things for him and daddy had to do others, and this was a
daddy thing. The man in the corner was so horrible that, if mummy
saw him, or he saw her, he might hurt her. He didn't think that the man
in the corner would hurt daddy, though.

"I am not taking you to your bedroom, Ed," said daddy angrily.
"You're almost six, you're too old for this sort of thing."

"Honey," said mummy quietly.

"What?" asked daddy, but mummy didn't reply, not out loud at least.
Daddy lifted himself back on one elbow and even though he couldn't
see him, Edward knew that he was looking over Edward and down at
mummy. For a minute, daddy and mummy didn't speak, but Edward
could almost hear a conversation happening somewhere above his
head. It passed between mummy and daddy, and although Edward
didn't know the words, he knew what it was about: him. About daddy
taking him to bed, about him having woken them up, about daddy
being angry and mummy not wanting him to be. Eventually, daddy
said, "Fine. Right. Come on, Ed, let's get you back."

Daddy got out of bed and waited for Edward, who slithered over to
the edge and then climbed reluctantly out. He tried to reach up and
hold daddy's hand as daddy walked out of the room, but daddy's fingers
were curled around into a not-quite fist, and he didn't open them, so
Edward stopped trying. Daddy didn't turn on the hall light either,
instead going quickly to Edward's room. His naked back was pale in the
grey darkness and Edward had to hurry to keep up with him even
though the hallway was only short.

"Into bed," daddy said when they were in Edward's room, and then at least helped Edward to snuggle down, tucking the quilt around his neck and making sure that Edward's favourite teddy, Mr Dog, was close at hand. "Now, where's this man?"

"In the corner," said Edward, "by the window. I can see him because the moon's coming in the edge of the curtains."

"Really?" said daddy, "That's funny, I can't see him." Daddy made a show of going over to the corner, peering around as though he was in a pantomime.

"Where is he, then?" said daddy, bending to look under the chair, fluffing the curtains out and looking behind them, opening the wardrobe and shuffling Edward's shirts and jumpers and jeans about. "The corner, you said? Well, I'll check again, but I really can't see him." Daddy went back to the corner by the window and made another funny little mime, putting his hand above his eyes and pretending to peer carefully around.

The man in the corner's smile widened as daddy looked straight at him.

The man was much taller than daddy, and very thin, and his face was very pale, almost white. He was grinning, his lips pulled back from his teeth, and was looking over daddy's shoulder at Edward, nodding ever so slightly as if to say, *We have a secret, you and I, don't we?*

Edward could only watch, helplessly, as daddy kept up his pantomime looking, peering all around the man in the corner but apparently not seeing him. The man's grin was, if anything, even wider, almost laughing at the great joke he was playing, making it so that daddy couldn't see him. Edward didn't know what the man wanted, but he was sure that he wasn't here to play or to be nice. His grin was like the grin the bullies had at school when they made the little children cry, the grin daddy sometimes had when he was really angry and was telling Edward off by making jokes that Edward didn't really understand but that he knew were nasty. Mummy had once said that daddy was 'cruel' when he did that. Edward didn't know what 'cruel' really meant, but it sounded right for how those jokes made him feel. 'Cruel' sounded long and narrow and pointed, just like the man in the corner.

The difference was that daddy wasn't cruel all the time, only when he was angry or when Edward had done something silly or bad, but the man looked like he was cruel every minute of the day and night. *He was probably even cruel when he was asleep*, Edward thought. The man in the corner, as though he knew what Edward was thinking, nodded slightly more firmly and stretched his grin even further around his face.

"Right, I'm going," said daddy suddenly. "There's no one here, Ed, there never was." For a moment, daddy was standing right in front of the man in the corner and although daddy was fatter, Edward suddenly realised that he was just as tall as the man, it was just that he normally walked leaning forward and with his shoulder hunched up so he looked shorter. Daddy's grin was wide and just as humourless as the man's as he said, "Go to sleep, Ed, and don't let me hear from you until the morning."

Before he left, daddy came and kissed Edward's forehead, although not very gently. Edward hugged daddy, hoping to make him stay, but daddy pulled Edward's arms away after not long enough and said, more softly, "Sleep, son, and we'll see you in the morning." Edward tried again to hold onto daddy, but daddy wouldn't let him. Edward couldn't help but make a little sound that wasn't even a word as daddy left, but he didn't cry out and he didn't move because there was no point.

The man in the corner grinned and nodded and came out of the corner, and Edward stayed quiet and hugged Mr Dog and wished for the morning to come.

Ectopic Enamel:

Enamel forming in unusual places such as the tooth root. In extreme cases, the newly forming enamel grows in long, spiralling threads that push up through the sinuses and pierce the front of the brain.

The Cotswold Olimpicks

Fillingham first saw the women by the dwile flonkers.

He had spent the day walking around Dover's Hill, the shallow amphitheatre where the Cotswold Olimpick Games took place and had taken, he thought, some good photographs so far. The place was heaving and he had captured some of that, he hoped, the shifting bustle as people flocked from event to event and laughed and shouted and ate and drank. The sound of cymbals and mandolins and violins and guitars filled the air about the crowd, leaping around the brightly-costumed figures and the smells of roasting meat and open fires.

There were five of them and they were watching as a circle of men held hands and danced counter-clockwise around another group of men. The men in the centre of the circle had a bucket and were dipping cloths in it and hurling them at the dancers; every time one of the cloths hit its target, the crowd laughed good-naturedly. When the cloth missed, arcing into the people beyond, a cheer went up and a man dressed in a costume of rags and wearing a hat that was too big for him would shout, "Ha! Jobanowl declares a penalty!" and the cloth thrower was given a large glass of ale to drink. The women were smiling as they watched, clustered tightly together, dressed similarly in white shift dresses and with their hair long and loose. Fillingham wondered if they were some kind of act and took their photograph, thinking that if he could catch another one of them later, in performance, it might make a nice pair, *Artists at rest and work* or something.

The women were definitely a group, seemed to be in tune with each other somehow, their heads bobbing to the rhythms of the music slipping through the air around them, their bodies turning in the same direction as though responding to invisible currents like birds wheeling through the sky. When one of the sodden cloths, the dwiles, came towards them, they danced aside as though choreographed. The crowd cheered again as Fillingham lowered his camera, a knot of people jostling between him and the women as they tried to avoid the dripping missile, and when they moved aside the women were gone.

Fillingham let the press of the crowd drift him along the field, taking more photographs, this time of men dressed in smock shirts and clogs kicking at each other's shins, and then of another team of men destroying an old piano as people around them cheered and chanted a countdown. As dusk crept across the valley, his images took on a sepia tone, bleached of colour's vibrancy, becoming timeless. This was what he was after, he thought, a set of pictures that captured some of the sense of history of this event, of people stepping back for a day to celebrate nothing but tradition and enjoyment itself. This was a folk event, owned by everyone here.

On the cusp of the gloaming giving itself to darkness, someone appeared as Robert Dover, the founder of the games sometime in the early seventeenth century. He was riding a huge chestnut horse and was dressed in a tunic with a heraldic crest on his breast. A yellow feather bristled jauntily from the brim of his wide hat, bobbing as he rode around. His face was a white mask hanging down from under the hat, gleaming like bone, and he was waving a wand above his head that glittered and spat sparks. It was a sign that the bonfire was to be lit and the crowd began to move back towards the huge pile of wood at the far side of the fields, following the horseman as he capered and called exhortations for people to hurry, to dance on. Fillingham took more photographs, catching a good one of Dover rearing his horse in the centre of a mass of people like some ancient leather-bound general, all buckles and gleam and leadership.

Moving with the crowd, Fillingham found himself walking behind the women in white and spent a few moments appreciating the sway of their buttocks under the thin dresses before realising they were barefoot; mud was spattered up the pale skin of their bare calves in dark, irregular tattoos. The hems of their dresses were damp and dirty as well, he saw, the material swinging in sinuous patterns as the women moved. It was surprisingly erotic, this shift of skin and muscle under skin and cotton and dirt that crept up to where Fillingham's eyes could not follow, and he suddenly felt guilty, as though he was peeping. Feeling himself blush and glad of the darkness to cover his embarrassment, he raised his eyes to deliberately look away.

The fire caught quickly, leaping orange into the sky and throwing its heat across the crowd, creating a fug of temperature and sweat. Dover cantered around the blaze, crying "To ale! To ale!" as people cheered and shouted, his motionless face reflecting the fire's colours. Fillingham took more pictures wishing, not for the first time, that his camera could somehow catch sound and smell as well, that it could trap the intensity of the heat and the noise and the scents of mud and flame and grass, and preserve them.

From huge bags on the ground near the fire, stewards in reflective tabards began to take long white candles and hand them out. The first few they lit and then let people ignite each other's, a chain of flames that stretched out in a long, snaking line as the crowds began to walk slowly back towards Chipping Campden. Fillingham declined a candle and let the line carry him, snapping all the while.

The procession ended up in the small town's market square, where more revels were starting up. Most of the shops were still open, filling with tourists buying souvenirs, and stalls along the sides of the square did a brisk trade in food and drink. Down the streets off the square, small canvas tents with open fronts nestled between the shops, offering people the opportunity to play chess and draughts, or games of chance like three card marney or craps. The square soon became busy, clusters of people spilling out into the surrounding streets, drinking and talking and shouting, filling the tents and shops, moving, and Fillingham photographed as many of them as he could.

He had been in the square for around an hour when he saw one of the women again; she was moving through the crowds holding a beaten pewter flask and stacks of small plastic cups. Fillingham followed her, intrigued; this wasn't what he'd expected. The women had looked like a singing group, as though they were about to launch into madrigals or choral songs at any moment, but now they were separated and were doing. . . what? The woman he was following, tall and dark, was doing little other than giving drinks away, pouring small amounts of liquid into the cups and handing them out. Fillingham took photographs of her, watching as she distributed the cups, dipping her head and saying something each time someone drank. Fillingham moved closer, hoping to get a clearer image and hear what the woman was saying, but he kept losing her in the press of bodies. Her white dress glimmered in amongst the shifting masses like a faltering beacon, and he followed.

The woman moved surprisingly quickly, without apparent effort, slipping along the alleyways around the square, darting through knots of people and giving out her drinks, nodding and speaking. Fillingham wondered where the other women were; doing the same thing throughout the crowds, he supposed, giving out their drinks and adding to the atmosphere. The day's games were over; now the celebrations started in earnest. He took more photographs as he followed the woman, of stallholders serving, of a group of Morris Men drinking beer from tankards, their bells jangling as their arms moved. Fillingham saw that the tankards were attached to their belts by lengths of string or leather cord; some of the Morris Men had more than one, spares hanging to their side as they supped. Children ran between the legs of adults, chasing and chased and laughing.

"Would you like a drink, sir?" The voice was friendly, the accent difficult to place, not local but redolent of somewhere hot and dry and surrounded by embracing blues seas. It was the woman, holding out one of her cups to Fillingham. He took it and sniffed at the liquid it held; it was sweet and rich and pungent. The woman was looking at him expectantly, but he held the cup back out to her. "No, thank you," he said. "I'm not drinking at the moment." Not drinking alcohol, he almost added, but didn't. Instead, he indicated his press badge in its plastic sheath dangling against his chest and gave her a rueful smile, saying, "I'm working. Perhaps later."

"The celebrations go on for many hours," said the woman. Above her, in the sky, a firework exploded, showering multi-coloured flames across the stars. "You can pay fealty at any time." Another firework tore open the sky, streams of colour painting the woman's shift blue and green, throwing their shadows downwards. For a moment, the woman's shadow-self moved against the shadow Fillingham, pressing to him, and then another explosion above them sent them dancing apart, wavering, their edges rimed with yellows and reds, and then the woman was moving again.

She stopped at the people next to Fillingham, offering them drinks which they took. As they drank, she dipped her head again and spoke, and this time he was close enough to hear what she said. It was doggerel, some old rhyme he presumed, intoned as though it were a prayer. *Atmosphere*, he thought, snapping a last picture of her before her head rose from its penitent's pose. On the screen in his camera's rear, she looked small and pale, the swelling of her breasts only just visible under the cotton of her dress, her hair draping down in front of her face, her neck exposed and delicate. She lifted her head, giving Fillingham a last look that he couldn't quite fathom, and then she was gone.

By the time Fillingham decided to go back to his hotel, the atmosphere was definitely changing; most children and their parents had emptied from the crowd, leaving only the adults who were drinking seriously. The amount of dancing had increased and the town square was full of moving figures and noise. Three or four different groups of musicians were playing, with more in the pubs, and the sound of violins and guitars and differing beats and voices was creating a discordance that Fillingham didn't enjoy.

The fireworks display had lasted for a few more minutes after the woman had left him behind, and had culminated in a huge explosion of reds and greens and blues and Dover using a megaphone to cry "To ale!" again, the wand above his head spitting like some giant sparkler as he waved it around, creating endless looping patterns in the air above him. Fillingham had taken more photographs, trying one last time to catch the feelings and the sounds and the smells of Chipping Campden, with its twisting streets and cobbles and stalls and olde worlde charm that managed, somehow, to seem vibrant and real and not clichéd or faked. After, he had put his camera in his bag and gone back to his room.

He was staying in a chain hotel, and not an expensive one either. He used the cheap chains unless he was on a commissioned assignment and could charge the room to someone else, and had grown used to their uniformity. Each room was the same; identical cheap veneer with its woodgrain pattern to make up for the fact that the surfaces were all plastic, identical small TVs bolted to the wall with limited numbers of channels available, identical beds and bedding. Everything the same, from city to city, even down to the pictures screwed to the corridor walls and the carpet with its not-too-subtle pattern of brown and skeined red. He had become almost fond of it, in the knowing what to expect and surpriselessness of it all. At this end of the market, there were no individual flourishes in the room, no soap or shampoos in the bathroom, only two sachets of coffee, two cartons of milk, two tea bags by the small white kettle that each room came equipped with.

Like most of the hotels Fillingham stayed in, part of the reason it was cheap was that it was out of the town centre. Chipping Campden was small enough to be charming at its heart, but even it had a business district and some minor industry, and the hotel was in this area, a ten minute walk from the cobbled lanes and town square. The view from his window was of a carpark for an office block and, beyond this, the corrugated roof of a garage. The garage was also part of a chain, Fillingham noticed, his mood oddly low; after a day amongst so many people, so many colours and tradition and vibrancy, looking out on identikit companies from an identikit hotel was depressing. It wasn't how he usually felt, and it was unsettling in a way he couldn't quite identify. Dropping the blind down, he went and lay on his bed. The mattress was unpleasantly soft and moved under him, his book and camera, lens cap on, bouncing gently beside him. He turned on the television, turned it off again after hopping through the channels and finding nothing but blandness. Finally, he sat up, sighing.

Distantly, the sound of revels reached him and Fillingham wondered about going back and joining them and then decided against it. By the time he had left, most of the people there had been drunk and pairing off, and he suspected that he'd feel left behind, standing to one side and watching but unable to join in. He'd end up miserable, wishing he'd brought his camera and seeing things in terms of their composition, their visual attractiveness as flat images; the lens stood between him and these things, even when it wasn't actually there. He sighed again and put his shoes on.

Although it was late, the shop along the road was still open and happy to serve him: Fillingham bought a bottle of white wine, taking one from the refrigerator so that it was cold. He didn't drink alone often, but tonight he would, and try not to think of the women in their shift dresses covering muddy legs and taut thighs and high breasts. There was no one to betray if he did so, no wife or girlfriend, he simply knew that thinking about them would make him feel worse.

Walking back to the hotel, Fillingham smelled the scents of the day's games and the ongoing party, burning wood and paper and powder, meat, malty beer, spices and wine. The skyline ahead of him glowed orange, the dark shapes of buildings painted in shadow between him and the bonfire at Dover's Hill. Here and there, tiny yellow flickers bobbed through the gloom as people moved distantly with their candles. It would make a good picture, he thought, fireflies of light set against the solidity of the angular buildings, skittering and indistinct, a perfect metaphor for the way folk traditions survived in the modern world. He wished he'd brought his camera, and then sighed again at his own inability to detach himself from his lens.

Fillingham's room was on the third floor of the hotel, the

uppermost, on the opposite side from the entrance. He was too tired to take the stairs so used the lift, emerging into a corridor decorated with featureless watercolours. He went past doors with Do Not Disturb signs hanging over their handles, past the muffled dissonance of televisions and conversations, before coming around the corner to the stretch that contained his room.

One of the women was at the far end of the corridor.

It wasn't the one Fillingham had spoken to earlier in the evening; this one was taller, blonde instead of dark, fuller-figured, but she too was carrying a beaten flask and had a bag hanging at her side. As Fillingham watched, she took a small plastic cup from the bag and poured a measure of liquid into it from the flask; the drink looked thick and viscid.

"A libation," she said, holding the cup out. Her voice was deep and mellow, filled with sly amusement. He glanced down at his bottle of wine, sheened with condensation, the neck cold in his fist, and said, "Thank you, but no. I don't like to mix my drinks." He sounded prissy, even to himself, but couldn't help it; it was late and he was tired and miserable, and whatever opportunities he had hoped the night might present felt old and lost to the past. This woman was a tendril of the event occurring down the road without him, reaching out, and her presence in the hotel was jarring, throwing his lowering mood into even sharper relief.

"You refuse?" she asked.

"Yes," said Fillingham, and went to his room door. As he unlocked it, he was conscious of the woman simply watching him; just before he opened it, she said, "It is a small thing, a simple toast. Join me?"

"No," said Fillingham again. Even from the other end of the corridor, he could smell the drink, pungent and spicy, and the mud that was smeared across the woman's legs. The odour was cloying, unpleasant, made saliva squirt into his mouth as though he was about to vomit. He swallowed, glancing at the woman to find her still staring at him and holding the cup out. Her nipples were prominent through the material of her dress and he had a sudden strong impression that she was naked under the thin cloth. She stepped forwards, still holding the cup out towards him. Fillingham swallowed his own spit, warm and swollen, and then opened his door, stepping into the room without looking at the woman again.

Its banality was reassuring. Fillingham poured some of his wine into one of the cheap white porcelain mugs and took a large swallow, unsure of what had just happened. Why was he so bothered? Ordinarily, the sight of an attractive woman, and she had been attractive, no doubt about it, would have pleased him. Even if nothing had come of it, he could have flirted, hopefully made her smile. Instead, she had disturbed him in a way that was unclear even to himself. She was out of context, yes, away from the games and celebrations, but that couldn't have been it. Her smell was strong, not pleasing but again, it couldn't have been just that. He took another mouthful of wine and realised.

Darkness. The woman had been in darkness.

The hotel, like all the others in the chain, had corridors whose lights did not remain on all the time; instead, they were triggered by movement, yet the woman had been standing in a pool of shadow. She had come into the corridor, moved along it as she spoke to Fillingham, and the lights had remained off. He drank more wine, was surprised to find he'd emptied the mug, and then started as someone knocked hard on his room door.

Hot saliva leapt into Fillingham's mouth and he swallowed again, tasting something like electricity and an afterimage of wine, and thought, *Why am I afraid? It's a woman, and a near-naked one at that! What harm can she do me?* He went to the door as the knocking sounded again, picking up his camera off the bed as he went.

The woman was standing away from his door, perhaps twenty feet along the corridor, still in darkness. Her dress glimmered in the shadows, a white smear topped by her pale face. Her lips were red, almost as dark as the shadows crowding her shoulders, and she was smiling.

"What do you want?" asked Fillingham.

"You to celebrate with us," she replied, holding out the cup again. The liquid inside slithering up and then down again and even in the poor light, Fillingham saw the residue it left on the clear plastic sides glistening and clinging like oil. "Devotions must be paid."

"What?" said Fillingham. "Look, I appreciate you've got this weird acting gig at the games and you're only doing your job, but please, it's late and I'm tired and I don't want to drink whatever that is."

"A last enquiry: you refuse?"

"Yes! I refuse! Now, just leave me alone." To emphasise what he was saying, Fillingham lifted his camera and took a photograph, the light of the flash filling the corridor with a bleaching whiteness that painted the woman into a colourless mass for a moment. As the dancing ghostlights cleared from his eyes, the woman nodded and then lifted the cup to her lips and drank the liquid it contained. Keeping the cup at her lips, she thrust her tongue out into it and Fillingham saw it writhe within, licking at the remaining drips of drink. It should have been erotic, he thought; he was sure it was meant as erotic, but somehow it wasn't, it was crude and unpleasant. Her tongue was dark and looked slimy, glittering inside the clear plastic walls of the cup. Finally, she dropped the cup to the floor, lowered her head and muttered something that sounded Latin or Greek. Before she could look up at him again, Fillingham shut his door.

Still unsettled, Fillingham sat at the counter that ran across the room under the window, shifting the mess of magazines and coins that he had dropped there and putting the camera in its place. He poured himself another mug of wine and sat, intending to look through the pictures he had taken that day. He always found it calming, seeing his images scrolling before him, seeing the life in them reduced to tiny rectangles of colour and composition like butterflies pinned to card. He hoped that he had managed to capture the sense and energy of the Olimpick Games and the celebrations afterwards, and anticipated that he could sell some of the pictures and use others for his portfolio.

The last picture he had taken, of the woman in the corridor, was the first one he looked at, and he saw immediately that it was. . . wrong. It was difficult to see it clearly on the small screen, but the air around the central figure of the woman was filled with shapes. No, with a single shape that had lots of pieces, he thought, something that writhed behind the woman with too many limbs to count. He wished he had brought his laptop with him in order to look at the image on its larger screen, but he hadn't wanted to carry the extra weight for an overnight trip, so he was left with the camera's display. Squinting, he tried to make out details; was that skin? Fur? Teeth? Hands, or clawed feet? There were things curling around the woman's legs from behind her, as though the dirt on her skin had gained mass and was lifting itself towards the camera. What was going on here?

The woman herself seemed normal except for her eyes, which were entirely black and much wider than he remembered them being; it made little sense, because if she was reacting to the flash, her pupils should have contracted not expanded. Quickly, he scrolled back to the earlier pictures, to the ones of the other woman distributing drinks and then to the ones of the five females standing together by the dancing men; the same distortions were evident in all the photographs, things fluttering and shifting in the air behind them. They were clearest in the picture he had taken of the woman bending her head after giving the group of people her drinks; it was still impossible to see what it was, but it gave an impression of limbs, too many limbs, claws that curved back on themselves, eyes that gleamed like dark bone, a pelt, or skin that was rough and ridged, or possibly feathers.

Fillingham pushed his chair back and went to rise and that was when the hands fell on his shoulders.

They pushed him down into his chair, clenching around his shoulders painfully. Fillingham tried to twist and managed to shift a few inches, craning his neck around. His room door was open and the five women were standing in his room; the blonde one was holding him and the brunette he had photographed earlier was by the door. The others were motionless by the bed. "What– " he started but the women, speaking as one, interrupted him.

"You must pay obeisance to partake in Dover's Bacchanalia," they said, a single voice from coming from all their mouths. "You refuse to partake in the tribute yet drink wine. This cannot be." One of the women, shorter and red-haired, reached out without appearing to move and lifted his wine from the table. She lifted it to her nose and sniffed and then upturned it, pouring the remaining liquid across his bed, dropping the bottle into the puddle when it was empty.

"Who are you?" Fillingham said, gritting his teeth against the pain of the grip; the woman's hands were extraordinarily strong and felt unlike a human hold, as though her skin were a mere covering for something else, something muscular and old and venomous.

"We are Dover's Children," they said, still in unison. Outside the room, something heavy crashed and the floor vibrated. "He is our father, the father of games themselves." There was another crash and a long, low noise like a howl scrambled and put back together with its innards showing.

"I don't understand," Fillingham said, still trying to twist free of the woman's hold. There was yet another crash from somewhere out of the room but closer, and this time everything shook, the wine bottle rolling to the edge of the bed and falling to the floor with a dull thud.

"The games were a gift to Dover from that which comes, given to him in dreams so that he might, in turn, gift it on," the women said. "A gift, and all that people need do on this one night is to take the drink in honour of the gift-giver, to drink and then to worship in inebriation and heat and the movement of flesh. You refused the drink three times."

There was another crash from the corridor, still closer. Another, and the door shuddered, dust vibrating from its top and hanging in the air. The lights flickered. Another crash and the lights went out completely. In the sudden darkness, one of the women moved and the blind was torn from the window, falling to the desk in a noisy tangle. Leaping orange reflections filled the room. *How is no one hearing this?* thought Fillingham, pulling uselessly against a grip that was getting tighter, was digging into him and tearing.

"It only comes for you," said the women, as though hearing his thoughts. "All others have given honour, or do not join the revels. All around, those who drank the tribute and heard the prayer are communing with each other through song and flesh and note, or they sleep undisturbed because they take no wine or beer." The room was suddenly filled with noises, with grunts and shouts and moans and tunes, with the images of dancing and clothed flesh and naked flesh, of people losing themselves to pleasure, and then the sounds and images began falling away, layer after layer stripped to nothing as though lenses were falling between Fillingham and them, distancing him, swaddling him away from the rest of the world.

"Give me the drink now," he managed to say.

"Offense is already taken," the women said, and the one holding him let go of his shoulders and stepped back. Fillingham snatched up his camera as he started to rise but something lashed into him, a hand tipped with claws or bone, and he pitched sideways into the wall, falling to his knees as he bounced away from it.

"He comes," intoned the women. There were more crashes from the corridor, closer and closer, faster and faster, and then the doorway was filled with a huge figure.

It was Robert Dover, only it wasn't. It was massive, having to stoop as it entered the room and the women took up a low moan, swaying. Its head brushed the ceiling as it straightened, the huge moon of its mask face glowing palely. Its eyes were completely black and in them

Fillingham saw something roiling and twisting about itself, something that glittered and rasped and sweated. It stepped fully into the small space, and green and red and blue fire boiled across the ceiling above it, gathering in streamers and falling to the floor in long, sinuous fronds. Fillingham screamed and tried to rise but again one of the women struck him, sending him sprawling. He managed to raise his fist, still holding the camera, and fired off a single picture. The glare of the flash leaped across the room and for a brief moment the fire was gone, the women reduced to pale shades, Dover to a ragged and spindly thing that capered in the light, and then the fires were back and Dover's shape was gathering, thickening, the mask dancing with the colours of the flames and it was coming towards Fillingham with its arms open wide in a lover's embrace.

I cannot tell what planet ruled, when I
First undertook this mirth, this jollity,
Nor can I give account to you at all,
How this conceit into my brain did fall.
Or how I durst assemble, call together
Such multitudes of people as come hither
  - Robert Dover, 1616

Christmas Eve, 5.24

"Can we sit? For a moment?"

Elise sat, smoothing her uniform. Illness affects more than the ill, she remembered, more than the ill. She was here not just for the poor woman in the room above them but for her husband as well.

He was old, and drinking red wine from a balloon glass, its smell rich and aromatic. He saw her watching him drink and said, "I don't usually do this." Elise said nothing.

A heavy bang came from somewhere above them, followed by a pause and then a series of quieter taps. Elise looked up at the ceiling, at the cobwebs in the corners and the lampshade with its skin of dust, and started to rise. "No," said the man, "please, I was up there only a few minutes ago. She does this all the time, bangs on the floor with her stick, calls for me. She forgets that she's just seen me."

Elise lowered herself back down into the seat. The room's only Christmas decoration, a tree half-covered in listless tinsel and drab baubles, drooped in the corner. Outside, it was growing dark; this was Elise's last visit of the day and she was looking forward to getting home. Around her, the house's night-time breathing was muted, all soft swallows and gentle settles. The man took another sip of his wine.

"She was so beautiful," he said quietly. "Still is, really. She was full of life, so quick, so sharp, until this thing came along and took hold of her. At first it was silly things, forgetting where she'd put something, calling someone the wrong name. We used to laugh about it."

Elise nodded; it was a story she'd heard before, refracted and refolded and in a range of different hues but essentially the same. People watched as their loved ones altered, disintegrated, became someone else. "Now, I'm all she has," said the man, "although she doesn't know me. She calls me, although she can't remember my name." As if to prove it, the thumps and taps came again from the upper room, following a long, dragging exhalation that might have been a shout. From some other place in the house, a clock started chiming; moments later, its companion on the room's mantle joined it.

"I watched and I couldn't do anything," said the man when the clocks had finished their mournful singing. "She forgot more, became duller and duller, then she started getting frightened and would wander. I had to lock the doors of our home to prevent her leaving in the night. She lost control of her body, couldn't toilet herself, started to need help to eat, to bathe, to dress." He took another sip of wine, a bigger one, and then tilted the remaining contents of the glass into his mouth. Another series of bangs came from above them and another cry, long and formless.

"She forgets," he said. "She always forgets. I go and clean her and feed her and sit with her and brush her hair and make her comfortable, and then I come down here and she calls me within moments because she forgets all the time I was with her."

"Yes," said Elise, business-like, and rose. "Perhaps I could go and see her?" Her watch swung against her breast like the tap of a tiny fist, the glints from its face catching her eye. Late, it said, you're late.

"Of course," said the man. "I'm sorry, I've been keeping you. I know you're busy."

"No, said Elise, not wanting to mean yes but meaning it anyway. "Shall I find my own way there?"

"I'll show you," said the man and rose. He was tall, taller than her but stooped, his hands and face as white as cuttlefish bone except for the red stains around his lips. He led her out of the room.

The banging was louder in the hallway, as were the calls. Elise had heard it before, the liquid slip of a voice whose ability to form or remember words was decaying. It filled the stairway around them like dark, oily waves.

"Sometimes, I locked her in her room, just so I knew where she was," said the man as they reached the top of the stairs. "Can you imagine, having to lock up the person you love like some kind of prisoner? She'd bang on the walls and scream and cry, but what could I do? I hated myself for it, and for being grateful when she finally couldn't walk anymore and had to stay in her bed."

The banging was louder now, more insistent. "Then she started to call me," he said, "constantly calling me, calling anyone, hitting the floor with her stick, hitting the walls. She used to knock over her table until I moved it out of the room. I sometimes think it's her, the real her, trapped in the centre of this helpless thing, trying to reach me, to find a way back. I can't stand it." The stick banged, the voice called out again.

Elise didn't know what to say. The man went to the nearest door and opened it. Through the entrance, she saw the old woman's wasted body lying motionless on the bed and the pillow covering her face. Her stick lay, out of reach, on a chair by the bed.

"I love her," said the man and began to cry, and the sound of banging grew louder and louder.

Hurting Words

Five. There were five.

Trevelyan counted the bundles of paper again, separating each from the others, and there were still five when there should only have been four. Sighing, he thrust them back into his bag. He did not have time to check them all now and would have to look at them later.

It was a simple idea; Trevelyan and four other staff members who had started at the university at the same time as him acted as proof-readers and critics for the various reports, grant submissions and research articles that the others wrote. It did not matter if they were from different disciplines, were in different departments, they simply made what comments they felt they could and the author did with them what they wanted. The previous Monday, Trevelyan had placed copies of his draft article 'Frankenstein's Monster: An Impression of Schizophrenia?' into four pigeon holes, and on this Friday afternoon, he should have had four replies. There were five.

It wasn't until that evening that Trevelyan looked at the papers. His original idea, that he had picked up a rogue paper or had photocopied one too many of his own article, he quickly dismissed. Each of the returned drafts before him was different. Jenni Grey had made a series of comments that were useful, and his fellow English Literature lecturer McTeague's return was, unusually, almost unmarked. Breen had, as befitted an orderly physicist, filled the margin with his notes written in lurid purple ink and Darber had simply listed all the typos and grammatical errors at the end of the article. And then there was the extra one.

Whoever had written these notes had spent time doing it; every page was covered in a neat black script that filled the space around his text. Here and there, words or phrases had been scored out and new ones written across them so that the paper had become a jumbled, uneasy palimpsest. The new comments were dry, academic, written in short sentences that speared their meaning quickly. On the final page of the article, the unknown author had written a longer piece:

My Dear Boy,

This is almost passable work, containing some ideas with facets that are not without interest but that need further work. I would caution you, however, against committing the great heresy of literary criticism: do not look back and impose your own culturally relative views on what you read. Frankenstein's Monster may well, to your mind, be a good metaphor for the creeping terror of schizophrenia, yet Shelley would have had no concept of schizophrenia. Madness? Yes. Bodily disintegration and the plight of the poor and ill? Yes. The workings of places like Bedlam and its unfortunate residents? Also yes. But schizophrenia? No. Ask yourself: had 'schizophrenia' as a concept even been 'invented' back when Shelley wrote her novel? Perhaps it might be better to say that Frankenstein's Monster is a good metaphor for illness generally, for decay and loss of control, rather than to tie it to such a specifically twentieth century concept as 'schizophrenia'?

DRR

"What?" asked Trevelyan, aloud. The earlier comments had been useful, but this last one missed the point entirely. His paper was about the way in which readers imported their own interpretations onto things, especially when the original writing was as powerful as Shelley's was. It was what made classics classics; their ability to be constantly reinterpreted and reinvented for the current age. Dracula, for instance, might be about the creeping influx of foreign cultures or the unstoppable march of science and technology, or it might be about the spread of AIDS, and in twenty years' time it might be about something else entirely. This was one of the themes that Trevelyan's article had sought to illustrate using Frankenstein, and it was this that his unknown critic had apparently missed.

It must be a joke, he decided, albeit a complicated one. The depth of knowledge displayed indicated someone with a good grip of literature and theory, which pointed to McTeague, but he was humourless and it did not seem to be his style, not really. Perhaps it was a way for McTeague to say all the things to him that he felt he couldn't in person? Unlikely; he was well known for arguing with his colleagues over the slightest thing, and did not shy away from outspokenness. It was more likely one of Darber's odd creations, thought Trevelyan. The psychology lecturer had the time and the sort of mind needed to find this sort of thing funny. He resolved to keep an eye on him.

The Five met every few weeks, and by coincidence their next meeting was that night. Jenni Grey and Breen, newly engaged, arrived at the bar at the same time as he did, and Darber came in shortly after, and they spent a few minutes catching up and exchanging news. When McTeague came in, he came straight up to Trevelyan and stood over him, saying "Stay away from me." He spat as he spoke, and his fists clenched. Trevelyan saw the fists and tried to move back, saying "Alex, what?"

"I know what you're doing," said McTeague. "It won't work."

"Alex, what's wrong?" asked Jenni, standing.

"He knows," said McTeague, nodding at a bemused and concerned Trevelyan, who was still watching the older man's clenching and unclenching fists. His hands were large, the knuckles prominent, the veins snaking around them like rope.

"Alex, sit down and have a drink," said Darber.

"I won't sit with him, nor drink with him" said McTeague, one finger jabbing towards Trevelyan. "Ask him why." And with that, he turned and ran from the bar.

"Alex?" asked Jenni softly to his retreating back. Once he had gone, she turned to the others, her face a question in skin.

"Strange," said Darber. "And what did you do to irritate him, Raymond?"

"I've no idea," said Trevelyan.

"He's–" said Jenni, but trailed off before starting up again, hesitant and quiet. "He's not himself recently. He's been acting strangely. He made some comments on a draft paper of mine. They were... odd."

"Be honest, they were rude" said Breen, and Trevelyan finally relaxed a little. Maybe it was McTeague who'd written his mysterious criticism after all. If he was about to burn out, it might explain it. McTeague, he thought. Poor, humourless McTeague, with his staid readings and articles on the classics and his dry lectures, has finally begun to lose his mind. It was a simple case of one of academia's smaller fish beginning to founder and Trevelyan, who had never really been that friendly with the older man, dismissed him from his thoughts.

That night, McTeague killed himself.

The funeral took place on a bright day, the mourners' shadows melting like tar across the grass and headstones. Trevelyan, sweating in his only dark suit, stood by Grey and Breen for the graveside service. Grey was weeping openly and even Breen looked sad, while Trevelyan was uncomfortably aware of how dismissive his last thoughts about McTeague had been; guilt lay in his stomach like undigested dough. Perhaps if he had gone to McTeague, spoken to him, he might not have climbed out of his fourth floor office window and thrown himself to the ground below, leaving his last mark on the earth in blood and flesh spattered across the concrete apron in front of the English Department offices.

Perhaps he would still be alive.

Trevelyan went to the memorial after the service, although it made him uncomfortable. He felt as though he bore a mark that let people see how he had treated McTeague, told what he had thought about him. Attending the gathering was a punishment for his inactivity, self-imposed, to make him feel better and he wondered if other members of the Five felt the same; they were all there. Jenni certainly did and cried almost continually, sometimes quietly and sometimes more noisily, cursing herself for not being a better friend to the dead man.

"I don't think you could have done anything," said Darber, wandering across from one of the loose groups of people by the buffet. "I saw him last week, before the incident in the bar, and he was being very strange then. Distracted. He told me that he was tired of being 'got at', but he wouldn't tell me who was getting at him."

"Did you try and help him?" asked Jenni angrily.

"No," said Darber, either not noticing or ignoring Jenni's anger. "There was no point. He and I didn't really get on anyway and I only saw him for a moment. I called into his office to give him back the draft of his paper; I'd forgotten to put it in his pigeonhole and I'd made some comments I thought he'd find valuable. He wouldn't take the paper from me. I thought it was odd, certainly, but not odd enough to make me worry. I tried to talk to him, but he seemed disinclined to speak."

Disinclined? thought Trevelyan as Jenni fell softly into more tears and Darber walked away. Poor McTeague, if that was one of his last human contacts!

During the next weeks, and as the bolus of his guilt receded, Trevelyan thought of McTeague less and less. The coroner's verdict came and went, confirming what everyone already knew: McTeague had killed himself as a result of unknown stress or stresses in his life.

His lectures were parcelled out between his colleagues and his photograph taken down from the Current Staff board. Trevelyan continued amending his article, correcting and reworking it according to the feedback he had received and thought useful. The Monday after it was finished, he took copies of it to put in the Five's pigeonholes, realising with a sad little jolt that they were the Four now, and that McTeague's pigeonhole had already been re-allocated; the strip of tape across its bottom edge now held a new name. He wondered if all the traces of McTeague's existence at the university were being erased as quickly and easily; certainly, no one seemed to want to talk about the man now he was dead. Even Jenni had not mentioned him the last time Trevelyan and her had met. Indeed, Trevelyan had the distinct impression that she deliberately avoided the subject. Perhaps her guilt, like her friendship with the dead man, was greater than Trevelyan's. He did not know.

That night, Jenni rang. She was crying, her conversation broken by sniffs and little animal hitching sounds and it took Trevelyan a while to calm her enough to explain why she had called him.

"You want me to what?" he asked after she had finished.

"Come with me to poor Alexander's office," she replied. "Now that the coroner's verdict is in, the police have released his things. The university want the room cleared, and they asked me to do it because they know I was his friend. You work in the same department, so you can help. Please? I need company, I'm not sure I can go there alone. I asked Davey, but he can't do it."

Davey? thought Trevelyan, before realising that Jenni meant Breen. Even Breen never used his first name, simply signing himself B or Breen. 'Davey' didn't seem to fit, somehow.

The foyer to the English and Philosophy Building was quiet, the air relaxing into the building's emptiness. Jenni was waiting for him, huddled into her coat, slumped back on one of the chairs that lined the walls. Her face showed the reddened signs of recent tears, although her eyes were dry. She smiled weakly, standing and saying, "Thanks for this. For coming with me, I mean. I couldn't have done this alone, not go through his things. It'd be like grave robbing. I mean, I know I'm not keeping any of it, but I'd feel really uncomfortable, you know?"

Trevelyan nodded, knowing exactly what she meant; the thought of searching through McTeague's possessions, of boxing them up and passing them on or back, felt insulting, as though they were sullying his memory. It was as if, by packing away his things, they would be packing away McTeague himself, constraining him and storing him like so much useless detritus.

At the office, Trevelyan let Jenni enter first, thinking she might need a moment alone. In the quiet, Trevelyan heard her sob once, and then a yellow lozenge of light fell through the open doorway, seeping across the hallway carpet like old honey. Briefly, Jenni's silhouette was caught in it like a fly in amber and then it was gone and Trevelyan followed her into the room.

It was a mess. The police search had left things in scattered, untidy piles and this, coupled with McTeague's own hoarding nature, had left an office claustrophobic with contents. The surface of the desk was lost under papers and books, ragged strips of torn paper sticking out from their closed pages as makeshift markers. Shelves lined the walls, the books they contained piled against each other like broken teeth; more books sat atop the cases, excess from the shelves that had no proper home. Magazines, also with torn paper markers jutting out from their closed pages, were stacked in uneven towers next to the bookcases. Two battered grey filing cabinets stood either side of the window, their drawers labelled with handwritten and peeling stickers. Next to the door, Trevelyan saw, the porters had left a stack of empty boxes.

"You look at the books," said Jenni quietly. "I'll start sorting through his desk."

The books were easy; almost all belonged to the department, so he placed them in boxes, sealing them when they were full, labelling them and pulling them into the corridor. The magazines he boxed separately; they would go to McTeague's mother. The filing cabinets were, oddly, almost empty. Once they were done, he was almost finished; only one more thing to sort.

"What's this?" Trevelyan asked, pointing to a clear bag by the waste bin. Jenni, just finishing sorting through the desk drawers, looked around briefly and then said, "The paper from the bin. The police took it to see if there was anything in there that might give them some idea of why he did it, but there was nothing. I think they hoped they'd find a draft suicide note, but there's just lots of academic notes, they said." Trevelyan noticed that, as she spoke, Jenni had looked at the window fearfully and then looked away. He had felt it himself, as he sorted and packed. It drew at him, made him want to open it and look down, to experience a little of what McTeague experienced, to see a little of what he saw. It had been raining that night, he remembered; McTeague's last view of the world had been dark and wet.

The carpet below the window was stained, and in amongst the remnants of the police fingerprint powder on the window ledge were tiny rings where the raindrops had dried and left behind their ghosts. As Trevelyan knelt to pick up the bag of old papers, something brought him up short. At first, he wasn't sure what it was except a sense that he had seen something out of place, something jarring, and then he realised.

Writing.

Inside the clear plastic bag, most of the sheets had been folded roughly, crumpled in the past and then smoothed again, and the wrinkles across their surfaces looked old and tired. Black type crawled across them, and webbed around the type were handwritten notes, and Trevelyan recognised the handwriting.

Using the point of a key, Trevelyan tore open the heavy bag. Taking out sheet after sheet of the paper, each different from the last but also terribly, awfully similar, he placed them on the floor. Finally, with perhaps thirty pieces spread out in front of him, Trevelyan leant back on his haunches and let out a long, uncomfortable breath.

"What is it?" asked Jenni, looking over at him and the paper.

"I'm not sure," replied Trevelyan. "I think it's what Alexander was working on when he died, but look," he said, gesturing at the paper about him. Each piece was covered in comment, written in the same brittle handwriting Trevelyan recognised from the additional copy of his own draft research paper. Sometimes, the comments appeared helpful and considered. Trevelyan read one that said, 'This sentence seems overly long: perhaps you could split it into three sentences?' Others were shorter, more terse: 'Lazy writing! Be concise, man!'. Trevelyan saw one sheet where an entire paragraph had been scored out with a heavy black line and the word 'NO!' written in the margin next to it.

"I got one of these," said Trevelyan. "I think Alexander wrote it, as well as his own normal feedback. It was strange."

"It's not his writing," said Jenni. "Besides, why would he write those things to himself? Some of them are downright nasty." She was holding a sheet upon which a series of sentences had been crossed out and the phrase *Have you learned nothing from earlier comments? Idiot.* was written.

"If he was stressed and suffering," said Trevelyan, "he might have done it to try to make himself feel better."

"How could this make anyone feel better?" asked Jenni, dropping the paper back onto the floor. "It's horrible stuff. Have you finished? Can we go?"

Trevelyan took the papers home with him in the end. Sitting in his study, he read them again and finally thought he could discern their order. If he was right, they showed an increasing aggression to the handwritten comments and a concurrent deterioration of the quality of McTeague's typed text. The handwritten comments became bullying, hectoring and finally downright unpleasant, and it made him sad to know that McTeague, Alexander, had essentially bullied himself to suicide. The sheets were a mute testimony to it, a goodbye note written in oblique parts, desolate and angry and bitter. He sealed them in an envelope and placed them in his drawer; he would pass them to Jenni and let her decide what to do with them.

He spent the rest of the night making his final changes to his Frankenstein paper and printing it. No more feedback, he decided; now this stands or falls on its own merits. Leaving it in the centre of his desk, he went to bed. It had been a long day and sleep felt like a reward for labours completed.

When he picked up the envelope from his pigeonhole, Trevelyan didn't have time to read what it contained, instead putting it in his bag with his other paperwork. The envelope was large, had neither sender's address nor stamp on it and only his name on the front in block capitals: R E TREVELYAN. He didn't remember it until the following night, carrying it into his lounge and opening it whilst lying on his sofa, tearing away the flap of the envelope and upending the contents onto his chest. Trevelyan caught a whiff of something dry, as though the envelope held long-untouched air full of dust and powder, and then a sheaf of white paper tumbled out.

At first, he couldn't work out what he was seeing. It was his work, his paper on Frankenstein, but covered in markings. Was it a rejection? No, there was no enclosure from the journal, not even a standard 'Thank you but no thank you' slip. Besides, the journal's editor and he had discussed his paper before he submitted it, and whilst it wasn't quite a commission, it wasn't a blind submission either. Had the editor sent it back with his thoughts written on? No, surely any comments or revisions would have been written up properly, or he would have rung Trevelyan to talk them through? He looked again at the comments and as realisation dawned he sat up and the papers fell to the floor in an untidy pile.

He recognised the handwriting.

It was McTeague's, or at least it was the writing he had assumed was McTeague's, and it should have died with him, buried in a near-anonymous graveyard that Trevelyan was sure the man had never visited in life. And yet, here it was scrawled over the paper, his paper, in cramped, obsessive lines. It was almost too dense to read at points, the letters tangling together and overlapping so that the words themselves were squeezed, as though whoever was writing was desperate to fit as much on the page as possible. The underscores and crossings out were so thick that the ink had bled sideways, feathering into the surrounding words like gathering stormclouds.

Trevelyan's first thought was that he had put the wrong paper into the envelope, had accidentally sent an earlier one to the journal, but he dismissed that idea straight away. He knew his own work and what he could see of the typed text under the handwritten commentary was the final version of the article, and he had only printed one copy. So how had it got here? And how had someone managed to scrawl over it?

The comments themselves were as vitriolic as before, he saw. One sentence, Lazy material, man!, leaped out at him immediately, and he found many others like it. There was a barely-restrained fury to the comments, to the parade of words (no! weak! idiot!), that made them difficult to read. On the last page, Trevelyan found another addition, written in a space of its own and larger, as though to ensure it was read:

You have listened to nothing, learned nothing from my earlier comments and suggestions. As a result, this paper is flawed and lazy, and I cannot allow it to go to publication. When you have the good grace to make the amendments that I have suggested, perhaps then I may be more amenable to allowing it to face public scrutiny. Until then, however, I insist that it stays unread by all except you and me.

DRR

After he had finished reading, Trevelyan very carefully put the papers back into the envelope, stood and went to his study. He placed it in his bag and went to leave the room, but stopped. In the half-dark, he thought about the paper, about the comments, about McTeague and Jenni and himself, and then in a low voice, he said, "No. It's my paper. It goes in the form I want." And then, trying not to think at all, trying to pretend that things were normal, he went to bed.

He didn't sleep. In a darkness that felt brittle and full of edges, Trevelyan lay in his bed and helplessly teased at the situation like he would a holed tooth with his tongue. If not McTeague, then who? And it wasn't McTeague, couldn't be; messages from dead men were the stuff of stories, the things he read and wrote about and taught, not things that happened in the warmth of a campus summer. So, another member of the Five (*Four*, he thought sharply. *the Four*)? But if so, why? What was the point? It didn't make any sense; at least with McTeague, there had been a kind of obscene, degraded logic to it, but not any of the others. Breen, Darber, Jenni, none of them stood to gain from it, and none had shown an inclination towards cruelty before. And besides, how had they intercepted it from the post, preventing it from reaching the magazine? Trevelyan was baffled, drawing his knees up to his chest as the night crept about him.

Sounds came from downstairs.

At first, he thought it was the midnight rhythms of the house settling, but it wasn't. It had none of the languid spread of normal night noises, none of the unwinding ease of them. Instead, it was a hurried, tenser sound, a chittering that made him think of palsied teeth. It was lurid, feverish, growing louder, more urgent, filling the room and pressing the darkness down against him like old, damp sacking. He reached out and turned on his bedside lamp, but the wan electric light made no difference; the sound shivered around him.

Eventually, Trevelyan had to move; it was that or remain frozen in his bed all night, he told himself, nestled under his quilt like a child, and he would not do that. No. No. This was his house, his home, he had bought it, was paying for it still, had arranged things within it the way he wanted them. It bore his imprint, held his reflection, was his place, and he would not be trapped within any part of it by something as simple as sound. Taking hold of his irritation, his tiredness, his fear, Trevelyan rose from the bed and went to the door. Quickly, before his sense of anger faded, he opened the door.

The hallway was filled with a shifting darkness, the shadows flowing across the walls like oil on the surface of water. It was words, Trevelyan saw, words creating themselves out of nothing, flowing black lines expanding and forming, some collapsing down to unintelligible strings of shapes that could be letters but that were so tiny it was impossible to make out individual characteristics. They moved, wormlike and sinuous and impossible, their noise the frantic, dry scratching of branches against old glass.

The lines swirled now, funnelling around the doorway but never quite crossing the edge of the light that fell out around him, remaining just beyond it. When they came close to the light's glimmer, the words and sentences and paragraphs reared away, rising from the floor like threatened insects, Devil's Coachmen showing their armoured bellies or scorpions lifting claws that glinted half-seen and dull. He saw words form and disappear in the tangles, close enough now to read, paltry and ill-thought and once simply NO in heavy, rigid capitals. Trevelyan couldn't scream; the words seemed to have dwindled his voice and breath to little more than a failing wheeze. They clustered, closer and tighter, closer and tighter, until they were dancing near Trevelyan's feet, filling the whole of the hallway.

Very slowly, Trevelyan shut the door and stepped back into his room, into the cradling arms of the light from his bedside lamp. Lines of words, writing he knew, crept under the door before the light drove them away, stupid looping alongside confused and pointless. Now on his bed, he pulled the quilt up around his chest. Words continued emerging and vanishing under the door as, silently, he prayed for morning.

The sunlight, pale and weak and clean, came with summer's earliness, for which Trevelyan was grateful. The sour darkness that had trembled and bled under his door only retreated with its arrival, and was completely gone by the time he risked looking into the hallway. The walls were unmarked, the floors clear, and the noise had faded like the last static of a dying radio. Going downstairs, the house itself felt tired, exhausted after a long and aching battle, and the closer to his study he came, the greater this impression became. The room throbbed, the bitter centre of an infection that had taken root during the night, and when he opened the door, it smelled sickened and dry and old.

The room was dark, but the darkness contracted as Trevelyan watched, swirling like ink flowing down a plughole until only a dense patch remained gathered around the envelope on his desk, and then this too was gone. Weary, Trevelyan shook the papers out onto the desk without touching them; they were still covered with writing, different from the previous day, thicker and more layered, some of the words faded and others glaring and new. Using a pencil to lift each sheet, he flicked through the pages until he came to the last one. The longer comment had faded down to a dusty, wretched grey and over it, written in large, black letters, was a single savage NO.

Campus was busy, buffeting Trevelyan as he walked. He was exhausted, and had the feeling that his world was shifting, bucking under him like the deck of a ship that he had not even known he was on. All these people, have they got any idea? he wondered, looking at the students around him, and thought that they didn't, couldn't. How could they? If he tried to talk to any of them, would they think him mad? Probably. Were it not for the packet of papers in his bag, he might have suspected that himself.

"Do you think it's funny?"

Trevelyan started, his reverie broken by Darber, who had stepped out in front of him, blocking his path. Darber looked different and for a moment, Trevelyan couldn't work out why, and then he realised: he was angry. His face, normally so smooth, was twisted into an ugly snarl Trevelyan couldn't remember Darber ever wearing before. He couldn't remember him showing any emotion, really, other than a kind of faintly amused disdain. The man wasn't just angry, he saw, but dishevelled as well, his suit wrinkled, his shirt unbuttoned. He was tieless, and was holding something, waving it at Trevelyan as he spoke.

"I don't appreciate this sort of thing. You and Grey may be upset, that's fine, but I couldn't have helped the man."

"I don't know what you're talking about," said Trevelyan, but he thought that perhaps he did. It was papers that Darber was holding and shaking, a sheaf that rattled like snakeskin.

"Nonsense," said Darber, an attempt at composure showing on his face. He shook the papers again and Trevelyan caught sight of printed text covered with the now-familiar writing. "I mean, is it a joke? If so, it's not funny, it's just offensive. By all means criticise me to my face, but to attack my work like this, work that you clearly don't really understand? It's childish." Darber danced the papers under Trevelyan's nose again, and he smelled the sour, trapped odour of age even though the sheets that Darber held were a new, bright white. Even upside down, he made out the words You are a fool, man!

"We didn't write those things," said Trevelyan but Darber only grinned, his face grey and wretched.

"You and her have always hated me, I know that, but I thought you could be professional about it."

"We don't hate you," said Trevelyan. "We didn't write those things, I promise you. Look, I got one myself," and he reached in his bag and withdrew his article, holding it out for Darber to see. Darber knocked Trevelyan's outstretched hand down without looking at it.

"I don't give a fuck," said Darber. "Just stay away from me, you and that bitch too." And with that, he turned and strode away, not looking back even when Trevelyan called him.

After picking his scattered papers up, Trevelyan made his way to the department common room and as he went, he thought he could hear the insistent scratch of new words being created rising from his bag. He wondered what would happen when he opened it; would they burst out in a shower of ink, coating the room, or would he simply find the papers bloating obscenely, swollen with words that were not his? Would they have spread to the other books and papers in there? He looked around him and wondered about how far the writing would go, whether it would take over and eventually cover the world. Would everything he knew and valued and loved eventually vanish under a swirling, vehement black tide? He saw it then, saw himself staggering through a world where the shadows had become the lightest thing around him, paler than the ever-expanding blackness, saw himself climbing out of a window to escape it, or taking pills or slipping his head into a noose in an anonymous room and kicking away a stool, somehow finding a way to follow McTeague, and then he was angry again, and he opened his bag.

The envelope fell out onto the table in front of him. As he watched, it bulged and shook slightly, as though the papers within were breathing. He picked it up and upended it, shaking the contents loose. They fluttered out, falling to the table in scattered drifts. Trevelyan picked up the sheet nearest to him, seeing his own writing caged by new words. Moron caught his eye, as did imbecile and poor and, once, dolt. Dolt? he thought. Who speaks like that? Who uses that as an insult? Fully two thirds of his own work had been literally blotted out; thick black lines now lay across his own writing, obscuring it completely, and over it were new words, new phrases.

New ideas.

"My God," asked a voice from his side, "where did you get a Rathbone from?"

Severn was the oldest member of the department, if not the oldest member of the university staff. "That takes me back," he said, lowering himself into the chair next to Trevelyan without waiting for Trevelyan to reply. "May I see?" He was reaching, Trevelyan saw, for the papers, surprisingly fast for an old man, and before Trevelyan could move them out of the way he had hold of them and they were gone. Trevelyan wanted to say something, a warning, but his voice had abandoned him. He waited for the writing to writhe, to flow around Severn's fingers, to create new words over the old. For the man to scream.

"He was a nasty piece of work, wasn't he? Where did you find this? One of the old filing cabinets, I suppose?" Severn looked expectantly at Trevelyan who, confused, nodded.

"We used to dread getting one of these, back when I started. All that criticism and never a positive thing to say about anything or anyone. I tell you, I don't miss seeing these in my pigeon hole."

Trevelyan thought that he was probably gaping; his mouth was definitely open and he shut it with an audible pop. His brain leapt, darting back over what Severn had said, trying to drag some sense from it. "You recognise it?" he managed to say. "The writing? You know it?"

"Of course," said Severn, looking more closely at Trevelyan. "Are you all right? You look pale."

"I didn't sleep well," replied Trevelyan. "Please, tell me about—" he tailed off, waving his hand at the paper. He still didn't know how to describe it; Criticism? Abuse? Attack? All those and more.

"It was written by a man called Rathbone, David Robert Rathbone. Look, he signed this one DRR, but he sometimes used to put DR Rathbone, which used to make us laugh, only never so he could hear us. We used to joke that he hoped that people would read it as Dr. Rathbone. He wasn't a doctor, you see, only a lecturer, and not even a good one. He was a glorified administrator, really, good at pushing pencils and forms around but less good with the academic end of things. You know the sort." Trevelyan nodded again terrified of interrupting Severn and slowing the flow of information. There were no answers yet, but Severn was finally giving him a framework for his questions.

"He was here when I started, and he was the strictest man I ever met. The department was run by Nixon, who was mostly old and senile, like me." Severn looked slyly at Trevelyan, waiting. Trevelyan merely returned his look, hoping his expression conveyed the message *Of course not, Severn, you're as sharp as ever* without needing to say it. He liked Severn well enough, but sometimes he could be difficult if he thought you weren't deferential enough to him.

"Rathbone was Deputy Head, but essentially he ran the department. He was a tyrant, controlled everything. What's that modern phrase? Micro-managed, that's it! He micro-managed things. Everything had to go through him, every order for books or stationery, every change to timetables or the syllabus. He made us all show him our research papers, journal articles, book chapters, what have you, before we were allowed to send them out. He claimed it was to ensure that the department's reputation wasn't adversely affected by poor work, but really it was because he was a critical old woman who couldn't stand the thought of someone having ideas better than his own. I don't think he even wanted to take credit for the ideas, not really. I think he just wanted to stop anything coming out of the department that he hadn't made his own in some way, moulded it the way he thought it ought to be."

Trevelyan watched as Severn held the paper up before him, waiting for the lines of text to move. They remained still, their heavy black print visible through the paper like veins under skin. Severn was looking at the writing, making sad little laughing sounds as he read it. Finally, he lowered it and looked at Trevelyan and said, "Have you read this? It's terrible isn't it? That he could be so vicious, I mean, and no one challenged it."

"What happened?"

"To Rathbone? He retired in the end, and no one was sorry to see him go. The department was a miserable place under him, especially at the end."

"The end? Why?"

"Because of his book," said Severn simply. "Because of the reviews it received."

The volume wasn't hard to find; there were several in the library, one of which Trevelyan stole.

It was slim, a 1970s paperback, and it was dusty with lack of use. It smelled of old thought, of fustiness and abandoned shelves and it left its marks across Trevelyan's fingers in grime like the powder from moths' wings. He flicked through its brittle, cheap pages, feeling the waft of air across his face and tasting the paper's shedding skin. Its pages, he noticed, were unmarked, which made him smile grimly. Its cover was a light blue, decorated with a line drawing of a quill and parchment. The picture was badly executed, or maybe badly reproduced, and it looked rough and cheap. On the rear cover was a grainy head and shoulders picture of an unsmiling man in a shirt and tie. Rathbone, in all his grim glory.

Trevelyan tried to see into the man's eyes, but they were lost in the poor print quality of the photograph, mere dark ovals hanging under a pale forehead and black-slash eyebrows. He ran his finger across the picture, not sure what to expect, but felt only the not-quite-smooth cover of a poorly bound and produced book. Where had such malevolence come from, he wondered? Where had that hate birthed?

How could it still be here now?

Even in print, Trevelyan thought he might have known that Rathbone was the author; the tone of the essays that formed each chapter of the book was dismissive, showing in the way in which he swept aside earlier ideas about the various works he was analysing. Rathbone was a man of absolutes, leaving no space for discussion. The problem was, most of his ideas were at best unoriginal and, at worst, old and stale. They would have been dated at the time the book was published, thought Trevelyan. In his introduction, Rathbone said they were "a summation of many years teaching and thinking", but Trevelyan found little evidence in what he read of anything original or creative or progressive. If this was the pinnacle of Rathbone's career, it was a stunted, low thing and it left little legacy.

In his office, Trevelyan took his article from his bag and put it on the table beside the book. It was now almost entirely black with additional text, illegible marks covering illegible marks, and he felt a wave of helpless fury. Even now, as he watched, swirling lines of words were creeping out over the edge of paper. They looked like the shadows of distant airplanes as they slipped across the surface of the table, like the x-rays of broken limbs made fluid and animate. They slithered around the edges of Rathbone's book, gathering about it but not touching it, until the tabletop was black with them, was bucking like the surface of an ink sea.

All except Rathbone's book, which was an island of pallid serenity on the table, a blue square of stillness at the heart of pulsing, malignant motion. Trevelyan gazed at it, hating it, hating Rathbone, and not knowing what to do about it. He reached out, lifting the book from the table, letting the shifting words rush in to fill the space it left behind so that the desktop was entirely covered, and held it in front of his face, flicking through its pages again.

"What are you?" he murmured. "What are you, and what do you want from me?" There was no reply. He wanted to ask it again, but didn't; if he was to escape from Rathbone, from the criticism and the bullying and the impossibility if it all, he would have to find his own solutions.

Trevelyan placed the book back onto the table, watching as venomous words shifted out from under it, clearing it a space. He reached out, knocking the book further away from him so that it slid across the tabletop and Rathbone's writing danced out of its way and flowed in behind it, always leaving it unmarked. Trevelyan tried to think; what had Severn said? That it was the book that made things bad? No, not just the book, but the book and the reviews, and as he remembered he thought that maybe, just maybe, he might have a chance.

Trevelyan listened as the department went to rest around him, as his colleagues locked their offices and called their goodbyes and trailed out, their footsteps like the pock of rain on cold stone. The lights dimmed, turning the corridor beyond the frosted glass wall of his office into a shadowed thing and the passing staff into edgeless, moving shapes. As he watched, Trevelyan wished that he could be on the other side of the glass, could be walking along the corridor with them, unaware of writing that created itself, of long-gone academics and their savage opinions.

One of the dark shapes stopped by his door. The edges of it rippled against the mottled glass, and for a moment Trevelyan thought it was some new aspect of Rathbone, writing that had plaited and formed itself into a figure, was coming for him on spindle, text legs. He tensed, and then the shape knocked on the door and opened it without waiting for a response.

"Hello," said Severn. "I saw the light and thought I'd pop my head in."

"Hello," said Trevelyan, his heart shuddering.

"I've been thinking about your Rathbone papers," said Severn. "I wondered what you had thought you might do with them? He might have been a terrible man, and I didn't like him, but he's still a part of this place's history." He waved a vague hand at the ceiling, somehow taking in not just the department but the building and the campus beyond. "History isn't always pleasant, is it? But we have to treasure it."

"I don't know," said Trevelyan, feeling a dreadful black humour bubbling in his throat. "Maybe the university library might want them, or I may give them to his estate. I haven't thought about it."

"Estate?" said Severn. "Oh, no, you misunderstand me. Rathbone retired years ago, but he isn't dead."

The room was dim but not dark, the light warm and diffuse. "This is very unusual," said the care assistant whose name Trevelyan could not remember. "Mr Rathbone hasn't had a visitor for such a long time, and he's such a sweet old man."

"Sweet?" asked Trevelyan, startled.

"Yes," said the care assistant. "I mean, he doesn't speak much these days, but when does he's always polite and he's so kind. And generous! He helped Mary's son with his homework last year when he heard her talk about how he couldn't understand the book he was reading."

I'll bet he did, thought Trevelyan bitterly. *I'll just bet.* "Can I see him?" he asked.

"If he's awake," the young man replied. "It's late, but it'd be good for Mr R to have a visitor."

Mr R? thought Trevelyan as the care assistant went to the huddled shape in the chair on the far side of the room. After a moment, he turned and beckoned Trevelyan over. "Mr R," he whispered as Trevelyan came close, "you have a guest. Someone's come all the way from the university to see you. Isn't that nice? Well, I'll leave you to talk. Not too long, now, we don't want you getting too tired, do we?" The care assistant shot Trevelyan a look as he went past, stern and sure and protective.

Trevelyan wasn't sure what he expected, but the grizzled, hunched figure in the chair wasn't it. All the way to the rest home, driving through streets that were filling with the night, he had imagined some unholy terror lurking in a room that smelled of candles and incense, but the man in front of him looked delicate to the point of frailty, shrivelled, his skin sallow and thin. He didn't look frightening, simply pathetic, a hunched and decaying thing whose eyes, crusted and rimmed with the dry, raw touch of age, hadn't focussed on him.

"Can you hear me?" Trevelyan asked, and was surprised to hear tenderness in his voice. This man had terrified him, tortured him, and yet Trevelyan felt the anger that had helped drive him here slip away in the face of this withered, pathetic thing.

"Hello?" he said, and withdrew the article from the envelope in his bag. The pages were creased now, and the ever-moving writing was clumped in the creases as though it had flowed there and was struggling to escape. "You wrote this," Trevelyan continued. "You keep writing it, and I need you to stop. It has to stop. You have to stop." Rathbone did not reply. The only indication that he had heard, that he knew Trevelyan was there at all, was a brief nod of his head, birdlike and fragile, when he saw the papers.

"Please," said Trevelyan. "This is my work, and you're destroying it. You're frightening people, frightening me. Someone I know has already killed himself because of what you're doing. I don't know how you're doing it, I don't know why, but please stop. Please." Rathbone still didn't respond and, frustrated, Trevelyan crouched by him, dropping the paper onto the man's legs, stick thin inside shiny, worn suit pants. At the sound of their dry rustle, Rathbone tilted his head down. A line of spittle slipped over his lower lip and trailed down to the edge of the uppermost sheet, glinting. One trembling hand came up and drifted across the sheets and then jerked violently, sending them wafting to the floor about his feet. He wore check carpet slippers, Trevelyan saw, and felt that black mirth roil again in him. A demon who wears slippers, he thought, and then, with surprising speed, Rathbone's hand darted forward and clasped around his wrist.

"It's not me," said the old man, in a voice like pages turning. "Not me."

"It is," said Trevelyan, trying to pull his wrist away but unable to, and surprised by the man's strength.

"No. Not me, not any more. I was that person, but no more." Rathbone coughed as though he wasn't used to speaking, swallowed, and carried on. "No one comes, no one visits. I'm alone, because of what I was. Was I so bad? Yes. Yes, I was, but no more. I try to be kind now, to not be the person I was. That," and the hand finally let go of Trevelyan's wrist and waved at the paper on the floor, "isn't me. Whoever it is, it isn't me."

"It is," said Trevelyan. "It's you. It's how you were."

"Yes," said the old man, and Trevelyan was horrified to see tears roll from his eyes. "I was him, but not now. I'm old and I'm so lonely here and I have so much time to think. I look back at him, and I don't recognise him even though I know who he was. I've tried to change, to be different. Tried to be the person I should have been all these years and I am, I do it, but it's not enough. I can feel it, every time that other me does what I used to do. It hurts. It hurts so much. I'm here, but I'm out there as well, and I don't want to be. I'm so tired.

"Please, can you stop him?"

"I don't know," said Trevelyan. "I was hoping you could."

"No," croaked Rathbone. "Not me. I can't. I haven't the strength, I've tried, tried to stop it but I can't. I'm too old, too weak. You have to. Promise me. Promise."

"I'll try," said Trevelyan.

"Promise," said Rathbone again, drool slipping once more from the side of his mouth and slicking across his chin. Trevelyan watched as tears gathered and spilled from the older man's eyes, their rheumy blue irises lost in sclera that were yellowed and exhausted. The room lights reflected on the trickling liquid as he spoke. "Promise," he murmured again. "Promise."

The door to McTeague's office was locked but the keys Trevelyan had taken from the departmental office opened it. Once inside, he shut the door and locked it again. He did not turn on the overhead light, instead flicking on the desk lamp. Its pale yellow light crept across the walls and ceiling, making the shadows huddle together in the corners. The office looked bigger now that it had been cleared out, the floor bare and the walls like old ivory. The bookshelves, free of their tottering masses of books and magazines, stood sentinel against the walls, and the desk, its scarred surface bare, had been pushed back into the far corner. Dust had gathered across the surfaces and a smell of neglect and abandonment had gathered in the few days since Trevelyan had been here with Jenni.

Trevelyan dragged the desk back to its place in front of the window, deliberately not looking out at the courtyard below. Even in the darkness, the paved ground that had been McTeague's landing place glared up in mute appeal. He removed his article from his bag, shaking it out of the envelope and placing it on the desk. Most of the additional comments had faded down to grey slivers now, so that in the dim light his writing looked scarred and weary. A tight smile on his face, he took a pen from his pocket and then, very deliberately, crossed out one of the extra comments with a heavy black line. Underneath, he wrote the word 'Nonsense' and then recapped his pen and put it back in his pocket. Sitting back in the chair, Trevelyan waited.

It did not take long. Around him, the air seemed to thicken. Shadows that had, only moments earlier, been light suddenly darkened to a gravid, opaque gloom. The temperature dropped, raising gooseflesh on his arms, and the lamp flickered, guttering like candlelight before catching again and returning to full strength, buzzing and humming as it did so. Trevelyan tried not to shiver, removing Rathbone's book from his bag and clutching it; its solidity was oddly reassuring. *This has to work*, he thought. *This has to work.* He repeated it silently, rolling the book tightly in his fist. The word he had written on the paper seemed to glow, gleaming blackly. He rolled the book tighter, twisting the cover and pages around into a dense tube, and then relaxed his grip and let it spring back into shape. It flapped as it did so, sending a breath of old paper across his hands. He rolled it again, released it. Rolled it; released it. Rolled it, and there was a noise, of fingers dragging across stone and of insects rattling their wings, and Rathbone stepped out of the far shadows and into the light.

It was the Rathbone of the cover's rear, an anonymous-looking middle aged man in formal clothes with short, bristling hair, not the shrunken thing he had been earlier that evening. He wore a neat suit, in a sombre grey that spoke of conformity and rigidity. His shoes shone, clean but not ostentatious, and his shirt collar clutched tightly at his wattle neck. His bearing was controlled, his hands held clenched in front of him, one gripping the other as though to stop it flying away like some bone-white bird of fury. He looked respectable, conservative, unobtrusive.

Except in his face.

Rathbone's pupils glinted out from the pooled shadows that hung below his brows, and in that glitter was fervent anger. His grave-worm lips were pressed together, tight and thin and sour, and his chin sloped away from them as if to escape their bitter attentions. The lamplight flashed across the lenses of his spectacles, glinting. His hair was swept back and thick, shiny with pomade, and the smell of it was cloying and sweet. He stepped forwards and Trevelyan saw that, at his very edges, Rathbone was blurring slightly as though he was continually being made, unmade, made again from the shadows around him. His feet made no sound as he stepped forward.

"You ignore my advice?" asked Rathbone, pointing at the paper on the desk. His voice was dry. He took another step forward, his hand trembling as he continued to point.

"Advice given freely, meant only to help, and yet you consider it 'nonsense'?" He came forward, leaning over the desk so that he was between the light and Trevelyan. He cast no shadow, Trevelyan saw, but the light falling through him onto the desk was hazy, splintered. This close, Rathbone's edge was impossible to define. Strands of him, of his substance, unknitted from his body and trailed away, growing thinner and indistinct the further away from him it went. It gave him a greying corona like an aura gone desiccated and lifeless.

"You believe my advice to be flawed?" asked Rathbone, with dangerous politeness. "Incorrect in some way? Do you believe you know this subject better than I?"

Trevelyan didn't reply. Instead, he reached into his bag and pulled out the sheaf of photocopies and printouts, dropping them onto the desk in front of him. It had been a hard job to find them and copy them, and now he would see if it had been worth it or not. He leaned forward, ignoring how close he was to Rathbone, ignoring the way his skin prickled as though there was a source of electricity nearby, and chose one at random, picking a sentence and speaking it aloud.

"'A man with no valid ideas.'"

"What?" said Rathbone. Trevelyan felt a wash of cold, writhing fear jittering across his skin and into his belly. He pushed the paper aside and picked up a new one.

"'Empty of originality, dull and likely to illuminate no one.'" *I'm reading to something that's not even a ghost,* he thought. *It's a fragment of one man, his vitriol, let loose and made independent.*

"I beg your pardon?" said Rathbone, and when Trevelyan risked looking up at him, he saw that he had backed away a step. His edges were blurring further, mutable and frenzied, and Trevelyan thought his expression had changed, shifting from anger to a kind of cold dismay.

"'Broadbrush arguments that never hit the mark',," said Trevelyan, reading from another paper, and then "'a mystery why this work has been published'" from a fourth.

"They were fools!" hissed Rathbone, his edges dancing like the tips of ocean waves. "They didn't understand what I was saying!"

"Not nice when the tables are turned, is it?" said Trevelyan, leaning back in his seat. His heart yammered so hard that he felt sure Rathbone would see his shirt trembling above it. He felt brittle, dangling above a place both vast and desolate, with only one way forward and no way back.

"It's so easy to feel under attack, isn't it?" Trevelyan lifted another of the copied reviews from the desk, smiling as insolently as he could manage, and read "'Feeble ideas swimming in writing as dull and lifeless as day old custard'. Now, that's harsh, isn't it?"

"How dare you?" shrieked Rathbone, his voice like flies battering against metal. "How dare you?" and he dashed forward, those eyes seeming to sweep up all the light in the room and draw it in until Trevelyan could focus on nothing else, not papers nor print nor walls nor the lamp at his side. There was simply Rathbone, grey and bristling.

"They were fools, all of them!" hissed Rathbone again, his voice dropping now to a sibilant whisper. "They know nothing. I spent my life at this university, reading and listening and understanding and I know those texts better than those people ever could."

"Really?" Trevelyan managed to say. Rathbone's face was all, a vast cold moon hanging before him.

"Yes! And you, you choose to ignore my advice and yet you take that of your friends? Some of them not even in the English department.

What understanding have they of the written word? Of art? Of literature? Scientists!"

He's not touched me, thought Trevelyan and his confidence suddenly, shockingly, felt genuine rather than a brittle carapace, *because I don't think he can! It's all words and written savagery, an intellectual violence not a physical one!* He grinned, leaning forward. Rathbone fell back as though they were in some stylised gavotte and Trevelyan grinned more widely. He let the book fall from his fist and reached for the last time into his bag. He continued looking at Rathbone, whose entire body was breaking apart and reforming now, only his face remaining constant, hanging above the shifting, dust-cloud shadows that swirled below his neck.

"It's your book, isn't it? Your creation? Your life's work? Only it's not very good, is it?" asked Trevelyan. He felt a rough edge under his fingers and clasped the last object he needed, lifting it from his bag. It rattled as he placed it on the desk by the book. His grin was painful now, stretching at the edges of his face and pulling at his muscles. He reached for the book, knowing that Rathbone was watching. The maddening scritch of new words being written came from his article again, lost to sight now, buried under other papers. He ignored it. Without looking down, keeping his gaze firmly on the figure ahead of him, Trevelyan lifted the book. Rathbone's face was growing again, filling the room. It came towards Trevelyan, the crown of the head brushing against the ceiling and the chin grazing the surface of the desk, ruffling the papers. "You dare to stand against me?" Rathbone asked, and his voice boomed around the room like the rattle of closing doors and dropping lids.

"Yes," said Trevelyan simply, and tore a page from the book.

It felt good; no, it felt *wonderful.* The paper made a noise like a ragged exhalation as it came away from the binding, and Rathbone screamed, wordless and terrible. Trevelyan tore another page away, dropping the two into the metal bin by his feet. He tore another, then clamped his hand around a wedge of pages and yanked at them, feeling them tug loose from the cover like teeth from diseased gums. He dropped them, seeing them flutter like butterflies at the edges of his vision and then Rathbone was over the desk, crashing back to a more normal size and shape, a stiff, weary man screeching helplessly, "No, no, no" over and again as his hands waved around in a semaphore of anger and despair. Trevelyan risked looking down, sweeping the papers off the surface of the desk and into the bin before dropping the remains of the book on top of them. He picked up the last object he had taken from his bag and shook it; the rattlesnake chatter of it sounded good in his ears. Pushing open the box, he removed a match.

When he struck it, the dancing light was somehow brighter than that of the lamp, a shimmering flame that filled the room. It washed across Rathbone, pushing him back even further, scoring his face to a sickly orange and withering his body to little more than a smear in the glare. Trevelyan held the match for a second, twisting it so that the wooden stem was truly alight, and then dropped it into the bin with the paper.

The sheets ignited with slow, lazy grace. The flames moved along one page and then stepped across to another, pirouetting as they went to catch more in their grip. When they came to the book, they burned more brightly, as though fed by unseen fuel. First, the cover shrivelled from blue to brown, curling, and then the pages within it caught and burned. Trevelyan heard Rathbone yowl, inhuman and thin, and then more loose pages were swallowed by the growing conflagration and the yowl turned into a scream of pure vitriol.

Rathbone was tearing apart. Pieces of him were ripping loose, spinning away to the corner of the room, leaving sooty trails behind them. They smelled, not the healthy scent of flame but the greasy stink of uncooked meat. His voice rose, staggering up through registers of sound until it became something stabbing and toneless, bitter, and Trevelyan had to cover his ears. The flames leapt at his legs and he moved away, watching as their frenetic jig encircled the rim of the bin and blackened the thin metal. Still Rathbone sounded and pieces of him, smaller and smaller, whirled away to the walls, old grudges being released and the distant smell of rottenness filling the room. Trevelyan watched the sheets curl, blacken, disintegrate, ashy fragments detaching and swirling up, carried by the breath of the fire. They capered around the last of Rathbone as he broke apart and was dashed away until only eyes and a mouth remained, and then only a mouth, dwindling, shrieking, the scream falling away to nothing and at last, it was done.

The office smelled of burned wood, but there was nothing Trevelyan could do about that. At some point, the flames must have crawled over his hand; there was an ugly pink blister across his knuckles and the hair had been scorched from the skin. The flames had also blackened and charred one leg of the desk, and had buckled the bin into an irregular, ballooning shape like a frozen cloud. Of Rathbone, there was no trace, except some darker streaks across the walls and a smell under the burning of something old and decayed. One of the scraps of paper that had danced loose during the fire was from Trevelyan's article and on it, he saw the printed words 'the Monster's greatest purpose'. Above them, in Rathbone's tense writing, were the words terrible fool. Trevelyan crushed the damaged paper to nothing with his uninjured hand and then left the office. Exhausted, he went home.

He slept badly, and in the early hours Trevelyan rose from his bed and walked away from dreams in which flames licked at figures whose faces swelled and twisted. He went to his office and printed a new copy of the article, placing it in an envelope and addressing it, and then he made himself coffee and waited for sunrise. After it came, he showered and then checked on his article; it was unmarked. He sealed the envelope and wanted to feel happy, but didn't.

The drive was long, through heavy morning traffic, and he arrived later than he hoped. He was made to wait in the reception area before being shown through to the manager's office.

"Did you know Mr Rathbone well?" the handsome black woman behind the desk asked.

"No, not really. We were acquaintances, I suppose you'd say. Can I see him, please? I have some news for him."

"Mr Rathbone didn't have any family, as far as we know," the manager continued as though he hadn't spoken. "If you hadn't visited him yesterday, I wouldn't be telling you this, but really, I can't see the harm. Mr Rathbone died in his sleep sometime during the night."

"I see," said Trevelyan, not wanting to ask if Rathbone had gone peacefully, whether the smell of burning had filled the room. "Thank you for letting me know."

"He had some papers, and we think that his will leaves them to the university. May we call you to collect them once the formalities are complete?"

"No," said Trevelyan, rising. "Call the faculty office. Call anyone but me." He left the office and walked back across the foyer, wanting to be gone from here, to leave Rathbone and everything he had created behind. He wanted to go back to his house, to plan boring lectures, to mark essays, to read and think. To get his life back.

Behind him, Trevelyan's feet left dusted black marks on the floor.

Hyperdontia:
The uncontrolled growth of many teeth. In extreme cases, newly emergent teeth fuse with existing teeth which are then pushed against the skin of the inside of the mouth, eventually erupting through the skin of the cheeks and jaw. If left untreated, the fused teeth can emerge to form permanent interlocking bony extrusions that can prevent the sufferer's mouth from opening and can affect the ability to eat, as well as leaving low moans and grunts the only available vocalisation.

The Pyramid Spider

[The following letters are the only contemporary record of Arnold Klein's research trip to Papua New Guinea. Klein, a postgraduate student with the University of Lancaster School of Languages, went there in July 1957 to further the work on his thesis, reassessing and re-evaluating the work of the nineteenth century German linguist Heinrich Jaekl. Klein stayed in Port Moresby, the capital, for 9 days, and it is known that he spent this initial period in an apartment and using an office that had been secured for him by a local agent. It was during these, the last dates that Klein's whereabouts can be verified, that the first four of the letters were written and sent. The last two, assuming they are real, were written after that time; Klein's whereabouts during this period remain unknown. These last two letters were never sent, but were discovered in papers of the private safe of the agent, Dischoff, following his death. How they got there, and why he kept them for over fifty years, must remain conjecture. At the request of Klein's family, the letters are recreated here in their entirety.]

03.07.57

An office in the middle of nowhere

Hi Jimmy

Well, it's as bad here as you insisted it might be. This place reminds me a little of what you said about Mexico – it's very colourful and not a little desperate; you'd hate it. The poverty's fairly extreme, and it'd offend your delicate socialist sensibilities, ha ha! Actually, joking aside, it offends my sensibilities a little. It's hard to see kids crippled and begging in the streets while idiots like Dischoff lounge around in offices bigger than some of the houses I saw on the way in. Speaking of which: Dischoff. I met him on my first afternoon here, and he's a fool. He was genial at first, and very accommodating, but I was getting nowhere with him. He wouldn't tell me anything, and then I worked out why – he wanted a bribe! I mean, the amount of paperwork and 'grants' that've bounced between the department, his office and the German consulate, the amount of form-filling we've had to do, not to mention all that communication with Jaekl's family, and after all that, he sits on his fat behind smiling like a toad and expecting payment. I'm afraid I lost my temper a little (well, a lot) and may have said some fairly unpleasant things to him. Can you let Millner know that he may be receiving a complaint about me already? That'll cheer him up!

Anyway, once Dischoff realised that he wasn't going to get anything extra from me, he took me to the office. Half the things that were agreed aren't here; there's no typewriter, hence this being handwritten, half the background documents we were promised aren't in the files, the travel visas are incomplete or missing (although Dischoff insists that the ones I do have will get me "anywhere", although God knows how or where I'd want to go, I'm already feeling I stand out like a communist at a God Bless America rally). There's a reel-to-reel, thank God, and a stack of old New Yorker magazines, which should keep me occupied, assuming I wanted to read about the cold war, or the weird details of American suburbia. Incidentally, the office is in one of the government buildings and I'm surrounded by what appear to be civil servants, who look at me very strangely whenever I leave the comparative safety of my room. I can't help but feel putting me here is deliberate, a subtle way of reminding me that I'm a visitor. Which is, I suppose, fair enough, seeing as I am. The advantage of it is, of course, that they deal directly with things like my administrative needs (need more paper, sir? Certainly!) and my post, speaking of which I'd best sign off if I want to get this in this week's airmail bag.

Take care and be in contact again soon. Hope Marie's okay.
Arnold

07.07.57

Jimmy

It's taken me three days, but I finally got the tapes from Dischoff. And guess what? There are only two of them! That's right, after all the bureaucracy that we went through to see the original thirteen tapes from Jaekl's collection, only two still exist. Two! When I queried this (lost my temper again), Dischoff simply shrugged and gave me one of those Teutonic 'This is what happens when you let inefficient people run your archive', looks. There didn't seem much I could do, so I brought what I've got back to the office and started work.

Firstly, I've made a straight translation without referring back to (and therefore hopefully not being influenced by) any of Jaekl's published work or private notes. The first of the tapes (labelled "2") deals with the day-to-day life of the Kaloni tribe. The speaker (the Kaloni chief? it isn't clear) talks about hunting, the tribe's history, its arts and literature, etc. The quality of the tapes isn't great, and there are sections I've had to listen to over and over again just to decipher the words. It doesn't help that a crowd surrounded the main speaker when the recording was made, who sometimes chip in with extra information. Every now and again, Jaekl comes in, asking a question. It's odd, hearing his voice after thinking about him as the enemy for so long. He sounds like a pleasant guy.

The second of the tapes ("12") is about the Kaloni's religion and myths. The crowd behind the chief (I'm going to assume that's what he is; what else can I do?) are far quieter on this tape, which means it's easier to make out what's being said, and already I'm fairly sure that I'm onto something. Jaekl's always claimed that the Kaloni's religion bore such striking resemblances to Christianity that it must prove the absolute reality of the Christian stories, yes? The creation, the flood, the saving of man through the sacrifice of God's child – he said all of these were in the Kaloni's religious beliefs, didn't he? Well, they're not, not according to my translation anyway. Rather, their beliefs seem to be that the world was spun or extruded from out of the chaos somehow, and is watched over at all times by a creature resembling a huge spider. There is a flood mentioned, but only peripherally – water is supposed to be the only place of refuge from this spider God (who lives in a giant pyramid structure, incidentally). There's no talk of its children coming and being sacrificed either; the Spider leaves one child here to keep mankind in check, and it demands sacrifices. I'd like to think that Jaekl's theories stem from simple ignorance, or a lack of skill in translating the language, but you and I both know that's not the case. His work on the field in legendary, and there's enough research material by him published at the turn of the century to show that he knows the language well enough. No, Jaekl was trying to force everything he came across into a shape that supported his hard-line Christian views, and I'm positive that that's what I'll find when I compare his own direct translations to mine. I may make a name for myself in this game yet!

Arnold

10.07.57

Jimmy

I have him! After my last letter to you (which I've realised will probably arrive at the same time as this one, seeing as they'll both go in the same mailbag), I spent the next couple days comparing Jaekl's translations to mine, going back to the tapes where we differed. There are so many things he's done, my God, you wouldn't believe it! At one point, the chief talks about the creation of the world – you know I said that they believe God to be a sort of spider? Well, the Spider God doesn't exactly make the world, but rather, tries to overcome it or conquer it. The chief's words are "...covered the land with terrors from inside of his belly stretched out in a web that lay thick and caught the dust and dirt over itself to form the ground we walk on." And how does Jaekl translate this? "...making the world out of dirt, even the spiders and their webs."

The chief talks a lot about how water is the only place that this Spider God can't go, saying things like "..and the sea cannot hold his [God's] weight..." and "...we must flee to water when he comes from his temple for the depths contain other Gods that may harm the Spider God...". And Jaekl's translations of these two passages? "..the sea is from God.." and "...the sea is also his temple...".

The worst though, Jimmy, the worst of all is the passage about the sacrifice of God's child that Jaekl used to argue so forcefully for the religious supremacy (read: actual existence) of Jesus as the son of God. The chief says "...and the God left a creature like himself but small enough to walk through the trees and on the land, and He made him a temple which rises to a point [a pyramid?], and sacrifices must be made to Him. When the temple appears in the appointed place, the sacrifice is taken into the temple to be wrapped in His cords, until it can provide no more sustenance. With sacrifice, God will leave the world untouched." Jaekl, however, translated this bit as: "...and God's child was came to the earth and worshipped in temples, and was sacrificed and will come again to make his mark upon the world". The arrogance of the man! To simply ignore what they were saying in order to make it fit his own views! And it's not simply poor translation skills; quite apart from his earlier work, his translation of the first tape is perfect. This is deliberate manipulation of material, and I can prove it.

Incidentally, the Spider God and the things in the depths do have names, but I'm not even going to attempt to write them down. They're full of altogether too many consonants and too few vowels – even saying them's hard. They've got glottal stops and plosives that feel all wrong for my vocabulary and vocal cords. Speaking them aloud is like trying to swallow something unpleasant and spit up something spiky all at once, and I swear that it leaves a bad taste in my mouth when I try. Weird, don't you think?

One other thing: I had an odd conversation with Dischoff today. He came to the office, and at first I thought he was prying, but it seems to have been quite the opposite. I think that he may have been shamed by my complaints (and I do know you've just thought "temper tantrums" to yourself, old friend!), and he's offered to help me. Apparently, some of the Kaloni still live out in the jungle, and he's going to see if he can arrange for me to visit them and talk with them. He says that the visas we have permit that kind of travel – I hope he's right. I have enough money to cover the extra costs, so may take him up on it. While he was here, he let slip that he was descended from the Kaloni, so I wonder if part of this is him trying to regain his people's religious beliefs for themselves, rather than leaving them as a sidestory in the Jaekl Christian Crusade?

Anyway, I'm going now. I think I deserve a whiskey, don't you? Love, as ever, to Marie.

Arnold

11.07.57

Jimmy

Fast message as I want to catch the mailbag, so you'll get three letters at the same time, you lucky soul! Good news! I'm going with Dischoff tonight and he's found a phonetic transcript of another tape. Tell Millner I want a bonus when I publish proof that Jaekl was deliberately lying.

Speak soon, love to M.

Arnold

13.07.57

Jimmy

I'm writing this letter in a hut in the jungle, because I'm here with the tribe – I'll post it and anything else I write when I get back to the comparative civilisation of Port Moresby. Last night, Dischoff picked me up and drove me a weird little slum suburb, where a funny looking guy took over looking after me (money changed hands between him and Dischoff – wonder what I'm worth?). The new fellow drove me for hours in silence, heading out of the town and into the wilds. It was a bit unnerving at first, but I soon got used to it and used the peace to translate the transcript (although the roads out here are little more than tracks, so the bouncing didn't make things easy – we were driving in an old army jeep, and it was very uncomfortable). I'm fairly sure that the transcript must be of tape 13, as it follows on closely from tape twelve, and talks about the ceremonies and practises of the Kaloni religion, and it's genuine as far as I can tell. The paper's old, and although it's typed, it's covered in handwritten German notes. There's a longer note at the end (also in German) basically attesting that it's an "accurate and correct transcription from the tape in the phonetic Kaloni dialect", signed by Jaekl.

Most of the transcript concerns the activities in and around the temple and has to do with appeasing or escaping the God, which returns to this earth whenever it needs a sacrifice (it and the temple apparently appear and disappear at will, coming back when the God needs more sustenance). I haven't brought my other Jaekl translations or papers with me, but I don't remember anything like that in them – just lots of stuff about making promises to God, although I'll check that when I get back. The Kaloni religion is more violent than Jaekl's Christianity: there's lots of stuff about blood offerings and needing to keep the Spider God happy. The chief says, at one point, that without the offerings to the "creature in the temple" (that seem, incidentally, to act as a distraction as much as an offering, helping to keep its eyes off the rest of the world), it would "walk to the towns and eat its fill". I'd love to hear the original tape, rather than just read this transcript, though. I get the impression that the Kaloni are frightened of their God, and that they don't worship it so much as try to keep it happy and occupied.

What's clear already is that the Spider God exists as part of a much wider mythology, full of terrible things (demons? fallen angels? I'm not sure, to be honest, but certainly monstrous and destructive whatever their classification) whose sole aim appears to be to feed off "...the creatures of the lighted world..." (i.e. us!). The Spider is one of a group called "old ones" (sometimes "deep ones", it's a little confusing) who at some point broke through (I can't translate that any better, sorry) and were somehow repulsed by the Kaloni in the past, leaving them with the sacred duty of guarding against their return.

I reached the Kaloni village late at night, and I'm hoping to talk to the chief (or anyone) later today.

Wish me luck! Speak soon.

Arnold

16.07.57

Jimmy

It's taken me days, but I think I finally gained the Kaloni's trust. I'm not sure Dischoff told them who I was, not properly at least, and they were quite aggressive at first. It took me a while, but I realised that they thought I was a colleague of Jaekl's, that I'd come to carry on what he started and he's not at all popular around here! Anyway, I've spent a good couple of days talking and taking notes and reassuring them, and I'm sure now that Jaekl lied in his reports. Their religion is massively complex, far more so than I first understood.

So: the Spider that created the universe came from outside it, according to their beliefs, from another place, (another dimension, I suppose you'd call it). The creature that got left behind isn't its child, exactly, more like a part of itself that it left here to see if there's a way to force an opening again for an invasion (again, this is hard to translate – it could also be 'annihilation' or 'consumption', I'm not entirely sure); like Jaekl's Christian God (and this may be the only similarity the Kaloni's religious beliefs have with Christian beliefs), there's an ongoing and everlasting battle between good and evil, which is as real to the Kaloni as the physical world. It's no wonder Jaekl wouldn't report the Kaloni's beliefs accurately, very little of it tallies with the heterodox Christian stories. There's no redemption here, no love or understanding, simply horrors and violence and misery and the constant threat of these things returning to the world and enslaving or slaughtering everything upon it! Hardly very Christian.

The Kaloni have proved a contradictory bunch as well. After the initial tensions, I think I've won them over and they're mostly pretty friendly, but sometimes I catch them looking at me when they think I can't see them, and they look almost sorry, as though they pity me. Heh, maybe it's because they've heard about England and think that their lifestyle (which is a mix of traditional and modern things, a little like the Amish but with fewer clothes and higher humidity) is far more preferable to mine. Of course, given how dull and small England is, they may be right...

This morning, they brought me to the temple. It's an astonishing structure, far more impressive than I would have expected. It's a pyramid, built in the trees on an island in the centre of a small lake. It stretches up from just above the ground to the top of the canopy. The sides are (I assume) made of trunks lashed together, but it's impossible to tell as they're covered in leaves and branches. None of the villagers would come in with me when we first arrived – they rowed me over, dropped me off and left me to investigate by myself, saying that they'd be back later. Anyway, I looked around the island itself after they'd gone (no wildlife, thank God!), and then wrote up more notes (sitting in the sun drinking warm water from a canteen, which isn't exactly heaven but beggars can't be choosers) before coming inside the structure itself.

I'm writing this sitting inside it, in the shade, which is very heroic of me, don't you think? There's not much in the way of decoration in here, but when I've rested I'm going to have a proper look around. One thing I want to check out is some sort of hanging figure near the apex of the temple, wrapped in cloth or rope – I imagine it's a representation of the sacrificed man, left to dangle until it falls apart and gets replaced at the next ceremony (a bit like those corn Christs that you can sometimes get at harvest-time). This one looks pretty far gone, to be honest, and is mostly ruined, but it'll be interesting to see it more clearly.

Past it, there's another figure, this one much bigger – the Spider God itself, I think. It's huge, quite creepy and surprisingly realistic, given that it must be made from branches and leaves and creepers – it's hidden in the shadows, so it just looks like a real giant spider, sleeping in the top of its web. I'd love to know how they've managed to get it to the very top of the pyramid. It's high enough to catch the breeze from outside, as every now and again, its legs shiver as though it's moving and once, before, it shifted around as though it wanted to look at me more closely. They've used shiny rock or something for its eyes, which look for all the word like they're glittering and alive and staring at me. Below the eyes there's a hole that might be its mouth, and I think something's made a nest in there because I'm sure I saw something wriggle in the hole, twisting and turning; a snake, maybe, or a few of them all crawling around whatever they've used for the Spider's teeth. Its skin is very dark, made of leaves or something else that's mottled and patched with mould and it smells, of rottenness and dust and something else, something that smells like the taste trying to say the various demons' names left in my mouth. I really don't like it at all!

The breeze must be picking up, although I can't feel it down here; the spider just moved again, turning and dropping slightly, and its legs are shifting about. It looks like it's stretching and waking up! See, this is why language students should stay in the lab and not venture into the field – we give ourselves cases of the fits, shivers and blind staggers! I hope my guides come back soon - apart from the company, they've promised that they'll take these two letters to Dischoff so he can get them onto the mail plane. He'll be pleased I'm rescuing the mythology of his people, don't you think?

Anyway, see you soon. Love to Marie.

Arnold

[No trace of Arnold Klein has ever been found. An investigation, carried out at the time following a request of the British government, uncovered no evidence of his whereabouts after the 11th July and his notebooks have never been found; his paperwork was removed from the rented office and apartment and has also never been located. Pietre Dischoff denied ever arranging a trip for Klein, and the Kaloni villagers denied that he ever visited them. No pyramid structure has been recorded in the jungles in or around the Kaloni land.]

Periodontal Masking:

A second layer of enamel grows over the teeth, thickening them and pushing them out of shape. This can distort the shape of the mouth and lips and lead to difficulties eating, speaking and, in some cases, breathing.

Vernon, Driving

Vernon drove.

He did not drive with a destination in mind, but let the roads and traffic choose for him. Along with one stream of cars, across another, stopping here and going there, just driving and yet leaving nothing behind. Around in circles. At first, he had tried to drive with the radio on, but its chatter became wearing so he turned it off. Then, however, the silence allowed his thoughts to swell, fill the car and press against his skin like thorns, so he turned it back on and found a classical music station with little talk. That kept the thinking at bay.

Vernon had first met Jay, and introduced him to Scott, at a reading in the library's committee room late the previous year. It was one of the few perks of Vernon's job; working in the library was rarely exciting, but occasionally local authors would agree to attend groups or give readings, and then Vernon would experience a small break with his established routines, and could have fun. Jay's reading was actually shared with two other up-and-coming local literary figures, a poet whose work had won small press rave reviews and a novelist whose intense, angry prose alienated as many people as it impressed. The three had amused Vernon, although he had not let it show. They looked similar, all in jeans and jackets and boots and t-shirts with prints on, and they had acted as though what they were reading, what they had written, was going to shake the pillars of the earth. In truth, of course, it was only Jay who moved the pillars, and then not with his writing.

Eventually, the constant circling began to grate on Vernon's nerves and he began to follow a route rather than simply driving. He started to make decisions, making choices and following roads although he still did not know exactly where he was going. Out, certainly. Out of the town. Somewhere. Anywhere. Away. As he drove, he wished that he could shed the hurt behind him in chunks, discarding it out of the window like old cigarette butts and the empty chocolate bar and pre-packaged food wrappers that lined the sides of the road wherever he went these days, but it was not to be. It stayed, clinging with fingers like old clicking bone and growing like some malignant ulcer in his belly, pressed up against his solar plexus and compressing his breathing into hard little bullets.

The poet and the other novelist, who made little impression on the assembled crowd in the library, were soon finished and then it was Jay's turn. Vernon had to admit, he was a good looking boy even if he wasn't Vernon's type; tall but not too skinny, his hair long and pushed back from a smooth forehead. His black jeans and jacket hung nicely about him, framing rather than hiding his figure, and his smile, which he did too rarely, was open and engaging. He had introduced himself briefly and then, leaning over the lectern casually and looking down at his typed sheets only once or twice, started to read.

The denser buildings of the city centre finally fell away and became the more widely spaced homes and shops of suburban living, the gardens and houses chained and docile behind fences that crept up in height each year as the world became a less friendly place. Vernon had lived out here once, but had moved at Scott's behest, transplanting them to an apartment high in a building that had no garden, surrounded by other buildings that had no gardens but did have underground parking and CCTV in the lobby monitored twenty four hours by faceless security firms. Vernon had hated it really, but had coped because of Scott. Because he loved Scott, loved him for his energy and youth and passion, for the way he talked about each day as though it were something special, had some new gift just ready to unfurl for him, for the way he kissed Vernon goodbye whenever he left and hugged him hello when he returned. Vernon tried to approach things the same way Scott did, but never felt he managed it; his age, his attitude, seemed to prevent him, made him slower, always behind Scott encouraging and loving but never partaking. Now, the spaces between the houses seemed to mock him for ever leaving, for ever thinking that someone like him could exist happily in the claustrophobic depths of the city. In their open, capricious shadows, Vernon saw a mockery of the space he thought he and Scott had carved for themselves and the pain bloomed, bitter and raw.

"They came," Jay read, "from their places on the far side of reality, tearing open the thin barrier between their vast, cold plane of existence and ours and dragging themselves towards us and they were as inexorable as the movement of the abyssal oceans or the final setting of a sun gone hidden and dark. As they passed, the walls were sucked free of life and grew brittle and were marked with their text, words written in blood and unreadable by any human eye. Their bodies filled the streets and their foul, flailing limbs clutched at any place they could gain hold, clutched and held so that they could not be dislodged. Men went mad at the sight of them, their hair becoming white as ash as they gazed upon their faces and at their bloated flesh. Terrible and ancient and scarred with the endless cold of space, the terrible and ancient things glistened with frozen moisture and colours played across the surface of their skin, colours that were never meant to be seen on earth. Before them, humankind could not stand and instead fled or fell beneath claws or teeth or arms that had no bones and yet a million grasping limbs, were taken into the shadows of the world where the gnashing things could feed, twisting and writhing about the ripped and torn flesh of men and the opened bellies of women. On the other side of the shadows more of them gathered, waiting for their time, for the moment when the world would open itself to them like a gutted thing, rolling and submissive in its own horrors and the stench of its own defeat. They came, and more came after, wearing the night's darkness like a cape."

Vernon grimaced as he drove, remembering Jay, remembering his intensity and the way he leaned over the podium like a preacher in a revivalist meeting. It was undeniable that he had charisma, had dominated the room. He had, at that moment, taken all of Vernon's life in his hand.

Jay had read more in this vein but Vernon thought it was terrible, over-written and preposterous. Scott, however, loved it, said later that he loved Jay's reading and the way his voice filled the domed room until it sounded like echoes of other, more distant voices. Vernon watched his partner, rapt as Jay read, and felt a swell of emotion. He had arranged this; Scott's pleasure was Vernon's pleasure, and he had pride that he had a hand in it.

Driving through the night, Vernon tried to pinpoint where things had started to go wrong. When he had asked Scott if he wanted to attend the reading? When he had first sent the tentative email to Jay to ask if he would interested in doing the reading? When he had first read about Jay in a local writers' magazine? When he had first met Scott and opened himself to this terrible, aching hurt? No. Not then. Whatever the end result, he must never think of Scott as a mistake, never think of Scott as something that shouldn't have happened. Scott was the highpoint in a life that had been lived along staid, repeating lines for its entire length, was the one genuine passion that Vernon could lay claim to. Not blameless, to be sure, Scott was at least not a regret. This ache in his soul Vernon could place squarely at one person's feet: Jay.

Following the reading, Scott became one of Jay's biggest fans. He would tell Vernon in breathless, excited tones about Jay's progress. Not about the stories themselves, which Scott seemed to consider a private pleasure, but about the writer's progress. How he had sold a story to this magazine or that anthology, how his work was building on ideas of earlier writers but would soon eclipse them entirely, how he had been nominated for this award or how that magazine had given Jay a glowing review. Vernon had listened to it all, happy that Scott had something to enjoy. Even when Scott and Jay began to converse more and more frequently via email and then started to meet, he had no concerns. Scott came back from the meetings, if it was possible, even more excited and started talking about setting up a website for Jay, somewhere to collate all the good news and give his fans somewhere to talk no matter where in the world they were. He would work late into the night, no longer coming to bed with Vernon and appearing only late in the mornings bleary-eyed and grumpy until he checked his emails and found a new message from Jay.

Gradually, the urban landscape changed, shifted. The roads narrowed and began to climb over hills whose grass seemed bleached to grey in the darkness. The valleys between the hills were pools of inky shadow and the reception on the car radio worsened slightly, overlaying the music with a light cobweb of static and interference. Vernon turned his lights to full beam, seeing how they splashed over the drystone walls that lined the edges of the fields about him, picking out some details and losing others in the gloom, and was reminded horribly of how the pictures had looked.

It was, oddly, exciting. He never really believed that Scott was having an affair with Jay, but it was fun acting as though he was. It was his imagination; it had to be, didn't it? He and Scott were in love, were a couple, and had been for years. Why would Scott need to have an affair? Surely Vernon gave him everything he needed and wanted? But still, those tiny suspicions moved wormlike in him. Why did Scott, a longtime opponent of mobile phones, suddenly get one and why was he so secretive about the texts and calls he received on it? Why was he meeting Jay so often, and why did he come home so late and so tired after the meetings? Vernon acted like a cuckolded husband in a bad drama, looked through Scott's drawers and letters when he was out, tried to listen in on his calls, and once tried to follow him but lost him in the bustle of the shopping centre. When Scott was at home, Vernon would drop references to Jay in the conversation to see how he would react, secretly pleased when Scott did nothing suspicious. In the end, he had no evidence but a heart full of suspicions and it ceased to be fun, ceased to feel an enjoyable roleplay and became sour and grim. He handed it over to a professional.

Once he had thought of the pictures, reminded himself of them, Vernon couldn't stop seeing them. They played out across the overlapping circles of the headlights and slipped among the trunks of the trees that sometimes stood sentinel at his sides as he drove. He turned up the radio, trying to drive the visual from him with the auditory but could not. He pressed down harder on the accelerator, letting the car leap forward and feeling the throb of the engine travel through the pedal and seat itself in his body and, hating himself, he thought of the pictures.

"I'm sorry," said the man quietly as he passed over the brown envelope. Vernon felt the world tilt and whirl under him in that moment, heard in the man's tone the cracking and splintering of the thin veneer of the reality that he had built over the years and had held on to so strongly for these past weeks. "Oh Scott," he murmured because if he had let his voice out louder than a murmur he felt it would grow and grow until it was filling his skin and tearing his throat. The man, a private investigator that Vernon had hired never expecting him to find anything, rose delicately and left Vernon's office. Vernon, his hands shaking, opened the envelope and let its contents fall across his desk. There were so many, most taken at a distance and with their edges blurring; Scott and Jay in a cafe innocently sat apart and drinking coffee or tea from white cups, Scott and Jay walking in some nondescript street their arms around each other, Jay leaning against a wall as Scott took money from an ATM, Scott driving as Jay leaned against him and both smiling. So many and most of the pictures, and there were dozens, could be explained innocently. Except for the last three; Scott and Jay, in a room somewhere, fucking.

Faster and faster, Vernon let the car suck the road into itself and spew it out behind. What fragile control he had was splintering, was failing, and he had a sudden image of glass falling into an abyss, its sharp edges catching the light as it fell, turning and turning and turning and turning and never stopping. It welled up within him, this blackness and the pain until he was moaning as he drove, an animal cry of misery that drowned the already-loud radio and gibbered like some living thing alongside him in the car.

Of the three, the worst picture was the first. In it, Scott lay on a bed naked apart from his pants. The picture was taken from a vantage point, presumably a window, to the side so that Vernon could see all of Scott as he lay. Jay was stood at the foot of the bed, visible in profile, naked. He was grinning and his erection jutted out in front of him. His cock was big, bigger than Vernon's, and the look on Scott's face was one of terrible, animal anticipation. His own erection was visible inside his underwear, straining against the tight cotton. The digital time printed in the corner of the photograph showed that it was the middle of the afternoon, and every detail in the photograph was clear and incontrovertible. Vernon and Scott had never made love in the idle of the afternoon; Vernon could not ever remember Scott having that expression on his face when he was with Vernon. Until he saw the photographs he would have said that Scott, his sensitive and beautiful love, was incapable of making that face.

Finally, Vernon tore at the wheel of the car and dragged it off the road and onto one of the single lane tracks that splintered out across the fields from time to time. Ahead was a small forest scattered with picnic areas and deserted clearings and he came to a halt in one of them, switching off the engine and taking the key from the ignition so that the car and radio both fell silent. The only sounds where the ticking of the engine as it cooled and the warring whoop of his own breath and anguish in his ears. He understood now that he had not been driving entirely randomly, but that some long distant memory had been setting out his path, pressuring him to come to this place, and he knew why. He had brought Scott here early in their relationship, hoping to show him the beauty of these wide-open spaces, but it had not been a good day. Scott was bored and frustrated and Vernon could not properly communicate how glorious this landscape was, how with the solid earth underneath and the vast and impersonal sky above he gained a sense of perspective and felt humbled and within the grasp of the infinite. He simply had not the language for it, nor the imagination to do it justice.

They had come home early and not spoken to each other during the journey. And yet, here he was. The night gathered about the car.

Vernon left work early; the pictures had affected him like a punch to the stomach and left him feeling sick and hollow. Oh God, for that feeling to have been all he felt that day! But as he walked the streets, unsure of anything in his world any more, the hollow space in him filled with the poisonous burn of grief and fury and helplessness and Vernon had known then that everything had changed. He wondered how unseemly it was for middle-aged men to cry as they walked the streets and found he didn't care. In the distance, he heard the sound of something terrible happening, saw flesh torn and battered and the barriers between worlds falling, and then he was driving.

The picnic table was sagging gently in the middle, the wood beaten into submission by countless hard winters and wet autumns. Vernon ran his finger along the grooved wood and let his nail carve into the bloating surface. Why had he come here? Because it was a place he had been hurt in before? What did he hope to gain? He did not know. Sighing, he looked up at the clear sky above him. Jay was a fool, he thought; it looked nothing like a cape. Instead, it was as though he had thrust his face through the surface of some great inky pool and was looking into its chill depths. The stars glittered, sharp and impersonal like the eyes of sulking dolls. He let its weight bear down on him for a moment, letting its cold seep through the thin material of his shirt, and then he returned to the car and opened the boot.

At some point on the journey, Jay had choked to death. Crumpled in the small space, he had vomited behind the gag that Vernon had drawn about his head and into his mouth, and the vomit had escaped from the around the edges of the material and spattered across his face in long tendrils. They had dried into a pale scurf like the shed skin of some writhing snake and the smell was sharp and sour. Blood had soaked down from his nose and then dried to a hard, brittle shell that flaked as Vernon pulled at Jay's stiffening flesh. He saw that Jay's hands were still bound but that, where they had simply been turning blue when Vernon had pushed the unconscious boy into the car, now they were torn and bloody. Looking at the underside of the boot lid, he saw smears and spots of blood, pieces of torn skin clinging to the dried liquid like tiny insects feeding. Grinning, Vernon said aloud, "There's your unreadable text, Jay! What last message where you trying to send?"

and then he was on his knees behind the car and crying, his bruised hands clutching at the metal rim of the boot and his head against the cold kiss of the bumper. He screamed, hating Jay even more, if that were possible, for the alien world he brought Vernon to the edge of, made him enter.

Eventually, he stood. His cries trailed off, lost and pointless and dying in the darkness. He dragged Jay from the car, dropping him to the earth where he lay like so much spoiled meat. Vernon looked down, filled with a sudden wave of sadness. "Oh, Jay," he said softly, "you never understood, did you? Those terrible creatures? They're not coming from any far place, they've been here as long as we have."

Private Ambulance

Elise drove a private ambulance.

Unlike most ambulances, this one was dressed a monotone, sombre grey, had no sirens or flashing lights, and the patients it carried were beyond treatment or help or hope of recovery. There was no need for rush, no pressure on Elise to arrive at her destination quickly, there was simply smooth movement of the world rolling past the windows and the knowledge that in the vehicle's chill rear, her passengers rode in silence. She never turned the radio on when she drove, despite the fact that the ambulance's cab was separate from the back section, feeling somehow that it would be disrespectful during these final journeys. Elise gave the dead serenity and grace wherever she could, quietness after life's noise.

These night-time rides were the ones that she enjoyed the most; there was little traffic, especially out here where the buildings had given way to farmland and the ground rose to hills, and she could drive without effort or concentration, letting her mind reach out into the sky and land around her and find shapes and scents and sounds that, she thought, few other people ever felt or smelled or heard. Old Man Tunstall's funeral parlour was out in one of the villages, serving the isolated communities scattered throughout the farmlands. Actually, they maybe weren't isolated communities, Elise thought, but one huge community stretched thin and laid across the hills and valleys and fields like a net, hundreds of individual strands twisting around each other in links that stretched from farmhouse to terraced street to barn and back to farmhouse. Few people escaped the area, once arrived, not for any length of time; Tunstall had once told her that most of his business was what he called "in-house", people from the area dying at home and being buried in the land that had sustained them. It was only occasionally that Elise was called on to take a body from the hospital in the city to Tunstall's, and the runs were always at night.

Outside, the ground was dusted with frost and occasional banks of snow. It had been bitterly cold these last few weeks, the earth hardening, becoming frigid, and Elise drove slowly, letting the vehicle's weight give it grip on the iced surface. The roads glistened in the dying moonlight and, around her, the fields drowsed under a caul of ice and the journey was all that mattered, this last journey between the places of life and the places of death.

Elise carried only one traveller that night. "He killed himself," the morgue attendant had told her in a voice somewhere between glee and horrified awe, "and we don't know who he is!" The man had apparently walked to the banks of the river that wound down from the hills, passing through the town on its way to the sea, stripped, knelt down on the ridged and furled mud at the bitter water's edge and frozen to death. His clothes were in a bag next to Elise now, neatly folded, the top of the bag rolled and held down with tape.

"He was frozen solid," the morgue attendant had said, "and we had to defrost him like a piece of chicken!" Elise had met people like the attendant before, people for whom the mechanics of death were the most fascinating part of the journey, for whom the biology of things was the most important. There had been the paramedic who had told her, voice rich with undisguised fascination, about the suicide who had jumped from a tall building and landed on the ground at an odd angle. Their head, said the paramedic, had connected hard with a kerbstone and cracked open and their brain had burst free and slithered, almost intact, across the road "like a big pink snail"; he had asked her out for a drink after telling her this. She had refused, politely, and taken the suicide's body into her private ambulance to begin its next stage of the procession into the ground. For Elise, death wasn't a moment; rather, it was a string of moments, a set of markers that led from life to burial or cremation, to earth or fire, and she saw herself as a companion and guide to these, the most significant of journeys.

The rear of the ambulance shifted slightly as she went round a corner, the wheels slipping over ice, and she slowed.

The dead man was being delivered to Tunstall's Funeral Home simply because Tunstall had a council contract to deal with the unidentified dead; there were spaces in the graveyards out here. In the cities, space for the departed was rapidly being filled and the real estate of passing on carried heavy costs that the council couldn't pay, so people like Elise's passenger were sent out to where populations were lower and the grounds cheaper.

The rear of the vehicle shifted again. There was a noise as it shifted, a gentle knocking.

Elise slowed again, dropping smoothly through the gears, letting the engine quieten. There was another thud from behind her, and a slight shiver ran through the vehicle. Had she run over something in the road? A rock or branch, maybe an animal? She glanced in her wing mirror but the road behind her, painted in fragile moonlight, was clear. She let her speed creep back up, happy that all was well. Elise took the dead man on.

Another thud, another slight shiver. Movement in the rear of the vehicle.

Elise's first thought was that something had come loose back there, one of the straps holding the man's coffin possibly, that it was flapping, but no; the thud had been too loud and the shiver too heavy to be caused by a simple loose strap. Perhaps the coffin itself was moving, slipping on its base and banging against the vehicle's wall when she went around corners?

Another corner, slower now, but no accompanying shift or thud, the road straightening, letting the ambulance speed up and then a definite bang from the rear. Elsie started, the tyres shimmying across the surface of the frozen road before she grasped the wheel and brought the vehicle back into line. The bag of belongings next to her fell from the seat into the footwell with a rustle of plastic and sound that was almost organic, like an owl opening its wings and stretching. Making sure the road was straight ahead for a while, Elise turned and tried to peer in through the small observation window between the cab and the refrigerated rear section. The glass was dark, throwing back a reflection of her face, eyes inked pools below her pale forehead.

She turned back to the road, lifting her foot from the accelerator and taking the vehicle gently left, in towards the roadside. When it came to a halt, she put the ambulance in neutral and unclipped her seatbelt, turning properly to the observation slit. Cupping her hands around her eyes, she peered into the blackness that travelled at her back. It was almost absolute, a gloom that was broken only vaguely by pale edges and shapes.

Something moved loosely in the dark and then the engine of the ambulance abruptly cut out.

Elise jerked back from the glass. What had that been? She twisted back around and turned the key, starting the vehicle again. The engine sputtered for a moment, caught and slipped, caught again and grumbled to full life. She opened the driver's side door and stepped out, leaving it open so that the cab lights fell across the road. There were no other lights out here, no streetlamps, no cars or trucks barrelling along the road, just the stars above her and the moon dipping low as the night came to its end. She made her way to the rear of the ambulance, reached out and took hold of the handles, felt the cold bite of chill metal against her fingers and palms, felt rather than heard something bump behind the doors, and then swung them open.

Everything was in its place. The coffin and its inhabitant were still on the lower ledge on the right side, where she had placed them, and the straps around the wooden box were still tight and fastened. She climbed in, crouching and pulling on the padded nylon cables; there was no give in them. She looked around, seeing nothing that shouldn't be there, nothing loose that would have explained the movement or the sounds. Experimentally, she placed her hands on the end of the coffin and pushed, wondering if the noises had been caused by it moving up and down rather than swinging sideways, but the casket remained still. Something inside it, then? No, she had watched as the dead man had been placed inside, the padding arranged around him to prevent precisely the kind of movement she was wondering about.

There was nothing on the other ledges, three of them, that could have moved. The rear of Elise's ambulance was, as ever, neat and clean and a fitting cradle for the dead on these, the last of their courses.

The engine, then, or something mechanical underneath the vehicle. She would simply have to drive carefully and hope she made it to Tunstall's, then make a judgement there about whether it was safe to drive back. She returned to the front of the ambulance and climbed in, shivering in the warmth. With the door shut and the belt back across her chest and securely clipped she pulled away, keeping her speed low. The road was rising now, curling around one of the fells. It would fall and rise several more times before she reached Tunstall's, she knew, and wondered if the ambulance would make it. She dug her phone from her pocket and checked it; a good charge but not much signal.

Another curve in the road and this time something definitely moved in the rear of the ambulance, banging hard against the side and setting the vehicle rocking outwards on its axles before it fell back to stability, distorting the vehicle's balance for a moment. This time, the bang had been accompanied by a noise that might have been a sheet tearing or something flapping, a long low noise only just audible over the sound of the engine. Her foot jerked on the accelerator, sending the ambulance lurching forward and onto the other side of the road before she could bring herself and it back under control, return them to the right side of the centre line and to a better speed.

Before Elise could do anything else there was another bump, this time even harder, jolting the vehicle and making the wheel twitch in her hands, and a long, drawn out noise like something dragging across metal from somewhere behind her. The dead man's bag of belongings slithered across the foot-well, the top pulling open and spilling the contents out. There were jeans and a dirty brown coat, pieces of paper covered in writing, and feathers. They must have been in the pockets of the jacket, dozens and dozens of them, hundreds of them, small and large, black and white and brown, speckled and plain, floating out in drifts. The smell of them, of the clothes, was rich and earthy, grimy with sweat and death and cold. One of the feathers settled on Elise's hand and she shook it off violently, not liking the greasy feel of it.

Another bang, another moment where the ambulance belonged not to Elise but to itself, another correction and control regained and still they were travelling on, Elise wanting to get to Tunstall's now, to get out of the ambulance and into light and company. Feathers drifted around the cab, dancing and spinning, as she pressed down on the accelerator, urging the vehicle to gather up the road and loose it out behind them, now sure that the problem wasn't the ambulance or its engine but whoever was in the ambulance's rear, whatever was in the ambulance's rear.

She risked a glimpse behind her. As she turned, there was a long cracking noise and the unmistakeable sound of wood splintering and something falling, the vibration of it rattling through the floor, heavy against her feet. There was a dash of pale movement in the slit, a pallid shape that rose behind the pane and then fell again, not a hand or a face but something indefinable, as though it was wrapped in linen or muslin.

The engine cut out as Elise jerked back from the glass and then she was reaching out to turn the key even though she was still coasting forward, gears in neutral and nothing, nothing, no reaction from the ambulance except to slow and slow, inertia and the slope bringing it to a halt soon, too soon. The internal lights clicked off with a sound like a gunshot, the dashboard's glimmer suddenly extinguished. She put the handbrake on, ignoring the increasingly loud, repeating sound of flapping behind her, not looking at the glass, not looking at whatever might be peering through at her, turning the key again and again trying to start the vehicle.

And then the thing with the head like a dog seated next to her turned and drew back lips from teeth that were huge and which were the colour of old, tarnished ivory.

Elise shrieked and jerked back from it, fumbling for the handle and opening the door and falling out into the road in a single frenzied jumble of flail and cry. Her shoulder struck the gritted concrete and an off-colour bolt of pain leapt through her upper body and she cried out again, helpless.

A series of taps and shudders ran through the vehicle, tiny vibrations that she could hardly see, visible only as a shiver against the distant night. Feathers, more feathers than she had ever seen before, more than could have possibly been in the bag, drifted out after her, curling and circling in thick clouds, floating upwards instead of down, rising on breezes Elise could not feel. There was another bang, this from the centre of the ambulance, as though something had struck the partition between the space of the dead and the space of the living, then the long drawn-out groan of something opening and the unmistakeable sound of coins falling into a dish or cup.

For a moment Elise had the terrible sense of having offended something vast and old and she screamed, a wordless apology wrenching out of her. In the now-dark cab of the ambulance, the dog-headed thing shook its head and grinned and held its arms out, and from all around her she heard the sound of beating wings.

Fusing Periodontia:

The upper and lower sets of teeth fuse together, setting the jaw into a single position and meaning the mouth cannot be opened. Teeth need to be broken to allow the sufferer to eat, and the condition is likely to recur, leading to several interventions being required over a person's lifetime.

Photographs of Boden

Boden was searching through the old photo albums in the loft for pictures of his dad when he first found it. There was a particular image he remembered from his childhood, of Dad pulling a face at the camera with Boden and Sally and mum standing behind him, that he wanted for the wall of shame. He knew it had ended up boxed in the loft, and finally came across it in an album with a maroon cover and a curling sticker on it that read '1977- 1979'. *One album for three-years-worth of photos*, he thought as he brought it down the ladder, *Christ, we could fill an album with the photos we take during one day out now, if we printed them all.* He had thousands, literally thousands, of pictures of him and Chrissie, far less of his parents and very few of his grandparents, who hadn't died that long ago. There was only one existing picture of his great grandparents, a stiffly formal thing taken in a studio showing two people who weren't even memories to him.

He couldn't use the picture in the end. His dad was clear enough in it, tongue out and hands forming comedy horns at his temples; no, the problem was the image of Boden himself. It had darkened, a blurred cloud of mould or damp-affected chemicals obliterating his face and neck. Rubbing the patch did nothing to help; if anything, it was larger when Boden lifted his thumb. Flicking through the rest of the album revealed that another couple of nearby pictures had been affected in the same way, one of Boden sitting on a bench in a park somewhere and the other of Boden on a beach holding a plastic bucket. In both his face had gone, lost to a dirty smear that looked greasy even though, when Boden touched it, it was dry.

Eventually, he found another picture of dad looking stupid, this time asleep in a chair one Christmas day with a pint balanced on his belly, and the wall was complete.

"How many pictures is it?" asked Chrissie that night as Boden scanned and printed the last of them before sticking it to the long strip of card.

"Sixty," he replied. "One picture of dad looking like an idiot for each year of his life."

"It's a lovely idea," said Chrissie. "I'm sure he'll be very grateful."

"He won't, he'll be embarrassed," replied Boden. "But it'll make him smile and he's supposed to smile on his sixtieth."

"Speaking of smiling, have you heard from Sally? Is she coming?" asked Chrissie.

"No, and I don't know," said Boden, and he could hear the chill in his voice even as he didn't want it to be there, especially not with Chrissie. His sister had caused enough family tensions and arguments over the years and he was determined she wasn't going to spoil dad's big day.

"Where is she?" asked Chrissie. "Can you ring her?"

"Still in London, I think, and I'm not ringing her. I've sent her messages and emails, and she knows when the party is. She knows she's welcome to come if she behaves. Hell, I want her to come and she knows that too, but I'm tired of chasing her, trying to get her to act like a decent human being and be a part of this family."

"I know," said Chrissie. "I just keep hoping that something'll change."

"Me too," said Boden and despite all of the anger and all of the disappointments and arguments, he meant it.

The party was a success, the wall of shame made everyone including Dad laugh, and by the time the last of the guests left he and Boden were both drunk. They, and Chrissie, were sitting at Dad's dining room table, and Dad had just mentioned Sally.

"I'm sorry, Dad," said Boden, "I did tell her, she knew about tonight. I hoped she'd come, but you know what she's like."

"I do," said Boden's dad, Roger, his voice laced with whisky and sadness and age. "She's like your mother was, hot-headed, sure of herself, convinced she's right all the time."

"Hot headed? She's rude, self-centred and a liar," said Boden, unable to help himself. "She expects everyone to do things her way, the way she wants, and when they don't she sulks like a baby. She's not come tonight because it clashes with a night out with her friends, and I wouldn't rearrange it. After all, why should you be allowed to have your sixtieth birthday party on your actual birthday if it interrupts Sally's social life?"

"Elliot," said Chrissie softly, warning.

"I'm sorry, Dad," said Boden, trying to let it go, to be calm. "But it annoys me. She annoys me. She never thinks about anyone but herself and she's never done anything for anyone if there wasn't something in it for her."

"She's young," his dad said. "She'll learn. Besides, you weren't so perfect, oh son of mine, not by a long way!" He proceeded to tell a story about Boden having a teenage tantrum because he'd been grounded after coming in from a concert late, and his telling of it had Chrissie laughing so hard she cried; Boden's dad's impression of a furious, teenage Boden was both affectionate and sharp and even Boden laughed.

It was a good story; the only problem was that Boden had no memory of it, and was sure it wasn't true.

It didn't matter in the end, not really, and Boden remembered the story only as a good part of the end of a great evening, something his dad and him and Chrissie had shared, something private and special. So his dad was remembering something wrong, or making it up for the sake of being a raconteur and to impress Chrissie; Dad could be a smooth sod on the quiet, Boden knew, and frequently turned on the charm around attractive women. Besides, he also wouldn't have put it past Dad to make up something as a way of distracting Boden, of telling him without actually telling him *Don't judge, don't let other people's pettiness or smallness make you petty or small, let it go.* After all, it was only a story.

The weekend following the party, Boden went to his dad's, this time without Chrissie. There was no real reason for the visit, just a pop-in to see how things were going, a quick coffee and then he'd be gone. He did it most weekends, and he usually enjoyed it. This time however, as he sat in the front room with Dad and caught up, something nagged at him, something subtle that drew his eye; not towards itself, no, but away, as though his vision was sliding off something that it should be able to grip. It was only as he stood to go that he realised what it was.

"Where's the picture?" he asked, surprised.

"What picture?" asked Dad.

"The one of us at the zoo," said Boden. It had stood on the mantelpiece as long as Boden could remember, an image of Boden and his mum and dad posing in front of a lion cage in a zoo somewhere, taken when Boden was perhaps four, a couple of years before Sally came along. Boden liked the photo because his mum was laughing in the image, wide and free, and both he and his dad were grinning broadly.

"Zoo?" asked his dad.

"When I was a kid," said Boden. "You and me and Mum. We had a good day. The zookeeper took the photo with that old Instamatic thing of yours that you had to wind on after taking each picture, remember?"

"No," said his dad after a moment. "I mean yes, I remember the camera and I remember a trip to the zoo about eighteen months before Sally was born, is that the one you mean? Because I don't remember a photograph."

"That's the day out, yes," said Boden, and went to say more but stopped at the frown on his dad's normally placid face.

"That was a horrible day," his dad said. "You cried and cried all day, and refused to be cheered up. You did that a lot when we had days out. Your mum used to joke that you were determined that we shouldn't have a good time. We did take photos that day, but none of them were much good when we developed them. Your mum, she looked fit to explode in them, and you were crying or all puffy-faced from crying. I don't think we ever put any of them out on show, did we?"

Maybe it's behind the cards, thought Boden, going over and moving a few of the sixtieth cards and peering behind them. There was a picture there, in a plain wooden frame, smaller than he remembered the zoo photo being and differently oriented, portrait rather than landscape. He lifted it, not sure what he expected to see, hoping that it was his memory, or maybe dad's, at fault, and was faced with a picture he had never seen before. In it, his mum and dad were standing in a garden, their old garden he thought, the one at Highmore Terrace, smiling at the camera, and in front of them was Sally.

Boden was not in the picture.

"That's a nice photo," said Dad from behind him. "But it wasn't taken at the zoo."

"No," said Boden. "It's Highmore Terrace, isn't it?"

"That's right," said Dad. "I suppose I should change it really, it's been up years, but it was one of your mum's favourite photos and I haven't the heart to take it down. It'd be like I was, I don't know, disrespecting her or something. Silly, really."

"No," said Boden.

"We never did manage to get one of you and Sally and us all together that looked nice, you were always so grumpy, wouldn't ever smile."

"Yes," said Boden, putting the picture down, thinking, *No, that wasn't me that was like that. Not me. Sally.*

"You were a terror, son," said Boden's dad. "A real terror!" He laughed as he said this, patting Boden's shoulder in an *It's okay, that's what children do, I still love you* gesture.

"Yes," said Boden again, and then, "Dad, I have to go, Chrissie's expecting me" and even to him his voice sounded hollow and the lie obvious and brittle.

That night, under Chrissie's bemused gaze, he brought all of the photograph albums down from the loft and began looking through them carefully. He had inherited them from Dad after Mum died, when Dad had moved to the flat and when Sally had said she didn't want them because she had neither the space to store them nor any interest in looking at them. He was looking for the photos from the zoo; the one on Dad's mantelpiece, the one that wasn't on Dad's mantelpiece, wasn't the only one that had been taken that day, it was just the best. The rest were in the albums somewhere, in amongst the other pictures of him and his parents looking happy, sitting in gardens in summer or in rooms on Christmas day or family birthdays. It was Sally who there were few photos of, Sally who never smiled, would deliberately turn away when someone pointed a camera at her, would grimace her way through family outings and events, not him. Not him.

Not him.

He found them eventually, the zoo photos. They were almost as he remembered them, pictures of mum in front of the elephant enclosure and dad drinking coffee from a Styrofoam cup at a table upon which half-eaten sandwiches were scattered, their greaseproof paper wrappings shed like snakeskin about them. There were fewer images of Boden himself than he remembered.

In each image, Boden's face was being obliterated by the blooming of something that looked like moss but which left no residue on his fingers when he rubbed it.

The stains looked like clouds of ink billowing in water, and they weren't completely black; there were hints of rich, deep reds and purples in them, skeins of light and dark that looked like vines wrapped tight around suffocated branches. The stains were not limited to the images taken at the zoo, however; in some of the photographs placed around the zoo pictures in the album, Boden's face had also started to be lost.

There was a picture taken at his cousin James' fifth birthday, a day

Boden remembered fondly as being good fun, in which his smiling, freckled face was already disappearing. A second, in a paddling pool at the age of perhaps seven, his smile spotted with flecks like oil spatters, while Sally looked on behind him, the image clean and unmarked and smiling. A third, taken from somewhere in the audience of a school play, him on stage acting in the nativity, being Herod dressed in a robe made from an old blanket with big silver stars sewn on it; dabs of maroon and black already gathering across his exposed skin. Boden had the strangest feeling that they carried on under the costume, rippling patterns of spots merging and blending, creeping across his flesh, hidden and invisible and stealthy. A fourth, in his school uniform. A fifth, running. A sixth playing football, a seventh, an eighth. A ninth, and more, and on and on.

The most affected pictures were clustered around the first one he had found, as though that were the focal point and the stains were spreading out from there. Some of his happiest childhood memories were from around the period of his life the picture showed, and the images of them were being entirely obliterated. It wasn't simply a physical process of contamination, Boden found; a picture close to the others in the album from a much later period was unaffected, yet other pictures from the same occasions kept in other albums were showing signs of the tell-tale marks.

That wasn't the worst of it, though; no, the worst was when Boden tried to recall the occasions in the photographs, the zoo or James' birthday. His memories themselves seemed odd and weirdly dislocated, as though there were two sets of things being recalled at the same time, the one that he actually remembered and another laid over the top, uneven and scab-like, changing the shape of what lay under it, tightening it, puckering it into something new and alien.

Corrupting it.

Boden tried rubbing at one of the patches again, not liking the way it felt under his thumb, warm and somehow slick, warmer than the surrounding paper, and liking less the way his rubbing achieved nothing. *Out, damned spot*, he thought to himself, and then *No, you're being stupid and over-dramatic, it's old chemicals reacting with damp or something. It's nothing.*

During the next few days Boden felt that he was permanently on the edge of something, although what he couldn't be exactly sure. He spent the time deliberately not looking at his old photographs and trying to not to recall memories that felt increasingly tender when he did accidentally probe them. He found himself more aware of how people spoke to him and the things they said. They angled their bodies towards him differently, hands folded across chests and stomachs as though protecting themselves. Surely this wasn't how people normally were with him? He prided himself on being relaxed, open and approachable, yet people were defensive around him, acting as though he was prickly, prone to aggression and attack. It made him uneasy, and he found himself over-analysing and over-reacting to things without knowing quite why. Even Chrissie noticed, accusing him of snapping at her after a conversation about some mundanity or other whilst they were lying in bed together.

"I'm not snapping," he said.

"Aren't you?" she asked. "Funny, you could've fooled me. What's wrong?"

"Nothing," Boden said, then paused. "Everything. Things feel like they're changing, I feel like I'm changing, and I don't know why nor how, and I don't like it."

"Is it us?" she asked.

"No," he said, surprised. "Christ, no. Why would it be? We're okay, aren't we?"

"I hope so," Chrissie said. "Really, I do. So, what is it?"

"I don't know," he said helplessly. "I don't."

"Have you argued with your dad again?" Chrissie asked. "You always get like this after you've argued with him, you know. I'm not sure you realise it, but you do, every time."

Boden didn't reply. Chrissie came over and lay with her head on his chest and soon fell asleep, but he remained awake. *Maybe what Chrissie said has some validity,* he thought. *She should know, I suppose, she's the one that lives with me and sees how I am after every argument I have with him. Maybe I'm just feeling bad after arguing with dad?*

Only, he hadn't argued with his dad, not recently. Not ever.

The blotches were worse, covering more of the photographs. No, covering more of him in photographs, his skin and smile and eyes and hair lost below a creeping, flecked darkness. Almost all of the pictures in the first album were affected now, all of the ones with him in anyway.

Those furthest away from the picture of dad making the face, the furthest away in time, were the least affected, with only one of two tiny blemishes appearing. *Like spots*, he thoughts, *like my photo has acne or a rash or something.*

There was one picture, of him in a family group with his mum and dad and auntie Jean and uncle Bill and Sally and their cousins Adrian and John. Boden's memories of the day were good; Sally hadn't been too tantrumy, Mum and Dad had been happy and had sat laughing with Jean and Bill most of the day. Jean was dead now, as was Bill, and Adrian lived somewhere in America, but John was still around. Boden rang him the evening after first seeing the photo, making small talk for a few minutes before saying, "John, do you remember an afternoon we all spent together when we were kids? In our back garden, I think? There are photos of us together?" His voice stumbled over the word photos; he hoped John didn't notice.

"I think so," said John after a moment. "It wasn't a birthday, was it, just a get-together?"

"That's the one," said Boden. "What do you remember about the day?"

"That's a strange question," said John. "You losing your memory or something?"

"Sort of," replied Boden, forcing a laugh that sounded, to his ears, hollow and flat. "Just humour me."

"Well," said John after a second's silence. "It was fun. We had a laugh. We played cricket, if I remember rightly. You were a bit of a whinge because your dad wouldn't get the paddling pool out, but that was pretty usual so we all ignored you."

Boden clenched, felt himself stiffen and then forced his tongue to loosen. "Thanks," he managed to say. He made small talk for another minute and then disconnected the call.

He didn't remember whinging, but as John had said it, something like a memory occurred to him, spongy and unreal. It overlaid the actual memory of a day in which it had been Sally who'd moaned about not being able to have the paddling pool out because the boys were playing cricket. In this new one, he was the one moaning, pleading with his dad to get the paddling pool out and his dad was refusing. Adrian and John played cricket in the garden while he whined, and eventually he joined them and every time he hit the ball he imagined he was hitting his dad with the bat and making him groan. No, that wasn't real, it wasn't what had happened.

No.

Yes. Yes, because even though he was sure it wasn't real, he had a memory of it, a memory of how he felt and the smells and sounds of the day. The photo album was on his knee, but he didn't want to open it. Had to open it.

Couldn't.

Had to, and opened it. His fingers found the family photo quickly, leafing through pages of thick, coated card to find his face lost under a rippling, crusted stain. It had grown in, what, twenty-four hours? Swelling, spreading, completely covering him, making what had been his space in the picture a space for something else, something impenetrable and uncontrollable.

No, Boden told himself, not uncontrollable. I will not be a slave to this. The question was, what could he do about it? Fight it, he told himself, fight it. It's changing everyone's memories of your childhood, so fight back, remind them of the reality, your reality and not the reality being made by that black growing thing.

He rang his dad first, asking him the same question as he'd asked John. "God, you were a horror that day," his dad said. "Going on and on about the paddling pool even after we'd said you couldn't have it out."

"'A horror'?" Boden repeated. "No, Dad, that was Sally."

"What?" asked Dad. "Sally? No."

"Yes," insisted Boden. "Sally, moaning about the paddling pool while I played cricket with Ade and John."

"It was you," said Dad. "You're my son and I love you, but it was always you, just like it's you now, blaming Sally when it's you. All those days out, those family events and trips and holidays that were spoiled, had to be changed, just because you didn't like something about them and made it impossible for anyone else to enjoy them until you got your own way."

"Christ, Dad, that was Sally, not me, can't you remember?"

"So now it's my fault? I'm going senile, perhaps?"

"No, that's not what I meant, Dad, but I never made things difficult, it was always Sally, that–".

"Enough," Boden's dad interrupted, and he sounded weary. "I'm not talking about this again. I'd hoped you might have grown up a bit by now, learned to take some responsibility for how you were and how you are, but clearly not. Fine, that's your choice, but I won't be a part of it." He finished talking, made a noise as though he was going to say something else but didn't, and then broke the call off.

By the time Boden had spoken to his dad and then tried to pull himself together after the call, the blackness had spread. It was now crawling across the photos in the albums either side of the '1977-1979' volume, darkening its way through 1976 and 1980, its tendrils already slipping into 1975 and '81. It was so fast, appearing to leap from image to image, from memory to memory, in the shortest of instants, corrupting them as it went. Now Boden could remember whining about the paddling pool as clearly as he could remember not whining about it, two layers of memory flapping like threads in his mind and waiting for one to achieve dominance, to take root. It's not real, he told himself, but knew that he was wrong, it was real because people remembered it, not just him but others as well, and people believed it. Whatever the black thing was, it wasn't just corrupting the photos, but his life as well, his past and his present and his future.

In the new reality, he thought, *I argue with Dad, I've always been a whining bastard, Sally was a good girl and no trouble, I make people wary and they don't like me.* The question was, how far would it go? How much of his past could it affect, blight? His early years? His teens? Already, those new early memories had changed people's perceptions of him, changed how they reacted to him. What would happen if his entire past was changed? When would it stop? When it had eaten its way through his twenties? His recollections of university? Work? Meeting Chrissie?

All of it?

Panicking, Boden set aside the old albums and went to the bedroom, pulling his and Chrissie's wedding album from its place in the wardrobe and rifling through it quickly. The pictures were unmarked, thank God, his face still smiling and clean, surrounded by people looking at him without a trace of tension or reserve.

Could it be reversed? Could he somehow turn it around by persuading people of the truth? Of his truth, rather than the truth being made by the blackness? His experiences with Dad made him think that he couldn't, but perhaps he could stop it spreading. It was in the years 1974 through to 1985 now, from pretty much his eleventh birthday back to his birth. A thought suddenly struck him, rose up and refused to be ignored. If mum was alive, would her memory of the day I was born be affected? Changed from something that always made her teary and proud when she spoke about it and she'd had a drink, to something that she hated? Boden had been an easy baby, she had always said, but would that truth be lost now? Would her memories of him be of a difficult labour? Of an unpleasant, hard-to-settle, graceless child, the way his memories were of Sally? And would the resentments and stresses that this new childhood caused back then have burned their way through the rest of his mum's memories, so that she reacted to him differently? He suspected probably so. *Thank fuck she's dead*, he thought, *I don't think I could cope with that.*

He started with the pictures closest to the affected ones, moving rapidly through 1985 and 1986 until he found one from 1987; it a group shot of him and a number of friends, taken on a school trip. The picture was as-yet unmarked, and he was still in touch with some of the people in it. Picking one at random, he rang them.

"Ollie? It's Elliot. Elliot Boden."

"Christ, Elliot, hello! How're you? God, it must have been years."

"A few, yes. I'm sorry for ringing out of the blue like this, and this is going to sound strange, but I wanted to ask you something."

"Yes?"

"Well, ask and maybe remind you of something," Boden said, casually flicking back the photo album pages and then stopping. Black spots had already started appearing on the earliest photographs, tiny but noticeable. *It's speeding up*, he thought, *speeding up, growing, spreading out.* I don't have much time. "The school trip we took? To that castle in Wales? Do you remember it?"

"Bloody Hell, mate, that's going back a bit, isn't it? I do remember it, though, vaguely. Why?"

"Did we have fun? I mean, was I fun to be with, or a pain?" Closer now, he could see the blackness spreading through the album, watched it bloom across his flesh like some grimy flower.

"You were fine, mate. I mean, when we first met a couple of years earlier you weren't so good, quite a moaning sod, but you were okay by then. Why?"

"I can't explain, Ollie, I'm sorry. I don't have time. Will you do me a favour?"

"If I can, I suppose."

"Try to remember that day, that I wasn't a pain, that I was okay, will you? Please?"

"Elliot, you're worrying me now, what's going on?"

"Later, Ollie, I promise. Just remember."

"Yes."

"Remember."

He spent the rest of the day on the phone, ringing as many of the people in the photo that he could track down. All of the conversations were reflections of each other; yes, he'd been fun to be with that day, yes, they'd try and remember, what was going on, no he couldn't tell them but he would if he could, and all the while the blackness slipped its way through the photographs. Finally, when there was no one left to ring, he could only sit and watch as the black spots came closer and closer to the group photo, finally appearing on the other photos on the same page, shadows gathering across his smile in the first picture and then the second, clustering around his eyes and disappearing below the neckline of his Bon Jovi T shirt. *Remember*, he thought, *all of you, remember*.

It came into the neighbouring photo now, the one at the side of the group picture, blossomed and spread, taking the picture of him in a garden somewhere and drawing it into itself, unmaking him, recreating him as a changed and sour thing. The stain gleamed, rich blacks and maroons, warm when he touched it, the edges feathering out to absorb all of his picture skin. He turned his attention to the next image, and remember and remember and please, please remember

The darkness got no further.

"Yes!" Boden cried, and actually punched at the air. He'd stopped it! Healthy memories, the actual memories of him and his friends, the ones they were holding in their heads, had stopped it, halted it in its tracks. He felt a rush of joy, but following on its heels was a realisation that brought it crashing down: how on earth could he stop it all? He'd have to go through every photograph, track everyone down, call them or email them or write to them, ask them to remember the good things about him. Jesus, it was a lifelong job!

Perhaps I don't need to, he thought. *Perhaps if I can get one or two key people to remember me the way I am really, that might be enough. Perhaps the good memories can be set in, like an inoculation, and stop it getting any further.* But who? Chrissie, for a start, but who else? Dad was already gone, infected by whatever this thing was, Mum was dead and there was no one else who he'd known for long enough, whose memories would have the strength to turn this thing aside, to fight it off.

Oh, no, God, wait, yes there was. There was one person, and he needed her now, much as he hated to admit it. Sighing, he reached for the phone.

"Sally?"

"Well, if it isn't big brother!"

"Sally, can I ask you something? Something important?"

"Of course, you can, Big Bro!" said Sally. She sounded happy, relaxed, not inclined to argue, to take umbrage at some imagined slight or at some message read into a tone of voice or word used. 'Doing a Sally', he and Dad called it when she did that, when she found offence in things that weren't there. Used to call it, he amended sadly. Now, Dad probably calls it 'doing an Elliot'.

"Sally, what was I like as a kid? As a teenager?"

"You were like most teenagers, and most big brothers, I suppose," she said. "Protective, a bit annoying, didn't like me pestering you. You were okay."

"Did we have good times?"

"Ell, what is this? Have you and Dad been at it again? Christ, can't you two leave it alone? You're like two walruses banging your fat together!"

"No, it's not that," Boden said. *It's got that, then, even with Sally,* he thought briefly, *me and Dad argue. That's a truth now. My past has altered.*

"Well what, then?"

"What were you like?"

"Me? What do you mean? Ell, what is this?"

"How do you get on with Dad?"

"Fine, Elliot, we're fine. What's wrong? Please tell me."

"Fine? You're sure?"

"Of course I'm sure, Ell; Dad and I get on fine, just like we always have. Christ, is this another of your paranoid trips, another 'they love my sister more than me' days? I haven't got the energy for it, Ell, I really haven't."

"What paranoid trips?" he asked, but already he could feel new memories crusting over his own, ones where he rang up and screamed at Sally instead of her screaming at him, ones where he hated his parents and his sister rather than loved them, and he fought the memories, fought them but they rolled on, growing, smothering, wetly claustrophobic

"I'm not getting into this now, it was bad enough in the run-up to Dad's birthday," Sally said. "All the accusations and rants, and you know what Ell? None of it's necessary, it never has been. Mum and Dad love you, despite what you do to them, what you did to Mum before she died, and I love you too. God help me, you're my brother and I love you even if I don't always like you a great deal. I'm going now. Try and ring Dad and make it up, please."

He couldn't fight it, it had got too far, had worked its dank fingers into too much of his past to be stopped, he saw that now. When he looked back at the school trip photo, it had started to blacken. He had started to blacken. *They're forgetting, or the weight of those other memories is corrupting this one,* Boden thought. He wondered about ringing them all again, but abandoned the idea. There seemed little point; he'd fought it and slowed it but not beaten it, and now that memory was infected, he'd never get it back. He remembered running across the grassy courtyard of the castle on that day, laughing furiously; and he remembered standing at the side of the courtyard sulking as his friends ran without him, one memory crowding and surrounding the other, thickening around it, replacing it.

Tired, Boden packed up the photo albums and put them back in the loft and then went and lay on his bed. After a few minutes, he picked up his wedding album, seeing with little surprise that black spots had started to pinprick their way across his skin in the earliest images in the album.

He thought about his and Chrissie's honeymoon, about the times they'd spent in bed together, about their laughter and the conversations and the future they'd planned and hoped for, and he wept. Already, new tendrils were worming their way into the memories, a raised voice on the honeymoon, a fist, flowers and apologies between the conversations and then more raised voices and fists. He tried to think about the good times, about the wedding and the love in his heart, felt it corrupting, swelling into something new and unwanted and tawdry, and he wept more.

When Chrissie arrived home from work, he had finished weeping, had nothing left to cry out. He greeted her with a kiss, and she flinched away from him, and in her eyes he could see the fear of the man he was newly become.

Ellis' Wart:

Triggered by a reaction to commonly occurring chemicals in the environment, the dentine undergoes rapid and uncontrolled growth, pushing forward and back against the enamel of the teeth and causing it to crack. The appearance of the teeth changes, becoming swollen and wart-like (a visual effect resulting from the cracking surface of the enamel). If left untreated, the dentine itself eventually begins to crack and flake, exposing the nerve and pulp of the teeth, causing constant pain. Anti-allergens can bring some relief to the sufferer but the long-term prognosis of this condition is poor, and in most cases all the teeth need extracting.

Rough Music

Cornish was awake, and he wasn't happy about it.

He wasn't sure what had woken him; the pressure of a bladder that needed emptying or a faint noise that he could hear coming from outside the house, perhaps. He looked at the clock, which told him in its dispassionate way that it was just after three in the morning, and then rolled onto his side and buried his head down into the pillow, trying to ignore both the noise and the need to urinate and failing at both. He rolled again, wondering if a new position might help, and came up against Andrea's back. She mumbled something and waved a hand to push him away. Sighing irritably, he gave up and rose from the bed.

Pissing seemed to take forever, a never-ending stream flowing out from him and into the frigid porcelain of the bowl. *The perils of having beer in the evening*, Cornish thought to himself ruefully. As he got older, he was finding that he couldn't hold his drink as well as he used to; not in terms of drunkenness, particularly, but in terms of his bladder, which seemed to be shrinking. Even Andrea had noticed, commenting on how often he went to the toilet once he'd had one, and he'd snapped at her for it. It was pretty much what they did these days, her saying something and him snapping.

Eventually, his stream dried to a trickle and then to drips that he shook from his penis without looking where they landed; he hadn't put the light on and it was too dark to see without it. Finally, bladder satisfied, he went to find out what or who was making the noise. Naked, Cornish went to the spare room rather than back into the master bedroom, so that he didn't disturb Andrea. There was no point in them both being awake, and he didn't want another argument. Besides, the guest-room gave a better view of the large, irregular circle of grass in front of the house that everyone called The Green.

The space was lost to the almost-dark of too few street lamps, the dirty orange light made filmy by rain that was practically mist hanging in the air. Glancing around, he saw that no other lights were on. Either people hadn't heard the noise, a sharp metallic clanging, or they weren't bothered by it. Or maybe they were, but they slept naked as he did and were leaving their lights off as they investigated in order to protect their modesty. *Thank God*, he thought, grinning, *I'd hate to see old Burley or his wife naked. Although if the woman at number 24 decides to show herself, I wouldn't mind.* She was newly moved in and he didn't know her name but she looked good, attractive and succulent. Her husband looked like a fool, though.

At first, he couldn't see any cause for the noise. There was just The Green, and the circled houses facing out onto it, silent and motionless; no gates shifted, no wind blew, the trees at the centre of the grass were still. There was just the noise, quiet, sharp, insistent. It sounded like something wood striking something metal, and Cornish was convinced it must be a gate clanging or a garage door that hadn't been closed properly. He could see most of the houses well enough that he dismissed them as the cause of the noise. His immediate neighbours, perhaps? He pressed his face to the glass, trying to see the houses adjacent to him, and as he peered, something flickered at the corner of his eye.

It was on the far side of The Green, beyond the light, hidden by it. Nothing as recognisable as human or animal, but a mere suggestion of movement in time with the noise. It was like watching something turn under water, impossible to make out, visible more as a shifting of the water itself or the swirling of currents. Occasionally, it came to the edge of the light, but never revealed itself fully. Was that a hand? A face emerging into the illumination of the streetlamp for a moment, pale and smooth and appearing to look at him with flat, dead eyes before falling back into the darkness? Even as he watched, the movement slowed and the noise faded to nothing. Confused and irritated in equal measure, Cornish waited for a few minutes, looking out into the night, but when the noise and movement didn't recur, he went back to the bedroom. Andrea had rolled and taken over the bed, and when he got back in moving her proved impossible. Finally giving up the unequal struggle to shift her sleeping weight, Cornish lay awake for a while, in part thinking about his day, trying to let his mind relax and feel sleep's rhythms again. Partly, though, he was waiting to see if the noise would come back, almost hoping it would so that he would have a reason for the anger he felt, have something to aim his irritation at; it was a trait he recognised in himself without really liking it and without quite knowing how to stop it.

The next morning, Cornish was scratchy and brittle from his broken night's sleep. He snapped at Andrea over breakfast when she asked why he was checking his mobile for the third time in as many minutes, and they ate the remainder of their meal in a silence that had small, sharp edges. Work was no better, the office feeling airless and cloying, and his colleagues' questions and small talk seemingly more asinine than normal. Despite his checking every few minutes, he received no messages or calls. Of course, he told himself, he wasn't expecting to, checking was a mere reflex and not an indication of anything other than habit on his part.

The evening was better, and he made an effort to stay calm and not snap at Andrea, to not give his anger its head. At one point, he found himself laughing with her and for a moment he could almost pretend that the last six months hadn't happened, that they were back to where they had been not so long ago, when laughing was a commonplace occurrence. It made him happy and terribly sad at the same time.

That night, the noise came back again.

It was louder, jerking him from sleep like a tautening cable, a dull metallic tattoo that shivered the air about him. Beside him, Andrea slept on undisturbed and Cornish felt a wave of helpless frustration at her. He considered waking her, just to share in the annoyance of being awake at...what? Just after three again, according to the clock.

Instead of waking his wife, Cornish rose and went straight to the guest-room. The rain had drifted away during the day and the night was clearer, revealing in the hazy orange light of the street lamps the stolid faces of the houses around him and the tangled, winter-grass surface of The Green. On its far side, as on the previous night, the darkness beyond the light bulged as someone moved through it, but tonight they revealed themselves much more quickly and completely. It was a man, tall and thin and dressed in nondescript pants and a shirt that hung smock-like past his waist. He was holding a pan, old and battered by the look of it, and was beating it deliberately with a wooden spoon, jigging slightly to the rhythm he was creating.

The man's face was pale and rough and his eyes were huge and black, and at first Cornish thought he was disfigured or suffering from some terrible disease because his head was bald and twice the size it should have been. Was he one of those water-head cripples, wondered Cornish, one of the patients from the nearby council home escaping at night to play games that made sense only to them? No, he realised, the man's head wasn't swollen, it was a mask, a large one covering his whole head like a giant goldfish bowl, a crude creation of papier-mâché or something similar.

As Cornish watched, the man danced slowly forward until he was fully in the light, still banging the pan, holding it out ahead of him and smacking it with the spoon slowly and emphatically. Still no lights showed in the other houses, there was simply the man with his pan and spoon. Cornish looked at him again, saw that he was barefoot and that each time he beat the pan he performed an odd little skipping jump that made his head bob slightly. When he reached the very centre of the light, he stopped moving other than to continue his beating. Cornish couldn't see his eyes but he could have sworn, would have bet, that the man was looking directly at him from the depths of that half-formed mask on which the nose and mouth were mere indentations but which still looked uncomfortably familiar.

As though waiting until he was sure he had Cornish's attention, the man gazed up at the house for a long moment and then gave a low bow, sweeping the arm holding the spoon out in a wide arc as though accepting thanks from an unseen audience. Then, with another delicate little hop-skip, he retreated back into the darkness and was gone.

"You didn't hear it?" Cornish asked Andrea the next morning. He had struggled to fall asleep after the noise had finished, and had spent time in bed thinking about the man and his mask but coming to no conclusions about what he should do.

"No," she said. "I slept like a baby."

"Sexiest baby I ever saw," replied Cornish automatically, and was startled to see Andrea colour slightly. Was she blushing?

"What?" he asked, smiling at her.

"That's the first time you've said something like that in a while," she said. "I thought you'd forgotten how to give compliments, or that you'd gone off me."

"No," Cornish said, thinking back. Was it really so long since he'd complimented his wife? Yes; yes, it was. Months. Six months, in all probability. Since June third, in fact. "I've not gone off you, I've just been..." What? Distant? Otherwise engaged? Busy? What could he say to her? "I've been distracted," he finished lamely.

"And now?" Andrea said. The colour was dropping from her cheeks, the laugh was gone from her voice and she was serious now.

"I'm not distracted anymore, and I love you" he said, and was surprised to find he meant it.

The man was back again that night, still beating his pan and wearing his preposterous mask, only this time he wasn't alone. Although he couldn't see anyone, Cornish could hear them, hear more pans or drums or dustbin lids being beaten, hear the atonal metal clatter of them. The darkness behind the man sighed with movement, its edge occasionally broken by pale hands or the glimmering crescent arcs of heads that were too big and too pale, rough and bald.

Cornish was honestly at a loss, an unusual experience for him. What was this? These weren't the local youths, who did occasionally see The Green as a convenient place to drink, fuck and generally make a nuisance of themselves, but who could usually be dealt with by a phone call to the police. This had the feel of something more, although what he wasn't sure. There was a sense of organisation to it, a sense of something directed and intended and choreographed, but why?

The whole thing lasted almost half an hour this time, and still no one else seemed to see or hear it, the houses around remaining closed and somnambulant. Andrea slept on in their bedroom; he could hear her making that noise that wasn't quite a snore, the one he had found so endearing when they first met, and suddenly he wanted to be back in bed with her, cuddled up against her and warm. The noise was scraping at Cornish, not loud precisely, but possessed of an intensity that came from intention rather than volume. The man did his odd little skips again as he beat at his pan, staring at Cornish and bobbing that watermelon head and, despite the fact that the mask's features were frozen, Cornish could have sworn that it was grinning, wide and mirthless and cold.

Cornish slept through his alarm in the morning and it was Andrea who woke him by leaning over him, kissing his cheek and shaking him gently. "There's a coffee," she said, indicating the cup on his bedside table. "You've never slept through your alarm before in all the time I've known you. Are you okay?"

"Why didn't you wake me?" said Cornish.

"I thought you might need the rest. How did you sleep?"

"Badly," said Cornish but didn't mention the man in the mask. It felt silly, and oddly personal and private, as though what he was seeing and hearing was meant for him and no one else. Besides, what could he say? *Sorry darling, a man in a big-head mask banged a pan at me, and last night he'd brought his friends but I didn't see any of them?*

"Poor darling," said Andrea, perching on the edge of the bed. Her skirt rode up, revealing her thigh, its smooth curve catching in Cornish's eye and refusing to leave. He reached out and stroked it, letting his fingers trail up under the edge of her skirt as he reached out with his other hand to brush her hair away from her face. She looked at him, not smiling.

"I have work. So do you," she said after a few more moments and as his hand stroked its way further up her thigh.

"We could both be late," he said and sat up, careful not to lose his contact with her skin; the connection felt suddenly vital, as though losing it would mean losing the moment, losing something more than the moment. He leaned forward, letting his lips brush against her neck and trailing them up to slide across her jaw and cheek.

"Your coffee will go cold," Andrea said, but didn't sound bothered. His fingers found the edge of her panties and tickled along it gently. She opened her mouth as he leaned in further, speaking as she kissed him, saying, "Be nice, please. Be nice."

After, they lay wrapped in each other, and Cornish tried to remember the last time he and Andrea had made love as opposed to just fucked. *Six months*, he thought. *Since June 3rd, remember?* He had found her rhythms again easily, though, just as she had found his, and they had slipped back into each other in the nicest way. With the sweat drying on his skin and the taste of her orgasm on his tongue, Cornish felt as though his past was coming back into focus, that he was remembering not just the snapping and the arguments of the past few months but the Andrea and the relationship with her that he had valued from before that, from before June 3rd. From before Gill.

"Are you okay?" Andrea asked, her voice muffled into his shoulder so that he felt the words as much as heard them.

"I think so," he said. "I know I've been a shit recently, and I'm sorry, truly I am. I don't know why I've been so horrible to you, or why I've been treating you so badly, but I know I have been and I'm trying to stop it. I'm sorry."

"You have been a shit and you aren't forgiven yet," Andrea replied, "but carry on being nice and you might be." She didn't ask why, although he thought she might when she was sure things were improving; it was how she tended to deal with things. It gave him time to come up with reasons, to point to work or money or something else, to find faults in her that he could highlight and make her feel guilty about, so that they could get over this. The longer until she asked, the better; each day was a day further away from June 3rd, and from the six months that followed it which had ended a couple of weeks ago.

It should have been comical, he thought. A group of people standing on the edge of a circle of grimy light, all wearing bulbous papier-mâché heads adorned with crudely moulded and painted faces with holes for eyes, all banging pots, pans or lids with wooden spoons. There had been a comedian that dressed like that, he remembered, with an oversized head; Cornish had seen him when he was a student and had laughed a lot. There were maybe twenty of them now, in addition to the original man, who had taken up his now-usual place within the circle of light as though he was dancing below a spotlight. Funny figures, doing silly things.

Cornish wasn't laughing.

It was just after three again, and the din was incredible; he couldn't understand how Andrea was sleeping through it, how it wasn't waking everyone up. Tonight, the noise was huge, discordant, everyone beating out of step with each other, making a sound that was at once ragged and somehow intimidating, the voice of a crowd grown restive and aggressive. The crowd, in this case, was standing in a rough semi-circle, forming a chorus around the original man, who Cornish was unaccountably starting to think of as his. His man had given up his pan and spoon tonight, was performing an elaborate mime instead, pretending to be seated and drinking with exaggerated gestures, turning that huge head this way and that and looking about him with a predator's eye.

Predator? Yes. Cornish wasn't sure how he knew, but he did; the man was eyeing up invisible prey around him. Even as he watched, the man made a new movement, a kind of subtle double-take and a darting of his head, bobbing it forward so that it wobbled oddly, his shoulders narrowing and his neck elongating. *He's found his victim*, thought Cornish.

The man didn't do anything, however, merely carried on miming drinking and watching, those hollow eyes following his unseen target. The noise escalated, jabbing and harrying the air around Cornish, making the glass of the guest-room window shiver as the man raised another drink, tilting his head and draining his glass with a decisive, snapping movement. *Now it starts*, thought Cornish, but it didn't. Instead, the noise reached a crescendo, climaxing in a violent swell of clatter and battery, and then stopped abruptly. The crowd stepped forward as one, clustering around the man in the centre of the green, and they all looked up at Cornish. He started to step away from the window and then thought, *No, they can't see me*, and forced himself to stand still. His man led the crowd in a long, sweeping bow, the ridiculous heads bobbing and nodding down, and Cornish could have sworn that he recognised some of them, that they were somehow familiar although he couldn't tell who they were exactly or why he thought he knew them. Then the crowd, as one, raised itself up from the bow and stepped back, losing itself in the darkness. His man bowed again, lower this time, before standing straight and then doing more of those curious little skips, backing out of the light and out of view.

When Cornish went back to bed, Andrea half-woke as he climbed in and rolled over to him. "Are you okay?" she asked, her voice mumbled by sleep.

"No, I'm sodding not," he said, and then "sorry." He was snapping again, could hear himself, and it wasn't her fault. He had to be careful, they had only just started to rebuild whatever it was between them that had broken, and it was delicate and liable to crack easily.

"I'm sorry, I'm not sleeping well," he said after a moment. "I know it's not an excuse, and it doesn't explain why I've not been very easy to get along with these last few months, and not nice to you, but I love you and I'm going to improve it. Improve me."

"What's brought this on?" Andrea said, the sleep slipping away from her voice. She raised herself onto one elbow next to him, shapeless in the bedroom's darkness.

"I love you," he said again. "I think I may have forgotten that over the past few months, but I'm remembering it now."

"Good," she said simply, "because I was beginning to think I might be better off without you, and I don't want to think like that." She leaned over him and kissed him gently, and he could feel her nipples press against him through her thin nightdress. He rolled towards her, pulling her into a longer kiss, and tried not to think about how much better she tasted than Gill.

Afterwards, he didn't ask if she had heard the noise; he thought that he already knew the answer.

His man was joined by two new figures that night, as well as the crowd.

The first was a woman, standing a few feet away with her back to him, her head bowed to her chest. Like him, she was dressed simply in a smock and leggings, her feet bare, and her head was huge. Unlike the man's, it was painted across its rear, clumsy brushstrokes of muddy brown that made it look, from Cornish's viewpoint, as though she had thick, twisted knots of hair. *I bet that'd look great spread out across a pillow*, he thought, and was shocked at himself. *I'm going mad.*

The noise was savage that night, atonal spikes lurching out from the insectile hum of the battering morass, faster, more frenzied than previously. The second new figure was standing at the end of the crowd, not beating a pan or lid, nor holding a spoon. They were at the edge of the light, worrying at the darkness, shuffling back and forth so that they were visible, invisible, visible again, never still. Her movement made it hard to see her clearly, and Cornish could make out her moulded features only in fragmentary moments, here a nose, there eyes, now ears, then a mouth.

Her? Yes, she was female, that he could tell. There was a suggestion of swelling breasts under her smock, and although he saw no painted hair, there was something feminine about the set of her face, what little of it he could make out. Her hands were clasped, forming a protective cup in front of her, and she was concerned about something.

The man was continuing with his elaborate mime, no longer drinking but dancing over to the female with the painted hair. He was offering her something, producing it like a magician from behind his back. *Flowers*, thought Cornish abstractly, *it'll be flowers*. Clichéd, but they work. As if in response to his thought, the female mimed taking a bouquet from him and sniffing it, raising her shoulders and going up on tiptoe in a sharply accurate representation of joyfulness. As the second woman watched, oscillating between the light and the dark, the man continued to give the first woman gift after gift until eventually he took her in his arms and the two began to whirl about the light in a wild dance that eventually led them completely out of the circle.

After a moment, the man and woman reappeared, walking separately now, and as the noise grew, becoming savage, unburdened by either rhythm or delicacy, they bowed to Cornish. The crowd raised their instruments over their heads, letting the noise grow even further, increasing the speed of their beating – Christ, couldn't anyone hear this? – and then they stopped, all at precisely the same moment. In the sudden, piercing silence that followed, they stepped back, vanished, all except the second woman who remained, her body language telling the tale of her misery, and then she, too, stepped away from Cornish's view and was gone.

What was going on here? wondered Cornish, sitting in his lounge as dawn broke. He had been unable to sleep after the people on The Green had left, so he had gone downstairs and sat in his favourite chair, thinking. What was happening made no sense, though, had no structure that he could grasp, no path he could follow, predict or head off. There wasn't anything to solve. Cornish liked targets and achievements, resolutions and progressions. Gill had been a target and then an achievement, and then ending it quietly, without fuss, had been another target. Leave her happy, leave his marriage intact, manipulate Gill into thinking that the end was her decision, better for both of them, a good resolution. How many things had he done, said, in tiny dripped increments, designed to get her thinking that she liked him but no longer wanted him? Three or four weeks of fun, of fucking and coming, and then four or five months of disengagement, of balance, of distance and retreat.

And now the new target was Andrea and his relationship with her, them finding their way back to where they'd been. He thought carefully; contrition, yes, he'd started that and meant it to some degree. He could hang some of it on work pressure, also true to some degree, and some more on Andrea herself, make her responsible for segments of it as well. Andrea was, he was beginning to realise, the best thing that had happened to him, she was his life and he wanted to keep her; she just wasn't all his life. The trick was to keep one part from knowing about the other, to maintain a blissful, ignorant equilibrium.

Which left the people outside.

Who they were was less important, Cornish decided, than getting rid of them. Apart from not understanding what they were doing and not being able to control them, their continued appearance and volume was disturbing him, tiring him, and if he was tired and disturbed then he would take his eyes off the ball, would make mistakes. He had to make them stop, and he began to work out how to do it and tried to ignore the memory of the sound of wood hitting metal.

It was, in a sick sort of way, quite interesting, Cornish thought.

Tonight, the man and the first woman continued to dance, slower and lazier, while the second woman looked on and the crowd created the soundtrack to what was happening in front of them. It was like watching a mummers' play, all over-exaggerated gestures played to an audience who preferred things simple to follow.

Played to him? *Well*, thought Cornish, *it ends now*, and he flicked the guest-room light on.

The curtains were open, and he knew that the people on The Green would be able to see him as clearly as if he had turned on a spotlight. He was naked, outlined in a lozenge of light that fell from the house to the ground in front of his man and his partner. As he watched, they danced through the uneven rectangle of illumination, stepping over his shadow, and as they did, he could swear that the man looked up and nodded, as though acknowledging the arrival of a colleague or friend. Cornish's nudity didn't seem to bother him, nor the fact that Cornish was making it clear: I can see you. I can hear you.

As if in response to Cornish's appearance, the second woman stepped more fully into the light, holding her arms out to Cornish's man. He swirled past her without acknowledging her presence, his face now pressed against the face of the woman who danced with him in his arms. They were kissing, Cornish realised, mouth against mouth and he had a sudden image of tongues made of dried paper grinding against each other, rasping furiously back and forth. The couple continued to dance, the crowd providing them with a stuttering beat, the second woman holding beseeching arms to them, and then they were gone. For a moment the crowd continued their noisemaking and then they, too, stepped back, falling silent as they did so. Soon, the second woman was the only figure left in view, her shoulders slumped. She turned to look up at Cornish and he saw that her eyes had been shaped and painted so that they were crying, fat tears rolling down her cheeks. He recognised her, he thought, but didn't know where from. He felt a wave of sadness for her, and anger at that sadness and their manipulation of him, and then she, too, went backwards and was gone.

This time, both women and the man bowed after coming back into the light, and the rest of the cast, orchestra and chorus, waited behind them. *Why not*, Cornish thought, *she's becoming as important as the other two. Credit where it's due, after all.* Bowing took a minute, maybe less, and then they were gone again and the night was quiet. Looking out into the darkness, gooseflesh erupting across his arms and belly, Cornish made a decision. If he couldn't get rid of them, he'd get rid of himself.

He still woke at just after three, conditioned to do so by almost a week of regular disturbance, but when Cornish looked out of the hotel window his view was uninterrupted by people and the only noises were the distant hush of cars and an owl hooting. He returned to bed happy, happier than he had been in months; he and Andrea had enjoyed each other's company and their sex had been long, lingering, rich. Perhaps better, though, had been the long hug after and the conversation. It hadn't been about anything, not really, just two people re-measuring each other's edges and depths, and discovering that they still loved and liked each other.

On the second night of their impromptu break, Cornish and Andrea didn't have sex, but just cuddled and talked again. For the first time in what felt like months Cornish was relaxed, relaxed enough to think that everything might be okay. Gill was gone, Andrea was warming, he was sleeping again. Life could be good, be like it used to be. Whatever the figures on The Green meant, whoever they were, his non-appearance at the window would surely show them that it was over? Without an audience, they would surely grow tired of whatever it was they were doing, and leave?

The first night they were home, the people were there again.

The noise was astonishing, a thing almost physical in its weight and texture, surrounding the crowd and the three figures in the middle of the semi-circle they made. It was raining again and the dancing couple sent splashes up as they cavorted, drenching the smock and leggings of the second woman, who was still holding her hands out like some melodrama heroine pleading for mercy. Cornish went to the bedroom to find his phone, quietly so as not to wake Andrea and, aware of the irony of that action, returned to the guest-room. With the light on so that they could see him, he scrolled through the phone's memory until he came to the name he wanted. Not the police, but George, the fussy old man from number twenty. George would hate to be disturbed but he could easily be persuaded to look out of his window and see the people on The Green, if Cornish told him that there were youths there. George and his neighbourhood-watch ambitions could be relied upon.

There was no answer. George's phone rang and rang until eventually

Cornish disconnected the call, wondering if something had happened to the old man. He still lived there, of that Cornish was sure; even as distracted as he'd been, surely he couldn't have missed people moving in or out of the houses around him? After all, he recognised the new woman from number 24, didn't he? *Because she has good tits*, he thought sourly, and turned his attention back to the figures.

The man was fucking the first woman. That is, they were pirouetting, dancing, grinding against each other frenziedly like dogs in heat. The second woman was still holding out her hands, reaching for them as though she hadn't noticed what they were doing, and continued to do so after they vanished. Finally, she too left the light, returning a moment later with the others to bow, another performance accomplished. When they had gone, the crowd stopped its drumming, letting the hands holding spoons fall away from the pans, lids and pots. Gradually, as the noise faded, most of them stepped away, this time leaving one of them to stare up at Cornish. This figure moved forward into the light, making sure its painted face was tilted back so that its features were clear, before nodding, turning and walking way. It was only later, lying in bed and trying not to let the churning in his head keep him awake, that Cornish realised something.

The figure had looked like George.

"Do you want to talk about it yet?"

Andrea was sitting opposite Cornish, their coffees and breakfast plates between them on the table. She had leaned over a moment ago and taken his hand, and in that small gesture warned him of what was to come.

"Talk about what?" he said. "There's not much I can say. Work's tough at the moment, lots of pressure."

"There's always work pressure," said Andrea. "There always has been. What's been so different recently?"

"I don't know," said Cornish, deliberately not thinking of Gill. "It's just hard. I try not to bring it home, but I know I do."

"You could always talk to me about it."

"Can I?" Time to turn it around a little, to share the pressure. "You have your own work, and when I tried to talk to you, it seemed like you had other things on your mind." Not true, not true at all, but Andrea would take it to heart; already, her face was creasing in the expression he knew so well, one somewhere between concentration and anger, all pointed inwards.

"Besides, you have your own work, and I didn't want to burden you." Pull it back, be contrite. "I'm sorry."

"I'll try harder," said Andrea.

"No," said Cornish, "I will."

This time when they fucked, it was more perfunctory. There was no whirling or frenzy, the activity drowned rather than raised up by the noise that surrounded them, the constant drumming dampening the man's lusts if not the woman's to something approaching boredom. As soon as the coupling was over the man walked away from her and off into the dark, leaving her holding her hands out in a curious mirror of the second woman, who was still staring after him. Perhaps thirty seconds later, he reappeared, seeming to glide across the wet grass, held up by the noise, and went to the first woman. Already, his attitude had changed further, and although he mimed giving her another gift, it was done with less ceremony, less delicacy. Soon after, they mimed sex again, fast and hard. There was no sense of partnership in the act, of two people joining together, but only of the man using the woman to satisfy himself. He dragged her around like a ragdoll during the act and they did not kiss.

Before they disappeared, Cornish recognised more members of the crowd, all banging their pans furiously. As well as George, the woman from number 24 was there and old Burnley and his wife, or at least, masks fashioned to look like them. Others, as they came and went through the light, made him think of people he knew. Of his neighbours, the people that lived around The Green, people whose faces he saw and who he might nod to in the shops or as they passed on the street, but who he had never bothered to really speak to.

The next night, the man and woman didn't fuck; instead, she pleaded with him, falling to her knees and wrapping her arms around him. He disengaged from her as the crowd's accompaniment whooped and soared around them; there was George, or at least the figure in the George mask, beating at his pan savagely, there the woman from number 24, tits jiggling as she hit what looked like an old-fashioned dustbin lid so hard that splinters of her wooden spoon spun away with each strike.

Cornish watched with dull misery now; he couldn't remember the last time he hadn't felt tired. During the weekend break with Andrea? Probably. Was it only a few days ago? It felt like an age away. His body felt thick and slow, his brain muddled and somehow facing in the wrong direction. He had snapped at Andrea tonight, lashing with his tongue and sounding, even to himself, like the stranger that he had used to be. She had told him it didn't matter, but it did, and she had rolled away from him in bed and presented her back to him. It was like going backwards, back to when he had been thinking about Gill at night rather than his wife, about what fucking Gill had been like or, more frequently, how to get rid of her with the minimum of fuss and damage. How much energy had he spent on Gill, a woman whom he had liked, but never loved? How much time had he spent getting out of something that had only ever been meant as fun, as something quick and pointless? How much damage had he done to himself, to Andrea? To their marriage? He wanted to pray, but didn't know how, that he might somehow correct it all, make it right, make up to Andrea the wrong that she didn't know he had done. He wasn't perfect, couldn't be, but he could be better, couldn't he?

Couldn't he?

The man had walked away, only to come back with more gifts. His mime grew more elaborate as he gestured a conversation, a tilted head of attention, a sympathy that the set of his shoulders gave away as something he didn't feel himself, even as the woman wept. The second woman was walking in circles now, in and out of the light, there and not-there, waiting and hoping. Finally, all three went into the darkness, only to come back to take their bows, mummers at the end of a long and complex performance. Their orchestra let their music sail, higher and higher until it could go no further and it peaked, climaxed, became so loud as to mean nothing and then collapsed in on itself like crumpling paper. Cornish recognised almost all of them tonight, the masked, blank expressions of his neighbours and work colleagues staring at him from below like a portrait gallery drawn by a child.

Later, in bed, he wept, and didn't know what or who it was he was weeping for.

At the climax of the next night's mime, the man went to the second woman, took her hands in his and pressed his face to hers as the first woman slumped to the grass behind them. This time, it was she who remained as the man and the other woman went off and did not come back, her shoulders shaking with racking sobs that Cornish couldn't hear but could almost feel.

The drumming was so loud now that it wasn't even noise anymore; noise was too small a word to contain the maelstrom of sound being produced. It came in waves, ascending and descending but never lessening, and finally the woman leaned back, looking up at Cornish, and he saw her face clearly for the first time.

It was Gill; no, not Gill, but a mask of her, swollen and distorted but her nonetheless. There was something about the tilt of her nose, the shape of her eyes, that he recognised, something about the way the mouth had been painted downturned with tears, that spoke to him of Gill's mouth that last night when she had tried to not cry as she agreed that them not seeing each other again was a good thing, the right thing. Gill.

That bitch! he thought, *that utter bitch! She told me it was okay, that we were okay, that it was fine and I didn't have to worry! And now this crap!* He went to his bedroom and took his phone, returning to the guest-room at an almost-run, punching in her number as he went. The sound of the ringing was harsh in his ear, fighting against the din from outside but somehow still audible, and then she was answering with a voice that was thick with sleep and wariness.

"Gill, what the fuck is going on? What are you doing?" She didn't answer, her silence injured, pointed, but he carried on. "What, we fuck and then split up and you think it's okay to get people to come and wake me up every night?"

"I don't know what you're talking about," Gill said, cold.

"I can see them now!" he shouted. "They're right outside, banging pots and pans and making a fucking horrible noise, waking me up. Please, Gill, get them to stop. I'm sorry it didn't work out, that it hurt you, I hurt you, but you knew I was married. I love my wife, I never said I didn't, I never lied to you, I was always open that we were just fun, it was just fucking, wasn't it?"

"I don't know what you're talking about," she said again, and disconnected the call. In the silence that followed, Cornish heard his breathing catch, felt his heartbeat in his chest, slowly calming, slowly falling back to normal.

"Who's Gill?" said Andrea.

Cornish turned; she was standing in the doorway to the guest-room, looking at him. There were tears in her eyes. As he turned, he caught a glimpse of the people on The Green; they were all bowing, moving back into the darkness. Vanishing.

"Who's Gill?" she said again.

"No one," he said, trying to think of a way out, a way through. Nothing. Nothing came, nothing presented itself. He was naked, lost. Helpless.

"A no one that you fucked," said Andrea tonelessly.

"No," said Cornish, and opened his mouth to say more but Andrea interrupted him, hissing fiercely, "You lying shit! I heard you!" She stepped forward and raised her hand as though to strike him but then let it fall, turning and running from the room. He didn't follow her.

Cornish heard Andrea sobbing in the bedroom, heard drawers and the wardrobe opening and banging closed, heard her call a taxi even though she could hardly speak for crying. He tried to call to her, to tell her that it was all a mistake, that she was the one he loved, that she was half of him and he was sorry, so sorry, but his voice was lost under the sound of wooden spoons beating metal.

SEE THE BAY AS IT SHOULD BE SEEN!

FOR A SINGLE EVENING ONLY THE

POOR WEATHER CROSSINGS COMPANY

IS RETURNING TO MORECAMBE! BOOK NOW TO CROSS THE BAY IN THE WORST OF WEATHERS AND SEE ITS TERRIBLE MAJESTY AND PURPOSE AT CLOSE QUARTERS. FOR A SELECT FEW, THIS IS A ONCE-IN-A-LIFETIME OPPORTUNITY, AS THE COMPANY HAS NO PLANS TO RETURN TO AREA FOR MANY YEARS. WALK WITH THE KING'S GUIDE TO THE SANDS AND HAVE THE EXPERIENCE OF YOUR LIFE!

CALL FOR DETAILS AND TO BOOK A SPACE.

Sykes found the advert on a night out towards the end of summer, in one of the pubs on the seafront thick with noise and sweat and the odours of stale beer and cheap perfume. It was a hand-printed poster stuck to the wall, the sort of thing that he always thought of as American: an A4 sheet with details printed across most of the paper's face but with the bottom sliced into fingers to tear away, each with the number to call printed along its length.

He tore a finger off and stuffed it in his pocket, not really intending to do anything about it, and found it the next morning, crumpled and beer-stained, in amongst his change and masses of other flyers and leaflets. He looked at the number for a moment and then picked up his mobile. *What can it hurt*, he thought? *It's something new to do, after all.*

"Welcome, welcome!" cried the little man, doing an odd hopping, skipping dance in front of the small crowd as he spoke. "You are most welcome!"

They had called Sykes out of the blue that day, almost two months after he had registered with them, telling him that the crossing was to be that night. At first he was going to turn them down but then he thought, *What else will I be doing? Sitting in front of the television watching programmes about houses or antiques? Sitting in a bar I don't like, drinking with people I don't really know? Walking like a ghost through Morecambe, wishing I was somewhere else?* And, almost without intending to, he heard himself agreeing to go and nodding when they told him where to meet the rest of the walkers.

As well as Sykes, there were three Japanese students waiting by the side of the road, an old man wearing a bright yellow raincoat and a sou'wester, a couple with a child who looked to be about nine – all three wrapped up in wet weather gear that creaked with newness – and a group of five that he thought might be from one of the seafront hotels that specialised in coach holidays for retirees. Around them the autumn night squalled, spraying them with rain as fine as exhaled breath, cold and tasting of brine and sand.

And there was the man.

He was small, not even reaching Sykes' shoulder, and dressed in a pair of black trousers whose cuffs he had rolled to his knees, a white granddad-collared shirt and dark waistcoat, and a cape that looked old, made of oilcloth. His hair was long, falling from a balding pate in straggles, and he had mutton-chops that dripped with rain. He was barefoot.

"Ladies, gentlemen and young folk," the man called, "if I can have your attention. Shortly, we will set off across the bay, but first: rules! There are always rules, are there not? Rules to obey, rules to know! You must stay close to me, and do not wander off. Stay within sight of me, and of each other. Do what I say, go where I go, for the bay is filled with quicksand and has a voracious appetite for those who stray, and it would be a terrible shame to lose any of you before our purpose is fulfilled."

"Is it safe?" asked the female half of the couple, putting her hand on the child's shoulder. She was American, her accent rich with nasal cadences. "I mean, it's getting dark. How will we see where we're going?"

"Madam, the bay is lit by the lights of moon and stars and by my knowledge," said the man, "and as King's Guide, your passage to your destination is mine to oversee." Sykes looked up; the sky was a swirling mass of grey/brown clouds and leaden distance and spiralling, white narwhal tusks of rain. He couldn't imagine the stars or moon would be visible tonight.

"I thought it was the Queen's Guide to the Sands," said the old man, his sou'wester rustling like liquid rolling over tarpaulin. "He's written books. I have one of them."

"Ah, yes, that fellow," said the little man. "He is the Queen's Guide, yes, to take people safely across the sand. Cedric is an honourable and venerable man and he does sterling work, has done for many a year, but he walks the daytime hours through the light of good weathers, taking the masses across the bay. Mine is a much older, more exclusive position. We only walk the seas in the worst of conditions, with small groups, and only ever as evening falls. I, friends, am Mister Calcraft, and I am the King's Guide to the Sands; not just these sands, but all the sands there are. Now, shall we go?"

They were at Hest Bank, on the gravelled car park above the foreshore. Behind them, the fence separating them from the tracks of the West Coast railway line murmured to itself in metallic whispers. The beachfront café, shutters down, was silent, an uneven apron of the parking areas almost empty of vehicles. Calcraft set off, walking down the steps to the foreshore, an expanse of seagrass and rocks that stretched out to either side and in front of the group, fringing the mudflats that started out in the bay proper. Instead of heading out into towards the distant humps of Barrow, however, Calcraft turned and began to walk parallel to the coastline, his cape fluttering about him, his hair dancing in the increasing breeze.

"The bay is one of this country's great natural events," he called back over his shoulder, "nearly two hundred square miles of intertidal mudflats and sand connecting Barrow all the way around to Heysham, and its history is long and its produce bountiful."

The group passed a small square of chain-link fence enclosing a stream emerging from the bank that dropped from the foreshore to the mudflats. "The Red Bank Outflow," said Calcraft brightly. "Allowing exit for the water that runs down from the hills, channelled through the earth to prevent erosion of the roads that line the shore. Two workmen died in its creation when an incorrectly supported wall slipped and smothered them. They were trapped for hours, in the mud, before they were found suffocated, their fingers raw and their mouths full of filth from their struggles to live."

The rain fell harder, furring Calcraft's words in a low caul of noise. The little man stepped nimbly across the ground, leaping over obstacles with apparent ease, dancing ahead of the group; the tide had done odd things to the earth here, cutting it down so that chunks of solidified mud protruded like giant building blocks from the ground, surrounded by small sinkhole pools whose surfaces constantly fractured and reformed, reflecting what little light there was. The group moved past two old fisherman's cottages, closed and empty, and then they were away from the buildings and there was simply open ground to their right and the bay to their left, flat and painted in shades of darkness. Sykes looked back over his shoulder as Calcraft began to lead them out over the fractured landscape and towards the deceptive smoothness of the sands beyond. The buildings behind them were little more than hunched, shadowed shapes against the sky and for a moment, he didn't like it; it felt as though they were walking away from civilisation.

No, worse; it felt as though civilisation had turned its back on them. Sykes had done one of the more normal cross bay walks when he first moved to Morecambe, back when he and Kelly were together and Morecambe had been his hopeful place and not just a grey jumble that lay around him, as cloying as an old coat. What he remembered most about it was the way the mud rose up his legs and clung, working its way inside shoes that had been so filthy after the walk that he had had to throw them away, and the way the bay had opened up around them the further out into it they had gone. The Barrow headlands ahead of them and the costal stretch of Morecambe and Heysham to their rear had wrapped around the long line of people like sunlit, comforting arms, leaving them to walk across (or, more accurately, through) a flat expanse of mud and sand that was cut by huge yet oddly gentle upheavals and valleys, and channels of fast flowing water. With the sun above him and the distant hills of the Lake District to his face, Sykes had felt tiny and insignificant and yet curiously cheered, like some explorer walking the plains of some vast and new land, discovering with every step something that he would carry with him forever.

This walk was nothing like that.

For a start, there were so few of them; whereas before he had been part of a huge snake of hundreds of people, holding Dee's hand as they waded and strode and shuffled and stared about them like tourists (which, he supposed, they had been), now there was only Calcraft and the little group. Its smallness meant that they were soon strung like beads on wire, Calcraft lithe at their head and the rest of them dragging behind him. The sound of the rain was a constant aggressive susurrus, pattering against the damp earth and the waterproof materials of coats and trousers, the air smelling of seaweed and something else, something thick and faintly rancid; old fish, or vegetation exposed by the retreat of the tide, or deep water, Sykes supposed. And then there was the view.

Or rather, there wasn't. The distances opening up between the people on the walk were filling with rain that drifted like smoke and thickening brown darkness in which darker patches emerged and then faded. It hemmed them in, reducing Sykes's vision to a ragged circle around him, not the coming of night because that was an hour or two away yet, but the obstruction of the evening by clouds that stretched all the way from sky to earth. By his reckoning, Sykes could see maybe two or three hundred feet, and could make out nothing of Barrow or Heysham and little of the closer land behind them or to their side. Most of what he could see was featureless and brown, mottled and shifting as though somewhere just beyond his view something was moving through the bay alongside them. Even the air was a dripping, sullen khaki, stained to a watercolour blandness by the weather.

"The oceans are this planet's lungs and heart and soul," Calcraft called from ahead of them. "Mankind has investigated almost none of the water's lightless depths, choosing for the most part to remain on its fragile surface and pretend that it is his domain and that he has mastery of it. Even on land we are surrounded, though, never far from water, and the earth has millions of miles of coastline, places where the seas breathe in and out to reveal something of themselves and the things they cover.

"Sometimes, like tonight, some of us are allowed glimpses of the things that the oceans normally keep hidden."

Somewhere behind Sykes someone called out, but when he turned back there was simply a line of eleven shuffling figures, following in the widening, blurring footprints of Calcraft, drab in the gloom.

"The coast here is a treacherous one," Calcraft continued. "As far back as maritime records go, the bay has taken its share of sustenance from the land and from those that try to work its beds and surfaces. Gales come in from the Irish Sea, tearing the surface to violent shreds, and its bed is uneven, littered with hidden banks and beset by fast-flowing tides and cross currents. In the days of sail, it was as dangerous when the gales died away and boats were left becalmed, drifting towards obstacles with slow, inexorable grace.

"The first wreck of note here was up at Fleetwood, when a vessel whose name most have forgotten but that was called the *Geomerung* was caught on a bank and then routed and set afire by royalists. Its crew were all killed, of course, their bones and the skeleton of the ship itself long since swallowed by the mud.

"Morecambe became 'Morecambe' in 1844; prior to that it was Poulton, and it was mentioned in the Domesday Book, although then it was called Poltune, and until 1820 it was a port town. That was the year the first recorded tourists arrived, responding to an advertisement offering a cottage for hire as an excellent base for sea fishing. Until then, the relationship between the inhabitants of the sea and those of the land was clear; when tourists began to arrive, however, things became somewhat confused."

They were far out into the bay now, Calcraft taking a path that led them slowly right, curving northwards. They came to a channel of water, flowing quickly. "As people who didn't understand the contract between the water and the land – who didn't live each day holding the water in their hearts and being held in its – arrived at the coast, boundaries blurred and became fractured, broken. The sea became another commodity, to be used rather than respected. And thus does change begin."

The group had come back together at the edge of the channel, waiting. The rain was harder here, heavier, a shimmering wall around them that sounded like dropping coins and tearing card.

"Look around you," said Calcraft. "This is how very few people see the bay. This is how very few ever see any ocean; dark, torn by poor weather, its lips drawn back and its teeth exposed, tongue writhing around them. Imagine this place as it was before the arrival of tourism, the skears rising from the water and topped by sickly trees, the low waters around them covering great mussel beds, a home for crabs and migratory seabirds, fished by locals who used coracles to get to them and who would return to the mainland as the tides came in, dragging sacks of the ocean's bounty for sale or to feed themselves and their families. For thousands of years, settlers in the area have used the skears for food, and their voices filled the airs and their thanks were heard at the greatest of heights and the lowest of depths. Now, onwards!"

Calcraft stepped out into the channel, the water breaking against his legs in small waves. "Follow, please," he said, his voice loud and clear now that Sykes was closer to him. "This cut isn't deep but the waters flow fast. Be confident and hold each other for safety if you wish. Madam," the guide said, turning to look at the family, "you might wish to hold your child's hand for the next few moments. Such flesh as he might easily be swept away if it is not anchored by a mother's love and solid grip!" And then they were off again.

The water was cold, but not as cold as Sykes expected. It pushed against his legs, insistent rather than bullying, and his feet sank into mud where he put them down; the sensation was strangely reassuring, as though he were creating temporary foundations for himself against the pressures of the tide. He stayed close to Calcraft, attempting to keep up, interested in the near-constant litany coming from the guide, ignoring what sounded like raised voices from behind him.

"There are one hundred square miles of intertidal zone in the bay, one hundred square miles of land that is periodically exposed and then lost again by the movement of the tides, a hinterland between the twin kingdoms of water and land. What nature fills and empties twice a day without thought would take a modern tap running at full flow over a million years to fill."

The water was up to the man's waist now, was brushing at Sykes at about mid-thigh, and Calcraft was speeding up. He was over half way across the channel, a small dark shape ahead of Sykes, still talking as he went, his voice all around them. The rain had softened slightly, falling now almost as mist, fingers of it spiralling down in the distance and glimmering silver against the browns and blacks of the approaching night, its sound a throaty whisper. When Sykes looked back, the group was once again spread out, the couple and child closest to him, both adults holding the child's hands and making him walk between them. The boy stared at Sykes from inside his tubular hood and Sykes grinned at him and winked. The boy smiled back briefly and then dropped his eyes.

Beyond the family, the Japanese students were walking together and behind them, three of the coach party were strung out, perhaps five feet apart and moving through the water like bobbing dinghies.

There was a flash of lightning as Sykes turned back towards Calcraft, and for a moment the distant mass of the Barrow headlands were black solidities against the moving, sodden sky. Silvered light leapt about them, coating the channel and the wet mud of its far bank like smearing nitrate, and then it was gone, leaving behind after-image phantasms of itself in Sykes' eyes. Someone behind Sykes made a noise that might have been surprise or fear, or even an appreciative groan, and then fell silent again.

On the far side of the channel, Calcraft stopped once more, turning back to his party, still following him through the water. "From here, the esteemed Cedric would begin to curl us back in towards the waiting safety of Arnside, but we are made of sterner stuff, are we not, and have to go further out before we can come back in. The charter of the Poor Weather Crossings Company, of the King's Guide, is to show the bay at its most elemental, out in the places where people do not usually go. We carry this task out across the world, our destinations dependent on weather and date and the darting of the schools of the silvery fish and the lazy shift of whales, and it is my humble honour to be its Guide and to fulfil its responsibilities."

As Sykes came up the bank of the channel, Calcraft had already reached its upper edge and was heading away. Sykes waited, offering the couple and the boy his arm to come up the slope, and then ushering them past him and waiting for the three students to offer them help as well. Two were female, one male, he saw, and all smiled at him.

"He's too quick," said one of the girls in perfect, accentless English, nodding at the receding figure of Calcraft.

"Yes," said Sykes, thinking about Calcraft's instructions to stay in sight of each other, of the old man in the yellow slicker, wondering if he'd be able to keep up, wondering about the coach party group and how safe this little jaunt really was.

"Will you...?" said the male student, interrupting Sykes's thoughts by holding out his camera. Sykes nodded, glancing at the still in sight Calcraft, and took it.

He stepped back and took several photographs of the three standing together at the edge of the strip of flowing water. After the lightning, the camera's flash seemed puny and faint, its pallid light catching the students and freezing them into the tiny screen on the camera's rear. Behind them, the flash showed Sykes the group of three from the coach party just beginning to make their way up the bank.

There was no sign of the man with the yellow sou'wester.

Actually, there was no sign of the man with the sou'wester, or the other two from the coach party. Sykes went back to the edge of the water, ignoring the student's attempt to take back his camera, and held it up high. He took several photographs and then looked at them on the tiny screen in its rear; the pictures weren't good, the flash struggling against the expanse of the bay, catching the fragmenting glitter of rain, but they all showed essentially the same thing; the expanse of water, visible across most of its width, uninterrupted by wading humans. "Shit," he muttered.

The student tapped Sykes on his shoulder, his smile faltering, and Sykes handed him his camera back. Leaving the boy and his friends he went quickly away from the channel, looking for Calcraft.

There was a shape moving through the mist ahead of him but it looked too large to be the guide, a shadow that stretched up above Sykes's head and then melted away as he pushed forward, seeming to slip sidelong and vanish into the fluttering ribbons of water. The constantly shifting mist and rain and spray was doing odd things to the light, what little there was of it, creating dancing figures at his sides that kept pace with him and distorted shapes ahead of him, smaller and more distant. Where was Calcraft? Where were the others?

There.

The guide was still walking briskly along, his feet doing little more than indent the mud that Sykes' feet were sinking into, and he was still talking. "Of course, it's not simply the bay that takes its toll, the whole coast here, the coast everywhere, it levies a cost, a price, that we must pay. The sailors of the yawl Arlette found that out in 1920 at Walney, as did the crew of the Crystal at Horse Bank, and a thousand others over the years. The Vanadis went down in the next bay along this coast early last century and its skeleton can still be seen at low tides such as we have tonight, the ribs of it blackened and its cargo of hard wood from Norway long since floated free." The little man skipped up a shallow rise, his feet kicking up licks of spray, as Sykes finally caught him up.

"You have to stop," he said. "We've lost someone. A few people, I think."

Calcraft wheeled about. From atop the rise, he looked down at Sykes, his edges blurring in the rain. It had thickened again suddenly, was so heavy now that the falling water was kicking up a secondary splashes as it hit the water-logged earth, curled skeins that lifted in the wind before merging with each other like tangled pleats of cord.

"Lost someone?" repeated Calcraft. Gradually, the rest of the people on the crossing were closing in, gathering around the man. "No, I don't think so; no one is lost. Everyone is precisely where they should be."

"The old man in yellow," said Sykes. "Some of the group that arrived together. I don't know their names. Are they ahead of us?" He turned to the approaching group.

"Where are your friends?" he called. "There were five of you at first. Who's missing?"

"We weren't together," said the first of them, an older man who had mud spattered across his skin and who looked tired, his face a pale moon of worry in the darkness. "I mean, we're on the tour together but we aren't friends, none of us really know each other. They were behind us and now they're not, that's all I know."

Calcraft didn't speak. Instead, he walked down the short slope and moved back towards the channel. In the scoured light the shadows coalesced into moving shapes and then fragmented again and for a moment something huge seemed to be capering just out of sight, given form by a trick of gleam and water, and then it was gone. The wind lifted its voice, became the choral song of something moaning through lips that were inflexible and taut, the rain the sound of tombstone teeth grinding, and then it, too, was gone.

"Well," said Calcraft after he reached the water's edge. "I see nothing to concern us here."

"What?" said Sykes. "There are people missing! You need to call someone!"

Behind Calcraft, the family pulled closer together, the mother's arms sneaking around her child, keeping him pressed flat back to her belly. The students had also clustered to each other, forming a little tableau like the statues in military graveyards.

"There's no need to call anyone," said Calcraft. "They are not missing."

"Then where are they?"

"The full crossing is not for everyone," said Calcraft. "All along its length, people who struggle, those who fall behind, are collected."

"You mean you have helpers?" asked Sykes, relaxing slightly. Outriders, on those little quad bikes, or a tractor maybe? He'd seen them in the distance, sometimes, harrying the edges of the walks that went across the bay in the daytime, shepherding people back to the column or letting them ride on the rear of the vehicles if they were getting tired. That would explain the figures that he kept seeing at the edge of his view, just out of sight but not out of perception, moving fast around them.

"Oh, no," said Calcraft, "not 'helpers'. I am their assistant, not they mine. I am the goat of the crossings, the King's Guide, a mere servant to their masters."

"Are they safe?" said Sykes, growing irritated with Calcraft's florid oratory. "Are we safe?"

"They are gathered together," said Calcraft. "And as for you, you are my ward, sir." He tuned again, heading on. After a moment, Sykes and the others followed.

"Fishing has changed, as all things do," said Calcraft as he walked. It was harder going here, the earth slick with water and clumps of grey/green seaweed that lay in wide, dank tangles. The earth itself was the consistency of thick mud, the boundaries between earth and pool less clear, and Sykes's feet were permanently under the surface of water so that walking was more like a skier's shuffle. Sykes was moving as fast as he could, trying to keep Calcraft in sight, the man a fluttering shape in the space ahead of him, his voice a thread that Sykes and the others followed.

"Catches came to be taken from further out, dragged from the depths into the bellies of ships that were made of steel rather than wood. Tourism spread its fingers further out from the coasts, across the waters themselves, in yachts and liners of increasing grandeur and opulence, safe and fast and clean and steady. Yet even now, safety is not assured; the ocean can reach out and fish even as it is fished, crews dragged from the fishing boats or the boats themselves dragged under, vast liners or tramp ferries sometimes gored or overturned, spitting their passengers into freezing seas or polluted estuarine deltas. In the wars, crafts as sleek as sharks and as stealthy as the tides themselves proved little protection for the men that crewed them, the seas remaining as demanding a master as they had ever been. Even now, in the lightless deeps, their metal skeletons sit quiet and abandoned, their corridors patrolled only by creatures that have never seen the surface of the world they inhabit.

"Trawlers still fished these waters in the war, sometimes catching unexpected cargoes, ships like the Murielle, torn open and sunk with all hands lost by a mine near the Morecambe Bay Lightship. No more was it a simple trade of fish for man; now, complexities multiplied and the Company was called upon more and more often to lead its tours to places rarely seen."

Sykes was exhausted, trying to keep up with the little bastard; the man seemed to be fucking dancing over the pitted earth, skipping through water and mud alike without appearing to even notice it. He seemed almost dry where Sykes was soaked to his belly, cold and anxious, and what about the others? Turning, he saw the students and the family close by, heads all down and churning forwards, and behind them the members of the holiday group. Only two of them were in sight now, pallid shapes in the distance against a background that constantly writhed and rippled. Even as he watched, the rain and turmoil thickened, coagulating into something solid, and came closer, seeming to reach out and swallow the rearmost of the two. Sykes waited for the weather to loosen its grip and release the figure, but it did not.

Something splashed off to his side, big enough to be heard over the constant rain. Sykes looked but saw nothing; nothing except air the colour and texture of saturated muslin.

He turned about, losing Calcraft in the distance and then finding him again. He was on the edge of Sykes's vision, tiny and indistinct, still darting along. The family and the students were up ahead of Sykes as well, having both passed him as he looked back. They were hunched in to each other in two small groups, the students closer and slower, their wet-weather gear turning them into reflective pepper-pot shapes in the gloom. Sykes peered up; high above, the clouds were tearing apart and reforming and then tearing apart again, revealing patches of inky sky. There were no stars.

There was another flash of lightning and then, like an echo, the students' camera flash went off. Caught between the two flares, Sykes's eyes clenched. Something flashed again, puncturing his eyelids with glare, and then it was gone. He opened his eyes cautiously, his vision dancing with yet more movement, black and red patches shifting in amongst the brown and silver shimmer around him. Rain rolled around the rim of his hood, gathering and spilling inside his coat, snaking down his neck in cold trails. Calcraft and the family were even further away and he hurried after them, stepping around increasingly dark pools and slick, greasy ridges of mud.

The camera was on the ground, half buried.

Sykes only saw it because it was facedown and the power LED was on, a tiny red dot in the night. He bent and picked it up, looking around. Was that the students ahead and to the side, shadows in the downpour?

There seemed to be more than three. Had they found some of the elderly group? Joined up with them? He blinked, trying to clear his vision, but it didn't help.

"Hey!" he called, hoping to attract their attention, holding their camera up. The figures faded away, their shapes lost again. He started to jog, his feet splashing through the water, the tang of salt in his nose. The skin of his face felt tight and stiff, as though he was wearing a mask that constantly cracked and resealed itself. "Hey," he called again, but his voice sounded tiny and depthless against the noise of the bay, swallowed by the wind and the tattoo beat of the rain.

The students appeared again in the distance as he came closer, distorted, magnified by some trick of the water and wind so that they appeared to be tall, taller than the houses they had left behind them on the shore, and then they were gone. Sykes broke into a run.

There was no land now, just mud covered by a thin but deepening layer of water. How far out had they come? Calcraft was up ahead, still walking on, apparently impervious to the weather. The little bastard was still speaking, Sykes heard, carrying on oblivious as Sykes tried to catch his breath to call him.

"Out here, the bay is still fecund despite the years of depredation," Calcraft was saying. "Huge beds of cockles line the ocean's floor, exposed at low tides such as these. The bay, generous as ever, offers itself to man. The seas offer themselves to man, and they ask little in return except that they are occasionally acknowledged."

"Calcraft," called Sykes. "We have to go back, this is getting dangerous."

Calcraft stopped and turned, beckoning the family and Sykes in to him. They came together in a huddle, gathering around the little man. Sykes was far taller than him, was looking down at the man's dripping scalp, pale under worms of hair.

"The tides here are quick, moving like quicksilver to surround the unwary. The waters have become crafty in how they take their reward, have had to become crafty, subtle in their appetites. They bay tries to take offerings most years, is sometimes successful and sometimes not. It almost took three children and their dog in 1967 but was beaten by the speed of the helicopters of the coastguard, has missed others who were more wary or simply luckier, morsels missed or spat out, but it would be a mistake to underestimate the grand majesty of the water. It takes fishermen looking for worms and tourists unused to its terrible speed, swimmers caught by riptides as strong as the hands of the devil himself. Not much, we might think, for how much it gives, and we would be right but remember; occasionally its hunger is voracious. Think of those twenty-three Chinese cocklers, their last moments on earth not on earth at all but in water, thousands of miles from home and their loved ones, all around them cold and grey and the stink of brine in their noses and the taste of the ocean in their mouths as they screamed their last."

"Did you hear me?" asked Sykes, holding out the camera to Calcraft. "We need to go back. This weather, it's too dangerous for us to stay out here." The father said something that Sykes didn't hear and tried to grasp Calcraft's arm but the man pirouetted out of the way.

"From the beginning, the creatures of the land and the creatures of the sea have had a contract, ancient, forgotten by almost all," said

Calcraft as though Sykes and the father had not spoken. "By almost all, but not by all. Even if man forgets, the King remembers."

"For Christ's sake," said Sykes and then the rain shifted, solidified and the darkness reached out and lifted the child off his feet and snapped him away.

The mother screamed, the sound stopping abruptly as something that might have been a tentacle but might equally have been an arm or a finger or a fin wrapped around her and sucked her back into the night's mouth. Sykes cried out, trying to run but stumbled, falling to his knees in a spray of brine and wet, clinging sand which sprayed up around his face and neck, and then he was up.

Someone behind him shrieked, the noise of it long and ululating, rising in pitch as it fell in volume until it was gone, and then the only sound was Sykes's own breathing and the fall of his feet into earth that was more liquid than solid.

His clothes were cold and wet, chafing and tugging as he ran, as though he was wearing someone else's skin, old and ill-fitting. The air curled about him, given shape by the rain and spray, twists dragging about his feet, the liquid slathering his face, dripping into his eyes and mouth. Where was he running? Away from Calcraft, but was he headed back to the shore? Sykes didn't know, just ran.

It was hard, the ground uneven, pools opening up before him at the last moment so that he had to dodge clumsily to their sides or run through them, slow and irregular. There was no moon above, nor stars, yet there was a luminescence in the air around him, the dank rain lit as though from within by a queasy sepia glow.

"Random chance selected you the moment you called us," said a voice from by Sykes's ear.

He yelped, staggered in surprise and stumbled again, falling and rolling through a patch of weed that smelled of salt and decay. Cursing, he clutched at the plant and hauled himself up, running on.

Calcraft ran at his side.

"At its heart the contract remains simple, even if the methods of implementing its conditions have become more complicated," said the small man. He ran as nimbly as he had walked, seemed to shiver across the surface of the puddles and skate over the undulating earth like an insect. His voice was conversational, neither breathless nor ragged. "The seas provided and occasionally they took, reaching out with a wave or a storm to swallow down boats and sometimes the crews. A reciprocal arrangement, fishermen and fished, neat and tidy.

Sykes leaped over a tussock, landing heavily the other side in water that came to his waist, thinking briefly that he might have to swim before the footing underneath him became solid enough to hold his weight.

"But there are fewer fishermen and fewer boats, and those that take to the water are larger, harder to take to the bottom than the coracles or longboats or wooden schooners of the years gone by. What were my masters to do? The contract changed, not by them but by you, taking more and more and giving less and less, and so the Poor Weather Crossings Company was born. I am the King's Guide and I lead you out, I entice you with tales of wondrous views and of not-to-be-missed opportunities, I tell desperate immigrants of cockle-beds where fortunes lie simply waiting to be claimed, I whisper in drunken ears in public houses that night-time swims can be so much fun, I encourage dogs to jump into stormy seas so that their owners might follow. I am Calcraft, the King's Guide to the sands, the Judas Goat, and I serve my master well."

All around Calcraft, figures swarmed through the rising tide, half-seen and blank-eyed.

"Your sacrifice will keep the seas at bay, protecting those on the shore. Be honoured," said Calcraft, running closer to Sykes. Sykes lashed out, missed and fell, his clothes ballooning with water, the weight of it holding him, rolling him onto his back so that he was staring up into a sky that seemed only feet above him, the colour and texture of decaying shrouds. He fumbled in his pocket, rooting through sodden layers for his phone. His fingers were cold, lost their grip on it as he pulled it out and it fell into the water.

The slight noise of it entering the tide sounded huge, echoing, curling around Sykes's rising moan and carrying it up into the clouds where it was lost in the wraiths of rain. Calcraft leaned into his vision, smiling.

"It wouldn't have worked anyway," he said. "Out here, you are beyond the reach of technology and there are only the truths of history and a covenant made when the first man lifted a fish from the water on the end of hook or spear. We have shown you the bay at its most glorious, shown you the seas laid out in a way that few ever see them, rewarded you for the offering you will make, but now the tour is done and the sacrifice due. We must finish, for the Company is needed elsewhere."

Over Calcraft's shoulder the rain fell harder, thicker, the water forming shapes that stretched to the ceiling of clouds above. The little man stepped back, nodding a last time, leaning back and opening his mouth to the rain and drinking the drops down. Sykes opened his mouth to scream but the tide flowed over his lips and choked his voice to nothing, and then the King was above him and taking hold of him and he was gone to the court where no light ever shows.

Teratoma:

A slow-growing, usually benign cyst that often contains teeth. Cysts can occur anywhere, including the ovaries, sinuses, brain, stomach or bowel. As the cysts are most often benign they often go unnoticed until they either begin to obstruct another bodily function or they rupture and the contents escape, at which point the teeth can emerge in a variety of ways. There are recorded incidents of people sneezing teeth from sinus cysts or evacuating their bowels to find several molars in their stools.

Chapter Bank

"Can you come?"

Hollister's midnight brain didn't move as quickly as his mouth and he was still trying to work out who the voice at the end of the line belonged to as he said, "Hey, Sis."

"Can you come?" Bex said again and then her voice hitched itself down into tears. Hollister lay in his half-asleep, half-empty bed listening to her, wondering how long it was since they had last spoken. Eighteen months? Twenty four? Longer, thirty six at least; before he and Dee married, certainly. He shouldn't get involved, he knew. This was Bex's pattern, the big explosion over nothing, the long sulk and the silence and then the dramatic return begging for help, and it never ended well for anyone. He'd had it all his life, all of them had, he and Dad and Mum, and it was exhausting. Little Bex, so fragile and mercurial, so pretty and aware of her own prettiness, so helpless. Whatever this was, he should say no, should disconnect the call and roll over, go back to sleep. He looked over at the empty half of his bed, the sheets rumpled and shadowed and cold, and did not move the phone from his ear.

"Please, Richard," Bex said, her voice sounding distant and lost, reaching out to him from every Christmas and Birthday of childhood, from every Sunday meal and summer holiday, from every argument and every good time, taking hold of him and pulling, just like it always had. "Please, Richard, he's following me and I can't stop him. I'm frightened, Richard, so frightened, please come, please help me."

"Where are you?" he asked, sighing.

"I'm at home," she said, her voice echoing in the space between them.

"I'll come tomorrow," he said and it was only after he put the phone down that the reality of it came, hard and raw and cold and crashing him into wakefulness; Bex was dead, and had been for nearly three months.

The next morning's light was bright enough to make Bex's call seem dreamlike and thin, something half-imagined and not entirely real, and Hollister wondered what he should do. He couldn't pretend that nothing had happened, much as he might want to; either he had imagined it, in which case he had to assume it was his unconscious telling him he was ready to deal with his younger sister's death in some way, or she had rung him from some place he didn't want to contemplate because she needed help. Whichever it was, he supposed he would have to go. What else could he do? Whatever her faults, whatever the problem, she was his sister, and he would go to her because she asked. How could he not?

He was packed and on the road by ten, and arrived at lunchtime.

Chapter Bank was tiny, a cluster of houses and shops miles from the nearest town, lost to everything except itself at the end of a road that curled and twisted over the brows of hills and through the river-cut valleys. For the last part of the journey, the road became a dark, single lane strip cut into the earth and Hollister wondered what might happen if he met something coming the other way as he drove, but he did not; there were no cars, no trucks or bikes, no people, just sheep grazing the grassland that hemmed around the road and a blue sky filled with cottony clouds above him.

How had she ended up here, Hollister wondered as he pulled into one of the parking spaces that lined Chapter Bank's small green. Bex, who hated the countryside and being bored, who liked lights and noise and things that glittered and sparkled, how had she come to this place? And why? After that last argument, when she had accused him and Dee of selfishness for wanting to marry and have children, why had she come here? She had lived like a recluse, he remembered the coroner saying, for the months before her death, rarely leaving her home, shopping online and having things delivered rather than going to the local shops. She had cut herself off from not just Hollister and Dee but from everyone, it seemed, existing in Chapter Bank for three years in a house bought with her part of their inheritance, and her death had been accidental, a fall down stairs whilst drinking that snapped her neck as cleanly as a piece of old wood broken for kindling. There were no suspicious circumstances, the police said, just another lonely person dying, found by the postman when he needed a signature for a parcel but couldn't get an answer at her front door and had peered in through the window.

Suddenly, Hollister was struck by a sense of loss and guilt so powerful that he felt faint, tears building behind his eyes, threatening to spill down his cheeks. How could he have lost contact with her so completely? Why hadn't he made an effort to find her? Because she and Dee didn't get on? Because life was quieter, easier without Bex in it? Because he was too wrapped up in his own grief over their parents' death? Because he was too lost in his own problems to think about anyone else's? All this and more, he thought, and now it was too late; Bex was gone, Dee was gone, his parents were gone and there was nothing he could do about any of it.

His mobile buzzed, distracting him from his thoughts. He pulled it from his pocket and put it to his ear, connecting to the call. "Are you coming?" asked Bex, her voice echoing, tearful. "Richard, are you coming? He's nearly caught me, Richard, he's so close."

"Bex?" he asked, his skin prickling. His mouth went dry, felt as cotton-filled as the clouds had looked. "Who's after you?"

"He is, Richard, the boy. The boy is coming," she said and then the call broke apart, wailing distortion before disconnecting completely. He held the phone away from his ear and then scrolled through its menu to the recent calls listings. The name at the top of the list simply read SIS. What would happen if he pushed the Call button, he wondered? Would she answer? Would someone else answer and reveal this to be some kind of elaborate, unpleasant joke? Would it simply ring and ring?

His thumb hovered and then fell away, not wanting to know. *I'm a coward*, he thought. He looked at the phone for a long time before putting it back in his pocket.

When Hollister got out of his car, he discovered that Chapter Bank smelled good, the air fresh and clean and thick with grass and birdsong. He started to walk, wanting to stretch his legs, and thinking that he and Dee might have liked it here. He passed its one pub and several small shops, a butcher's and a newsagent's, before coming to the edge of the green. At its centre was a war memorial, an old and black piece of statuary with names chiselled into its front. Across the base, he saw, someone had sprayed SHE WALKS in bright yellow paint. Not only that, he thought, she calls as well, and despite himself, despite the situation, he grinned.

It was time to go to her house.

He had assumed that finally entering Bex's home would give him some kind of answer, present a solution to him, but it did not.

The house was an old farmer's cottage situated at the end of a narrow track that his car jumped and jolted along, the police tape still fluttered from one of the gateposts slapping into his window as he passed it. There were old bunches of flowers and wreaths scattered across the front garden and Hollister's car rolled over them as he parked. They stank of sweet decay when he opened the door, and slithered under his feet as he went through. Cards floated among the rotting leaves. He saw one that read, *We're so sorry*, and another, *Be at peace*.

Hollister picked this last one up. The card was sealed in a small plastic envelope, and it was clean, the bouquet it was attached to fresher, laid on top of one whose flowers were little more than black clenches of petals atop curling green stems.

This hasn't been here three months, Hollister thought. *A month at most, maybe less.*

Looking around, he saw other fresher bouquets amongst the older ones, as well as single flowers and one teddy bear, its fur bedraggled and faded. Looking back, he saw flowers had been tied to the stones along the top of the boundary wall and to the wooden struts of the opened gates; some were drooping and dead, others looked colourful, fresh. Dropping the card, he entered the house.

There were the remains of more flowers throughout the house, these in vases, and he thought that they were probably here from when Bex was alive. The house stank of them, and the first thing he did was to open all the windows and then find a refuse bag to put all the dead blooms in. He poured the stagnant water down the sink, running the water for a long time to clear it, and then threw most of the vases into the bag with the flowers, which he then sealed and placed outside.

By the time he had finished, Hollister had been in every room in what had been Bex's house; his house now, he supposed. It was small, two bedrooms and a bathroom over a kitchen, lounge and utility. He sat for a long time at the bottom of the stairs, in the place where Bex had died, trying to feel her, but felt nothing. She wasn't here, not now anyway.

There was old food in the kitchen, mostly packets and microwave meals that had gone out of date. Hollister threw it all away as well. The fridge was thankfully empty and disconnected from the wall, smelling musty but clean, and in the cupboard under the sink he found a mass of vodka and whisky bottles, some full but most empty. There was something sad about the dusty bottles, hidden away, and he felt like crying again. He opened one of the whisky bottles and sniffed at the peaty aroma that rose from it, debated taking a swig, and then replaced its top without doing so.

Bex's phone was by her bed, on a table that also held a glass from which the water had evaporated and left grey rings around its inner surface, and a strip of birth control pills. Four of the pills were gone and the phone held no charge. There were piles of paperwork in most of the rooms, unopened mail as well as bills and flyers and other documents. It was going to take him a few days to go through it all, he supposed, if he stayed here.

He thought again about the calls, about Bex's voice, and wondered why he wasn't scared. *Because, even if she's a ghost, she's my sister*, he thought. *What harm can she do me?*

He needed food if he was going to stay here. Hollister locked the house and went out into the warm air, treading warily over the carpet of flowers. They slithered under his feet, their scent rotten and thick, and he only saw the woman as he reached his car.

She was standing just inside the drive and he thought it was Bex at first, but she was older than Bex, somewhere in her sixties.

"Hello?" he said.

The woman dropped the bunch of flowers she was holding, the blooms scattering the ground around her, and turned, walking out of the gate and disappearing from his view. He went after her, calling again, but by the time he reached the road there was no sign of her. Crouching, he looked at the flowers she had dropped. The card tied around the stems read simply, *Rest peaceful*.

When Hollister looked up, Bex was standing in the doorway of the house.

She hadn't changed, not much. She was a little thinner, her hair longer and less styled than it used to be, tangled around her face in whorls and knots. She was holding her arms up, her hands open, reaching towards him, and she looked miserable. No, not miserable, terrified. She was speaking, her mouth mouthing, writhing, but he heard no sound.

"Bex?" he said, standing, absurdly aware of the sound of his knees popping and thinking, I'm getting old.

She didn't reply, not in words. Instead, she stepped towards him, her mouth still moving, chewing at words he could not hear. Behind her, lights began to show through the opaque quarter windows in the top of the front door. The light was bright, yellow, and as it fell on Bex's shoulders she flinched, hunching down as though it was burning her. She cast a glance back towards the door and then turned back towards Hollister, her face twisting, the bags under her eyes cast into black pools by the light.

"Bex," he said again and stepped towards her. His feet kicked aside petals and buds, the sound of them like silk slipping against silk. The light was building, growing brighter, glimmering not only in the windows of the door but also the other windows, as though the house itself was filling with it. It was brighter than the day around it, brighter than the sun above Hollister, and then Bex was gone, scurrying away from the door and collapsing to nothing as she passed through the shadows below one of the windows. The light was gone moments after she was.

It had been Bex, Hollister thought, *Bex. His sister. His baby sister, frightened and asking for help, and what was going on here? What?*

What?

"Have you come to take her away?" the man asked.

The drive back into Chapter Bank hadn't taken long, but Hollister felt as though he was being watched from behind every curtain and from every shadowed alleyway. People on the street turned to watch him as he rolled past and when he parked in one of the spaces along the side of the small square, he saw people standing looking at him from the other side of the grass. He raised his hand to them, but they did not respond.

Chapter Bank didn't have a supermarket, so Hollister went into the corner shop. It was cool inside, the heat kept at bay by a long, old-fashioned fridge that was full of meats and cheeses. He gathered an armful of food and placed it on the counter, following it with soft drinks and a couple of bottles of wine. It was as he was paying that the man behind the counter spoke.

"Pardon?" he asked, and then realised that the man was staring at the keys in his other hand; he had taken them out of his pocket to get to his wallet. No, he thought, the man wasn't staring at the keys, but at the address written on the brown card tag that dangled from them, attached by a piece of white cotton twine and spinning slowly. Bex's keys had been sent to Hollister as her only surviving relative, labelled by the police or the coroner or one of their solicitors, he supposed; she hadn't left a will and the only officials he had dealt with were the ones investigating her death.

"Her. The girl. Have you come to take her away?"

"I'm sorry," Hollister said again, "I don't understand."

"You have the keys to her house," said the shopkeeper, finally looking up and into Hollister's face. "She's here. She's always here. Every night."

"In the shop?" Hollister asked, aiming for a tone of voice somewhere between facetious and amused but suspecting he failed and came across as numb and slow.

"Everywhere," the man said simply. "All the village. Everyone sees her, and we all hear her. No one sleeps for long anymore because she comes to us. Please, can you take her away?"

"I don't know," Hollister said, picking up his purchases. *Oh, Sis, what are you doing here*, he thought, suddenly angry. *Where are you? What are you?* As if in reply, his phone rang again, the sound of it shrill in the shop. Behind the counter, the old man backed away, leaving the money where Hollister had dropped it.

Hollister reached inside his pocket and removed the phone, holding it in the same hand as the keys.

"Hello?" he said after answering the call and the shopkeeper began to moan, backing further away and bumping into the shelves behind him.

"Hello?" Hollister said again but the only reply was the sound of someone weeping, the sobs echoing and swooping and repeating, as though he was hearing them from a great distance. He didn't look at the display to find out who was calling; he already knew.

"Please," said the shopkeeper. "Take her away. Please."

As he left the shop, Hollister lost his grip on his food and some of it fell. One of the bottles of wine smashed on the floor and sprayed his ankles with chardonnay, the smell of it sweet and sharp. He stumbled, leaving the mess for the man to clear up, and went out into the sunlight. He felt as though he'd fallen into some weird fever dream, something unreal and hallucinatory. He dropped more of the food as he got outside, bacon and bread falling from his arms in ungainly arcs. His vision had blurred, tears spilling from him, hot and scalding. The phone in his pocket rang again, and he slapped at it, hoping to turn it off through the cloth, dropping the last of his shopping. A bottle of cola bounced and rolled, coming to rest against the feet of the woman who was standing at the edge of the pavement.

She was at the head of a group of six or seven people, all of them motionless, watching him. Hollister straightened, wiping the tears from his face, trying to ignore his phone's shrill call.

"It's her," the woman said. It was the woman who had been at Bex's house a few minutes ago, he realised. Her hair was grey and her face square and set and she looked tired; they all did, this little crowd that had gathered around him, closing in, tightening like a human noose, driving him back against the wall. Some of them were older than the woman, some younger, their only apparent link the exhaustion that was painted across their faces, sagging skin and bruised flesh under their eyes. They gathered around him.

"I'm sorry, genuinely, but I don't understand," he said.

"It's her," the woman said, and gestured towards his pocket. The phone had stopped ringing and its silence was almost as heavy as its noise had been.

"I don't–" Hollister began again but the woman interrupted him fiercely.

"You do! It's her! She's still here, she won't go. She runs through the village every night, through our homes and our dreams, always calling, always crying, never stopping. She's running from the light, desperate to avoid the inevitable, trying to hold on to something she's got no right to."

"No."

"Yes. You're her brother." It wasn't a question.

"Yes."

"You have to persuade her to go where she needs to go. She can't stay here, feeding on us. She liked flowers, so we take her flowers, but they don't satisfy her. You're blood, you can help her."

"No," but it was true, wasn't it? That was Bex all over, always running, always angry, never satisfied, turning her anger outwards and expecting people to simply carry it for her. He had a sudden image of her at the centre of a spreading pool of black, clinging liquid, starting at her house and gradually widening, covering the village, soaking everyone in it. A tendril had reached out to him because of a groove worn between him and Bex by their history, but how far could it reach eventually? How much sleep could she steal? How many dreams could she infect?

How many people could she hurt?

"I don't know what to do," he said.

"Love her," said the woman. "And persuade her to stop running."

Persuade her to stop running, Hollister thought when he arrived back at the house. *So easy to say, but how the fuck do I do it?* They didn't know Bex, didn't know the impossibility of changing her mind once it was set. If she had decided to run, to avoid the light, then she would run forever rather than change direction. She hadn't liked Dee, and nothing had changed her mind about that; hated it that he and Dee had talked about children, not because she thought that they would be bad parents but simply because she, Bex, didn't like children. Hollister had always denied it in the arguments with Dee, but suspected in his secret thoughts that Bex hated the idea of him and Dee starting a family so much because it would mean he wasn't as available for her.

My sister was selfish, he thought, the first time he had ever really allowed himself to think it. *Selfish, and shallow, and manipulative, but she was my sister and I loved her. I still love her.*

The evening was quiet. Bex didn't ring again and the thought that she was sulking because he hadn't answered her earlier calls, that she was a sulking ghost, made him smile, although it was a smile that felt weighted with tears.

He drank the wine that had survived his dropping it and ate some of the bread and bacon, chewing mechanically and not really tasting what he swallowed. He found the power cable for Bex's phone and charged it up, half wondering if he might be able to ring her on it, and then dismissed the idea; this would, as with everything else, be done to Bex's timetable. Instead, he read through some of the piles of paperwork, casting most of it into a bag for disposal.

Most were bills, their payment dates long gone, which he put on one side to see if they had been paid or not. There were leaflets and flyers, magazines still in their plastic sheaths about flower arranging and home making, brochures for local fast food delivery services, the detritus of months of deliveries. In one pile, he found a collection of letters tied together with a black ribbon; when he started to read them, he found that they were from a man he had never heard of. He stopped reading after looking over a couple of them because they were full of sexual innuendo and it felt as though he was snooping, opening up something private that should remain closed.

Sometime around midnight, Hollister went into to the kitchen to get himself a glass of water before sleep. Peering at the reflection of his face in the window over the sink, he saw himself pale and thin, his eyes droplets of ink on alabaster skin. *Here I am again*, he thought and then saw the glow in the garden.

There was a light coming from the far end of the lawn, fracturing apart his reflection, washing out his face and replacing it with the gaunt outlines of tangled grass and plants left to grow without attention. The glow filled the space in front of his eyes, brighter and brighter, fingers of light reaching out to him. Hollister pressed his face against the glass, cupping his hands around his eyes to try and see more clearly, but had to turn away because of the intensity of it. In the moment before he turned away, there seemed to be a figure at the centre of the glare, tiny and dark and moving forwards. He turned, expecting to see Bex, or to hear his phone ring, but there was nothing, and when he looked back, both the light and the figure had vanished.

Hollister didn't fall asleep but lay on the bed in Bex's room thinking. *It was a cliché, wasn't it? Dead people and bright lights? But just because it was a cliché didn't mean there wasn't some truth there, surely?*

Was Bex avoiding the light? Clinging to life, reaching out in dreams and through his phone, desperately trying to hold on to him, to someone, to something so that she wouldn't be dead? He could imagine her doing that, refusing to accept her situation, fighting it, making everyone else suffer just to help her achieve what she wanted, no matter how impossible. And where did that leave him? There was no way he could change things, he didn't think; he had never been able to change her mind about anything when she was alive, so why should things be different when she was dead?

Hollister wondered why it mattered to him, to get Bex to go into the light. For her own good? Maybe. To know he had helped her do this last thing? Maybe. She was his sister and he cared about her, yes, but he was, if he was honest, angry at her. She had placed strains on him and Dee that they had not survived, caused his parents all sorts of stresses and miseries, and yet always seemed to emerge from these situations as though nothing had happened; perhaps now he had a chance, a final chance, to give his sister the kind of peace she had constantly refused herself in life. She had set herself against the light, and would stay set against it as long as she could, which left only one option as far as he could see.

He would have to trick her.

The screaming started at thirteen minutes past two.

It was coming from downstairs, ragged whoops and cries of pain and terror. Hollister thought he recognised Bex's voice in the screams but couldn't be sure, so torn and split were they. He looked at his watch, remembering what the coroner's report had said; that Bex had been dead for perhaps six or seven hours when the postman found her at almost nine in the morning. Was this her death he was listening to? Some nightly recreation of her last moments? He went to the bedroom door, listening. The screams continued, hoarse, wordless.

I am not afraid, he told himself, *because she is my sister*. Then, taking a deep breath, he stepped out and looked down the stairs.

There was nothing there.

What had he expected, he wondered, as another scream tore the air? The spectral image of his dying sister? Bex shrieking and glimmering and holding out her hands, a ghost on the phone. Perhaps she could text him, Dear Bro I'm Dead Help me Thnx.

I'm going mad, he thought, and started down the stairs. He was halfway down when his phone rang. The noise, so normal, sounded shrill in the night-time darkness of the house, its forced jollity jolting Hollister, making him jump. He fumbled it from his pocket, looking at the display. It read simply, SIS. He looked back up at the house's upper floor, knowing that Bex's phone was in the bedroom he had just come from. His phone rang again and he pressed the button to connect to the call.

"Richard, are you there?" Bex said.

"I'm here," he said, and she sounded so scared, so distant, her voice echoing and repeating, that he sat down, his legs suddenly nerveless and weak. Light was beginning to bleed out from under the kitchen door, spreading in pallid streaks across the floor.

"He's coming, Richard," Bex said. "He nearly caught me but I hid, but he keeps finding me."

"Who?"

"The boy," she said.

"Come to me, Bex," said Hollister. He used the bannister to stand, keeping the phone by his ear, watching the kitchen door. The light was growing brighter, strips of it growing up along the jambs, the edge of the hinges silhouetted, casting angular shadows. The door began to open, more light falling out.

"Bex?" Hollister said and then she was in front of him, stepping out across the hallway towards him. The light was tautening, brightening, filling the doorway behind her. She looked back over her shoulder, her face drawn, her mouth twisting down. Her arms were out towards Hollister, her hands empty, and her voice crackled in his phone again, "Richard, help me."

"I will, Bex," he said. "Look at me, just look at me."

She looked back around, peering at Hollister. Her face was pale, her skin the colour of whey, her legs and hands streaked with darkness. In the centre of the light behind her, a black shape was coalescing, thickening just above the floor. Bex moaned as though she could feel it and Hollister said again, "Look at me, Sis, just keep looking at me. It'll be okay Sis, there's no need to be frightened."

The light carried on expanding, filling the hallway, blurring Bex's edges as she moaned again. Hollister could see nothing past Bex now, the kitchen doorway and the room beyond lost to the brightness. The black mark in the light's centre was growing, resolving itself into the shape of a child standing behind Bex with its arms outstretched.

"Richard!" she cried and stepped towards him.

"Stay still, Bex. Stay still and stop running. You don't belong here, you belong there." Hollister was crying now, seeing his sister properly for the first time in three years, remembering her face and her laugh, remembering the tiny kindness she sometimes committed, the time she had turned up with a bottle of whisky for him, the time she had called him and made him laugh telling him filthy jokes.

"Richard," she said again and the child behind her moved closer, the light knitted together into the shape of a boy, a toddler who was naked and chubby. His hands, fingers opening and closing, fastened on to her leg and she shrieked, kicking back.

"Don't be frightened," Hollister said. "Go into the light, Sis, go with it. Let it take you where you need to be. I love you, Rebecca," and he was no longer crying, he was weeping, tears falling from his cheeks, slicking the hand holding the phone, and his voice was thick and near-unintelligible.

Bex shrieked and the child pulled at her, tugging her back inexorably towards the doorway. The light flared more brightly, dissolving the two figures in the hallway into little more than wavering shadows, printing afterimage puppets across Hollister's eyelids. The phone in his hand, always Bex's preferred method of communication, wailed, the noise wavering and then dwindling forlornly. For a moment, she surged out of the light towards him, her hands out and her mouth open wide. One last, wrenching cry came from the phone and now it was coming from Bex as well, piercingly loud, full of anger and fear and then it, too, collapsed and she was gone, slipping back into the glare.

"I love you," Hollister said, and dropped the now-silent phone to the floor.

Ahead of him, the light folded in on itself, circling around to nothing, leaving only streaked shadows in its wake. The house settled and then relaxed, and only his tears remained

"I love you," he said for a third time, and then, "Rest easy, Sis."

He thought that would be the end of it, but it wasn't.

There was something wrong, he thought, something that didn't fit. He had done what was needed, the last thing he could do for her, helping her to accept and go into the light. Hadn't he? Only, he told himself later, sitting at the kitchen table with a coffee and peering into the garden as dawn crept across the edges of the world, she had never accepted it, not even right at the end when she was already within the light. She had fought and fought against it, clinging on as tightly as she could to whatever kind of existence she could grasp, but why? Why was she so determined to avoid the light?

Unless it wasn't the light she had been avoiding, but the thing the light contained; unless she was avoiding the child. 'The boy', she had kept saying, she was avoiding the boy.

Why should Bex be frightened of a child? Hollister wondered and then thought, as the world pitched beneath his feet, that he might know.

He retrieved the letters from the pile in the lounge and flicked through them; the last, dated not long after Bex moved to Chapter

Bank, was brusque, saying simply that if Bex refused to reply to letters or calls then the writer could only assume she no longer wanted to see him. He thought of the screams and gasps he had heard from the kitchen, the crying, and imagined blood lying across the cheap tiled floor, and sweat and pain and fear.

Hollister walked out into the garden. In the pre-dawn light, the air was chill and raised gooseflesh across his arms. The glow he had seen through the window had been coming from the far border, he remembered, and it didn't take him long to dig down and find the bones. He wanted to believe the child had been born dead, but he knew it hadn't. It had been born alive and buried holding its arms out for its mother, and his sister had spent the next years hiding and running and pretending that the world outside the walls of her home didn't exist.

Bex's dead child had come for her, born by light, and Hollister had forced her into its arms and told her he loved her even as she burned in the child's embrace.

He sat in the garden and wept, brushing dirt from the tiny bones, and all around him the light of a world that would never be bright again filled the sky.

Campbell's Degradation:

Teeth lose their rigidity and become plastic, often changing their shape numerous times over short periods. Treatment involves the application of heat followed by the removal and destruction of the infected teeth.

The Fourth Horse

"Hey, stop!" Atkins called, and started across the road towards the battered Land Rover. Although the driver's window was open, the crook of a tanned and brawny arm showing, the vehicle didn't slow down and Atkins had to run to catch it as it moved away from the kerb. He came up alongside the horsebox and was going to bang on the side when he saw, lost in the African shadows of its interior, a large chestnut horse. Not wanting to startle the animal, he jogged faster, the sweat trickling down his brow. Reaching the rear of the Land Rover, he banged on the roof, calling, "Hey," again.

This time, the vehicle jerked to a halt in a gritted and rusty squeal of brakes. Atkins stopped, taking a deep breath of air that was too warm to refresh him, leaning over slightly and resting his hand on the roof of the vehicle. The once-white metal was hot enough to hurt his palm.

"What?" said the driver, leaning out of the window and peering at Atkins. He was younger than Atkins, with skin the tanned ochre of someone who spent a lot of time outdoors, and his face glistened with sweat. His voice was ex-pat English, the original accent, from somewhere in the Midlands Atkins thought, threaded with the cadences of Africa. Atkins wondered if he sounded similar, his own Welsh lilt corrupted by the alien rhythms of his adopted country, and suspected it did. The years were blurring his edges, he thought, unmaking him and creating something new.

"What?" asked the driver again. Atkins sucked in another breath, as airless as the first, and replied.

"You've got a pipe loose," he said, "underneath. It'll tear loose if you carry on driving on these roads."

"Fuck," said the driver conversationally, and climbed out of the vehicle. He was taller than Atkins, bigger up and across and layered with muscle. Atkins took an automatic step back, removing himself from the man's shadow and out of his reach. His size was intimidating, his solidity casting pitch shadows across the vehicle's interior. The man saw Atkins' discomfort and smiled, revealing even, white teeth. His smile was friendly, open, and seemed to shrink him down to a more manageable size.

"Thank you," the driver said, crouching and looking under the Land Rover, and then "Fuck," again.

"Is it bad?" a new voice asked, female. Atkins looked over the bonnet of the vehicle to see a tall, slender woman emerge from the passenger seat. She was as tanned as the driver, her hair bleached a straw blonde by the sun and her eyes a faded blue. She smiled at Atkins and then disappeared from view as she, too, crouched. Atkins bent down by the man, pointing unnecessarily at the pipe that was dangling loose behind the radiator. Fat liquid dripped from the torn maw of the pipe, pooling darkly on the pitted road.

"Oil cooler," said the driver and rose. Atkins followed. Across the road, three of Colonel Nicholas' soldiers, dressed in ill-fitting uniforms and with weapons hanging at their hips or over their backs, were looking at them disinterestedly. One of them looked barely old enough to shave, but held his AK-47 with a practised ease. There was a barracks nearby, an outpost from the larger detachment in Kabwebwe, and the soldiers were on rotation from there. They changed every few weeks, although there had been more of them over the previous months, their number increasing slowly and steadily.

"Can you fix it?" asked the woman, also rising, her head appearing in the frame of the passenger window like a straw sun.

"No," said the man. "I've got spare oil but I can't repair the pipe."

"Fuck," said the woman. "We need to get him there, Mark. We only have three days." She looked over at the soldiers, who were still staring across at them. One of them smiled at her and she smiled back with her lips but not her eyes.

"I know that, Victoria," said the man, Mark. "I'm aware of our deadline, but this gentleman's right; if we drive like this, at best we'll break down and at worst we'll burn out the engine in the middle of fucking nowhere."

"There's a supplier in Chingola," said Atkins, "that'll probably have the pipe, but it'll take a day, maybe two, for them to get it here I'd imagine. Where are you going to?"

"I'm Mark, and this is Victoria," said Mark, holding out his hand and ignoring Atkins' question. "And you are?"

"Atkins," Atkins said, taking Mark's hand and shaking it. It was warm and dry.

"Just Atkins?" asked Victoria over the Land Rover's bonnet.

"Richard," said Atkins, letting Mark's hand go. "But everyone calls me Atkins."

"I think," said Victoria, "that I may call you Richard. 'Atkins' sounds very impolite. So, Richard," she continued, walking around the vehicle and coming to stand next to the two men, "what do you do?"

"That's why I was looking at you, because of the horsebox," said Atkins. "I own a gymkhana a few miles from here."

The inhabitant of the horsebox was one of the most beautiful horses Atkins had seen, almost as tall as him at the shoulder, chestnut around its head and forelegs, dappling to a light tan over its haunches. It was a contrary one, though, and at first wouldn't move from the horsebox, remaining motionless even when Victoria took hold of its bridle and pulled.

"Should I help?" Atkins asked.

"No, thank you," said Victoria. "He's being difficult to make a point but he'll come because he knows who his bosses are. He's called Ore, and he's bred from German stock." She tugged again at the lead and finally the horse began to move, stepping delicately down the ramp at the rear of the box and onto the ground.

"Strange name," said Atkins, walking ahead of the woman and the horse to one of the empty stables. Behind him, he heard the measured clip of the horse's hooves as they struck the concrete floor. It seemed very loud, somehow drowning out the sound of his own feet and those of the woman. The sun, behind them now, cast the shadow of the horse's head on the ground in front of him so that it appeared to be entering the stable block first, surrounding him. Elongated, the shadow of Ore's ears curved up like horns emerging from a head the size and shape of an enormous cockroach.

"It's kind of a joke," said Victoria. "His full name is much longer and harder to say, and very old, so we called him Ore because we got him from a mine in Kitwe." She walked Ore into the stable as Atkins poured water into a bucket for the animal and pulled in some straw from the bale in the corridor. In a stall opposite one of the others, probably Chime Bar, snorted quietly and stamped his feet. Ore stood quietly as Victoria removed his bridle. She didn't stroke or talk to him, Atkins saw, touching the animal as little as possible. The horse didn't move at all, showing no interest in the woman or his surroundings or the feed that Atkins offered him. Finally, Victoria backed out of the stall and closed the wooden half door. Strips of leather, tied into the animal's platted mane, swayed on either side of his neck as he finally turned to look at Victoria over the stable door. Another, thicker strip was threaded through his tail and he had what looked like bracelets tight around his fetlocks, something Atkins had never seen before, and he wondered if it was a custom local to Kitwe.

"He's very beautiful," he said as Victoria slid the bolt across to fasten the door.

"Is he?" she said. "I wouldn't know. He's just something I have to deliver."

After settling Ore, Atkins drove Victoria back to where Mark was waiting with their Land Rover. They arrived to find him in the middle of a small crowd of soldiers, trying to explain why he was waiting on Mayondo's only street.

"You were seen earlier," Atkins heard one of the soldiers say as he and Victoria pulled up behind the wounded vehicle.

"Stay here," said Atkins, turning off the engine and opening his door to climb out.

"No," said Victoria and climbed out after him.

"Hello, Sergeant M'Buzu," said Atkins. Mark, taller than the men around him, shot Atkins a glance, the expression on his face impossible to read. "Is there a problem?"

M'Buzu was the head of the barracks in Mayondo, and although Atkins disliked him, he had been careful to cultivate something that might appear to be friendship with the man, if neither of them looked too closely.

"Mr Atkins!" said M'Buzu, his voice cheerful with the hollow *bon homie* that surrounded the aggression at his centre like dough around a lump of ragged stone. "Do you know this man? My men tell me he has been lurking here all day, making calls from the payphone in the bar. He is up to no good, we think."

"Hardly lurking, if I've been out in the open," said Mark but Atkins shushed him. One of the other soldiers, one of the new ones that Atkins didn't know, stepped forward and knocked Mark in the chest with his rifle, pushing him back against the Land Rover. Mark winced but stayed, thankfully, silent.

"Perhaps it is a clever trick, to pretend not to be lurking when you in fact you are?" asked M'Buzu, his voice dangerously conversational. "And who is this with you, Mr Atkins?"

"This is Victoria," said Atkins, his tone dismissive, *This is men's work, pay no attention to her,* and hoped that Victoria would understand. She remained quiet, and he was grateful. Already, several of the soldiers had moved their attention from Mark to her, were eying her like the lions that he sometimes saw staring at him when he rode Chime Bar out from the gymkhana and into the open bush beyond his home. He had learned to judge when the lions had fed, knowing when it was safe to continue or whether he should turn and retreat before entering their killing zone; he wished he had learned the same trick with humans, whose lusts and drives he remained unable to judge. Their eyes were on her, crawling and lingering.

"These people are my customers, sergeant, but their transport hasn't stood up to our roads" Atkins said, trying to make his voice calm and business-like. *Look at me,* he wanted to say, *look at me and forget the woman and the suspicions that you don't have, but whose existence you're using as an excuse for your aggression.* All that violence, simmering in the African afternoon, clad in khaki and smelling of sweat and dust and gun oil and baking earth, and somehow he had found himself in the middle of it. He held out a placatory hand to the sergeant, the edge of a folded Kwacha poking out from his thumb and palm. "I'm sure you and your men must be thirsty, it's a hot day. Please, have a drink on me, and I'll help my guests get on their way."

"You have to be tough out here, eh? Africa is not kind to you if you underestimate her, her roads or her wildlife, yes?" said M'Buzu, shaking Atkins' hand and removing the note in a single gesture, clapping him on the shoulder with his other hand. "Customers, yes? Are you sure? She is a looker, my friend! Perhaps you hope to be her customer? I'll bet you have to pay her, my friend, although not too much, eh? Not too much!"

Atkins felt Victoria tense beside him and spoke before she could say anything. "Ha, sergeant! She is out of both our price ranges, I suspect, but we can dream, no?" He heard himself mirror M'Buzu's hearty tone and careful speech patterns, heard the soldiers laugh around him and felt himself begin to relax even while he disliked himself for playing the game. The note, spirited away now into a pocket somewhere in M'Buzu's fatigues, had bought them peace.

"My friend Mr Atkins has explained," said M'Buzu loudly, peering around his men. His face had a clumsy, too-false expression of understanding on it, a bad actor playing a poorly-written part. "There is nothing for our concern here." With a final, hard stare that took in Atkins, Victoria and Mark, M'Buzu walked off across the street, his boots dragging tiny zephyrs of sand and dust with them. His soldiers followed, most throwing looks back at Atkins and especially Victoria as they went. He did not completely relax until they had all disappeared into the darkness of the nameless tavern fifty yards down the street.

"Thank you," said Mark after they had gone. "I've been here all this time, years now, but I've never got used to it."

"It's just Africa," said Atkins. Most expats understood that, the phrase they used to convey their helplessness in the face of corruption and violence and poverty and heat and dirt and brutality. *It's just Africa*, and walk away and don't rise to it and lock the doors between you and it and look at each other knowingly and say again, *It's just Africa* on a kind of disgusted, downbeat exhalation. Africa, in the hands of people who had no idea, control slipping away from the old masters to the new, and wouldn't it be better if things could be different?

"Yes," said Mark, with the same tone "Just Africa."

"They're getting worse," said Victoria, and spat into the dust at her feet.

"Yes," said Mark again, and then after a moment, he added, "but not for much longer."

Night came quickly, as ever, slipping across the land and swallowing the ground beneath it voraciously. When it came to the gymkhana, it spread itself around the stable block, Atkins' small home and the various utility buildings, held back by the light falling from the kitchen windows and the lamps that he had strung out along the fencing to keep the night's predators away. He looked out at the block now, wondering about the strange day he had had. Ore was the club's first new horse for over a year, joining its three long-standing residents, only two of whom Atkins received payment for. The third, Chime Bar, was his horse, a rescue from a farmer out in one of the provinces who had found the animal abandoned in one his fields one morning but couldn't afford to keep it. The Kwacha that Mark had given Atkins, currently piled loosely on the table and held down under a pepper mill, would pay for feed for Chime Bar for several weeks.

If there was something that Atkins loved most about his life in

Zambia, it was the African night. It was absolute, crowding in on his meagre lights with cathedral vastness, spreading out and absorbing everything about it. It was so different, umbrella black and greater than anything he had experienced in Wales. If he were to go outside, he would hear it as well, hear a silence that was stately in its solidity, punctured only by the distance cries of nocturnal animals and horses in the stables whinnying and moving. Safe in the fragile bubble of his home, he marvelled at it, distant and deep.

One of the lamps on the far fence went out.

It wasn't unusual. Atkins had wired the lamps himself and the bulbs, cheap African things, went often. What was strange, though, was when the next bulb along went just after the first, leaving the end of the stable block nearest the fence in a pool of darkness. Another bulb blew, and then another, a chain reaction that spread quickly along the fence as he watched. For a few moments, the stables were outlined in brutalist shapes and then the lights behind them must have failed as well, and the building was lost to the night. He looked up the ceiling light above him, which flickered slightly as though teetering on the edge of collapsing, and then flared back to life. Looking back at the window, he saw himself reflected in the glass and was uncomfortably aware of the fact that anyone out in the darkness would be able to see him clearly. He thought about the money on his table, and the soldiers who had heard him tell M'Buzu about customers and payment, about greed and violence. Then he went and turned the lights off.

The night had made its way to the other side of the glass. In it, he could made out the faded shapes of the stables and the huts that contained the generator and his tools, but little else. There were uncountable stars above him, scattered across the heights of the sky, but they shed little light. He peered out, trying to spot movement, but saw nothing. If it was burglars, they would attack soon; home invasions were swift and blood-stained and often ended in flames that scoured the earth clean of evidence. He made no attempt to find a weapon, reasoning that any resistance increased the chances of being killed. The best he could hope for was that whoever it was would break in, tie him up and the take the money and leave; he didn't want to contemplate any of the worse scenarios.

As he waited, Atkins heard a low stuttering moan that rapidly rose in pitch until it became a shriek, layered and atonal. It was like the hooting of the klaxons heard through a storm, but the air was calm and the nearby the bushes still. Another sound joined it, a staccato tattoo like fat sticks beating brittle ones, faster and faster until it became one blended noise. Atkins peered through the window, seeing only gunpowder shades of night, hearing only that which made window itself shiver slightly.

Within the cacophony, Atkins thought he heard the ragged whinnying of horses.

"Jes-sus," he exhaled, and wanted to go to the loved animals that were his livelihood, but he dared not. He was old, frightened of the people out there who were making his horses nicker, and he wanted to live. Instead of moving, he watched, expecting any moment to see the darting movements of people approaching the house.

They did not come.

The noise rose, all fractured siren wails and savage battering. Over in the stables, the horses were screaming, he thought, screaming in voices that were almost human. He had only ever heard horses cry like that once before, when the stables of his childhood home had burned along with every animal within. Then, the shrieks had torn the Welsh night apart. To forget the smell of charring hair and horseflesh was impossible; for years, he saw in nightmares the frenzied whirling of the creatures in their stalls as the flames beat back his father and brother, preventing them from opening the doors for escape.

This was worse. There were no flames; there was simply the howl itself and the night around it and then, finally, something moved near the stables. Whatever it was, he shouldn't have been able to see it; no light remained, and yet he did see it, a blacker patch against the darkness, roiling out from the stable in spastic lurches. There were no details for his eyes to catch, only the contractions of the thing as it squeezed itself out from the building, the upper half of the door bending out to an angle that Atkins would have sworn was impossible. The noise increased, if that was possible, raging against the glass in front of him, formless and torn.

What was emerging from the stable finally loosed itself from the door, falling to the ground where it flipped over and scuttled towards the house. It seemed to grow as it came, and although blacker than the evening around it, part of it glowed as though lit from within by guttering embers. Atkins couldn't tell its shape, only that as it came it swelled, that it had eyes that gleamed blackly and that it danced as it moved, jittering and capering. It covered the ground from the stables quickly, rising up so that it blotted out the stars above, towering above the house and still the bellowing came, Chime Bar and the other horses screaming and screaming, and something began to chuckle, sulphurous and low. "I'm lost," Atkins breathed to himself, sure that whatever it was, it was the last thing he would see. The laughter became louder, loose and shifting, not drowning the horses' panic but somehow magnifying it; Atkins closed his eyes and waited for his end.

After a few moments passed, and nothing happened except the continuing noise, Atkins couldn't help himself. He opened his eyes and it was there, filling the window, pulsating on the other side of the glass as though pressed against the side of the house, smothering it. Thickening liquid flesh was churning against the window, one moment covered in hair and the next naked, now scaled and now feathered, lips emerging briefly only to sink back and be replaced by eyes that blinked and glared. The air smelled of burning stone and dust and steam gone sour, the odour filling the room in fetid waves. It pressed ever closer against the window, and the glass shuddered and bulged, and still the horses shrieked, and then the thing fell back. The sound of it changed, the chuckle giving way to a noise like the grinding of teeth, and the house shook once, as though the thing had given the building a swift, savage shake. A blue pitcher in one of the cupboards near Atkins fell over and shattered and the kitchen table jerked, the pile of Kwacha fluttering loose as the pepper mill weighting them down fell over and rolled away. Atkins' beer bottle slipped from his fingers and broke on the floor, sending shards of glass and warm beer spattering around his feet. A metallic crash came from one of the other rooms. The thing at the window writhed around and was gone.

~

There was a charcoal-hued cobra on the road, just on the far side of the gymkhana gate, battered flat and surrounded by a halo of blood and intestines and loose scales like confetti after a wedding. Atkins found it, along with all the other dead animals, as he walked around the club the next morning, avoiding entering the stables. The horses had neighed for hours, finally tailing off during the night's lowest point, and all around the buildings that living abyss had pranced and jabbered. Sometimes, it disappeared from Atkins' vision, but he could hear it chortling and sniggering and feel the earth under his feet vibrate as it leapt and landed. Even after the horses had fallen silent, it had carried on, only ceasing before dawn. His last view of it had been as it squeezed itself back into the stable, pouring itself like oil into the building as the sunlight crept across the horizon.

Atkins had set a fire in a brazier behind the generator shed and he scraped up the remains of the snake and added it to the blaze, where it crackled with greasy flames. Other animals were already burning, the ones he had been able to carry. Outside the fence, which the thing had left untouched, the bushes and the ground beyond were battered down and torn. Larger creatures lay among the broken branches and foliage and once dry earth, two zebra and a duiker the only ones he recognised. Others were merely torn and bloodied piles of flesh, white fragments of bone emerging from the ruins like accusatory fingers. The destruction ran in a swathe around the club, a wide circle of torn earth that stretched several hundred yards, dotted with the carcasses of animals that had been caught beneath the dark thing as it landed, and marked here and there with indentations that might have been the prints of clawed feet or suckered tentacles or something else entirely. Atkins walked it, trying to read meaning into the marks, but could find none; he felt numb, both physically and emotionally, as though he was observing himself from a long way off and through layers of glass that were scratched and muddied. Building the fire, picking up or dragging those animals that weren't too large, kicking dirt over bloodstains that, if left, would attract the daylight predators, all these things he had done with the automaton movements of the rootless men he sometimes saw in Kitwe, drunk or in a place beyond drunk, and a long way from any kind of reality. *It's Africa,* he told to himself bitterly, *just Africa, the place where the impossible can happen, where brutality and beauty walk hand in hand. Just Africa.* Finally, when he could put it off no longer, he walked to the stables.

His horses were still alive, just.

Chime Bar lay on his side, his breath coming in ragged, foamy bursts. Blood spatters ran up the walls of the stall around him, and urine and shit were strewn across the floor. His legs were covered in scratches and crusting rips; one of them was clearly broken. Thick strings of saliva tinged a ropey pink oozed from his nose and as Atkins looked at him over the stall door, he rolled his eyes, the whites bloodshot and inflamed. In the next stall, Siesta Glow was standing, but each of his legs was damaged and he had a series of cuts across both his head and flanks, as though he had tried to batter his way out of the stall. Atkins supposed he had. Opposite, Enzo had his head out over his door, his mouth dropped open to reveal bloodied teeth and a tongue that he had bitten through. Dribbles of blood hung from his lips and dropped lazily to the floor.

Beyond them, Ore stood in his stall, unharmed and motionless.

"I'm sorry," said Victoria from behind Atkins, making him jump, although not much. His reactions were slower, less taut than usual.

"What is he?" asked Atkins, looking at Ore, at the way the horse's eyes trailed both him and Victoria, its mane swaying under the weight of the woven leather strips.

"At the moment, he's a horse," said Victoria, placing a softly golden hand on Atkins' upper arm, caressing him gently. "I'm sorry, we didn't know this could happen. Mark and I will cover any costs that this causes, vet's fees or compensation. Here, I'll help you clear up and get the horses sorted."

"Vet's fees," repeated Atkins, looking again at Chime Bar. He felt tears well in his eyes, felt the weight of what he had to do press down on him. "No. I have something in the house that I can give him that'll end his suffering. Siesta Glow and Enzo may be okay, but Chime Bar's – "and then he was crying and couldn't carry on.

"Yes," said Victoria, "that's maybe best."

"I should give some to him," Atkins managed, nodding at Ore, his sobs hitching in his chest.

"You wouldn't get close," said Victoria. "If I couldn't stop you, he certainly would."

"What is he?" asked Atkins again, but Victoria merely shook her head and said, "Let's get the horses sorted."

It was late afternoon by the time they had the stables cleaned and the horses dealt with, and the sunlight was the slanting yellow of a tired day. The vet, a sallow, taciturn man called Pesters, treated Siesta Glow and Enzo and had taken Chime Bar's body with him; Atkins wanted to hope that his horse would be afforded some kind of burial but he knew that he wouldn't. Instead, his flesh might be sold for meat, or simply dumped away from the town where the wildlife would consume him at their leisure. *Just Africa*, thought Atkins again, as he watched Pesters drive away, Chime Bar's head lolling over the tailboard of his flatbed truck. It had taken the three of them several hours to drag the animal from the stables and winch him into the truck, and then another hour for Atkins and Victoria to clean the stall and wash away the streaks of blood that Chime Bar had left running along the stable floor. All the time, Ore stared at them, moving only the smallest amounts to keep them in view.

When they had finished, Victoria led Atkins back into his home and sat him down on one of his chrome kitchen chairs. She bent to pick up the Kwacha, still loose on the floor, and put them on the table back under the pepper mill. Then, she took two Mosi Lagers from the fridge and opened them, giving one to Atkins and sitting opposite him with the other. As she walked past him to sit down, she trailed one hand over his shoulder and then brushed his cheek lightly.

"He can't stay here," said Atkins eventually. "I don't know what he is, I don't want to know, but you have to take him away."

"We can't," said Victoria. "The Land Rover won't be fixed until tomorrow, and we'll take him then. Mark will come before nightfall, and we'll make sure that it doesn't happen again. Please." She leaned forward and placed her beer on the table, reaching out to take one of his hands. He took another mouthful of his beer and looked out of the window. The sun had stripped the sky to a rich, angry red now; nightfall wasn't far away. Victoria rubbed her thumb slowly across his palm, the nail tracing delicate lines towards his fingers, and said, "It's only another night." She had a mixed scent like night-perfuming flowers, gardenias, cereus and jasmine.

"No," said Atkins, feeling the pressure of her hand and fingers as a maddening tickle.

"We can take him tomorrow, we'll be gone for good and you'll never see us again, I promise. Unless you want to," Victoria said, leaning forward. The neckline of her top bowed away from her skin, revealing the top of her bra, a froth of delicate lace swirls. "We only need to deliver him, and then it's done."

"Deliver him? Who to?"

"Corporal Nicholas," said Victoria.

"You must have seen how it's been going?" she asked Atkins, still stroking his palm and leaning forward so that the upper edges of her smooth breasts and lavender bra showed even more . "How Zambia's following the other African countries? How many soldiers were there in Mayondo when you came here? When did you come here?"

"Five years ago. I took early retirement from the mine to set this place up."

"What was it like then? The town, I mean?"

"Quiet. Small. There was a garrison here then but it was only about 10 soldiers, and we hardly ever saw them except when they came to get drunk or play football."

"And now?"

Atkins didn't answer. Mayondo had changed, it was true, but it was only as he thought about it that he realised how much.

"How much has this country rotted? Since Colonel Nicholas' coup?"

"It wasn't a coup," said Atkins, helplessly, feeling that he was being talked back into the corner of a room whose walls he couldn't see but could feel pressing about him.

"Wasn't it? A sudden doubling of the army numbers? A doubling again after that? New garrisons? Places like this suddenly jumping from ten soldiers a garrison to sixty? A hundred? New weapons? New uniforms? And who controls them, Richard? Ultimately? The president, or Colonel Nicholas?"

"It's not a coup," said Atkins, watching a bead of sweat trickle down Victoria's neck and into the shadowed valley between her breasts. The side of his beer bottle trickled condensation over his fingers in sympathy.

"Maybe not an obvious one," said Victoria, placing her other hand on his leg. He glanced down at it, tanned and firm over his knee, the nails short and unpainted. Working hands. "No battles, no bloodshed, but the Colonel's the man in charge now in all but name. Only there has been bloodshed, hasn't there?"

Victoria's other hand had started moving now, and she leaned forwards further so that she could stroke Atkins thigh. More of her laced bra showed in the cleft that was exposed by her bowing top, and she licked her lips as she looked up at Atkins and continued speaking.

"Who's controlling the soldiers now? No one. Your friend M'Buzu, for instance? Who makes sure the bastard behaves himself?"

"He's not my friend," said Atkins.

"No, and he's not completely controlled either, which is how Nicholas wants it. A series of local fiefdoms where the only rules are what the commander decides; where that commander has almost total freedom. Rapes and burglaries, assaults, murders, they're all up, and the only absolute is that Nicholas is commander in chief, and his peccadilloes are law. Have you ever had trouble? Been attacked? I mean you're out here alone, miles from Mayondo with just the wildlife and the dust and the horses for company." Victoria's voice, which had becoming strident, fell at the mention of the horses. Her hand, crawling ever further up his leg, stirring in maddening rubs, stopped momentarily before starting again, each back and forth movement carrying it slightly higher.

Atkins thought of his fears the night before, of the home invasions and drunken savagery he read and heard about, of his friend Prescott who had been stamped so viciously in a fight not of his making that the image of an army boot's sole had been printed across his face in old bruises for weeks afterwards, and said "No."

"Why?"

Atkins didn't answer; it was a question he avoided even though he knew the answer.

"Horses," said Victoria, and now her hand was clutching as it rubbed, the tips of her fingers brushing his crotch at the apex of each circular brush, harder and harder. "You survive untouched because Colonel Nicholas likes horses, and the men, M'Buzu knows it. But most people don't have horses, do they? They don't have anything Nicholas likes, except maybe money or blood, or a body he can use. He never comes out further than Kitwe, he doesn't need to, because he hears, and reaches out and acts without ever moving. There may not have been a coup, but there has been a shift in power, you know it, I know it, Mark knows it, every poor sod who's been beaten or raped or had land annexed for the military knows it. You know it, Richard. But Nicholas, he loves his horses, and he likes people who love horses, and Ore is a gift for him. We just need another day to fix the Land Rover and we'll be gone." Her hand gave up all pretence of delicacy and jerked forwards, cupping around his scrotum and holding it in a warmth that was somehow hotter than the dying African day.

"Another day," she repeated, and squeezed gently. "Another night, twelve hours, and we'll be gone. Mark will take care of Ore, and I'll..." she let her voice trail off and started rubbing again, this time moving upwards. Atkins looked at her, at the intensity on her face, at the deep swoop of her breasts and the sweat the trickled down between them. Her tongue flicked out and licked her pink lips.

"We have a chance, but we have to be able to control it," she said. "The summoning binds it for three days, but the binding's getting weaker and it can escape at night. We didn't realise how much damage it can do, but just think. Think! What if that was in Nicholas' compound? What if it was freed, released from the bindings on the third night to do what it wanted? We could be free of him. We could have our country back!"

"Our country?" asked Atkins quietly. "We're guests here, nothing more."

For a second, Atkins thought she would slap him. Her face clenched, and her right hand jerked up as though to lash at him before dropping back. "Guests?" she said. "Guests? Without us, the people here would still be banging rocks together and roasting grubs. Still in the shit. We brought civilisation here."

"And gave Nicholas the guns to make sure everyone acts as civilised as he wants them to be?" asked Atkins.

"It's Africa!" snapped Victoria. "Just fucking Africa! They need us to protect them from themselves!"

"No," said Atkins again. "They need us to treat them like humans. I don't know what Ore is, what you've done, but I can't be a part of it."

"You already are," said Victoria. "You were seen with us, and the horses won't protect you if M'Buzu or someone starts to really think about you. Just a funny old man, living by himself with just the horses for company? If a man can't make love to a woman, what is he good for anymore? You're already in suspicious company, and what if they start to think you're gay? A queer? What if I were to drop into a conversation in town that I tried my hardest to give you the fuck of your life, but you wouldn't because you prefer boys? How long will you last then, Atkins?"

He remained silent, and his silence was answer enough: not long. Whatever protection the horses offered him, whatever carapace of civility M'Buzu wore and made his men wear, it was brittle and weak and liable to shatter at the lightest of pressures. So far, Atkins had maintained his safety by not being noticeable, being as insubstantial in people's memories as gossamer, but what Victoria was threatening would make him solid, would give him an existence he didn't want. Would make him a target. He wondered how long it would be before his tyres were slashed when he went into town, before the whispering started and then the shouts of "faggot" and "queer", before the shops stopped serving him. Before men came to the gymkhana and to his home with violence at the fingertips and on their tongues, and he knew that the answer was the same as before: not damn long.

There was a knock at the door. Atkins went to stand but Victoria simply called, "It's okay, Mark." Mark entered the house, looking at Atkins and Victoria and seeming to take in everything that had happened in one glance. He looked tired and there were streaks of grease and dust across his wrinkled clothes.

"I'm sorry it came to threats," he said. "That was never our intention, please believe us. One more night, and we'll be gone. I just have to bind it more firmly." He gestured to a heavy book he was holding, bound in leather so dark it looked like aged metal. "It's stronger than we thought."

Victoria leaned forward again, although this time she did so without revealing her breasts or bra, and kept her hands crossed over her legs. "I'm sorry too, Richard," she said. "You've been good to us, helped us when you didn't have to. Just help us a little more. Help everyone, let Ore stay. We'll move him tomorrow, take him as a gift to Nicholas and then we'll be gone, out of your hair for good."

"And after?" Atkins asked.

"After Nicholas is dealt with?" she said. "The thing in Ore has a night of freedom, those are the rules. It has one night and then at dawn it'll be gone, back to the place we summoned it from. It's freed in Nicholas' compound, destroys it and him and everything else there, and whatever mess it leaves will be put down to the usual insurrection or infighting or revenge. In the vacuum left by Nicholas' death the government can move quickly, reassert its authority. We can go back to where we were, to being a country that it's good to live in, where we can afford to not be fearful."

Atkins looked from Victoria to Mark and back again, and then nodded, once. What choice did he have, really? Ultimately, it all boiled down to the same thing, power and violence and the threat of violence, no matter who was making the threats. *Just Africa*, he thought. *If you let this blow over you like a dust storm out of the bush, you'll emerge dirtied and scoured raw, but you'll be alive.*

~

Just after nightfall, the horses began to scream again.

Atkins was at his kitchen table, looking again at the piled Kwacha, seeing it soiled and sweating and rank. Under the sound of the horses, he could hear Mark chanting and, taking up the descant, Victoria singing. When he looked through his window towards the stables, the night's opacity was shivering around it as though it was being disturbed by something moving under its surface but which couldn't find the strength to emerge. Finally, a new noise joined the cacophony, a fractured, roiling belch of a noise, furious and frustrated and so great that it made the Mosi Lager bottle in his hand shiver like a palsied infant.

In a life of choices made to remain unseen, Atkins had often wondered what he would do it ever presented with a situation where all of the solutions would make him visible. As he slipped in through the stable door, not making an effort to remain silent because of the noise coming from within the building, he began to understand himself better. *I've been blessed*, he thought, surprised at the sense of dawning revelation the thought gave him. *I was hiding so that I could have this place as long as possible, the gymkhana and the Africa I love beyond it.* Raising the shotgun wasn't hard.

Victoria hadn't really answered his last question, but had instead answered a question he hadn't asked. He imagined the roar of the horses magnified, made huge by the addition of more horses. How many was Nicholas supposed to have in his compound? Twenty? Thirty? Huge numbers, certainly; he collected them the way other men collected old paperbacks or paintings or mistresses. And who else lived in the compound besides Nicholas and his men? Wives, certainly; children, probably. What would they sound like when the thing in Ore got loose? Like the horses? Worse?

Beyond Mark and Victoria, Ore's stall was filled with flapping, with wings or claws or tentacles, with something for which Atkins had no name, long and fat and writhing. It was hoofed and sparks flew like greasy spittle when it hit the walls. Mark's chanting was ragged as he held the book out in front of him and Victoria danced in sinuous waves besides him. *Just Africa*, thought Atkins, and then, *but that's not right, not at all. It's not 'just Africa', it's God's Africa, the most luminous country there is, where the light is brighter and cleaner than any other, and if this place has a problem it's us, with our 'just Africa' and 'we know better' and 'back to what it was', all built on the backs of the poor dead bastards that we thought were in our way or that were somehow less than us.* He looked again at the thing fighting the horse's flesh, trying to escape even as Mark's chanting drove it back in and the other animals screamed around him, and he wondered how much damage it could do here if it got out. Not much, he thought, and sighted along the gun's barrel. It could trample the animals if it wanted, flatten the vegetation and tear the earth, but more plants would grow and the earth would heal and more animals would come.

The gun's explosion was insubstantial in the noise, but Mark's back and chest disintegrated nonetheless. Blood and torn flesh leapt out across the book and the stall beyond it in vivid strings. Victoria screamed and that which had been Ore let out a bellow. Without Mark's chanting restricting it, it was growing, metastasizing, taking a shape that Atkins' eyes couldn't hold on to. It opened its mouth: a tongue slickly massive, anchored in flesh born in some darker place, lolled. Smoke curled from it, clotting around the lights and dimming them. Victoria screamed again as the thing leaped and flowed from the stall towards them. The beautiful woman vanished into it with the sound of hair sizzling in open flames and Atkins had time to think, *Just Africa, just the place I love* and to regret that he wouldn't have the chance to ride a horse or see the golden, burnt-honey light of the African sun again before it was on him, pressing all about him and he was gone.

Qiqirn

Becker wasn't what Pollard expected. He was younger, for one thing, baby-faced and clean-shaven and without a tie, and there was no desk or drawers in the room, just the chairs and a small table that held a jug of water, a box of tissues and a small vase containing a single flower. Becker sat in an easy chair in front of the window and indicated that Pollard should sit in the chair on the other side of the room, a leather wingback that looked old and proved comfortable. He made no notes as they spoke and referred to no paperwork, simply steepling his fingers and looking at Pollard over the spires he had created, listening as Pollard spoke.

It took a while, because at first Pollard found it hard. His voice had dried, catching like dust in his throat, and he drank three glasses of water from the jug as he told Becker about what had happened, about the panic and the running and the cold. About the fear, and the thing that had taken up residence in his home. Becker kept nodding, not interrupting, not moving apart from those little bobs of his head, and when Pollard had finished, he said, "So this has been happening for a few weeks?"

"Months, really," said Pollard. "Building up. The last few weeks have been the worst."

"Tell about the first one again."

Pollard had been coming down his stairs when he first felt it, a prickle across his skin as though something had exhaled along the hallways of the house. Gooseflesh rose on his arms despite the warmth of the day and he shivered, suddenly cold. A quick, reassuring glance told him that the front door was still closed, things were in their places; nothing appeared amiss. So, why was his heartbeat increasing? Getting faster, harder, more urgent? Why was the hair across his body refusing to lie back down, the follicles tightening further so that his skin felt covered by hard little nodules like scales? Why did he feel cold? He took another step, down off the stairs and onto the carpeted floor, uncomfortably aware of the rub of his flesh inside his clothes, of the accelerating movement of his heart, of the way his hand, holding his empty cup, was shaking. What was this? The hallway was empty, the sunlight dropping into it through the open doorway from the kitchen, the house as silent as it had been these last months.

There was something in the kitchen.

As soon as he thought it, Pollard knew it was true. Something was in the kitchen, something awful, hiding just on the other side of the doorway, out of sight and waiting for him. He gasped, unable to help himself, his hand flexing sharply, opening and closing so that he dropped his cup. It bounced on the thick carpet, unharmed, knocking against his foot, and the cold porcelain bite made him scream and the next thing was, he was running.

"And you stopped where?" asked Becker.

"At the end of my path. I was barefoot and I must have trodden on something. It, I don't know, startled me back into myself or something because suddenly I wasn't scared or cold anymore, and I couldn't remember quite why I'd felt the way I had."

"How did you feel?"

"Embarrassed, mostly, in case any of the neighbours saw me; I was only dressed in my pyjamas. They all pity me anyway, and I don't want to give them other reasons to talk about me. The sympathetic looks and little nods of concern are bad enough."

"And when you went back in the house?"

"It was fine. The feeling that something was in the kitchen was gone. Everything was normal." Pollard paused before saying the word normal, and then wondered if Becker had noticed. *What's normal any more*, he thought? *There's no such thing.*

"Good. Mr Pollard, what you're experiencing isn't pleasant, but I can tell you, it is entirely typical. The feelings and reactions you describe are symptomatic of panic attacks and phobic reactions; in your case, although it's unusual, I'd be inclined to treat this as a phobia. Your panic is related to a specific thing, to a fixed point, yes?"

"Yes."

"Each time?"

"Yes. Every time, there's something that frightens me, terrifies me, and it's specific. It's in the kitchen, or the lounge, or the hallway or landing, just out of my sight. I just don't know what it is."

"Then, for all intents and purposes, it's a phobia, and we'll deal with it as such. There are two main ways for dealing with phobias: flooding and graduated hierarchies. Flooding involves, essentially, placing you somewhere with the thing causing your phobia and not letting you leave until you simply can't sustain the panic anymore and you calm down. Quite apart from the fact it's not at all pleasant, it'd be hard to achieve with you because we don't know what specific thing the phobia is focused upon, so that leaves graduated hierarchies. We approach the thing that's causing the feelings small step by small step until you have the ability to deal with it, to not panic anymore."

"That'd be good," said Pollard, remembering the fear he had felt, the sheer terror. "I'd like to not be frightened anymore."

"There'll be homework each week, a new step to take" said Becker, "things for you to think about and come prepared to talk about. This process will be hard work, and will only work if you're honest, you understand?"

"Yes."

"Good. I'll see you next week, and we'll talk a bit more about how these phobic attacks make you feel, what happens to you when they're occurring."

Pollard had risen, was at the door, when Becker said, "And Mr Pollard? I know we've not talked about your wife at all, but we will. Next week, Mr Pollard."

"So, how have things been?"

"Awful," said Pollard, "much worse. I've had three attacks, each worse than before." The office was warm and bright again, Becker in the same place and the same position, everything the same except for the addition of a piece of folded paper on the occasional table, held down by a small glass paperweight. Becker made no mention of the paper.

The worst of the attacks had been the previous evening. Pollard had been making himself a cup of tea when, standing at the counter waiting for the kettle to boil, he suddenly knew that something was behind him. Its head was just at his shoulder, its breath against the back of his neck, cold and fetid. The temperature in the room dropped violently and he shivered, and then he had been at the door, knocking it open and dashing hectic and thoughtless into the hallway, accelerating along it and to the front door and out. Running had been automatic, uncontrollable, driven by something that came before thought, by an unwillingness, a desperation not to see the thing behind him.

"And you stopped running at the end of the path again?

"Yes."

"And when you went back in?"

"Nothing. There was nothing there, no feelings of anything. I made my drink and went to bed."

"Tell me about your wife," Becker said.

"Mary? She died," Pollard said automatically, "seven months ago." His standard response, the emotions practiced out of it.

"I know. Did you love her?"

"Yes. I still do."

"Did you get on well? I mean, were you friends?"

"Yes." Pollard was unsure were the questions were going, where they were taking him. Becker was leaning forwards slightly now, his hands no longer steepled but crossed loosely over his lap.

"Tell me about how the phobia makes you feel."

"Frightened," said Pollard. "Out of control, threatened. In danger."

"Tell me the three things you miss most about Mary."

Pollard didn't answer. Thinking of Mary was hard, painful, but he tried and eventually found things he could verbalise. "Her smell after she'd showered," he said, "it was so clean and fresh and nothing else ever smelled that way. Her laugh, how loud it was, too loud for someone so petite but never intrusive. The way she felt when I held her in bed and we talked."

Becker nodded, as though Pollard had confirmed something for him, and said, "Please read what's on the paper on the table." Pollard picked it up, unfolded it and saw, printed neatly in black, THE ATTACKS WORSENED DURING THE WEEK.

"I'm not showing off," said Becker. "What you're experiencing is awful but it's also understandable and to some degree predictable. I wonder, why did you have to pause before you could tell me the nice things about Mary but not before you told me about how the attacks feel?"

"I don't know."

"I do. It's because the attacks are the most important thing for you now, more important than your wife because they're more real, more immediate. All the good memories of Mary are tangled up with the unpleasant memories of her death; thinking of her pulls up not memories of the good times, but of the bad time, the awful time when she died. Those memories are like scabs covering the things you should be able to remember about her without pausing, the things that should be your primary memories of her, the good times and the happiness and the love. In a funny way, the attacks are healthy because they represent the positive memories trying to reassert themselves, trying to regain their rightful place of importance in your brain. In your life."

"Why are they so frightening?" Pollard said. "Mary wasn't frightening, I loved her. I still love her, I'm not frightened of her."

"No," said Becker, "but you are frightened of remembering her fully, because doing that means facing fully how much you've lost and how that makes you feel. It means facing the rest of your life without her. You're frightened because the way to stop these phobic attacks is to take control back, to face the panic and pain and fear and the terrible memories of Mary's death, peel them away and allow Mary, the memories of Mary and how she made you feel, to regain their rightful place in your mind and your imagination. Those are the steps you have to take to stop this happening. That's where we have to go, together. Next week, Mr Pollard, we talk about how Mary died."

"If the paper says 'had an even worse week'," said Pollard, nodding at the new folded sheet lying on the table, "then it's right." He felt greasy with tiredness; the attacks had been coming almost daily since his last session with Becker, at all times of the day and night. The previous night's had been repellent, leaving him ragged and queasy with terror and tiredness.

Pollard had been half gone, in that state between sleeping and wakefulness, when his whole body spasmed violently. That, in itself, wasn't unusual; it was a lifelong, though occasional, thing, as though he was walking and had tripped. Mary used to laugh about it and say the startled look on his face as he popped awake was one of the funniest things she had seen. This was harder though, almost painful, a savage jerk that yanked him awake. He rolled, tangling himself in the duvet as he went and then thing sitting on the bed next to him shifted, leaned in towards him.

Pollard remembered screaming. He threw himself from the bed, the duvet clinging to him, and fell to the floor. He was cold, terrified, the muscles in his legs jittering spasmodically as he tried to kick away the heavy, tangling duvet, struggling out from under it as behind him something moved across the bed. It was huge, blocking the night's half-light coming in around the edges of the curtains as it came, and then Pollard was free of his bedclothes and he ran without looking back.

He had ended up in his back garden, standing naked at its far end in the shadows of the apple tree that he and Mary had planted when they first moved to the house over thirty years ago. His panic receded in shuddering waves, the world seeming to swim back into reality around him. He was still cold, although not as cold as he had been in the bedroom, and his legs ached from the running but had stopped twitching. Embarrassed, Pollard covered his genitals with his hands and went quickly back down the garden path and into the kitchen. Smells lingered, the residue of his food that evening, a microwave meal from the local supermarket. Suddenly, bitterly, he missed Mary, missed the smells of her cooking and the times they cooked together, peeling and slicing, chattering, drinking wine. The feeling was almost anger, rage even, hot in his chest.

"And the house? The bedroom?" asked Becker.

"It was fine," said Pollard. "I could feel even from down in the kitchen, the frightening thing was gone. I went back to bed, but I couldn't sleep. Although it was gone, every time I closed my eyes I saw it move again, the way it leaned over as though it wanted to get closer to me, to catch me."

"Let me ask you something," said Becker. "Why did you run to the garden?"

"Because I wanted to get out of the house," said Pollard.

"Did you pass your front door to get to the back door?"

"Yes," said Pollard. He hadn't thought of that before, had just run.

"So why not go out of the front door?"

"I was naked," he replied after a moment. "I didn't want to be naked in the street, people might have seen."

"So," said Becker, "even though you were terrified, the fear of being naked was greater?"

"Yes," said Pollard. "No. I don't know."

"You do," said Becker. "It might not feel like it, but you're making progress. The phobic reaction, the attacks, are getting worse, yes, but your inherent rationality is beginning to break through. All of the things you experience can be explained physiologically: you feel cold because your body, having entered an extreme 'fight or flight' reaction, is drawing the blood away from your extremities in order to protect and feed your muscles. The thing you saw moving was your eyes adjusting to opening and the pupils widening very quickly, the movement and change in the amount of light being taken in by your eyes being interpreted by your brain, an interpretation fed by fear and adrenaline. We make patterns where none exist; it's why we see shapes in the clouds. The pattern you made was fearful, terrifying, because that's how you were feeling at the moment of interpretation. Consider this, though, Mr Pollard: you went past one potential exit from your home to a further one not because it was a better exit, but because you're starting to take control, to set them within the context of your wider life. You didn't want to be seen naked, so even without realising it you were assessing the situation, considering your options, acting on them, reducing the possibility of that happening. You may have felt out of control, but you weren't, not really."

"But it was so real," said Pollard, remembering the weight on the bed, the shift of the mattress, the cold, the sight of it surging forwards at him as he struggled in his duvet.

"Of course it was," said Becker. "The feelings that are causing it, all the pain and fear, all the grief you feel about Mary's death, they're real. You don't want to experience them again, to even remember them; who would? So, unconsciously, you've trapped them down and converted them into this other fear, something powerful but ultimately irrational, an externalised point, a thing to flee from, to allow you a literal running away. The feelings fade when you run because you've vented them, released some of the pressure, but it builds up again. The attacks are a sign that, whether you realise it or not, you are ready to deal with those feelings now, to get rid of them, to uncover Mary and let her back into your memories. Not as a painful thing but as something good, something positive."

"Tell me how she died."

The question surprised him, caught him off guard, and Pollard couldn't speak. That day, that miserable, dreadful, awful day, was the most terrible memory he had, and it was scraped and raw when he probed it. Fragments of the day jumbled together inside him, fighting to free themselves, each one bad, worse, the worst; the phone call from the police, the trip to the hospital, the doctor in her white coat with the voice as sympathetic and absolute as cold mercy, being left alone with Mary but not for goodbye, no, for identification, to know that she was dead and to be able to confirm for the world that he knew she was dead. Mary, who joked she'd kill him if he went first, Mary who wouldn't eat olives but who loved anchovies, Mary whose mouth and eyes were open as she lay on the morgue's viewing room table as though she had been caught by surprise, frozen staring into the distance, mid-speech. Mary, who was already going cold when he kissed her for the last time. Mary, who was dead. "She had a stroke in the office behind the gallery, unpacking crates," he said eventually.

"This was an art gallery, yes? She worked there?"

"She owned it. She set it up six years ago, after years of working in a job she hated. She mostly showed contemporary artists, and imported and sold ethnic art. Most holidays these last years have been business trips." He smiled at the memories, Mary excitedly telling him about the new pieces she had found somewhere off the beaten track, of the deals she managed to do. "She was good at finding things that were unusual, that people liked enough to buy. She was successful, was getting a good name for herself."

"She had a heart attack?" asked Becker, gently steering Pollard back to the subject he was trying to skirt around.

"Yes," he said. "But it didn't kill her, not straight away. She fell. She was unpacking some Inuit pieces at the time, little stone carvings, and they fell with her. Most of them broke on the floor, all except one she was holding. Mary, she... she rolled in them, and the pieces cut her. She had scratches and punctures all over her arms and face, so many that the police thought at first that she'd been attacked and stabbed. There was an autopsy and an inquest before they decided she'd died of natural causes."

Pollard took a deep breath, painful and sharp, and said, "They think she was alive for at least a few minutes after the heart attack. There was a lot of blood and marks like she'd tried to crawl towards her desk, towards the phone. That's the worst of it, I think, the thought of her being alone and scared and in pain for those few minutes. I wish I'd been with her."

"Yes," said Becker, "I'm sure. Have you told anyone that before?"

"No."

"Then well done. This isn't easy, I know; you're peeling back these layers, all of those miseries, but it's for a good reason. Mary's there at the centre of it all, Mr Pollard, the positive Mary, the good memories. I know I keep saying it, keep repeating it, but I have to know you understand, that you trust me. We're getting there, getting closer."

"Yes," Pollard said. He was suddenly exhausted, sick with tiredness.

"Tell me, the object that you wife was holding, do you know what it was?"

"No. The police gave it me back once the inquest was over, but I've never looked at it."

"Then homework for the week, Mr Pollard, is to look at the object and find out what it is, and tell me about it next week."

The day before his next session with Becker, Pollard ate his lunch outside. The square in front of his office was busy with business men and women – scurrying, eating, talking, smoking. He liked it here, liked its busyness, the bustle of it. The concrete benches that ringed it faced in, which he and Mary had laughed about that lunchtime all those years ago. "Business only wants its people to look inwards, at other business sorts," she had said, "God forbid they look at the world outside even for a moment!" Pollard, who had worked in finance since he was sixteen and was used to her teasing, had laughed with her and kissed her and poured her another glass of champagne. Sitting here now, he remembered her leaning into him, whispering about the future, the smile on her face evident in her voice. Ah, but he missed her, more every day it felt like.

It had gone cold.

On the other side of the square, something black moved. It was large, stalking behind the curtain of people so that Pollard couldn't get more than a glimpse of it. He had an impression of flanks, of fur sleek with wetness, of a head that swayed from side to side as though sniffing at the floor.

Of eyes as black as obsidian and of teeth the yellow of ivory left in dark places.

It's an animal, he thought, although what, he couldn't tell. It was high at the shoulder, almost as tall as the people around it, none of whom reacted to it. Couldn't they see it? Feel it?

It was even colder now, and steam was rising from the thing as it moved around the edge of the square, coming to towards Pollard. A gap opened briefly between two of the hurrying people, allowing him to glimpse a head whose flesh was crenelated and raw-looking. Pollard dropped his half-eaten sandwich and rose, knowing that he had to go, to go now, to escape the thing, to not let it any nearer. He heard it, a noise like the snuffle of some giant carnivore scenting its prey, heard a sound like freezing rain hitting glass, and he ran.

"I don't remember much after that until I was in the office," said Pollard. "I must have run up the stairs, though, 4 floors. My legs still ache now." In fact, Pollard did remember one thing; as he knocked open the door from the stairway onto the fourth floor, startling some of his colleagues, the thing had been at the bottom of the stairwell. It was long and lithe, slipping around the corners with a sinuous grace, peering up at him. In the bright electric light, its black eyes glinted with flashes the colour of burning grass. The sight of it, of those glittering and depthless eyes, made his bladder clench and he had felt a hot splash of urine escape him.

"Did you do your homework?" asked Becker.

Pollard, momentarily startled by the conversation's change of direction but beginning to recognise Becker's tactics, didn't answer. Becker looked at him expectantly, forcing him to speak. "Yes," Pollard said. "I did my homework." *Homework*, he thought. *Some homework, to investigate the last thing my wife held on this earth.* He had opened the bag the police had given him several months before, tipping out Mary's purse and phone and the other thing, letting them tumble onto the table in front of him.

The thing was in his pocket and he took it out now, putting it on the table between himself and Becker. It was a small dog, carved out of dark rock. "It's an Inuit carving of a qiqirn," he told Becker. "I remember Mary telling me about it when she originally ordered them. Most Inuit art is stories, they were originally nomadic and didn't have much use for carvings and statues, I don't suppose, so she was excited to find them. Qiqirn are supposed to be malicious spirits, unpleasant, taking advantage of the lonely."

"A dog?"

"Yes."

"And the thing you saw, could you say it was a dog?"

"Maybe," Pollard admitted. "A big one. It's hard to say for sure."

"No, it isn't," said Becker. "You saw a version of the thing Mary was holding when she died, this Inuit qiqirn, not because it's real and not because Mary was cursed by it, but because it's a representation of her death. Those bad layers, Mr Pollard, they're fighting as hard as they can to stay in place but you're winning." He gestured to this week's piece of folded paper. Pollard picked it up and read A BAD WEEK IN WHICH YOU HAVE SEEN SOMETHING.

"We're getting closer, Mr Pollard, closer to the heart of it. Closer to Mary, moving through the layers of bitterness and mourning and anger and hurt that surround your memories of her. Those layers have helped protect you these last months, kept you safe until you have the strength to move forwards, but they've done their job now. These attacks are evidence of that, of that fact that the rational, loving part of you is beginning to assert itself, to free Mary from their shackles. Let me take a guess at something: the square in which you saw the qiqirn, it was somewhere that had significance to you and Mary?"

"Yes." It was where he and Mary had gone after she had signed the lease on the art gallery, where they had had the conversation a year earlier about her quitting her hated job and setting up the gallery. Where they drank champagne at lunchtime and smiled at other and looked forward to the future.

"The kitchen, the bedroom, other places of importance where this thing happens, the qiqirn makes its presence felt in those places because it's a thing of negativity and it can have its greatest effect in places that are most positive for you."

"It felt real," said Pollard, not sure which was worse, the idea that the qiqirn was real, or that he wanted to it to be real because the alternative was that was holding onto his negativity so tightly that it had made him see things.

"Of course it was, because it is real," said Becker. "Where our brains are concerned, our perceptions, there are no metaphors or similes, there's simply real and not real. Did it physically exist? No. Was it real? Yes, yes it was, a manifestation of all your unhappiness and loss and sadness and fear."

"I suppose," said Pollard, remembering steam rising off grey flanks.

"You're doing well, Mr Pollard, so well. Time for the next stage, I think. All the steps you've taken so far have been around the edges of the attacks. Important, yes, vital even because it's been about helping you to understand what's happening, but now we have to deal with the things themselves. Small steps, Mr Pollard, or in your case, no steps. When the attacks come, try to stand still for a second before you run, for five or ten or thirty seconds, as long as you can manage. Try to stand for longer and longer each time. Take control of them, rather than letting them control you. Will you try, Mr Pollard?"

"Yes," he said, and thought again of flanks and teeth and eyes that flashed through the darkness of four floors, black and cold and glistening.

"You look tired. I'm assuming this hasn't been a good week?"

"No," said Pollard, thinking that these sessions were making him monosyllabic. It had been a terrible week, with at least one attack each day and sometimes more. He had tried to stand in the face of them, he had, but they were simply too strong. The fear, the thought of seeing that thing again, the qiqirn, was simply overpowering and he had found himself running within seconds of the attacks starting. He had cowered in his garden, come to a halt in the street, even locked himself in the bathroom once, pushing towels into the gap between the floor and door and knowing as he did so that it was a ridiculous thing to do.

"I did some research on the Inuit, on the qiqirn," said Becker. "You were right, they're malicious dog spirits. Most cultures have similar things, from the Native American tricksters to the Japanese kitsune, even the Christian devil. They represent all those forces beyond our control, accidents and disasters and bad luck and the like. According to most mythologies, they latch on to someone when they're at a low ebb, when they're mourning or scared or upset, take root, fester. They cause fits, sickness, misery. Does that sound familiar?"

"Yes," said Pollard. "It's me. Mary and me, my memories of her."

"Yes. Qiqirn are supposed to be ugly, bald, vicious, to cause fear and panic and disgust, to carry the cold of their native land with them wherever they go, all the things you've experienced. I found something else out as well: the angakkuq, what I suppose we'd call the spiritual leader of the Inuit group, had advice on how to deal with a qiqirn if you found yourself haunted by one. 'Turn and face it', they say. 'Walk towards it, taking small steps. Be steady. Look it in the eye. Recognise it. Shout its name.' Does that sound familiar as well?"

"Yes. It's the advice you've been giving me."

"We think of psychology and psychiatry as new sciences, but they aren't, not really. The Inuit have a saying about their mythology: 'We don't believe; we fear'. It's how we cope, by fearing, by putting our fears into shapes that we can categorise, name, understand, and by doing so, we give ourselves the tools to overcome them. Religions, particularly older ones, have always understood that we have to force our fears into view to get rid of them. Each step we take away from them strengthens them, each one we take towards them weakens them. Walk towards it, Mr Pollard, using the smallest steps if you want, but walk towards it. This qiqirn, these negative emotions and fears, they exist because you're allowing them to and for no other reason. Keep walking, Mr Pollard."

"Yes," said Pollard, feeling a swell of helplessness. Becker made it sound easy, practically sweated confidence, but he hadn't seen it, hadn't heard the noises it made, hadn't felt the numbing fear and the electric twitch in legs that had to run.

"I know it sounds hard," said Becker. "It is hard, but it's not impossible. Call it a qiqirn, a phobia, a panic attack, whatever you like, but you can defeat it, Mr Pollard. You can."

Pollard didn't reply. He hoped Becker was right.

Pollard hit the door hard, yanking at the handle, but it refused to open. He had locked it earlier, he remembered, casting his eyes about for the keys. Where were they? He had locked the door and then gone to the kitchen, putting the keys down on the counter by the kettle. They were in the kitchen.

Where the qiqirn was.

The attack had come suddenly, faster than any of the others. Everything was fine, he was getting ready to go to bed, and then it was there, in the kitchen, behind him. He had a vivid, frenzied image of it sitting on its haunches, its black lips curled back in a grin from teeth that were slick with saliva, its bald head a pale, sickly pink, ridges of flesh crawling across its crown, its ears laid flat. The temperature plummeted. Pollard ran.

Hitting the locked door brought him back into himself slightly, the door's solidity and immovability cutting through some of the terror. Pollard heard a moaning sound, realised it was him and forced himself to stop. *This can't go on*, he thought, *I can't keep on like this, it's killing me. I want my life back. I want Mary back, she's dead and I want her back, not this, not this terrible fear.*

He turned, keeping himself pressed again the door. The kitchen was almost dark, the lights off inside, low illumination coming in from the night beyond the window, from the moon and the streetlamps and the stars. From the normal world.

Pollard took a step towards the doorway, his legs shaking so much that his knees actually knocked together. *I wonder if Becker knows that it's not a cliché?* he thought to himself randomly, and took another step.

Another. The thing in the kitchen growled, low and glottal.

No. There was no growl, there was no thing in the kitchen, no qiqirn, no trickster demon feeding on his pain and fear like some fat parasite, there was only air and memories buried under layers of grief and anger and sorrow. He took another step, and the urge to run was terrible, his muscles sick with adrenaline and unspent energy. He reached out, taking hold of the kitchen doorframe, anchoring himself. *I will do this*, he thought, *I will*. In the room ahead of him, claws clicked softly on linoleum as the qiqirn shifted and he imagined it readying itself for him, crouching, bringing its bald, ugly head close to the floor and drawing its lips back even further from its teeth to reveal gums that were flushed and dark, the colour of wet slate.

No.

There is nothing there, Pollard told himself again. I will step forward into my kitchen, my kitchen and there will be nothing there, no demons except my own and the empty spaces they create. He took another step, pulling himself against the doorframe. He was cold, the house was cold, his life was cold. More sounds from the kitchen, the spatter of saliva dripping from teeth and tongue to floor in thick, lazy strings, another low growl. *I will face it*, Pollard thought, and made the last step through the doorway.

In the kitchen it had started, gently, to snow.

Nahum's Taint:

Thought to be caused by as-yet-unidentified environmental factors, this is a condition in which the teeth become discoloured. The sufferer first notices a slight yellowing of the enamel, followed by rapid colour changes and a deterioration of the viability of the teeth, which crack and can grow and twist into strange shapes The teeth eventually become a colour that is impossible to describe.

Day 34

02.13 - Camera 1: Interior, Lounge. Pricey and Lucy are talking about Jamali. Lucy is on the couch, Pricey the floor. Lucy is playing with Pricey's hair as they talk.

They had the lowest ratings of the last 4 series, and their budgets had been cut as a result. Where before there would have been three or four of them on the overnight shift, now Anders stared alone at the multiple screens stacked above the control desk in careful rows, all displaying the inside of the house. It was late and two of the four housemates were asleep; in these weary hours, it was his job to simply review the images and decide which went to the live feed, and to mark anything that might be useful for that evening's highlights show. The conversation between Pricey and Lucy wasn't bitchy or unpleasant enough to be used, so he simply let it run and watched the other cameras.

02.17 – Camera 5: interior, large bedroom. Jamali is snoring; Ellie turns in her sleep, pulling the duvet around herself in a twist.

02.18 – Camera 13: exterior, garden. Dark shape crosses the lawn.

Foxes sometimes found ways into the garden and cats occasionally made their way over the lower parts of the wall, and once a couple of series back there had been a seagull that landed and waddled around the lawn before crapping a stream of chalky white liquid and taking off again. Anders rewound the film but the shape was too dark to see clearly, simply a moving blur of shadow. They used wildlife shots as inserts sometimes, overlaid with the sound of a camera's pan and zoom gears whirring, but this wasn't good enough quality so he forgot it and brought his attention back to the screens and the now that they showed. Lucy and Pricey's conversation seemed to be winding up, was increasingly punctuated by yawns and mumbles, so Anders drifted from it and let his vision loosen and blur, ceasing to focus on any one screen and taking in all of them en masse. If anything moved or changed in the images, he'd sense it rather than see it and could bring his attention back easily enough.

02.23 – Camera 6: Interior, large bedroom. Lucy and Pricey enter, hug and go to separate beds. Jamali rolls, stops snoring. Ellie twists again.

02.35 – Camera 6: Interior, large bedroom. Someone enters, although without lights they are little more than a silhouette. They go and stand over Ellie, bending so that their face is close to that of the sleeping girl's.

Anders blinked, sat upright. All four housemates were in their beds, asleep; he'd tracked them all night, they were in the bedroom and none had moved, so who the fuck was this? *An intruder? Jesus!* he thought, reaching out for the alarm; they had a direct line to the police in case of things like this. The programme generated strong responses in viewers, and not all of them were positive.

The figure was gone and the only thing above Ellie was the room's comforting, familiar darkness.

Anders rolled the recording back, the digitised sleepers disintegrating and then reforming as he sped up and then slowed down the film. There were Lucy and Pricey, conversation falling away as they entered the room, embracing (no romance though, despite the producers' hopes, and certainly no sex), climbing into their separate beds. Spool forwards, but no. No one else came in, no one stood over Ellie's bed. Had he imagined it, dozed off and dreamt of a figure whose head almost touched the top of the doorframe as it entered, making it nearly seven feet tall, a painfully thin figure stalking into the room with a step almost like a dancer's lope?

Yes, he must. He must have imagined it.

Anders rubbed his eyes, waited for the floaters in his vision to clear and then peered again at the images before him. Some of the screens showed the dark green of night-vision lenses, some the dark greys and blacks of rooms without light. The external images were brighter, the scenes lit by the wall-mounted security lights and the moonlight, and in none of them did anything move. He checked the images going to the live feed, but he hadn't changed it to the bedroom when the two housemates had retired; it still showed the lounge, so whatever he thought he'd seen had been a private twitch and nothing more.

03.16 – Camera 9: interior, small bedroom. Shadows in the corner of the room shift slightly. Something that might be the edge of a shoulder appears and then the top of a head emerges, caught by the pallid light from the garden entering window. The head is bald, the skin uneven and ridged.

03.17 – Camera 9: interior, small bedroom. Image pans left and zooms in, changing from normal to night-vision as it moves. The corner is empty.

Anders let the camera's gyros return it to its default position and depth of focus, but left the image as night-vision. It gave the small bedroom a dirty lime wash but meant he could see into all the corners except the one directly below the camera itself. After a moment, he flicked all the other cameras except the large bedroom and the gardens to night-vision as well, so that the interior of the house appeared before him as a fractured scale of greenery. Apart from the sleepers, the building was empty.

04.40 - Camera 3: interior, kitchen. Image pans left and then back right, sweeping the whole room. Nothing moves. There is a person, tall and almost anorexia-thin, standing at the sink. Camera jerks, overzooms and then pulls back.

04.41 – Camera 3: interior, kitchen. The kitchen is empty.

05.01 – Camera 2: interior, lounge. Something dark scuttles across the floor and disappears behind the sofa.

05.01 – Camera 1: interior, lounge. Opposite side of the sofa. Nothing moves.

05.01 – Camera 11: exterior, chill-out space. Cushions shift and tumble off upper bunk.

05.01 – Camera 19: exterior, isolation pod 1. Water suddenly ripples as though something has been dropped in it. The lid of the pod is closed.

Anders watched it all, or thought he watched it. The falling cushions and rippled water remained, caught by the cameras and recorded to the vast hard drives, but nothing else out of the ordinary appeared in the playback. There were no figures or scuttling things; there was simply the house and its occupants, now at the end of their fourth week of luxury imprisonment, watched by millions each night. Even now Anders could see from the viewer count under the live feed that over a million separate computers were logged in to the streaming images. Over a million, simply to watch a silent, motionless house and four sleeping fame-hungry housemates. He flicked the live feed to another camera, picking one at random, and sat back. He was tired; this shift tired him, and he thought this might be his last season with the show. He was bored.

05.13 – Camera 5: interior, large bedroom. Jamali is the first to awaken. He sits up, climbs out of bed and leaves the room.

05.14 – Camera 1: interior, lounge. Camera pans to track Jamali as he crosses the room to the bathroom.

05.14 – Camera 21: interior, bathroom. Jamali urinates (not on camera but audible), reappears in the image, washes his hands and looks at himself in the mirror.

05.15 – Camera 22: interior, bathroom viewed from behind mirror. The room is dark. Jamali is leaning close to the mirror, his face filling the image, removing sleepcrust from the corner of his left eye with one index finger. He yawns. As he does so, someone steps forward from behind him and a face appears at his shoulder.

Anders started, literally jerking back from the screens. The face was thin and, even in the low light, it looked sallow, the skin a dirty grey, lips darker and wrinkled back from teeth that were crooked and discoloured and terribly, obscenely large. Its eyes were invisible in the pools of shadow that gathered under its hairless, bone-ridge brows.

It was grinning.

Anders leapt forward, hand darting for the alarm for the second time, and then the face was gone. Swearing, he rewound, watching for a second time as Jamali dug the grit from his eye, and this time no one stepped close behind him and Anders watched and waited for a face that did not appear.

05.16 – Camera 2: interior, lounge. Jamali emerges from the bathroom and

goes to the kitchen, where he puts the kettle on and gets a cup out of the cupboard
to make himself tea.

05.17 – Camera 4: interior, kitchen. Jamali is stirring sugar into his tea.
Behind him can be seen the large glass doors into that lead to the garden, where
three figures stand motionless on the lawn.

05.17 – Camera 4: interior, kitchen. Image pans up and zooms, wobbling, but
the figures are gone. Another pan, blurring past a now out-of-focus Jamali, to
the other visible portion of the glass doors. Zoom out. The garden is empty.

Anders reached for the alarm again, then stopped. He was a director
and assistant producer, and APs had no authority. If he called the police
over nothing, he'd be fired. Above him in the pecking order was
Pearson, and above him a complicated tangle of production company
and television channel executives, all of whom could and would
oversee his removal without breaking stride or sweat. He hesitated,
undecided, hand hovering.

05.21 – Camera 5: interior, large bedroom. Ellie rolls, falls out of bed. The noise
wakes Pricey, who laughs at her. Lucy wakes, yawns, stretches, sits up. Pricey
says something inaudible and all three laugh. The fourth figure, sitting on the
far bed, simply watches them, clutching the duvet up around itself so that only
its eyes and one long-fingered hand are visible. Its nails are black and twisted.

Anders made sure the live feed was from the bedroom, that the figure
on the bed was visible to him in the feed, and then checked the
comments thread that constantly unspooled below the image on show's
website. For thirty seconds of the comment conversation no one
referred to the figure and then someone mentioned that the duvet
behind Ellie was "all rucked up like a person was there". Anders let out
a sigh of relief; someone else could see it too, although the responses to
the sighting showed that viewers thought it was either a trick of the light
or, possibly, something done by the programme-makers as part of the
housemates' next task or test, or simply to surprise them. The question
was, what should he do about it?

05.27 – Camera 6: interior, large bedroom. Pricey walks past the far bed, going to his drawer. He catches the bed with his hip, knocking it, and the duvet pile collapses. The figure is gone.

Anders' hand was shaking as he held it over the phone. To call or not to call? Either there were people in the house, somehow manipulating the cameras, or the image software or computers had been hacked. Or, worse, he was suffering some kind of breakdown and needed help. His jaw clenched, trying to keep the panic inside, his hand dipping, rising, dipping.

05.37 – Camera 7: interior, diary room. Lucy comes in to speak to the all-seeing-eye and omnipotent voice of the programme. She is still half asleep, slurring her words slightly, as she talks about her home and wanting to see her family. After six minutes in the room she gets up and walks out. A second person passes in front of the camera, following her.

05.43 – Camera 4: interior, kitchen. Lucy walks through the room away from the diary room. A tall, thin figure follows her. The kitchen lights are off and the figure is indistinct.

Anders' hand darted, away from the phone and to the alarm, pressing it before he could stop to think. Whatever this was, it was above his payscale, and he was scared.

05.44 – Camera 13: exterior, garden. Lucy emerges from the house. There is no one behind her.

05.45 – Camera 14: exterior, garden. Lucy walks across the lawn towards the hot tub. Behind her, lined up against the wall of the compound, are several tall figures. They turn to watch her as she passes. One reaches out and strokes her hair.

05.45 – Camera 14: exterior, garden. Image pans and zooms, jerky, losing Lucy and closing in on the figures behind her. For a second one of them is caught, face long and stretched, mouth open and tongue licking blackly at its teeth. It is the one who stroked her hair and it turns to look directly at the camera and it grins and grins. It pulls its hand back and sniffs its fingers and then it steps back and vanishes into the gloom. Image swings side to side but the garden is empty.

Day 34

Anders shrieked, hand hitting the alarm again and again.

05.45 – Camera 21: garden, looking down from corner turret of the fence around the compound. Lucy and Jamali are in the hot tub, both leaning against its side, talking. Between them, under the water, several figures are crouched. Through the rippled surface it is impossible to make out details, only a general outline: they are gaunt and dark. As Lucy leans back, arms stretched out along the tub's sides and eyes closed, someone enters the picture and stands behind her on the step. It is not Pricey or Ellie. It kneels and sniffs her hair.

05.46 – Camera 11: exterior, chill-out space. Pricey and Ellie are sitting on the upper bunk. A third figure is seated between them. It is thin and naked, its legs crossed, its skin a mottled patchwork of grey and browns like rotting leaves. It has one hand on Pricey's shoulder and the other high on Ellie's leg, under the hem of her skirt. It is stroking both of them. As the camera zooms in, it leans to the side and a tongue the colour of slugs emerges from its mouth and licks slowly at the strap of Ellie's nightdress.

05.47 – Camera 20: interior, isolation pod 2. The water in the empty, closed pod swirls and then something rises up. It smiles, its teeth the only thing visible in the darkness. They are long and uneven, sharp. Above them, after a second, a pair of eyes opens, the pupils slits that slowly widen.

05.49 – Camera 11: interior, chill-out space. Pricey stands up, telling Ellie he's going to go back to bed. As the camera pans to follow him, the figure sitting next to Ellie grins even more widely and puts its arms around the girl, leaning in to her face, its mouth opening wide, too wide, and its teeth are huge.

05.50 – Camera 13: exterior, garden. Pricey starts across the lawn, turning to Lucy and Jamali in the hot tub. He screams and starts running for the house.

05.50 – Camera 14: exterior, garden. As Pricey screams, one of the shapes under the water in the hot tub stands up. It is very tall, very thin. Lucy gasps, backs away and the figure kneeling behind her wraps its arms around her torso, one clawed hand clasping her breast and the other at her face. Jamali is frozen, only moving when the other figures rise up, water splashing. He tries to throw himself over the tub's side but the figures grab him and they struggle before dropping below the water. The figure holding Lucy topples forward into the water, still holding her. The water churns, its turbulent surface showing nothing but lights and ripples, and then clears. The tub is empty.

05.50 – Camera 4: interior, kitchen. Pricey can be seen through the doors at the top of the image running across the lawn towards the house. A tall shape steps in front of him and grasps him and they tumble sideways, out of view.

05.50 – Camera 13: exterior, garden. No one is visible. Nothing moves.

Where the fuck was everyone? Where were the police? Why hadn't the alarm gone off in the house, sending the housemates to the exits through the diary room or the eviction door? Anders banged his hand on the alarm again, then picked up the telephone.

Silence.

05.51 – Camera 1: interior, lounge. Nothing moves.

05.51 – Camera 2: interior, lounge. Nothing moves.

05.51 – Camera 3: interior, kitchen. Nothing moves.

05.51 – Camera 4: interior, kitchen. Nothing moves.

05.51 – Camera 5: interior, large bedroom. Nothing moves.

05.51 - Camera 6: interior, large bedroom. Nothing moves.

05.51 – Camera 7: interior, diary room. Nothing moves.

05.51 – Camera 8: interior, diary room. Nothing moves.

05.51 - Camera 9: interior, small bedroom. Nothing moves.

05.51 – Camera 10: interior, small bedroom. Nothing moves.

05.51 – Camera 11: exterior, chill-out space. A cushion settles, falls from the empty bench to the floor. Nothing moves.

05.51 – Camera 12: exterior, chill-out space. Nothing moves.

05.51 – Camera 13: exterior, garden. Nothing moves.

05.51 – Camera 14: exterior, garden. Nothing moves.

05.51 – Cameras 15, 16, 17, 18: exterior, differing views of house's walls. Nothing moves.

05.51 – Camera 19: exterior, isolation pod 1. Water ripples then settles. Nothing moves.

05.51 – Camera 20: exterior, isolation pod 2. Nothing moves.

05.51 – Cameras 21, 22, 23, 24: exterior, differing views from corners of compound's walls. Nothing moves.

Where were they? Anders viewed each screen desperately, hands automatically zooming and panning the cameras. Nothing. He reached out again for the phone but from over his shoulder a clawed hand came into view and pressed down on his own hand, squeezing. It was hot, burning, and he screamed.

05.51 – Camera A: interior, control room. Anders is screaming as the figure behind him leans forward and takes him in its arms. Its skin is peeling and raw, its mouth is open wide and it is grinning.

05.52 – Camera A: interior, control room. Nothing moves.

Tinea:

Caused by the drinking of water containing the eggs of the parasitic worm Adedo Shukeri. The eggs lodge in the gum line and gestate for several days before the worms hatch and burrow into the root of the tooth, where they grow and consume both bone and nerve. Sufferers report excruciating pain before the tooth falls out, pushed out by the destruction of the root structure and the increasing size and number of worms. When the tooth falls out, the worms spill from the hole, leaving trails of eggs that need to be removed immediately before they can implant and infect other teeth. The worms are poisonous and, if swallowed, death can occur.

A Place for Feeding

"Ah, ah, *aaah*," said the woman with the beige coat and the too-red lipstick, waving an admonishing finger in the air in front of her, and Angela didn't realise at first that the woman was directing it at her so she carried on.

Shaun had been good that afternoon, better than usual, but he had been getting squally these last few minutes. Knowing that he wouldn't stop, would only get louder and more demanding, Angela had stopped shopping and found a café, got herself a drink and was preparing to feed him. She undid another button on her blouse and then reached in and pulled down the cup of her bra. Then it was simply a matter of lifting Shaun to her breast and readying the large square of muslin in her other hand so that she could drape it over her shoulder to give both her and Shaun some privacy. It was as she moved Shaun's lip to her nipple so that he could latch on that the woman made the "Ah, ah, aaah" sound again, wagging her finger more forcefully, and then said, "You! Miss! Not in front of my children, you don't!"

Even then, Angela wondered what the woman was talking about, though that she was talking to her had become clear: she was looking directly at Angela as she spoke, and the wagging finger (topped, Angela saw, by a long nail painted the same too-red shade as the woman's lips) was stabbing now, poking emphatically at her. It didn't make sense, not at first; Angela wasn't doing anything, was she? Just sitting, having a cup of tea while Shaun fed from her.

So what, then? Angela wasn't doing anything to cause offence, nothing to generate such a strong reaction. The woman's face was actually wrinkling, her lips pulling back from her teeth and twisting her face into an expression of disgust, as though she'd smelled or seen something foul. Angela glanced down at herself, wondering if she'd spilled something or walked something in on her shoes, but no, there was nothing. Nothing except her long skirt and flat shoes, her coat over her knee and her plain blouse above them, and Shaun nestled at her left breast, partially covered by the muslin. He was content now that he was feeding, his cheeks expanding and contracting in sweet little ballooning motions as he sucked and swallowed. Just Shaun, and then Angela paused. Shaun? Was it Shaun, Angela wondered before realising that it was, it was Shaun, it was Shaun feeding that the woman had a problem with.

She was so surprised that she didn't respond, didn't move, and the woman said angrily, "Don't you ignore me, missy! It's disgusting, doing it like that, in front of people, in front of my children!" and she actually hissed the last word. Her finger stabbed forward, now no longer up vertical but a savage horizontal, jerking forwards and back as she spoke. The red nail flashed as the café's overhead light caught in it, streaks like the glint of fishes' scales darting across its surface. Angela looked around the café, hoping she would see a friendly face, but everyone seemed to be looking at her disapprovingly. One young girl was even nodding as the woman spoke, and that really hurt Angela's feelings; the girl had a small child in a buggy by her side, and Angela had hoped she, at least, might be on her side. The café windows were slick with condensation, misting the world beyond to pastel smears through which the shapes of people passing were little more than insubstantial blurs.

"I'm sorry," Angela started, meaning to tell the woman that she was sorry, she didn't understand what the problem was, but the woman interrupted before she could get any further.

"You ought to be sorry, exposing yourself to my sons like that!"

"Exposing myself? How? I don't understand," Angela stammered, but knew that she did. Behind the woman, two small boys glared at her; one looked to be about six, the other a little older, perhaps eight or nine. The elder of the two was peering intently at Shaun, at her almost-exposed breast.

"That!" the woman said furiously, jabbing her finger forward again, this time extending her arm so that it was at nearly full stretch. "We don't want to see you do that while we eat. It's disgusting."

"It's not disgusting," said Angela, not liking the way her voice wavered as she spoke. She wished that Steve was here, he'd have already told the woman what she could do with her fingernail and her "Ah, ah, aah" sounds and her ridiculous, upsetting attitude to Shaun feeding. Trying to gather herself, she went on.

"He's just having a feed, it's perfectly natural,"

"So's going to the toilet," the woman retorted, still hissing, "and we have a place for that and it's not in the middle of a café where everyone can see and where decent people are trying to take their sons out for a meal."

"Can see what?" said Angela, still trying to remain calm, to not cry, hating how this woman was making her feel, small and angry and strengthless. She had never been good at conflict, never liked standing up for herself, always wanted to try to walk away to avoid the fight if she could. "I've covered him, he's just having a feed. He's hungry."

"He might well be hungry. We're all hungry, you know, but I don't want to see him have his drink. You should do it somewhere else. It's disgusting," the woman repeated. "In public. And don't think that little cloth helps, either; we saw you before you put it there, and we know what's happening behind it now. I can hear him."

Angela couldn't speak; her cheeks burned in helpless, impotent fury. Shaun was four months old, was the sweetest, brightest thing there was, and being able to feed him herself was the thing she was most proud of in her whole miserable existence. All the struggles of her life before, all the terrors and pains of his birth and of her and Steve's hopes and wishes for him, they all fell away when he fed from her. She wasn't successful, she wasn't popular, she didn't think she was pretty although Steve said she was, she had neither a good job nor good prospects, she was just Angela who had got pregnant at nineteen and had somehow managed to have a perfect little baby and stay in a relationship with his father. Shaun needed them, needed her, and finally she had found something she was good at; she had taken to feeding Shaun easily, as he had taken to feeding from her. And yet, here was this woman, this cow, undermining her, attacking her, making her feel bad.

"It's the healthiest thing for him, it's so much better than formula," Angela tried again, hoping to somehow persuade the woman, make her see things from Angela's point of view.

"So you think you're better than those of us who chose to feed our children using the bottle do you, better than those of us who chose to respect other people's sensibilities?"

"What? No, I never said that," said Angela, feeling the tears start. She hated people like this, people who could twist what she said, who were quicker with words and who always had an answer, no matter what she said. "I just meant that–" but the woman interrupted her again.

"You just meant that you're better than me, that I should just ignore you because he wants it. Well, let me tell you, missy, if you let him have everything he wants as he wants it, he'll grow up spoiled. Perhaps I should let my boys do what they want. How about that, Oscar? Would you like to just do what you want, when you want it?"

"No, mum," said the older of the boys, still peering intently at Angela's chest. She could almost see the hope in his eyes, the hope that her blouse would flap, that he might catch a glimpse of something. Angela reddened more, if that were possible, feeling the burn spread from her cheek to her forehead and down her neck, knowing that a dark flush was appearing down her throat and spreading across the bony hollows of her collarbones.

"There!" said the woman, triumphant. "'No, mum'! He knows that he won't be able to live his life getting what he wants, he's not selfish. Both my sons had the bottle, had formula, not when they wanted it but when I wanted them to, and they've turned out fine. Better than fine, perfect! So don't give me your nonsense about 'better for him'!"

"But it is, it's the best thing for him, it's from me, how can it not be, the companies lie about how good formula is because it isn't, but my milk is, it's perfect for him," and Angela was crying now, tears of shame and anger rolling down her cheeks, fat and hot and corrosive. Out of the corner of her eye, she saw the manager of the café come out from behind the counter and start to thread his way between the tables towards her. *Oh thank God*, she thought, *he's coming to tell her to leave me alone*. She looked up at him gratefully as he arrived by her side.

"Miss," he said quietly. He was only small, she saw, short and slight and wearing a thin white shirt and a tie with a pattern of green and blue and red triangles.

"Miss," he repeated, and he looked down as he spoke, refusing to meet Angela's eyes. "You'll have to stop, I'm afraid. It's upsetting the other customers. Please. There's a room you can use, where you and he can have some privacy."

Angela felt like she'd been punched, and couldn't speak. Any sound she might want to make seemed suddenly trapped in her throat, swelling and painful. She tried to swallow and found she was unable, that her tongue was clumsy and dry in her mouth. Shaun suckled on, oblivious.

"Miss," said the man a third time and reached out for her, his hand stopping nervously between them and hovering before falling back to his side. "I'm really very sorry but you really can't do that here. It's offending people. We have a place you can go, please come with me. Please."

Angela wanted to say, What about me? I'm offended, for me and for my son, he just wants to have a drink and so do I, my feet hurt and I'm tired and I want to sit here and wait for the food I've ordered and for my son to be allowed to finish his feed, please, but she didn't. Instead, she inserted a finger into Shaun's mouth and gently prised him off her breast, slipping the cup of her bra back up with a practiced motion at the same time. Shaun grouched, but only a little; he would be content for a few minutes, but he hadn't finished feeding yet and would become demanding again soon. She lifted him to her shoulder, cradling him against her, using her other hand to hold her blouse together rather than rebutton it. She kept her head down so that the woman and the manager wouldn't see her tears, wouldn't see the expression on her face. The manager reached out to help her with her coat but she knocked his hand away, saying stiffly, "I'm fine."

As she followed the manager, Angela saw that the woman was sitting with her arms folded, a broad smile on her face. *It makes her look like a frog*, Angela thought bitterly, *a big horrible frog with a big ugly tongue. I'll bet kissing her must be horrible, I bet she tastes horrible, like old ponds and slimy plants*, and the thought made her smile. "Look at her," said the woman, "no shame. She thinks this is all a big joke." Angela hurried on, carrying Shaun and uncomfortably aware that she was leaving her bags of shopping and his pram by the table, and she wanted to be somewhere else, anywhere but in the café. She wished the ground would somehow magically open and spirit the two of them away, but beneath her feet the tired linoleum remained stubbornly whole. Ahead, the manager's skinny buttocks and curved back guided her on.

The room was a storeroom between the two toilets. It was half full of boxes and it smelled of cleaning fluid and musty air and old, pale urine. The bulb dangling from the ceiling was low-wattage and waxen, the light it cast a seeping yellow that showed the room in the colours of old photographs. The floor was plain concrete, gritty, and Angela heard it crack and pop under the soles of her shoes. It was cold, and there was no furniture that she could see.

The manager fumbled behind one of the piles of boxes and finally pulled out a folding chair, opening it and setting it against one wall. He had to shift one or two smaller boxes out of the way as he did so and he grunted as he pushed them, a little animal sound like the noise Shaun sometimes made as he filled his nappy. After the boxes were moved, he turned to Angela, his face a mask of misery. "I'm sorry," he said, "but there's nothing I can do. I'll make sure no one takes your table and that your things are left alone, and your food will be ready when you've... when he's finished. Can I get you anything else?"

"No," said Angela, not trusting her voice to say more. "Please just leave us alone."

Once the door had swung shut the room was gloomy, the darkness seeming to magnify the odours into a rich landscape that hung around her and Shaun as she sat down. The chair wobbled, Shaun griping as she clenched him tight. He could tell she was unsettled, and it disturbed him. She cuddled him for a minute and then tried to get comfortable in the chair, which wobbled again as she shifted. Finally, he calmed enough for her to try to let him feed; she let her blouse fall open and lowered her bra cup again, moving Shaun so that he could take her in his mouth. At first, he didn't latch on properly, so that the initial sucks he took were painful. Wincing, she repositioned him, trying to concentrate on him and not on the woman, not on the other people in the café or the manager, not on this horrible room or the smell, just on Shaun and feeding him and being what he needed.

The sound of a door closing came from behind Angela, making her jump. She twisted slightly, careful not to disturb Shaun who was latched and feeding better now. The wall was only plasterboard, she saw, more a divider than a wall. It looked damp and soft, and the sound from the room beyond travelled through it easily. It was the men's toilet, she thought, as she listened to heavy footsteps and then another door closed and there was a click she thought was probably a lock. "No," she whispered out loud as another noise erupted, a horrible bodily sound, flatulent and full. Someone groaned and then broke wind again and Shaun wriggled in her arms and she realised that she was holding him tight, her arms trembling. There was a third sound from beyond the partition, another groan, and then the noise of water splashing and Angela was on her feet and speaking out loud again.

"No," this time not whispering but saying it clearly as though she were talking to the person beyond the wall. "I will not feed my son listening to the sound of someone going to the toilet, I will not." She gently broke Shaun's latch, ignoring his emerging wail of protest, and lifted him back to her shoulder. Then, as calmly as she could, she buttoned her blouse back to the top and picked up her coat. It had wetness on it from the floor, dark patches standing out against the beige material. Steve had bought her the coat for her birthday and she was suddenly angry – no, not angry, furious. Not enough that they made her feed Shaun like this, like some animal, they had made her coat messy. It was hers, not theirs, and they had messed it up. Well, that was it. She was going to take Shaun back and go and sit at the table and she was going to show the manager her wet coat and explain to him politely about the sound of the man on the toilet and how she wasn't going to make Shaun have his food listening to it, and then she was going to eat her food and let Shaun feed and if the woman or her children didn't like it, they could go and eat in the cupboard. They could all eat in the cupboard if they wanted, and if they tried to stop her feeding Shaun, well, they'd have a fight on their hands. She had had enough.

As she got to the doorway, Angela heard the sound of the door further down the corridor opening again and footsteps coming towards her. She waited until the person, the man, had passed and she had heard the sound of a more distant door open and close, so that she knew he was back in the dining area, and only then did she come out of the cupboard. She went quickly, carrying Shaun against her front like her badge and shield and armour. Her heart fluttered in her chest, birdlike, and she wished she were stronger, braver, because she knew that she wasn't going to say anything to the manager, she was just going to sit and eat as fast as possible and hope Shaun didn't start to cry, and if he did she was going to get up and gather him to her, get her things and leave. She hadn't the words or the strength to fight, but maybe if she sat quiet they'd leave her alone. Taking a deep breath, she went back into the main body of the café.

Shaun's pram and her bags remained where they had been, untouched, but now there was a bottle on her table, a baby's bottle full of thick white liquid. Angela looked at it and then up, around the people in the café. The woman had her head down, was shovelling a forkful of food from her plate to her mouth. Oscar was looking at Angela with undisguised interest, his round face creasing into a frown of disappointment when he saw that her blouse was fully buttoned. The other child was also eating, his actions mimicking his mother's. There was an old man sitting at the table beyond the woman and children, his face red. Was he the one in the toilet? she thought, the noisy one? Glancing away, she saw other tables, other people. A younger man wearing overalls and a paint-spattered fleece, an older couple who were both reading, another old man who was peering at her, the light reflecting across the lenses of his spectacles. Other people had entered in the short time that she had been in that horrible room with Shaun: a group of young girls in fat anoraks covered in gold and silver logos, and a couple dressed in smart clothes like they'd just come out of an office. By the door, the young girl, the one with the child in the buggy, was looking at her. Angela caught her eye long enough for the young girl to look deliberately down and then back up; Angela repeated the action and saw the bottle again. She put Shaun back in his pram, where he gurgled happily to himself and played with the dangling fish of his mobile, and then looked at the girl again, who smiled at Angela. Picking the bottle up, Angela walked across to her and said, "Is this yours? I think you might have left it on my table by accident."

"No, it's for you. Well, for your baby," said the girl.

"No, thank you," said Angela politely, a feeling of unreality washing over her, "he's breast-fed, he doesn't need a bottle."

"Oh, I'd disagree," said the woman suddenly from behind Angela. From right behind her. "You can't fill boys, not with just the breast," she continued, her voice almost conversational. "They need something extra. Besides, it'll help him sleep through."

"No," said Angela again, trying to turn but finding her way blocked by the woman, who was really very close now. "Formula isn't what he needs; it's not as good as my milk. I don't want him to have a bottle. I'm the only food he needs."

"Nonsense," said the woman, reaching over Angela's shoulder and taking the bottle from her hand before Angela could stop her. "This young woman's been very kind to let you have this, you should be grateful. After all, it won't hurt him."

"No, please, stop," said Angela, trying again. She managed to twist part of the way around this time, but then the woman stepped further forward and bumped into her, knocking Angela back against the nearest chair and causing her to stumble. Her knees caught against the seat of the chair and she sat heavily, the upright of the chair catching her painfully.

"He'll like it," said the young girl. Her voice was breathy and excited.

"He will," said the neatly-dressed woman, and the man with her nodded. The girls at the other table giggled.

"No, wait, please," said Angela again and tried to rise, but then the manager was in front of the woman and was pushing Angela back into the chair. For such a small man, he was surprisingly forceful, and she had time to think that he was the only man besides Steve to touch her in over two years, and then she couldn't see the woman any more. She reappeared in Angela's view, was now by Shaun's pram and appeared to be leaning over and peering inside it. Angela saw that Oscar had beaten her to it, however, and had already taken Shaun out. Taken him out, was holding him, was holding her baby.

"Put him back," Angela shouted. Oscar ignored her; everyone ignored her except the manager, who said "It's for the best, really. We all talked about it, and we all agree."

"No, formula can give them poorly tummies, he doesn't need it, leave him alone, let me go," said Angela. Her voice cracked as she spoke, rising to a shout, and then she was struggling, pushing against the manager, trying again to rise. He forced her back down, calling out, and the younger man came over and sat in the chair next to her, leaning over to grip her arms tightly.

"Everything'll be fine," said the manager, but he wouldn't look at Angela as he spoke; his eyes were tightly shut and his shoulders were hunched up as though he were trying to cover his ears. She opened her mouth to scream and the younger man squeezed her arms painfully tight and said in a quiet voice, "Don't. You'll only make it worse. Besides, you'll thank us in the end."

"Please," she repeated. "He's my baby, I don't want him to have a bottle, I want to feed him myself, let me go and we'll just leave and we won't come back."

"It's okay, love," said one of the old men as Angela started to sob. "You don't want to listen to any of the rubbish the papers tell you. He'll be fine, he'll enjoy it, and it's better for everyone, isn't it? You can go anywhere with him if he's on the bottle, can't you?"

"Of course you can," said the woman, taking Shaun from Oscar. "You're only young, you think you know everything but you don't. I've had two, and this way is so much easier for everyone."

Angela screamed as the people in the café crowded around her, pressing her back into the chair. The smell of hot bodies filled her nostrils as she screamed, once, before a hand that was heavy and tasted of soap and grease clamped across her mouth. She couldn't see who the hand belonged too in the mêlée, only that it was connected to an arm that snaked away around the side of her head. Another arm wrapped around her stomach and pulled her hard against the chair. The manager let go of her shoulders and backed away, and just before the gap he left was filled with more bodies, Angela had the briefest glimpse of Shaun. He was in the arms of the woman, her face bent down towards his, and she was smiling widely and holding the bottle to his lips.

Message 3

She pressed play on the answering machine, stilling the flashing red light and listened to the messages. The first was her mother, asking how she was, and the second was a friend inviting her for a drink that night, which she'd have to turn down. The third was Mike, and in the background Davey and Meg. Meg was speaking but what she was saying was unintelligible, and Davey sounded upset. Mike sounded upset as well, his voice blurring at the edges. There was traffic noise behind the three voices. She looked at her watch; they weren't due back for another half an hour. Mike was, in fairness, precise about these things if nothing else.

"Ellie, I've tried, but I can't live without you, or the children. One lousy day every two weeks isn't enough, you're my world and it's not fair that I can't be with you all the time. It's not fair on me, or Davey and Meg. I can't do it. I won't. We belong together, we belong with each other, and I'll keep my children any way I can, I love them. I love you. I'm so sorry. "

The playback ended and for a moment, she was confused. Putting the phone down, she watched as a police car pulled up outside the house and a uniformed man and woman emerged from it. They looked about the street, focussing on her house after a moment, and the scream only birthed itself in her belly when she saw the look on their faces as they started up the path towards her front door.

Norman's Heart

"Are you looking at me like that because you're late inviting me to your wedding or because you didn't realise I was dying?"

Norman stepped back in to his hallway and motioned me in. I followed, cursing silently that my face had given away my shock, and guilty about how long it had been since I had visited the man who had raised me. He looked awful, his skin sallow and haggard, lined so deeply that it was like looking at him through cracked glass, and he was thin. Not healthy thin but too thin, somewhere down past gaunt, somewhere into the kingdoms of wasting and illness. He almost wasn't there, and the daylight shadows in his home seemed in danger of swallowing him whole. When he let himself fall back into his chair, he grunted tiredly.

"Why didn't you tell me?" I asked.

"What's to tell?" he said. "My heart is tired. It's dying."

"Who says?"

"A doctor."

I sat forward, the wedding invitation loose in my fingers, the embossed card in its vellum envelope growing heavier and heavier as I looked at the deep etching that Norman's face had become. "A doctor? You'll go to one of those damned quacks but not me? Norman, I'm hurt." I said it lightly, but I was being truthful. Norman's stubborn refusal to ask for my help, to even acknowledge that he needed help, meant that I rarely had the chance to repay any of the myriad kindnesses he had shown to me, never had chance to demonstrate to him the man he'd helped me become. He winced as my words struck a gentle blow.

"I came to ask you to be my best man, which I thought I ought to do in person rather than by post," I said, still keeping my tone as light as I could, "so I need you well. I'm going to check your heart myself."

"Don't worry about me," he said irritably, trying to stand, with just a flash of the Norman I knew and loved.

"Don't tell me not to worry," I replied, letting myself become just as irritable. "I'll decide what I worry about, not you, and now I'm choosing to worry about you and the advice you've been given. Now, shut up, sit back and relax." He didn't argue, in itself a worrying sign, but let himself flop again into his chair with another of those weary grunts. Norman never usually allowed himself to lose an argument, never backed down, and seeing him like this was causing worms of panic to wriggle in my belly, to turn and slip and slide around dank notions of illness and death and loss. I tried not to let the worms show in my expression but I don't think I did a very good job; Norman smiled at me and reached out, touching my cheek with a hand that felt like twigs wrapped in skin and said, more gently, "I've had a good life, David, so please don't fuss. It's my time, that's all."

"Nonsense," I muttered, as much to myself as to Norman, as much in hope as in certainty, and leaned toward him.

Once I had unbuttoned Norman's shirt to reveal his sagging chest with its scurf of grey hair, I pressed my right hand over his heart, palm flat and fingers splayed. In ordinary circumstances, I might have made a pass or two with my other hand, waving my fingers to suggest magic and intricacy but with Norman it was pointless; he knew that what I do requires no great mysteries and no supernatural devices but simply the will to do it and a sympathetic understanding of the flesh.

Norman's heart fluttered under my fingers, its skip and lurch irregular and weak. I pressed harder, feeling a moment's tender resistance and then my fingers parted the skin. Norman gasped and I realised that it was the first time he had ever let me inside him and I was momentarily ashamed. How had I let it go this long without showing Norman who I had become?

His heart fluttered again. I felt the traceries of capillaries around my fingertips and below them, musculature, warm and cabled. Parting the heavy folds of muscle, I wormed my hand in further. The ribs bent aside under my touch, coiling away from my hand like snakes on warm rock, and then my hand was around the heart. Its surface was scarred, pulsing in a way I did not like. I cupped it, letting it talk to me. Using my other hand, the fingers teasing and peeling, I opened the flesh around my wrist. It took me minutes to do it but I finally moulded the flesh back completely, letting me see what I was holding.

It's a simple muscle, really, this thing that keeps the blood moving around our bodies; four valves, arteries, walls. Exposed to the air hearts are a rich, vibrant red and they sing, songs of joy with tunes that reach from the ground to the sky, from past to future.

Norman's heart was streaked with grey and the sound it made was a low, keening thing.

I stroked it, listening. There were no words in what it sang to me, the heart, but its song was clear if you knew how to listen, to hear. Its voice wavered and grew faint, slipped back in louder, the beat of its walls finding rhythms and losing them again, attaining in its irregularity a curiously musical atonal beat. It had strength, this heart, somewhere deep inside it, somewhere at its heart. After a moment I let my eyes lift from it and looked into my friend's face.

"Your heart is tired," I told Norman, "but it's not dying. Doctors! Jesus, they shouldn't be allowed out of their nurseries, they're a fucking danger to everyone they talk to," and then I was drawing the heart towards me, pinching and blocking blood vessels and arteries with my other hand as I went, persuading the flesh to seal itself. Norman gasped and reached up but I very gently knocked his hands away.

"Your heart needs a rest from everything, including you. It needs to be by itself for a few days."

Norman did not respond. He was looking with a mixture of awe and terror at his heart, lying flat on my palm. I reached forwards and cupped his chin with my other hand, drawing his eyes to my face. Seeing organs detached from your body can be unnerving.

"I'm going to take your heart for a rest, but you'll be fine. Your body knows what's happening and it'll cope. Don't do anything that's energetic or stressful. I'll come every day and check you're okay."

"I can't–" he said, but I interrupted him before he could continue.

"You don't have a choice. It's not dying yet, but it will be if it doesn't get complete rest. Let me do my job, Norman, please. It will be a pleasure."

I carefully finished sealing the hole in Norman's chest and left him reading his favourite Melville novel, the wedding invitation opened and propped up on the side table, thinking, *All that rambling about vast whiteness and the terrible whale will keep him occupied*. I packed his heart in a bag of ice, not too much in case Norman felt its chill but enough to keep the flesh safe and then as quickly as I could, I drove to Denny and Rose's home.

Denny and Rose are a middle-aged couple I use sometimes; they're part of a network of fosterers, each offering different environments to be used in different circumstances. They live in a pleasant cottage that always smells of baking bread and roast dinners, of tradition and comfort. I can't imagine Denny or Rose ever having to deal with bills or arguing; it's why I like them. The hearts I take there need to forget, need to relax, need to beat to a lesser beat for a time.

When I arrived, Rose helped me lay Norman's still-beating heart on a bed of moss in the quiet room, the one I rent from them. The air in it was warm and humid and music played softly, the light provided by the room's hidden bulbs low but constantly shifting from colour to colour as though the space was open to the sun above, its glow refracting down through layers of crystal like the leaves of the trees in some vast petrified forest.

Here, the heart could rest.

For three days, everything was well. I visited Norman twice a day, enjoying his company and making sure he was safe; people in his state are slower and clumsier than normal and cannot perform complex tasks, but he could read and chat and seemed to be relaxing comfortably. We played chess, me winning easily and guiltily enjoying the experience even though it was only because of Norma's reduced attention span and concentration, we talked about old times and started to plan my wedding. Norman wanted me to wear a morning suit with hat and gloves, I wanted to wear a lounge suit; we compromised on no hat or gloves. He asked what I wanted him to say in his speech and I told him to be honest, but not too honest; he said he'd be as honest as he needed to be to make sure people knew how proud he was of me and how much he loved me, and I had to blink to hold back tears. I fed him, cajoling him to chew his food rather than forget about it and have it fall from his mouth, and we did something we'd not done for months or, perhaps, years; we caught up.

On the morning of the fourth day, however, it was clear that something had gone wrong.

Norman was unable to rise from his couch when I arrived, his breathing was ragged and shallow and he was covered in sweat. His fingers and legs spasmed uncontrollably, jittering back and forth, his slippered heels scuffing on the carpet with a noise like fingers slipping across coarse paper. When I spoke to him, he didn't respond but sang something under his breath, as though trying to accompany a distant jig that he couldn't hear properly. Those worms writhed again then, the worms of panic and failure, hollowing my belly; I loved this man as a father and yet he was suffering in front of me, seemed not to even know me. Had his heart been further gone than I thought? The flesh more corrupted by life and medicines and pressures than I recognised, further than I could help to pull them back from? And then... and then, watching Norman's constantly working lips, watching the tongue in his mouth trying to poke the air into the shapes of words, watching his feet shift back and forth, I had the most terrible thought.

Closing the heavy curtains so that the room was dark, I gently opened first Norman's shirt and then his chest, peeling back the skin and revealing the cavity where his heart belonged. Putting my ear very close to it, I could hear music, faint and distant and jangling. There were tiny flashes of light in the pinched-shut blood vessels, golds and reds and blues and greens. Sighing, I knew what was wrong.

Norman's heart had gone Vegas.

Neither Denny nor Rose answered their door when I knocked, so I pushed it open slowly. The house was dark and almost quiet and did not contain its usual smells of bread or family meals or comfort. Instead, there was a dull scent of unflushed toilets and mustiness and staleness and a sound on the edge of hearing, rhythmic yet unpleasant. Walking along their neat hallway, no longer so pristine, painted in dust and odour, I wondered what had happened here, about what I might find. Their home seemed darker, colder and I felt myself grow tense as I went along its deserted hallway. The noise I had been hearing resolved itself from the almost-silence, from the cusps of noise I'd been hearing since opening the door. It was coming from ahead of me, from behind a closed door, the metallic beat of something modern and garish.

I went to the room, the one where Norman's heart was supposed to be resting but from which now noise pulsed and shook, and opened the door. Instead of the quiet room of soft rhythms and live plants that I should have found, there was instead a dizzying mess of flashing lights and wild, energetic music, a tarantella of staccato tones and plosive beats. Brightly coloured bulbs dangled from new cables roped across the ceiling and around the door and new speakers were mounted on brackets fixed inexpertly to the wall. They vibrated in time with the volume and rhythm of the music, dust shivering out from drilled holes in the walls where screws poked out at odd angles. The air had become stifling, too warm, and Norman's heart now lay on moss that was dark and dry. Its surface had flushed to a rich, unhealthy purple and it flexed irregularly. It wasn't singing any longer, it was wailing, a frantic, exhausted yowl that sounded to me like distant cats at night. Its pain was almost tangible.

This needed fixing, and fast, before this Vegas became the place Norman's heart beat its last, closing around itself and smothering its song and its beat and Norman's life in one frenzied moment. I took both the speakers from their brackets and yanked the leads from them, stopping the music mid-note. Tracing the light-bulb cables back, I found the power-source and disconnected it. It, too, had been badly put together and I had to feel my way through a tangle of live wires and stripped plastic cables hanging from hooks unevenly drilled into the wall to turn it off. It sparked as I did so, the room's original lighting fluttering like the back and forth of a hummingbird's wing above me before shorting out in a swirl of ozone and smoke.

Turning back to the heart, I saw that it was already calming, jittering more slowly but still irregular, the rhythms wretched, its surface covered in tiny striations where it had dried and cracked. I found the plant mister lying on the floor, rolled against the wall, picked it up and sprayed it, letting the water drift down like mist, thankful at the way the heart responded to it, at the way the water trickled around the valves and tubes as it pulsed, at the way in which its colour began to fade and the moisture made the striations smooth out, and the heart's voice began to ring out again. Satisfied that it would be all right but growing angry with Denny and Rose, I left the room and listened; there was no other noise in the house. I went through to the kitchen, always their home's warmest place, and peered inside. The room was cold and the sour smell stronger here.

Rose was sitting at the kitchen table. She did not look around as I entered.

"Rose?" I said. She ignored me.

"Rose," again but louder, sharper, and finally she turned her head towards me. Her face was slack with disinterest and drool spilled from her mouth. I saw that she held a cup partway between the table and her mouth and seemed unable to decide whether to put it down or drink from it. Her hand shook, tea that looked grey and sickly slopping over the edge of the cup and trickling down its porcelain side and onto Rose's skirt. Great hanks of her hair had fallen out and lay draped in skeins over her shoulders and the floor.

I stepped to Rose, my anger draining away at the sight of that baggy, pallid face, pulling a chair in front of her and sitting, bringing my face close to hers. The smell of her was wrong, rotten and grimy and somehow septic, overlaid with the scent of too-sweet tea and milk going slowly off. Her eyes had paled over the past few days, becoming slate-grey voids in which I could see neither the skitter of interest nor sign of awareness. Veins bulged in her forehead, pushing out the skin, and I thought again of worms, of things writhing beneath the surface. In one of the bald spots on her scalp I saw an ugly, twisting wound where the flesh had been split and then raggedly healed, bunched together in two thick cables that squeezed against each other and merged like half-dried glazier's putty. The wound was weeping and what hair remained around it was knotted with dried and crusting pus. Pink streaks of blood ran through the pus, here and there dried to a cracked ruby carapace.

Someone had opened Rose's head and then not sealed it correctly afterwards; the edges where the flesh had failed to join properly, where the lips of skin overlapped or did not meet at all, were all too obvious.

"Oh, Rose," I said, more to myself then to her, and then I placed my hand against the wound.

The flesh parted, its wet edges sucking at my skin as though grateful to be freed from the unnatural shape it had been forced into. The inside of Rose's head was warm, too warm, near-feverish, as though she was burning out from some place near her core; in some ways, I supposed, she was. I stroked and pushed a little deeper, fingers brushing against bone.

The skull had been opened along a suture line but also had been closed poorly and it, too, opened for me with no resistance, and I peeled back the scalp and skull easily, as easily as unfolding the flaps of a cardboard box, and revealed Rose's brain. Clinging to it, now exposed to the light, was a small, dirty grey mass, is jellied edges curled around the crenulations of Rose's own brain. Touching it, I shuddered. Someone had placed dead brain matter in Rose's head and tried to encourage it to grow by folding its edges around her existing flesh. It was chill, this dead flesh, and smelled of infections that had burned themselves out and left only poison in their wake.

It was an easy job to remove it, for it had not taken root; I simply peeled it back from Rose's brain, wiping her clean as I did so, pressing her back into her own shape and sealing her as I removed my fingers. Once Rose's skull and scalp were closed and the scars smoothed to nothing, I dropped the brain mass to the floor and then placed her hair back onto her head, coaxing it to root and grow now that the alien presence was gone. She would always be thinner on top, I thought, but not noticeably so.

After just a moment or two, the focus came back into her eyes and she looked at me. "What happened?" she asked, and then her memories pulled themselves free from the morass of the last few days and linked together and, leaning forward, she vomited over the floor, dropping her cup. I pulled her into a hug and whispered to her that everything was fine, that everything would be fine, that she would be okay. My hands stroked her through her clothes and soon she was asleep in my arms, her flesh made drowsy by my touch.

Leaving Rose sleeping, slumped across the table with her head cushioned in her arms, avoiding the spilt tea and vomit, I went to the lounge. It was here I found Denny; he was sitting on the floor, his head bobbing along to sounds only he could hear. His fingers clicked, the sound slightly uneven as though his fingers and thumbs weren't quite lined up correctly. Like Rose, his hair was falling out in clumps and a thick wound crawled across his stubbled scalp.

"Hello, Denny," I said. His head snapped up and he glared at me. His eyes were bright, glittering, but their reddened rims betrayed his tiredness. "What happened to you and Rose?"

"I bought us some imagination," he snapped, his glare never lessening, "from a man who came to the door! He put it in for us. You never told me that having imagination was so much fun!"

I sighed. It was obvious once he said it. That pale lump in Rose's head could be nothing other than illegal tissue, stolen from the dead and dying, or worse, to augment the living. Door-to-door flesh, bought from morgues and accident scenes, unearthed from the graves of the recently interred, scavenged from the weak and helpless in homes and hospitals, held out and offered like the answers to questions you'd never asked, like an answer to a prayer offered at such a reasonable price. God knows how the salesman had persuaded the normally reliable Denny to buy it, but persuade them he had, and the result had nearly killed three people.

The reason I employed Denny and Rose was that they were perfect for me; they had a little imagination without being in any way creative. Providing a resting place for hearts is a careful business and I needed someone who could be trusted to follow my instructions without needing mothering. Rose knew to increase the humidity if it got dry and which sort of plants each heart responded best to; Denny knew when to replace the moss and when to lower the volume of the music slightly if the hearts did not like it. He read the hearts and changed the slow shift of the lights, increasing or decreasing play or vibrancy of the colours. They saw situations, both of them, and made tiny intuitive leaps; they used a little imagination.

The problem with having just a little imagination, of course, is that it occasionally it leaps further than anyone expected. Occasionally it can be worked upon by the unscrupulous.

Occasionally, it grows.

"Why did you change the room?" I asked, just to keep Denny talking. He was dangerous in this state, like a faithful dog on the cusp of a rabies madness, waiting for the trigger than would give him the reason to explode.

"The room was dull! That old heart looked bored just lying there doing nothing," said Denny brightly. "I thought it needed cheering up. It looked like it needed a holiday so I made it more fun."

"It was a nice thought, Denny," I replied as kindly as I could and before he could stop me, I stepped to him and placed my palms over his eyes.

He screamed, thrashing in my arms. He came up to a half-standing position, his feet pushing against the floor and driving us both backwards. I crashed into the wall, heard something fall, and then Denny's hands were clawing at my own.

Already, he was changing. The signals emerging from his brain were distorted and alien, warping his body into something new; claws sprouted from the ends of his fingers, splitting the skin in weeping red curves. I managed to dodge his first strike, which was clumsy, but his second was faster and slashed across my forehead, drawing blood that spilled down into my eyes. I blinked, twisted as he slashed again, and yanked him around, clamping my hands tighter across his face, one across his eyes and the other dropping towards his mouth, stepping behind him at the same time in an intricate gavotte of violence. Already my fingers were in his flesh, pulling apart the muscle and bone. I had no time for niceties, entered without delicacy, pushing aside his teeth and reaching beyond a tongue that had grown scales, was wrapping itself around my fingers and rasping at me, my other hand digging above his sinuses to get at what lay in the centre of his head. He was trying to scream again, the sound muffled and raw, and his legs were kicking back at me. His knees were bending the wrong way, his boots splitting as he grew another step further away from human.

I pressed on, finally through Denny's elongating nasal cavity and into his brain. It was cold in there, limbic and dank, alien, sharp. Something tightened around my questing fingers, trying to hold them together, to prevent them moving, but I spread them; the thing in Denny's head was still new, thank God, was still weak. It snapped at me and he screamed again, this time in pain, and then I was at the right part of his brain, my fingers against the sleep centres, and I squeezed, tight, pressing everything in on itself. Denny went rigid, the skin of his back rough against me through our clothes, something that felt like ridges of scale grating against me, and then he collapsed into sleep.

I don't like doing that, but sometimes it's the easiest thing.

I opened Denny's head more fully, letting his sleeping body sag against me. I reshaped his skull as I went, undoing the damage I had wrought on my journey into him. As I had guessed, the situation was worse in Denny than it had been with Rose. Here, the dead brain matter had taken, had started to grow and spread its poison throughout his head. I touched it and knew, from its heat and the texture of it that it wasn't human.

Jesus, it wasn't human.

The new brain matter felt alien, felt fucking reptilian, clung on to Denny's lobes with a blind tenacity when I tried to unwrap it. Each tendril reacted against me, trying to burrow deeper to get away, and each tried to form itself into tiny, sharp-toothed worms and to turn and bite me as I pulled them free and dropped them to the floor.

The central mass of it had managed to wrap itself around a huge section of Denny's brain, tightening threateningly when I reached for it. Eyes opened in it, milky and lidless, a mouth opening and snapping at me as I started to pull it free. Who had sold this, I wondered, who had sold this dank and rotting flesh? It was poison because it was dead, because it was inhuman, because it was wrong. Denny thrashed once more, weakly, and then was still.

It took me hours to untangle it all, peeling back healthy lobes and freeing clammy grey strands of new growth, teasing out strings of

corrupted tissue from between the valleys of Denny's own brain. I had
to stop several times to let my hands rest, to let the intruder flesh calm
down. Its eyes blinked at me, weeping grey tears, its mouth snapping
ineffectually at my fingers. As I worked, freeing Denny from its grip,
his body began to return to normal, the claws retreating into his fingers,
the skin healing down to white-scarred smoothness and the ridges on
his back sinking away like fins into distant water.

I dropped the pieces of dead brain on the floor next to me and
watched as they tried to crawl away. I crushed each one that made it
free and looked as though it had the strength to escape, not liking the
feel of it under the heel of my palm, not liking its smell or texture or
the way it bit at me even as it died. What had it been, this sold thing?
Had it once graced a creature in an African river or some South
America swamp? Or was it the last of some poor zoo animal, driven
mad by concrete and captivity and insane even in death? Perhaps it was
all three or more, a terrible blend of the grotesque and the savage and
the dead.

Eventually, I was finished. I sealed Denny's head and allowed him to
slump to the floor. With luck, he would have no ill-effects other than a
headache and bruises around his knees and fingers where his body had
been warped and then put back to its more usual shape. I was dripping
with sweat, my shirt soaked and becoming clammy against my skin as
it cooled. I used the bathroom to wash and to see myself in the mirror,
sealing the cuts across my forehead with a hand that shook. I went back
to the heart, to Norman's heart, and watched it beat for a long time,
letting its normality calm me. It had settled, had found a slow and
relaxed rhythm for itself, was a healthy cherry colour. In a few days, if
it was allowed to rest properly, it could go back to Norman and he
would be back to his usual, headstrong self. The thought made me smile
and I wanted to go home to sleep but could not. I was tired, but I had
more to do yet.

Before I left, I laid my hands on both Rose and Denny one more
time, persuading their flesh and bones to forget all that had happened.
They would wake tomorrow and simply get on, tidying the house and
seeing to the heart as before. On my way out, I buried the dead tissue
in the garden where it could rot to nothing and feed the soil.

There are no police for what I do, no rules except those which we
set ourselves or those which we agree with each other in gentlemen's

agreements or palm-shook, pinky-sworn and spittle-sealed deals, but there are standards. We do not use the flesh for profit, we do not mix the flesh, we do not augment the healthy. We open the flesh to heal, to lift the weights and the pressures, to create spaces in which people can remember how to breathe, remember how to fall in love, to open themselves to others and close themselves to the darkness. We do this because we have skills that few are granted, and now there was someone corrupting the gift.

Am I a monster? I have been told so, by people who were frightened of me; once, a girl I was in a relationship with broke off contact with me when she found out about my skill. "What if you open me up by accident," she asked, "while you're inside me, while you're touching me?" She was crying as she said it, her arms crossed in front of her and her hands clasped in front of her sex as though in a downward-facing prayer for safety. She was wrong, of course; opening is not accidental, not ever. It requires thought and will and touch; I could have traced my fingers between her legs an infinite number of times and done her no harm, but she would never believe that. Damage is done by deliberation, by commission.

By monsters.

Human flesh is easy to obtain, if you need it. The unscrupulous openers need simply to scan obituaries, pay cemetery attendants, cultivate friendships with hospital morgue staff or funeral directors or ambulance drivers; there's always someone in need of money, someone prepared to look the other way. It is easier and simpler to insert and coax into life than animal flesh, less violent, less resistant, but it is more expensive. What had been done here was foul, a perversion, a mutation and a lie, done for money and profit, done for coin.

I reached above me and opened the flesh of the sky, speaking. My fingers wriggled through the veins and capillaries of the clouds, seeking, and the words followed. The world, this complex beautiful thing, peeled back and exposed itself for me and I could see it all, see every part of it, from the swirling lightless depths of the ocean and the giant fish that swam there to the tiny spiders floating in the slipstream whose feet never touched earth and who fed on fleeting bugs so small they can only be seen through a microscope, and I touched everything and I searched, feeling for the taint of sickness and fever.

There.

He was a cancer, a blight, a man with a bag of dead animal flesh over his shoulder walking along a darkened road and then I opened more, opened wider and let the words chase out, let them dart like silver fish, let them wind and spin and the words were there about him and above him and opening the earth below him, and then the man fell and the man was gone and the bag was gone with him and I spoke the last word, the heavier one that moved like swiftly flowing oil and it swallowed the silver ones and closed the gaps they had made and I sealed and pulled back and the world healed and Rose and Denny slept.

Am I a monster? I do not know, but I know that Rose and Denny are safe, Norman is safe, no one else will be sold that corrupting, decaying flesh. I open, and I close, and that is the world I know and love and live in. This is me, and this is what I am.

Tired, I returned home and showered and went to bed and when I slept, I did not dream. Somewhere in the night, a heart that had shaped my childhood and laid the paths into my adulthood that I walked to this day lay resting and secure and its owner rested too. Am I a monster?

Six months later, I married and Norman stood by my side as best man, and his speech was warm and funny and made me cry and his heart was well and the sound of its singing was almost as loud as the sound of my own heart's song.

The Terrible Deaths of the Ghosts of the Westmorland

i. Arrival

"Welcome to the Westmorland, Mr. Nakata," said the man - boy, really - behind the counter, and handed Nakata a plastic keycard. Apart from the black magnetic strip along one side, the card was blank except for the word 'Westmorland' in small, neat letters. The plastic was scratched and worn, warm from being in the receptionist's hand.

"Thank you,' said Nakata, placing the card in his pocket. "Is Mr. Brook here yet?"

"No, sir. He's left a message for you, though. He says he'll be here later and that he'll meet you in the restaurant at eight. It'll be his pleasure to take you to dinner." The boy stopped talking and screwed up his face, rolling his eyes to the ornate ceiling above him, lips moving as though he was going over a script he was struggling to learn. After a moment, his face relaxed and he said, "No, that's all. Eight in the restaurant and he'd buy you dinner."

"Thank you," said Nakata again, bending and retrieving his bag from the floor by his feet. "

"Are you with him?" the receptionist asked.

"With who?"

"Mr. Wellman."

"Amos Wellman?"

The boy's face went slack, his eyes starry and distant. "Yes. I wondered if you were part of his team. I mean, I know he's in the hotel but I haven't seen him yet so I don't know who's with him and who isn't. Is he going to be working here? I mean, I don't know, no one's told us. Is he? If he is, then he might already be working. In the hotel, I mean."

"I suppose so, and no, I'm not with him," said Nakata and turned to go. Amos Wellman's dark, piercing eyes watched him from a poster adorning the foyer wall, following him as he went to the stairwell, and they only seemed to shift their attention away long after Nakata had moved out of their eyeline and started down the stairs to his room.

Room 116 was pokey, apparently formed around one of the pillars that ran up through the Westmorland's architecture so that the space seemed constricted around the centre of the room, breathless and tight and taut. The ceiling was low and Nakata wondered if the room was an afterthought, created out of previously-dead space to capitalise on the hotel's popularity during its more successful years. Now, it was an oddity in the Westmorland's depths, a double room designed as though for people who weren't quite all there. Only the fact that he was short, a gift from his father's side of the family along with a slight caste to his skin and the epicanthic folds that gave his eyes their sleepy, hooded appearance and marked him out as mixed race, meant he could move comfortably around the room and not feel hemmed in from above as well as from the sides. *Thanks, Dad,* he thought, smiling as he did so and putting his bag on the bed.

He unpacked slowly, putting his pants and socks in the slightly uneven drawers at the side of his bed and his shirts on the mixed hangers in the wardrobe, making the place his home, if only for the next three days. He put the papers he had brought to read on the top of the drawers, hoping to get to them later; although he wasn't at the university at the moment, was serving out his enforced sabbatical, he was keen to keep up to date with recent research.

Next to them, he placed Amos Wellman's autobiography, *This Man of Visions.*

The same picture that had been on the foyer wall graced the book's cover, the smaller size making the eyes, if anything, more intense, gleaming out from above a thin, straight nose and lips that were pulled back in something that might have been a smile but might equally have been a snarl. In the picture, Wellman's hair was swept back from a high forehead, the widow's peak a dark *V* that made the rest of the face aquiline and tense, a raptor spying prey. Nakata looked at him for a moment, trying to discern anything but show business glamour and media manipulation in the face, and then stopped. This was nothing but a frozen image, a face that he suspected bore little relation to reality; he'd find out soon enough, he supposed.

Nakata looked at his watch; just after three. He had hours before Brook arrived and he didn't want to sit in this windowless, below-ground room waiting. Instead, he left the cramped space and walked the Westmorland's corridors.

The hotel had motion-sensitive lights, flickering into life as Nakata ambled along the panelled hallways and clicking off behind him, so that he felt he was travelling in a bubble of his own illumination; light that fell on standard framed prints on the walls slid along the threadbare carpet with him and finally brought him to an T junction. Heading to his left would, if his internal map was correct, start him moving back towards the lifts and the reception above him, to the places he'd been before; to the right was unknown, a mystery. *Mystery*, he thought to himself and felt himself smile again, this time bitter and without humour. *You've surely had enough mystery, haven't you? So much mystery that the university have sent you on gardening leave while they decide what to do with you, and the press love to call you all kinds of fool. You've had mystery, mystery that led to dancing ghosts and dead children and a court not believing you when you told them ghosts were real, despite what you tried to show them. Let it go, man. Let it go.*

He looked to the left. Beyond the light darkness filled the corridor, stretching it out in a jumble of shadow and doorway edges before ending at another T junction decorated with a sign pointing to reception. To his right, another corridor rolled away in a fractured patchwork of liminal greys and blacks. *Mystery*, Nakata thought, and turned his back to reception and took his light sunwise, into the depths of the Westmorland.

ii. Dinner and Mr. Brook

"I'm still not sure why I'm here," said Nakata, laying down his knife and fork and looking at the man opposite him, plate empty.

Henry Brook put his own knife and fork down and said, "What did you think of the food?"

"Pardon?"

"The food. What did you think of it?"

Nakata looked around; he and Brook were sitting in the Westmorland's dining room, its old wood and polished brass exuding a weary, fading charm. They were the only ones in the room, and the meal they had been served by an unsmiling girl in a too-tight uniform had been good but not excellent; nothing to write home about. The conversation that taken place over the meal had been frustrating in its inconsequentiality. "It was very nice," he replied, "but as I said, I'm still unclear as to why you want me here."

"The food wasn't 'very nice', Mr. Nakata, it was passably adequate. The Westmorland has a long history of functional adequacy. The rooms are clean but plain, the décor is tired but not unpleasant, the service is unremarkable, not poor but nothing you'll remember afterwards. The Westmorland does not linger in the memory, Mr. Nakata, and this is the way the owners like it."

"The owners?" Nakata had assumed that Brook was the owner; it was from him that Nakata's invite had come, and he with whom all the arrangements had been made.

"The owners," repeated Brook. "They feel that the Westmorland has existed for a large number of years in its state of adequacy, a place that fulfils a function but never goes beyond its own simple remit, that of providing sanctuary and peace and a place to rest to anyone that needs it, for as long as they require it. It is their considered opinion that the Westmorland, having been successful in this task, should be allowed to carry on in this honourable, if anonymous, manner without interruption or obstacle. There is, they see, no reason to change."

It was like being at an academic funding meeting, Nakata thought, where everyone had agendas but wouldn't reveal them, and where the conversations moved in elliptical, tangential directions. The participants performed verbal sleights of hand, so that their actual meanings were shaped and created and obscured by the words they used, rather than exposed, and he was tired of it.

"Mr. Brook," Nakata said, "I appreciate the entirely adequate meal, but you brought me here because you said you had a proposition to discuss with me. Can we please get to the point?"

Brook looked at Nakata for a moment, and then nodded as though some internal agreement had been reached. "Of course," he said. "I apologise for what must seem like unnecessary delaying, but the owners value their privacy, and this situation is unprecedented. We had to make sure you could actually help us.

"You've heard of Amos Wellman." It wasn't a question but a statement. Brook's voice was toneless and hard, professional now.

"Yes. A little. You told me he'd be here at the same time I am."

"Just so. Amos Wellman has decided to visit the Westmorland. He has, in fact, been here for a day already."

"So I heard," said Nakata, remembering the picture in the foyer, the dark eyes following him as he went to his room, the star-struck reaction of the young receptionist. "I saw the posters in town before I came, and brought his book with me. I thought it might be amusing."

"Amusing? Well, possibly. In any case, he is here and he is not a valued guest. Mr. Wellman originally contacted the Westmorland's owners through me several months ago now, asking for permission to film here. He had, he said, gathered a considerable number of eyewitness reports about the Westmorland's 'apparitions and presences', and wanted to see if he could contact them, to 'help them on'. Naturally, we refused."

"Yet Wellman is here," said Nakata. *Now we're getting to it*, he thought.

"Indeed. Mr. Wellman and his small team booked in under assumed names several weeks ago, and then once ensconced announced their presence loudly, making sure people knew of their arrival, making sure all the staff knew, and then told everyone that they were filming here whether we liked it or not. We do *not* like it, Mr. Nakata, not at all, but we found ourselves in a difficult position. Removing Mr. Wellman at that point might have created more fuss than leaving him here; certainly, that's what he threatened us with. The Westmorland's anonymous adequacy was threatened by this intrusion, Mr. Nakata; our carefully worked-for space and the things it contains were at risk."

"I'm sorry," said Nakata, "I can understand your concern, I can, but I still don't understand what you want me here for. I'm an academic, not a bouncer or a PR manager. I can't see how I'm going to help you."

"Have you ever watched Wellman's show *The Spirit Guider*?"

"No."

"Amos Wellman is a showman, pure and simple. He goes to public buildings, determines that there are ghosts in attendance and then exorcises them. He terms what he does 'guiding them along the path to God', but it's an exorcism nonetheless, a showbusiness one with all the attendant whistles and bells. It usually comes along with what have now become trademark Wellman histrionics, gibbering and speaking in something that he'd like you to believe are 'tongues', sometimes collapsing to the floor, shrieking, pointing, seeing demons attacking the ghost's spirit as it tries to leave this earthly plain, that kind of thing. It's tawdry and unintelligent, and now he's brought it here."

Nakata waited. Wherever this was going the end was in sight, the explanation just behind Brook's lips.

"To prevent any adverse publicity and to try to keep control of the situation when Wellman first arrived, we discussed the matter and regretfully agreed that if he left peacefully, we would allow him and his team of three to return and to investigate The Westmorland for three days, this arrangement being dependent on his agreement to three non-negotiable conditions. Firstly, that all footage filmed within the Westmorland is viewed, and where possible agreed, by the owner's legal representatives prior to broadcast and that in the event of a disagreement between the two parties a final decision about what can be broadcast be arbitrated by an independent third party. Secondly, that neither Mr. Wellman nor his team speak to any of the Westmorland's other guests during their stay."

Brook paused, anticipating the question. Nakata, suddenly feeling claustrophobic, feeling the walls move in towards him, asked it. "And the third?"

"That Mr. Wellman co-operate fully by agreeing to be accompanied by you during any time he is within the hotel and engaged in his investigation, to ensure that nothing fraudulent takes place and to ensure that some level of decorum be adhered to."

And there it was, the reason for the last few weeks' cagey discussions, the reason for the offer of three nights' accommodation, the reason for the adequate meal, the reason for the mystery. Nakata stood, trembling, and then sat back down, still trembling. Mr. Brook remained silent, watching and waiting and really, what could Nakata do? He opened his mouth, closed it, opened it again but Mr. Brook interrupted.

"I know this is a surprise, but please believe me when I tell you we have only taken this course of action after considerable thought. The owners trust you to ensure that Wellman remains within acceptable boundaries. They trust you to protect the hotel, Mr. Nakata, and to make sure that Wellman does not use the Westmorland like some gaudy fairground ride. We know of you, Mr. Nakata. We *trust* you. Please, help us.

"We are, of course, prepared to make significant restitution for your time." Brook pushed a slim white envelope across the table. Nakata reached out but did not take it.

Do I want this, he thought. *Do I?* His hand hovered, dropped, rose, dropped again like a bird buffeted by lean winds. Silence surrounded him, a silence filled with the sound of shouting and tension and uncertainty. It filled his head, this fractured noiselessness, until he thought he might scream and he closed his eyes and his hand moved a last time, apparently without him telling it to.

After the meal with Brook, Nakata returned to his room. He was angry, at Brook and the way he and the Westmorland's owners had simply assumed his agreement and acted without explaining the situation to him first, but also angry with himself, angry that he hadn't stood up, nodded his polite goodbyes, and left. Sitting in the room, staring at the blank television and the faded counterpane and the cheap plastic kettle and the mug with the single sachets of coffee in it, at the envelope propped against one of the mugs, he thought *I'm an academic, a good one, not some assistant, not part of a TV psychic's sideshow. This can't be what I do next. I'm not a babysitter. I'm not this thing they think I am.*

And then that other part of him, the more realistic part, said quietly, *You're an academic who's likely about to be suspended by his university and whose recent appearances in the press have been reacted to with criticism and hostility. You investigate ghosts for a living, what did you expect? Besides, how is this any less a job than investigating haunted places for a lawyer? How is it any less important than appearing in court, staking your reputation on a jury? Telling twelve strangers ghost stories and hoping they'll believe you? Isn't Wellman simply another facet of this world you chose to walk in? You wanted mystery, but maybe this is the one you have to face next; the mystery of what do I do with my life now?*

Nakata couldn't breathe. The walls closed in, the air thickening, the room darkening until all he could see were his own hands, white and glimmering in the gloom and a voice that might have been his own muttered in his ear, quiet and distant. *Mystery*, it said, and then fell silent.

iii. Wellman

"You don't want to do this anymore than I do," said Wellman as he shook Nakata's hand.

Although he wasn't sure why, Nakata expected Wellman to be taller. Something about the way he was photographed for the posters, maybe, always from below so that he seemed to be looming, but the reality was that he was shorter than Nakata, compact and neat. Dapper, almost, dressed in a matching jacket and waistcoat, a plain shirt, dark jeans and formal shoes. He was bald, the skin of his scalp smooth and gleaming in his room lights and Nakata suddenly had the oddest image, of the man polishing his head lovingly with a cloth and oil so that it shone as bright as possible on the screen.

The note had been pushed under Nakata's door during the night, there for him when he awoke, stating simply *Room 372, 10.00am* in neat, tight handwriting. A summoning, and the last chance to say no, to turn his back on this task and all the things that it might bring to his life.

He was standing outside room 372's door at 10.05.

When he knocked, the door was opened by a scruffy man holding a camera at his shoulder, its red LED eye glaring at him. "Put that down," Nakata said. "I'm not to be filmed." The cameraman glanced back into the room, obviously received permission, and lowered his camera.

"Mitch," the cameraman said, "you Nakata?" Nakata nodded, was ushered in and then he was with Wellman.

Nakata had spent some time the previous night looking up the presenter on the internet, and then more time this morning on the telephone with Tidyman. He had seen Wellman's approach to paranormal investigation, a media-age version of muscular Christianity, charging up and down shadowy corridors and into gloomy rooms, seeing things that the camera couldn't catch and then holding a hand out and exhorting them to leave in the name of *God*, in the *power of God's love*. There were usually shouts, sweat gleams from Wellman's scalp, intense eyes and occasionally the intimation that the unseen spirit was fighting back, refusing to leave. As Brook had said, Wellman would sometimes lapse into other languages, making glottal sounds like fingers popping through mud and chanting something that might have been Latin or Spanish but might equally have been sheer nonsense. It was a gimmick, as old as snake-oil traders, no better than the television preachers with their shining suits and bouffant hair; Wellman had just climbed on the shoulders of other shows and made the investigations less neutral. He was there to remove the spirits, to banish the ghosts, and he did so with all the drama that the camera required.

"Read this and sign it, please," said Nakata, handing Wellman the document Tidyman had dictated to him that morning. Although it was handwritten, it was legally sound; Tidyman, who felt guilty about the way things had turned out for Nakata after the court case, had happily given Nakata the wording he needed.

"What's this?" said Wellman, taking the paper from Nakata.

"You're wrong, I'm happy to do this," said Nakata, not exactly truthfully, "because it's interesting. I'm interested in seeing how you work, and how your work fits or doesn't with mine, but I won't be in your film. I've had enough trouble with negative publicity recently, so this is simply your agreement that, whatever else your film ends up showing, it won't include me. I will not be mentioned or referenced in any way at all."

Wellman read the form and then, to Nakata's surprise, took a slim fountain pen from his inside pocket and signed it without comment. Handing back the document he said, "I have no problem with this. My presence here isn't about you, Mr. Nakata. In fact, I'm glad the Westmorland's owners asked you to watch me, it's simply a shame they've forced the issue in the way they have. It would have been nice to have been given the chance to arrange this without external pressure or the ultimatum hanging over us the way it is, which I'd have been happy to do. I've been interested in you for a long while now, and it's a genuine pleasure to meet you."

"You know who I am?"

"Of course. Everyone in my field does. We may appear to be fakers and charlatans, and some are I suppose, but there are some of us who are genuine. Anyone who works within this area wants to be vindicated, and your work may go some way to prove that we're not all liars and idiots. Ghosts are *real*, Mr. Nakata, you know that as well as I do. We just have to persuade everyone else. Now, shall we start?"

The second surprise was that Nakata found himself liking Wellman.

Wellman first introduced Nakata to his team members. Mitch nodded at him laconically while the sound man, Jay, ignored him and the PA, a small, elfin girl with long dark hair called Caitlin, bustled about him and talked over his head to Mitch about "fields of view" and "operative moments" and "audience connection points", their language an industry-speak code that Nakata almost understood the way he almost understood some dreams, grasping the broad ideas if not the specifics. Then, while the team planned that afternoon's excursion,

Nakata and Wellman sat in the corner of the room and talked.

Wellman proved to be witty and intelligent and seemed to be able to draw a distinction between the approach he took and the approach Nakata took, which other supposed psychics Nakata had met and worked with did not. He seemed to be up to date on the academic research and certainly knew about Nakata's court case and asked insightful questions about Nakata's approach and the results he had achieved. Wellman was open about his spirituality and background, telling Nakata a story he had heard a version of countless times before, a tale he had started to privately call "the psychic's lament"; of a childhood spent mostly apart from other children and with only one or two key adults present, of church attendance, of academic talent but little support, of feeling lonely and excluded, and of seeing the dead.

"They were everywhere," said Wellman, "and I didn't know they were anything other than normal. It was only as I got older that I began to understand that not everyone else could see what I saw. I began to keep it secret, and it made me feel awful, like I was doing something wrong, that the things I saw were shameful. When I brought it up at my parents' church I was told to be quiet, to say nothing, that I was imagining things, all in the same breath as exalting the greatest spirit of them all, God."

Seeing Nakata's expression, Wellman said, "Oh, don't get me wrong, I'm not complaining. I've long since come to terms with my past and the difficulties I faced. The important thing is that I came through it with an understanding that the dead were and are real, that ghosts exist, and that they need our help to finish their journey."

"Our help?"

"Well, if you're being pedantic," said Wellman, smiling, "my help. They're like children, the dead, waiting for guidance and structure, waiting for instruction." Nakata, thinking about the spirit of a racist old man and of Amy falling down the stairs, said nothing. There had been nothing childlike about the ghost in 24 Glasshouse.

"And you see them? The dead, I mean? When other people can't?"

Wellman paused and then said, "'See' is a very precise term, Mr. Nakata. Knowing the dead are there is more and less than a visual experience. It's a sight and a sound and a sense like a breeze blowing on my skin. It's like hearing something you can't see and seeing something you can't hear at the same time."

"That's not exactly scientific," said Nakata as Wellman smiled at him again. The man was warmer than he appeared on screen, had charisma and charm, and it was hard not to like him.

"I'm not a scientist," replied Wellman, "and I never claimed to be one. I'm a man of faith, and my faith leads me to believe the dead who remain need help to move on. I'm happy to work with scientists such as yourself, but I see no reason to try and prove myself because I know what I feel and what I do and how I help, and that is enough."

"So if I asked you to try one of your... what do you call them? Exorcisms?"

"No, not 'exorcism', that's a loaded and dangerous term. I deliver the ghosts on. They're, if anything, deliverances, or support or help sessions, that's all. Exorcism is a very different thing"

"So if I were to ask you to carry out one of your deliverances under more scientific conditions, would you refuse?" asked Nakata, thinking not of deliverances but of the term 'support sessions,' and picturing the dead sitting in a circle saying, one by one, "My name is Caspar and I'm a ghost."

"Not at all," said Wellman. "I'm not a scientist and I have no requirement to be justified by you or anyone, but I'd be happy to co-operate. My faith doesn't need explanation or proof but I realise your science does, so if I can help that in any well, all the better."

Caitlin appeared at Wellman's shoulder, waiting deferentially until he'd finished talking to Nakata before leaning forward. "Amos," she said, her eyes cast somewhere towards Wellman's feet.

"Yes?"

"We're ready." She held out a sheaf of papers to him, saying, "Do you want to see the plan?"

"No," said Wellman, standing, waving away the papers that, Nakata saw, were floor plans marked with pencilled notations and comments. "I'm sure whatever Mitch and Jay have come up with is fine to start, and we'll play it by ear from there. Mr. Nakata?"

"Richard, please."

"Richard, then. Shall we go?"

"Go?"

"Hunting, Richard. Shall we go hunting ghosts?"

iv. In Shadowed Corridors

They started just outside Wellman's room. Mitch raised the camera to his shoulder as Wellman stepped in front of him, speaking back over his shoulder as they moved along the corridor, Jay's microphone hovering at the side of Mitch's head like some squat, dark fly.

"We're here in the Westmorland Hotel," said Wellman, "a building with a long history of housing the unfortunate dead. Unlike many places, however, there are no references to this building in pre-Internet printed books or pamphlets and only scant reference to it online, but if you know where to look and who to talk to, you can find out the information that has so long stayed hidden. The ghosts here are neither as showy as some of those we have helped in the past, nor as angry as those that challenged us in, say, the Hyde Hotel, but they are here and they deserve our help.

"There's a girl, I'm told, walking the corridors with a bunch of flowers in her hand, always searching for her long-gone mother and father; there's a nameless shape that hovers in the dining room; there's the shade of a murderer who committed his crimes over a hundred miles away yet has ended up trapped here; there's a kitchen maid always washing clothes and sheets, and a business man from the eighties talking into a phone that he no longer holds. The Westmorland has its ghosts, ladies and gentlemen, despite its attempts to keep them secret.

"And tonight we will endeavour to send them on their way."

It was a different Wellman to the one he had been talking to in the room Nakata realised; this one was brasher, somehow larger and louder and more overtly in charge. He kept looking back over his shoulder as he walked, peering briefly each time into the single eye of the camera and through it into the eyes of his viewers, a move Nakata recognised from the clips he had watched of Wellman on the internet the previous night. He talked constantly, a stream of patter that flowed around them as they went, making Nakata think of fairground barkers or market stall traders, exhorting and inviting confidence whilst trying to sell the listener something they weren't sure they needed. This was the Wellman of the posters and book cover, the centre of attention, the pivot around which everything else, including Nakata, turned.

"Where are you?" called Wellman, moving into another corridor, the lights popping on over them, their shadows pooling around their feet. "Where are you?"

Nothing answered. Wellman's head was a stream of light in the corridor, covered in a sheen of sweat, the effort of searching for the ghosts (*or the impression of effort*, thought Nakata briefly) showing on his face, in the lines that pitted his forehead when he turned back. "They're hiding," he said, "because they fear what must come next, but they have no need to fear. We've had this before, of course, ghosts that cling to the earth, to the roots they laid down in life, under the mistaken belief that they belong here. Little dead things, caught between life's miseries and God's graces, and we will find them and we will assist them on."

It was the preacher Wellman now, the one whose eyes gleamed with belief, the one whose lips sometimes flecked with spittle, whose absolute assurance filled the screen with a terrible inexorability. It was the Wellman that Nakata suspected the Westmorland was desperate to keep out, the one who would rage along the corridors and whose absoluteness would fill the space around him. It was fascinating to watch, this shift and change, as Wellman pulled this persona around himself, dragging it up like a cowl so that it covered him entirely, so that he became it and it him, and then the man practically shrieked, "There!"

Everyone froze, just for a moment, but again Nakata felt it was a practiced thing, a pause designed to communicate surprise, tension, maybe fear, to pull the viewers to the edge of their seats because then they were moving and both Jay and Mitch were smiling, *grinning,* as they dashed in Wellman's wake.

"Spirit!" shouted Wellman, turning yet another corner. Nakata was lost now, unsure of where there had come to or where they were headed. "Spirit, wait!"

I wouldn't wait, thought Nakata, *in the face of this bald, shrieking man charging down the corridor.* Wellman looked positively feral, wild and furious, less like a saviour than damnation itself. "In the light of God, go forth!" shouted Wellman and Nakata saw that some swift sleight of hand had taken place, that Caitlin had handed a small bible to Wellman under the camera's distracted gaze, that he was now holding it above and ahead of himself as he ran. "Go to the grace! Go to the mercy!

"Go on, child, go on!"

"It's a child?" asked Mitch, the feed line perfectly delivered.

"A lost child," Wellman panted, "a poor innocent soul that needs to take but one more step to enter God's all-encompassing embrace." They had come to yet another T junction, left taking them along a corridor of more rooms, right towards a storage cupboard and a dead end. Wellman turned right, still holding the bible out, thrusting it forward at a patch of air that appeared to Nakata to be empty and still.

"Go on, child!" Wellman shouted. "Go on, go to God!" With his free hand, Wellman reached out and grasped something either invisible or non-existent. It was low, perhaps three feet up from the floor, and he shook it hard, his other hand bringing the bible about and jamming it close to his clasping fist. Nakata could suddenly imagine a child, held by their shoulder and being shaken violently, the bible filling their vision, held for as much as weapon as for comfort, Wellman's voice rising above everything like that of a revivalist preacher.

"Go on! There is nothing for you here, nothing but the remnants of a life that you must let go to find true peace! Go on, I tell you, go on!" The last word was a full-throated roar, making even Nakata flinch, and then the bible was being swung around, slapping through the air with a noise like ripping cloth.

"Go on, damn you, go on! Oh," and this was cast back over his shoulder, "she's fighting, resisting. She's a feisty one, this girl, but I will not be stopped, God's will will be done!" And Wellman shook the air again, stepping forward so that had a girl existed she would be trapped between the wall and his body, confined in a prison of noise and sweat and that bible slashing back and forth and then Wellman was reciting the Lord's Prayer and making it sound like a battle cry punctuated by plosive gasps.

"Our Father! Who art in Heaven! Hallowed! Be! Thy! Name!" And Mitch was stepping forward and jamming the camera over Wellman's shoulder and Jay was at his other side and behind them Caitlin was hectically scrawling notes on a pad and the bible was swinging again and then Wellman stumbled back, still clutching the unseen thing, still swinging the bible.

"Find God," he shrieked, "find God and go on! You are delivered! You are sent on!" He fell to his knees and Nakata was alarmed to see tears rolling down his face, the expression there one of unwavering compassion and firm love. "He is waiting, He is there for you, child! Go on and find Him!"

The bible swung again, cutting through the space where the child's head might be, and then Wellman let go and fell forward, onto his hands and knees, the bible skittering forward. He took a deep, whooping breath, and then straightened, leaning back on his haunches, eyes closed.

"She is gone," Wellman said, his voice quiet again. "I have saved another." He closed his eyes, his breathing slowly steadying.

"Amos?" asked Caitlin. "Do you want to carry on?"

"No. We're done for now," replied Wellman. "We'll try again later. Mitch, did you get that?"

"Of course," said Mitch. "It'll look fantastic, Amos, very dramatic. The light in here is perfect, and you looked great. This is going to be a brilliant episode."

"Good," said. "Now, I'm tired. I need to rest."

He stood, assisted by Caitlin, and then walked away down the corridor without a backward glance. Nakata watched as he went, wondering if anything else would happen, but it did not. There was simply a man disappearing into the light, head a sheen of sweat and slump-shouldered with exhaustion, but no ghosts to be seen.

v. The Staff Areas

They went out again a couple of hours later.

Because it was later in the day, Wellman told Nakata, and there was a greater likelihood of bumping into other guests, Brook had limited this excursion to the staff areas. Consequently, they were confined to the kitchens and laundries, vast yet cramped spaces that took up all the basement and sub-basement levels. Followed by the ever-watchful Mitch and his third, electronic, eye Wellman stalked through huge cupboards filled with canned and dried foods, through rooms dense with steam and the smell of detergent and the almost-burned sweetness of sheets scalded to cleanliness and then heated to brittle dryness. Here and there staff members watched them, the expressions on their faces either excited recognition or angry dismissal; Wellman seemed to incite equally strong feelings in both directions.

In the main kitchen, Wellman claimed to see a black shape above the cookers but it slipped away before he could engage with it, making him hiss at the camera in something that might have been anger or might equally have been pity. A few moments later, in the connecting corridor, there was a man who darted away and had vanished by the time Wellman reached where he had been standing. This time, Wellman practically howled, the veins on his neck standing out in photogenic frustration.

As they progressed, it was clear that Wellman was becoming more and more irritated, and that this irritation was genuine, his over-the-shoulder comments becoming terser and terser, crackling with anger. *He believes*, Nakata realised. *This thing he's doing, it's not a show at all, he believes in it.* He wondered how often this happened, the times when Wellman couldn't find the ghosts he was so sure were there. Not often, he suspected. Whatever dressing up Wellman used for the cameras, at its heart was a genuine belief that he was seeing ghosts, that he could help them on.

Did that change anything? No, Nakata thought, it didn't, except that it if this were an experiment being carried out under laboratory conditions it might change Nakata's approach. The longer he spent with Wellman, the more he realised that this was a task not so much about catching out a cynical fraud as it was about separating different versions of the truth from each other and seeing which was stronger. Seeing, more importantly, which could be observed and recorded. Seeing which could be *proved*.

"There!" cried Wellman suddenly and began to run, to *sprint*, and again there was that sleight of hand and he was holding a bible ahead of him like some shield of righteousness and lance of light. "I see you, I see you!"

They were in a corridor lined with huge wheeled trolleys, each filled with rumpled masses of dirty sheets, and for a moment Nakata was caught up in it, was sure that someone was standing at the end of the long passage, someone slight and bent, standing behind the last of the trolleys. Was that a curve of shoulder, twitching as Wellman bore down on them, a head dipping, the person trying to make themselves smaller but unable to completely vanish? A person hunching into the space between two of the trolleys? Yes!

No. No, it was just shadows and old, frayed light falling from the dusty strip lights above them and Mitch was running and Jay was there too and then Wellman was grabbing at the liminal air and hollering and screeching.

"Go on! Go on!" and he was shaking the air again, a dog snapping the neck of a thing that wasn't there, swinging his bible in vicious, jabbed arcs. "You do not belong here! You do not belong, go on! Go ON!"

Nakata was struggling to see past the cameraman and sound man and even Caitlin was in front of him now and the scene ahead of him was a melee of sound and shouts and lights jumping and darting, four people writhing around each other. An elbow snapped back out of the struggling mass and caught Nakata under the left eye and his vision filled with startled explosions, floaters and streaks that collapsed in on each other as he shook his head, concentrating on the four people ahead of him.

Five people, a glimpse of white dress and black ankle boot.

Four people, Wellman still shouting, sweat droplets now flicking from his head as he shook and thrashed, his entire upper body twisting and twitching.

Five people, that flash of white again, a grimy pale blur in the centre of the mass, Wellman holding not it but the air above it, the bible still scything back and forth and there was shouting and Caitlin dropped her pad and the loose pages sheaved away and fluttered in the air and there was another cry, a bellow and then a scream so high and long and desperate that Nakata winced to hear it.

And then it was gone, and over, and Wellman was slumped on the floor, leaning half back against the wall, dripping sweat and gasping. "Enough," he said and his voice was thin and hoarse. "Enough. I must rest."

vi. Over Drinks

"Well, what did you think?"

Nakata didn't reply, because honestly he didn't know *what* to think. What had he seen? Or heard? Nothing, or at least nothing that couldn't be explained by the situation itself, by the heightened emotions of the hunts and by the mild bang he had taken in the face. That Wellman believed was not in doubt, but as to whether he had actually helped the dead onwards with their journey was another matter entirely. Eventually, because Brook was clearly waiting for an answer, he said, "It was very odd. Loud and intense."

Brook nodded. They were in the restaurant, Brook having called Nakata earlier in the evening. Nakata and Brook had had another entirely adequate meal and we're now sitting at a table in the corner, their dishes cleared away.

"I'm not sure what you want me to report, or what I'm supposed to be doing," continued Nakata. "Wellman might be a showman, but he's honest as far as it goes, I think. I didn't see any sign of things being faked. I didn't see anything at all, in fact." *Except the edge of a dress, the top of a boot, and I heard a scream.*

"Yes," said Brook, and he sounded old and tired and somehow sick at heart. "That's rather what we thought, and rather what we feared."

"'Feared'?"

Brook didn't speak, instead reaching into his inside jacket pocket and withdrawing a square of paper which he placed on the table in front of him. He looked at it for a moment and then, using one finger as though touching it was dangerous, that it might be infectious in some way, he slid it across the table to Nakata.

It was a photograph; or rather, it was a blow-up of part of a photograph, recently made, but the original image was old, black and white. It showed a girl, her hair in pigtails, her face distorted into something shadowed and coarse by the poor quality of the original image and the effect of magnification. She was only half-turned to the camera, looking back over her shoulder, her eyes nothing more than black smudges under hair that hung in loose, angular waves around her face.

"This is the only photograph of her that exists," Brook said.

"Who?"

"She was nine when the photograph was taken," continued Brook, "in 1919. It was taken by a photographer who was reporting on the return of troops from the Great War. The girl was in the background of the picture, unknown for years and years, just a person in the crowd celebrating the safe return of the people they loved. She was not, in general, a happy child, Mr. Nakata. She came from an age when women and children had rights on paper but no rights in life. Her father was like a great many men of his age and background, not actively cruel or abusive but prepared to wield power and indulge in a myriad of tiny harshnesses day after day simply because he had been born a man and women were somehow lesser beings."

"I'm sorry, I don't understand," said Nakata.

"Her name was Alice Earnshaw," said Brook, as though talking to someone else, someone ago and away, "and her childhood was spent in war. Her father was exempted from service on health grounds and it gnawed at him, made him feel inadequate and bitter, to be called a coward by people on the street who didn't realise that he was infirm. Infirm, of course, was just as embarrassing. It meant being weak, being pathetic, being less of a man.

"Earnshaw took his anger out on his wife and younger daughter. Not physically, but emotionally. He was a man of sudden temper eruptions and sullen, pointed silences, of over-reactions and shifting moods. He made everyone walk on eggshells around him, bullying them terribly in private but as nice as could be in public. Alice grew up confused, desperate to please an increasingly remote and angry and unpleasable man."

Brook, lifting his eyes to look across the table and seeing Nakata open his mouth to speak, held a hand out. "I'm sorry, I'm getting to it, I promise I am. The thing Alice wanted most in her life was to be the bridesmaid at her elder sister's wedding. In 1919, her sister's fiancé was finally demobbed from the army and returned home, and the date was set. Arrangements were made. For those few months, Alice was probably at her happiest, the impending wonderful day shielding her somewhat from her father's moods and tyrannies. That was when the picture was taken, at the beginning of that period, waiting for her future brother-in-law to return, her heart full of light and excitement and joy.

"A week before the wedding, Alice caught influenza. Spanish Flu. She died the day she was supposed to carry her bouquet up the aisle behind her sister, and the same bouquet served as her funeral wreath and was placed in her coffin with her. She was buried in the rain. There were only six mourners at the graveside, and her father was the only person there who didn't cry.

"She came here in 1935."

It took Nakata a moment to piece together the separate fragments of information he had just heard but again, Brook held another preventative hand when he tried to speak. "The Westmorland is a place of ghosts, Mr. Nakata. That adequacy I told you about, the carefully cultivated veneer of averageness and conformity and anonymity? It exists because the Westmorland's true clients aren't the living but the dead.

"The girl in the kitchen didn't have a name, not one that she told us anyway. She was about nineteen when she died, came here in the forties and never spoke, just folded sheets for hours and hours, sheets we could never see. I think she enjoyed the peace and repetition of it, to be honest. Her life was, I believe, hard. The Westmorland offered her a place to be safe, just as it offers all the dead who come here the chance to be safe, to relax after what may have been a hard, distressing life.

"Alice came here with her father and chose to stay because she was tired of being tethered to his anger and his misery. Who the girl in the kitchen arrived with we don't know, but she was as welcome as all of the dead are."

"The dead live here?" asked Nakata. He felt dumb, heavy and stupid, trying to catch up. The dead?

A hotel for the dead?

"And now Wellman is here and he is not, to our great disappointment, a fake. However he does it, he senses the dead and then tears them from their lives here and sends them on whether they like it or not."

"I'm sorry," said Nakata, "but even assuming I accept what you're saying, what do you want me to do?"

"Do? I'd have thought that was obvious. I want you to help them, Mr. Nakata. I want you to save the ghosts of the Westmorland."

vii. The Waystation of the Dead

It made sense, Nakata supposed. If the dead lingered, as he believed they did, then surely there were places where their lingering was easier, places that were easier for them to gather and stay, places that were safe and hidden and welcoming.

And if he accepted that these places existed, which he surely had to because he'd been in them almost too many times to count now, places where the dead continued to cling to their existence, then he had to accept that the dead had choices, some of them at least, that they chose to congregate in the places that made them feel safe, in the places where they could most easily hide, places where they could live out their remaining existence until they faded away or went on.

Places like the Westmorland.

And if the dead existed here, in this hotel that provided them with a resting place and that functioned as a waystation on whatever journey they were on, if they were *real* then people like Wellman must also be real. Nakata remembered Wellman swinging his bible back and forth, shouting and exhorting and sweating, and thought of a girl called Alice.

A little girl, permanently nine years old, being attacked by a grown man with a bible and volume and anger and such absolute surety. How frightened must she have been? How *terrified*? As Wellman, convinced of his rightness, bullied her and attacked her, driving her from safety to whatever came next? Savaged her with his faith and his bible and his cameras and his implacable certainty? As he killed her?

Could you kill the dead?

Yes, because Alice and those like her might be dead but they lived on in some way and Wellman was taking away their choice, taking away their existence, taking away their *life*. You could kill the dead, you could bully and batter them, make them scared and helpless, make them let go even if they didn't want to.

You could murder the dead.

Nakata stood, paced his room, feeling dizzy and sick. If he had been able to see Alice or the girl in the kitchen, properly *see* them, what would he have seen? A man beating two girls, grasping them and battering them, hitting them with his holy book? Did ghosts bleed or bruise? Would their ghost skins have torn, would their ghost teeth have been loosened or lost?

Would he have seen murders?

Nakata sat, hard, on the bed, the springs squealing in metallic protest beneath him, and leaned forward, putting his head in his hands. Nakata didn't believe Wellman was evil, but what he was doing was surely a terrible thing, was vicious and violent and grotesque. There was no way of stopping him, though, of this Nakata was sure. Wellman was convinced of his own rightness, as were so many people of faith, and would accept no deviation from his chosen actions. He was helping the dead, removing their confusion, nothing more. Wellman, and people like him, were never wrong, never unsure; even without the cameras and ratings and celebrity endorsements and sponsorships deals and the books and posters, Wellman would do what he did because it was a mission, a calling. And if the price of the calling was the death of the dead? Then so, Nakata assumed, be it.

Jesus. *Jesus.*

So, then, how did he prevent any more deaths?

His first thought was that he could simply take a piece of the Westmorland, a brick or piece of woodwork, and place it in another building so that the ghosts had somewhere else to go, but he quickly dismissed this idea. The ghosts in the Westmorland weren't there because they were tethered to it; quite the opposite, in fact. They were there by choice, because the Westmorland offered them a place to exist, to that point at least, in peace and safety.

Could the dead be encouraged to hide?

Presumably, yes, but if Wellman's powers were genuine then they risked being found, much as Alice and the girl had been found, and Nakata suspected that they had already *been* hiding, or at least keeping a low profile, and it hadn't saved them. The whole thing, Nakata realised, would become, already was, like some grotesque, lethal game of hide and seek, where *Tag, you're it* meant a death beyond death.

There was a knock at the door and Wellman's voice came through the thin wood, slightly muffled but still recognisable. "Richard, are you ready? We have another hunt to go on."

That morning, two more of the dead died, and this time Nakata saw them as blurred things tearing and ripping and fluttering loose and heard their screams as clearly as if their lips had been pressed against his ear.

"Do you mind if I take pictures?" asked Nakata, reaching into his bag and removing a cheap digital camera that he'd bought earlier that day. It was the evening of Wellman's second allowed day of investigation, hours after the first hunt with its attendant hysteria and shouts and Wellman's sweat and aftershave scent filling the corridor as he jerked those invisible spirits around and beat them and sent them on.

"For what purpose?" asked Wellman, not apparently concerned but inquisitive, eyes crinkling slightly. "Are you hoping to catch spirits in your camera's eye?'

"No," replied Nakata, meeting Wellman's gaze.

"Then evidence of fakery, perhaps?"

"No. Whatever's happening when you hunt, you aren't fraudulent, of that I'm sure."

"Thank you. I appreciate that, Richard. It means a lot coming from you."

If there was ever a time, it was now. Could he persuade Wellman to stop? Try to get him to see the fear and pain he was causing? Get him to see the murderousness of it, the sheer naked violence?

No. Even now, at his calmest, Wellman's eyes were the *surest* Nakata had ever seen. There was no compromise there, no leverage, because how could you compromise a truth when the truth itself was the lever you used?

"I'm not sure my word means anything," said Nakata eventually, "and the pictures are just for me, to act as an aid memoire."

"That's fine, as long as I have your word they won't be used in any public forum. No websites, articles, blogs, whatever, without getting my clearance first."

You have my word," said Nakata.

"And that's enough for me," said Wellman, turning away and starting to talk to Mitch.

Nakata waited, bag hanging on his shoulder, camera held in his hand. Years of patient waiting for often no-show spirits had taught him to be calm, to find a place in himself to stave off boredom and achieve a thing he sometimes thought of as 'ghostwaiting zen', and he did it now. As Wellman and Mitch and the other two moved around the corridor, milling from space to space and playing with lenses and lighting, dabbing at Wellman's already perspiring pate, Nakata simply stood. This would either work, or it wouldn't; this was the end of it, one way or another.

"Well, Richard, are you ready?"

"Yes," said Nakata and made a show of lifting his camera and taking a couple of shots. They were just for show, of course. He had no urge to keep a record of what was about to happen. What was important was the bag.

"Good," said Wellman. "Everyone? Let's hunt."

viii. A Lack of Ghosts

"Fucking nothing!" Wellman raged.

They were back in his room, and the presenter was furious, his face and scalp mottled to a dark, ruinous purple. It was late, the evening closed about them like a shawl, and the hotel was, apart from room 372, quiet. "Nothing!" Wellman snarled again, and swept a pile of papers off the top of the cheap desk to the floor with a contemptuous noise. Any doubts Nakata might have had evaporated then; this was a man who didn't just want to do what he thought of as good, he wanted to be *seen* to do good, to be seen to be the helper and guide and mentor. He wanted to be praised for it, to be held in regard.

To be loved.

"The whole place was empty?" asked Caitlin?

"What the fuck do you think I've been saying?" snapped Wellman. "There was nothing. Do you think I make this crap up, Cait? Well? Do you?"

"No, of course not," said Caitlin. "I just wondered if you could... well, you know?"

"No, I don't. What would you like me to do, Caitlin? Enlighten me, please. Should I conjure ghosts just so I can send them away? Play act for the cameras?"

"No, I just—"

"Get out of my sight. We're leaving in the morning. There's no point in staying if there's nothing more here to find. Tell Brook, he'll be fucking ecstatic I'm sure."

"I'll leave you," said Nakata, rising. He put the camera, full of pictures of Wellman and his team dashing along dark corridors and looking increasingly frustrated as the hunt went on, in the outside pocket of the bag that was still hanging over his shoulder. He didn't want to open the main zipper yet.

"Richard," said Wellman, visibly bringing himself under control. He held out a hand, which Nakata shook. This was the most dangerous time, this moment now when Wellman was focused entirely on him, not on the hunt or the missing ghosts or the fact his unstoppable absoluteness had crashed against the immovable object of the dead's absence. Nakata shifted, pushing the bag back over his shoulder so it fell behind him, swinging at his buttocks. Hiding it.

"Thank you for your time and your open mind," said Wellman. "I hope we meet again."

"Yes," said Nakata, not sure if he meant it or not. Wellman was undoubtedly fascinating and would make an interesting test study, but his brutality in the name of goodness was unpleasant and Nakata wasn't sure he wanted to come within its orbit again.

"What will you tell Mr. Brook?" asked Wellman, not letting go of Nakata's hand. The bag swung slightly, tapping at Nakata like the urgent finger of a child.

"The truth. That you're honest, and I saw no evidence of trickery or faking, but that I equally saw no provable evidence of ghosts while I was with you."

"None of us saw much, did we?" said Wellman, finally smiling, a rueful grin that made him look younger, more like the man whose company Nakata had enjoyed when they first met.

"No."

"We may still salvage a show from this," said Wellman, "with what we filmed. It might be good to show me not finding as much as I expected, of course. It'd help people understand that what I do is real."

"Yes," said Nakata.

"And we'll make sure you aren't mentioned or shown, of course. Well, goodbye Richard. Take care."

"You too," said Nakata, and this he meant and it felt good to leave on a statement of truth. As he backed out of the room, the bag swung and its weight seemed to be growing and its mass swelling.

The secret was in the perception, of course. It had come to Nakata as they hunted that second morning, as he watched Wellman dash along corridors and grasp at things that no one else could see. For Wellman, the ghosts of the Westmorland, the ghosts of everywhere, were physical things to grip and yank and hem in and send on, but for Nakata they were very different, things of energy and glimpse and hint. *We create them,* he had realised, *not initially, of course, because we're talking about the leavings of the living as they die here, but we give them a form in which to fit. We shape them, mould them into what we want them to be.* Perhaps, he wondered, they were like Schrödinger's poor cat, in all states until someone opened the box to see if it was dead or alive and its state collapsed into a singularity. Ghosts were energy, sentient or otherwise, that responded to the will and observations of the living, and Wellman's personality, his *need,* was so strong that he made them into something real that he could bully and instruct and order.

Which meant he could send them on, casting them forward like a stone skipping across still waters until they vanished into the depths.

In the corridors there had been five of them looking but it had been Wellman's vision of how the dead were that triumphed, meaning that his personality was stronger than Nakata's, Nakata supposed. It made sense; it was how he had pushed himself into the limelight, of course, that will to be seen, to succeed, even if success was on the back of the murdered dead that he had saved. And if Wellman hadn't been present? What would Nakata's ghosts have been? Emotions and energies, things prickling at the corners of his eyesight and brushing against his skin without actually touching him? Things that spoke, could hold conversations, were capable of forming relationships?

Things that allowed him the hope that he and Amy might one day be allowed to be together again?

And what did they mean for his research, these Schrödinger's Ghosts? That it was pointless because if he ever did manage to show anything, to prove anything to himself in laboratory conditions, those results would be different for anyone else trying to achieve the same thing and thus rendered useless? Was everything he had done pointless, a waste of time?

No.

Nakata nodded at Brook, who unzipped the bag. They were in one of the lower corridors, a staff-only space that had been cleared of everyone except themselves, and Wellman and his team had been gone half an hour; they had left it this long in case they came back for anything.

In case they saw.

Wellman needed the dead to be a certain way, had forced the ghosts into a form that approximated the physical, and in doing so had given them the means of their saving. As physical things, they could hide in the one place Wellman would not be concentrating on – Nakata and the bag he carried – and that realisation had made things simple. Well, maybe not simple; it had been a dash to go and buy a camera and bag, the camera mere dressing to allow him to carry the bag, and then to get Brook to encourage the dead into the bag before Nakata went to Wellman's room the previous evening. They had them all, every spirit and spectre from the Westmorland's corridors and rooms, and Nakata carried them with him the rest of the day.

They weighed nothing, and they weighed everything, because if he failed they might all be torn from this life and sent on into nothing.

He had carried them with him around the hotel, hoping that Wellman would be too focused on the hunt to realise the things he sought were only feet from him in a cheap nylon shoulder bag, a gamble that had paid off and as the zip eased back the first of them emerged, a haze that shimmered before vanishing. Then another, this one darker and smaller, then another and another and another and before long Nakata had lost count. Two of the ghosts wrapped themselves around each other before disappearing and Nakata thought, *That could be me and Amy, one day.*

Maybe it wouldn't, of course, but it didn't matter. He would keep working to see if he could find a way back to Amy, to see if there was a way to bridge the seemingly impossible space between the dead and the living. As Nakata watched the ghosts of the Westmorland go safe and free, he smiled and he dreamed.

And, most of all, he hoped.

Post-Mortem Hyperdontia:
The continued growth of teeth after death. In some cultures, this is thought to indicate that the dead person was, in life, possessed by a demon.

No evidence has yet been found to contradict this.

This collection has been, for a number of reasons, a long time coming.

The last short story collection I wrote prior to *Diseases of the Teeth* was 2011's *Quiet Houses*, (although in terms of publication dates, *Strange Gateways* was a more recent publication, coming out in 2014 even though it was written across 2009 and 2010). The stories in *Quiet Houses* capped a number of years' intensive story writing, and by the time I'd completed and submitted it I was ready to focus on something longer. The 'something longer' turned out to be a novel, *The Sorrowful,* that would eventually be published by Del Rey in the UK and Doubleday in the US under the title *The Devil's Detective,* and then there was another novel to do, and somewhere in all that novelling I stopped writing shorts except for one or two commissioned pieces, in the process forgetting how much I enjoy them. This collection, originally pitched and accepted in about 2012, was originally intended to be a resting place for a lot of writing done during that last frenzied burst of short story-telling but a number of things (publisher issues, me not writing the final story, a poor conjunction of ley lines just under my office) stopped it appearing and I, deep in Hell and then deeper in Heaven, first stopped worrying about it and then forgot about it entirely.

But collections, like dead horses in Nick Cave songs and alien spacecrafts under tube stations, don't stay buried for long. Early this year, I started thinking about short story collections again, remembered that I had one pretty much ready to go and, intrigued, revisited the stories I collected together pre-novel and was pleasantly surprised because although some of them were now five years old or more they still seemed fresh enough to consider putting out. I wrote some new stuff to add in, tweaked the existing stuff to remove some errors, picked a title that made me feel uncomfortable (working on the principle if it made me twitch, it'd make other people twitch too) and then sent it out, sat back to watch where it landed and hoped it would take seed.

Which brings us to this point. I've written the damn thing, got the lovely Steve Shaw of Black Shuck Books to publish it (interesting coincidence - my first ever published story, in 2007, was about Black Shuck so it's a nice feeling of coming around full circle. Don't know who Black Shuck is? Go find out) and now I have to explain myself. So, settle back. I might ramble, I might present myself in the best (or worst) lights possible, I might repeat myself or simply dawdle off into tangential space, but I'll probably get there in the end. If you're interested, this is how these stories came about.

INTO THE WATER

A commission, for Stephen Jones' *Weirder Shadows over Innsmouth* anthology. In the months before I wrote this, the world had been flooding, and I simply wanted to see if I could fit the various floods into the requested Cthulhu mythos story. It was written over the course of a bitterly cold but entirely wonderful weekend in a lodge in the Lake District with the woman who would eventually become my second wife, and it came out pretty much fully-formed. My favourite scene in the story, the four tainted things sitting around an underwater picnic table leisurely eating, came from swimming over an upturned garden table in Salford Quays (don't ask) and wondering why it was there, and having a sudden clear image of four Innsmouth folk sitting around a similar table and one of the things reaching out, spearing a fish and eating it. David is based on my friend Andrew's dad, although as far as I know he's not turned into an underwater beastie yet.

LEFT BEHIND

I used to do Halloween readings for the Cancer Research shop in Morecambe and one year I thought it would be a good idea to stay in the shop one night, sitting in its gloomy loft and all alone in the building, and write a story by torchlight that I could read at one of the events. I hoped to soak up the atmosphere of the deserted shop full of donated and unwanted things and channel it into something nostalgic and sinister, and 'Left Behind' is the result.

2.23 A.M.

Probably my worst fear.

LITTLE TRAVELLER

Another commission, this time by Mark Morris for the *Spectral Book of Horror Stories* series. There were no guidelines for the story other than 'horror' so I was pretty much free to write whatever I wanted, which is a nice feeling. I'd seen a news report on the Somalia piracy situation (the waters around Somalia, at the time of writing considered a failed nation-state, were usually agreed to be the most dangerous in the world because of the various gangs that sailed there attacking boats, stealing cargo and kidnapping or killing crew), which mentioned that most of the pirates were high on drugs, most were orphaned or displaced, and that the violent gangs they belonged to were almost like a replacement family for them. The gangs offered them, the report said, the stability and sense of belonging they needed, and it chimed with something inside my head. I felt, oddly, a sense of sympathy for the pirates because much as they do appalling things, how awful must it be to find your stability in those unstable, dangerous and violent circumstances?

The other element was the attraction of doing something set on the ocean. I've always responded as a reader and viewer to aquatic horror stories (there's something that creeps me out about all the flat distance, and the knowledge that hidden under that flatness is a world of monsters and teeth and tentacles and poison) so I thought I'd see what happened when I wrote a story about a modern-day pirate, displaced and high and scared and lost, meeting something that might (or might not) be a supernatural threat afloat upon the ocean and very far from safety.

N IS FOR NOODLE

I was invited to contribute to the anthology *M is for Monster*, in which every author was given a letter and asked to write about a monster that began with that letter. I came to the party late and was offered the last remaining letter, *N*, and because I can sometimes be a contrary bugger I decided to write about noodles (I think, I *think*, I made a joke to the editor about it, if I'm honest, about how all the good monsters were gone and I might as well write *N is for Noodle* or something, at which he laughed thinking I was joking and I got bloody-minded and decided to stick with it to see if I could do it). I'm pleased with the final story, which I've read aloud at story readings a couple of times and which always goes down well. The last line, incidentally, is a tribute to the late Karl Edward Wagner and the last line of the first (and still my favourite) story I read by him, the brilliant and unsettling 'Where the Summer Ends'

CHILD

An updated version of the first good thing I ever wrote, this came directly from the experience of my first wife and I losing a pregnancy. Although the original version (written for a creative writing class) isn't that good, it always had something in it that I liked, and I took the opportunity to update it a few years ago and submit it to Andy Cox' excellent *Black Static* magazine. I like this new version a lot, but the old version (unpublishable though it is) is still one of the pieces of writing I'm proudest of because it was the first thing I'd written that other people liked and in which I could see the seeds the author I wanted to be.

H IS FOR HRACE

There was obviously a spate of 'letter' anthologies a few years back (I was in three of them all at around roughly the time), and this story was from one of them, *Demonologica*. It grew from a genuine incident that occurred when I was in the Lake District walking up a hill and saw a man ahead of me, about halfway up the same hill and pointing to its summit. I lost sight of him as the path I was on bent across the hill's flank but when I emerged onto a new stretch and saw him again he was still in the same place pointing, apparently not having moved. Each time I lost sight of him because of the curves of the path or overhead foliage, when I emerged out into the open he would be in the same place and pointing, and I was starting to wonder if there was a problem and what I'd find when I got to him. Finally, the path took a last bend and curled back on itself and when I came out from a low cover of trees, the man had gone.

When I reached the top of the hill, it was approaching dusk, the weather had worsened and it had begun to rain and the colour of the reflected sky in the puddles across the summit was a grimy, leaden shade of bruised red. That, the man and a sudden image of the clouds above me opening like a huge mouth, led to this story. Hrace is the old English word for 'throat' (or 'throat gorge'), just in case you're interested.

THE MAN IN THE CORNER

Just written because I wanted to write it. This was written in a time in my life where I wasn't very happy, and if I were given to psychological self-analysis I'd say it represents my fears about how good (or bad) a dad I was turning out to be. I'm sure it does represent those things, but I also just wanted to write something short (which it is) and creepy (which I hope it is) and in that sense, it's just a short creepy story.

THE COTSWOLD OLIMPICKS

Written after being invited to contribute to Paul Finch's *Terror Tales of the Cotswolds*. I'd wanted to write a folk horror story (something akin to *The Wicker Man*) for ages, and when (during research for inspiration as Paul's deadline approached and I'd got precisely nothing written) I came across the story of the genuine Cotswold Olimpicks, I knew I'd found my inlet and had a way of writing about folk traditions, chain hotels and why you should never refuse drinks from attractive women. Robert Dover's poem that finishes the story is real, by the way, as are the games described in the story.

CHRISTMAS EVE, 5.24

I can't honestly remember why I wrote this, other than at the time I was experimenting with much shorter pieces to see if I could find the key elements of horror or ghost stories without all the narrative padding and this was one of the things I produced. It didn't have a home for a long time, just sat on my Mac's hard drive and lurked, sulking, before eventually being published in *The Association for the Scientific Study of Anomalous Phenomena's* magazine. ASSAP is a great organisation, and if you have any interest at all in the scientific study of and coherent approach to the study of ghosts and all manner of other supernatural phenomena, you should join and get involved.

HURTING WORDS

In some ways, the story in this collection that was hardest to write. It was originally called 'The Thirteen' and was started years ago, and although the central storyline was the same, it had far more terrified academics in it (thirteen, to be exact, although one dies at the beginning). I could never get the story past its midpoint, however, despite numerous attempts, so it kept being abandoned and the returned to and then abandoned again. Barbara Roden, of Ash Tree Press, gave me the sage and sensible advice to trim the central number of characters and then Stephen Jones, editor of distinction, told me to get my finger out and finish writing it. I did, coming up along the way with the unexpected revelation about Rathbone, and I'm pleased with the result. It might have taken years, but the delay was, I think, worth it.

The Pyramid Spider

Very originally, I wanted to write this story on a typewriter because I'd always envisaged it as belonging to something like the *Pan Book of Horror Stories* (and I must have assumed at the time that everything that appeared in the Pan books was written on typewriters). I know I even started, using an old typewriter I'd been bought as a gift, but it was too slow and boring to complete that way (I word process, which makes me quick and makes editing far easier but, I suspect, also makes me lazy).

I did eventually produce an early version of the story for a creative writing class, who seemed to enjoy it (although one of the pieces of feedback that I received I found written across the top of a returned copy of the story said simply, "It is time to stop with the frippery and write something adult"!) and it then went through various iterations (there was a modern version written in emails, an earlier-set diary entry version, a version designed to be done as a reading at the British Fantasy Convention presented as a series of telephone answering machine messages [with my wife Rosie providing the voice of the answering machine, fact fans] and a version with less Lovecraftyness) before this final version was arrived at and published by Mike Davis in his excellent *Lovecraft Ezine*. This might feel like a fairly slight story but I still like it because I like stories like this, that function purely to scare and disturb, and I think it has enough going for it for me to be happy with how it turned out.

Vernon, Driving

In the immediate aftermath of my first story being published in an actual book and then nominated for a World Fantasy Award ('The Church on the Island', in *At Ease with the Dead*), I assumed fame, fortune, inevitable critical adulation and an untimely death through exhaustion due to excessive book signings lay in my future, so when Ellen Datlow invited me to submit to a new anthology she was putting together, *Lovecraft Unbound,* I also assumed anything I sent her would be received with open, accepting arms. Confident in my authorial prowess, I sent her a story... which she duly rejected. So I sent her another, which she rejected even more quickly. So, ever the trier, I sent her a third which boomeranged back so fast I think my cursor was still hovering over the 'Send' button when the rejection hit my inbox.

Sulking, I decided that my stuff was clearly too something or other for Ellen to appreciate, and gave up submitting to her.

Until an odd thing happened. About 2 months later I was thinking about Lovecraft, about what his cold, glacial horrors might actually mean in a human perspective and this story appeared in my head absolutely fully formed. It was written in one sitting on a train journey from London to Lancaster, sent to Ellen the next day with almost no editing and, to my astonishment, accepted. It's in some ways the most cynical story I've written, and certainly one of the saddest, and I still like it a lot.

PRIVATE AMBULANCE

A story that had been knocking around inside my head for ages before I actually wrote it (for NewCon Press' *Noir* anthology), this came out of one of those weird images that take up residence in your head and won't leave until you've worked out why they're there. In this case, I kept seeing a woman open the rear door of a private ambulance and birds flying out. Although that specific image didn't make it into the story exactly, working out why the woman was there was good fun, and the rest of the story turned out better than I'd hoped.

The line from the paramedic, incidentally, about the brain shooting out from the head like a big pink snail? That was a real occurrence, as told me by the paramedic.

PHOTOGRAPHS OF BODEN

Written for Willie Meikle's *The Unspoken*, a charitable anthology in aid of cancer research charities. I like my old family photos, maybe because there's so few of them (they were taken in rolls of 24 and cost a lot to develop, remember?), and wanted to use them as the basis for something creepy and upsetting. I also wanted to try and explore the insidious, stealthy stalk of cancer, and the effect it might have on the people it affects and about how it corrupts and stains and distorts. It's a story that represents (like so much of the other stuff I write, I'm beginning to realize) the fear I have that I'm not a good enough man, not a good enough husband, because I worry that as much as I might try to be decent, one day a truth I haven't even realised exists will emerge and I won't like it at all.

Rough Music

I took my son to the small museum in Lancaster and in one of the posters on the wall was a description of a practice called 'rough music', where people in a village would bang pots and pans outside the house of a cuckolder at night as a kind of community punishment. I was absolutely entranced with the idea and by the time we got home I'd got the story in my head.

If you want a point of reference, the papier mâché head people in the story all look like relatives of the late, lamented Frank Sidebottom.

The Poor Weather Crossings Company

I've done two cross-bay walks across Morecambe Bay in my time, one of them in absolutely terrible weather and one in bright sun, and both were excellent fun. This story was an attempt to catch some of the soggy brilliance of poor weather crossing on paper, with added ancient monsters (or possibly gods). The Queen's Guide to the Sands is a real position, the King's Guide to the Sands I'm less sure about. It was written for Paul Finch's *Terror Tales of the Seaside,* and all the facts about Morecambe and its bay and the deaths and shipwrecks in it are true, by the way.

Chapter Bank

My sister said she wanted to be in one of my stories doing something horrible or dying, so I obliged her when doing for a story for Hersham Horror's *Siblings* anthology. Sis, this one's for you.

The Fourth Horse

I'd already stolen my Uncle Barry's name for my sort-of hero's name for my first Zambia-set story, 'Mami Wata', written for Danel Olsen's *Exotic Gothic 3.* When Danel asked me to contribute to *Exotic Gothic 4,* I revisited Zambia and remembered a story Barry had told me about stopping a horsebox because it had a loose brake cable, only to discover that the horse was intended for delivery to Joseph Kabila (google him if you're not sure). I stole his story, wondering a lot about what it might be like to live somewhere you loved but that was gradually being corrupted and how far you might go to save it, added a horse demon, and this is the result.

QIQIRN

Written for another of those '26 letters' anthologies, this time Dean M. Drinkel's *Phobias*. Stupidly, I let someone else choose my letter, and they gave me 'Q'. Bastards. It was only when Johnny Mains (author, researcher and editor of great taste) told me about the Inuit spirit Qiqirn, and when I saw a documentary about counsellors helping people deal with their internal demons by writing letters to their more destructive or desperate selves, that various ideas came together and I wrote 'Q is for Qiqirn'. It's another story about sadness and loss, which I clearly wrote about a lot in the period before my first marriage crumbled, and I'm very proud if it because it seems (to me at least) to be psychologically as accurate a thing as I have ever written.

DAY 34

Written for Alex Davis' *Reality Bites* anthology of stories about reality TV, this one's a simple exercise in trying to be as scary as possible. Decide for yourself if I managed it or not.

A PLACE FOR FEEDING

It's always struck me that oppression takes all sorts of forms and that lines of power are sometimes obvious but are often more subtle, although no less awful for those on the shitty end of them. When I was asked to contribute to the anti-fascism anthology *Never Again*, edited by Allyson Bird and the late Joel Lane, I started to think about small fascists and small fascisms, and about things that from the outside might not look too bad but from the inside would make you feel like you had no control, that you were small and insignificant and used. I'd heard dreadful things about how people react to women breastfeeding in public, and those stories became the springboard for this one.

MESSAGE 3

Every now and again you hear about a divorced or separated man who kills his children rather than be parted from them and it must be the most heartbreaking thing, to be in involved in a situation like that whatever your relation to the dead man or dead children. This was written after hearing about another of these incidents, and occurred in my 'let's try and keep it short phase', which ended with this story.

God, but this story has been through so many variations! It's an old one which I revisit every year or so and, frustrated that it still isn't what I want it to be, rewrite and edit and generally fuck about with it. This version is the most recent, and the one I think might be the final edit. For now.

THE TERRIBLE DEATHS OF THE GHOSTS OF THE WESTMORLAND

I'd kind of left Richard Nakata, the hero of my portmanteau short story collection *Quiet Houses,* hanging at the end of that book, and I'd always wanted to revisit him to see what he did next. I like Nakata a lot because he seems to be a reflection of a me that I aspire to be – inquisitive and honest and prepared to stand in front of the screaming darkness and sometimes faceless ghosts alone and armed only with his faith (I try to ignore the fact that, if he's the version of me that I'd like to be, it probably says something very odd about my psyche that I keep hitting him with tragedy). Plus Nakata allows to me explore various aspects of the ghost story, placing him in a variety of odd situations and sometimes following his investigations to places even I never expected. This story was originally started for an anthology whose deadline I failed to meet, put aside whilst I started an as-yet-unfinished Nakata novel (I'll come back to it at some point) and then completed because Nakata felt like the right person to finish this anthology with. He's still a decent man, and I still like him a lot.

Made in the USA
Las Vegas, NV
04 June 2021

24180364R00206